STACKS

3 9077 01006646 5

W9-CKH-658

LITERATURE DIVISION   1 - 6465

Getz, William.

Sam Patch

R

$17.95

DATE			

Literature Division
Rochester Public Library
115 South Avenue
Rochester, New York 14604

STACKS

DEC 17 1986
© THE BAKER & TAYLOR CO.

Sam Patch

SAM PATCH

Ballad of a Jumping Man

BY WILLIAM GETZ

FRANKLIN WATTS   NEW YORK   TORONTO   1986

1-6465

Library of Congress Cataloging-in-Publication Data

Getz, William.
Sam Patch: ballad of a jumping man.

I. Title.
PS3557.E89S36   1986   813'.54   86-11171
ISBN 0-531-15026-7

Copyright © 1986 by William Gietz
All rights reserved
Printed in the United States of America
6   5   4   3   2   1

It seems that he [Sam Patch] had some misgivings of his fate, for a pet bear, which he had always taken with him on his former break-neck adventures, and which had constantly leaped after him without injury, he on this occasion left behind, in the care of a friend, to whom he bequeathed him "in case of his not returning." We saw the bear, which is kept at the principal hotel; he is a noble creature, more completely tame than I ever saw any animal of the species.

Frances Trollope
Domestic Manners of the Americans
1832

Prologue

A low, plaintive whine brings me to myself. She sits opposite me at a respectful distance, gazing at me with anxious, pleading eyes. The rain drips from her nose, as it does from mine, and mats the soft fur on her face and throat into mournful streaks and patches down which the wet courses like a flood of tears. Stirring eagerly as she sees she's roused me, she lurches forward a few inches and plumps back down again in the mud of the pen, panting invitingly and soliciting a sign to approach. She's very pretty. Even bedraggled and frightened as she is, and still marked with the crusted blood that the rain has not washed away from the wound the trap has made over her ankle, she's pretty. But her looks have no power over me. They're like a tug on a limb that has lost feeling. I myself am a limb that has lost feeling. She moves me no more than the rain does, which I see rather than feel, or the gnawing in my stomach, which signals its want of attention with such single-minded persistence and does not appreciate the novelty of being ignored.

I slip away from them all, the dreary rain, my indignant stomach, and her pleading eyes. None of them can hold me. I slip away, back into the waking dream from which my penmate has so briefly drawn me. I slip away and her pursuing wail quickly fades, dissolving in the plash of the rain and the swirl of images that arise to greet me as I reenter the dream. I give myself up to these gratefully.

We're old friends. They're the ghostly remains of the time before I lost all feeling—when indeed I had as much feeling as anyone and was perhaps happier in its possession than most.

First stop: this morning. It was raining then, too, and I sat out in it only slightly less preoccupied than at present. Bill Cochrane's yard behind the Recess Tavern was my venue then, instead of this disgusting sty where my ever-falling fortunes (and Bill) have lately brought me. I could still think about the future this morning; not having been brought here yet, I still theoretically at least had one. So I sat placidly—numbly, if you will—in the wet, chained to my stump by Bill's stable, watching the drops dapple the puddles and smooth the glistening mud, and divided my time about equally between thinking about my future, such as it was, and my glorious, uncommonly happy past.

It was because my past was ever so much more prepossessing than my future, even then, that I consented to remain chained. I could have "escaped" any time. The chain would have been no match for my once-personable five hundred pounds. I could have snapped it like a string of sausages. (—That, I imagine, will be my stomach talking again. It's a very persevering stomach, as are all of them I've had any acquaintance with; and it has no heart. If it had, it would mute its demands. But no, on the contrary, it insists on my giving these pride of place; insists there can be nothing more important than its own well-being; that satisfaction of other claims is a luxury to be entered upon only when its own demands are met. I'm sure there's a moral there someplace. In any case, a thoroughly unsentimental creature, is a stomach.)

Yes, I could have walked away a free bear any time. I could have "escaped." So why didn't I? And why do I say I could have, so ironically?

Because it was only my present I could have escaped, and since all other presents I could imagine led to the same future, escaping seemed an idle business.

I could have walked away from Bill all right, and he would not have been sorry to see me do it. I was an albatross around his neck, if you'll forgive the image of someone draped with a five-hundred-pound bird. I reminded Bill constantly of Sam. Sam had entrusted me to Bill, and for four months Bill lived up to the trust. I don't hold it against him that he finally disencumbered himself this morning. He's not to be blamed. But first off, just as Bill only kept me as long as he did for the memory of Sam, so too I stayed partly for the same reason: Bill's was the last place I'd gone with Sam; it was the spot where I'd left him, or he'd left me. While I stayed, I maintained contact—ever more tenuously, I grant you, and hopelessly, as of course Sam was never coming back—but contact it was. I hadn't the will to leave, to put Sam behind me—to bury him. It was more than I could do.

Then, too, I had nowhere to go. Society has no place for the single bear. This truth has been repeatedly impressed on me since my first introduction to what passes for civilization. The life of a bear alone where men and dogs are about is all too apt to be nasty, brutish and short. I would need a sponsor, a protector; and while I probably could have found someone to take me away, how pale a thing life would be on the road again without Sam! The memories and contrasts, the constant reminders of my fallen estate, would be unendurable. Sam's relict, I would feel every slight—and they wouldn't be few, a bear's lot being what it is in this life—as if it were an offense against Sam or his memory. I'd sicken, or I might become vicious. To travel with anyone new would be the end of me.

A quiet retirement, then—why not that?

I thought of it. Slip away into the woods, press on till the woods become forests, leave forever behind the clamorous scenes of my life with Sam, and with them all reminder of my bereavement. Yes, that idea had some appeal for me, I confess. I saw myself, a lonely, tragic figure, stalking the solitudes of the wilderness, living in the past, keeping bright the memory of Sam and our triumphs together. I thought of that. But sooner or later Crockett would hear I was on the loose again and come for me. I know he would. I'm surprised he hasn't come before this, just to look in. I think he hasn't only because I sat chained to my stump and the chain protected me from him. But if once I were free, I know he'd drop everything in Washington, fetch his best dogs from Tennessee and come for me even if it meant letting the British pile kindling against the White House again.

No, there's no relief for me there. I'm blocked at every turn. And it doesn't matter; without Sam, I have no desire to go anywhere else, do anything else, anyway. This new place Bill brought me to this morning (after an ominously fine breakfast) is as good a place as any to conclude a life that's already over. I could wish I had the accommodations to myself—the pretty female, so forlorn, so puzzled by what's befallen her, distracts me with her pleas for comforting; she leads my thoughts away from Sam and would start me

—3—

having feelings again if she could—but I can't be choosy. As for yielding to her importunings, that would be doubly futile, suspecting what I do what's to become of us. I have no desire to open a new chapter after Sam, and if I did it would be a pointless desire in any event when that chapter is so likely to be closed so soon and ignominiously. Dust to dust, ashes to ashes, the service goes. In our case I think we're destined, she and I, to become Sears Famous Bear Grease before we pass on to the more conventional terminus. I don't mind. In this new incarnation I'll visit and revisit the scenes of my earlier happiness with Sam—haunt them like a fragrant ghost embodied in boots, harness and tackle—and keep my sundry fleshly envelopes as supple as my memories.

Well, so be it. In the meantime I travel those roads and revisit those scenes in my mind. I slip away down a path only I can follow. The pleading eyes and questing nose of my poor pretty penmate recede into a mist that sounds of rain, and then the sound of the rain recedes and the mist covers all, and at last the mist itself recedes, evaporates to reveal a trackless forest and leaves tranquilly shimmering on the trees, and a purer air and a cleaner world generally, and the stage is set again for the beginning of it all, the beginning of that chain of events that led to my meeting Sam. And I wouldn't change a bit of it—not at the price of missing Sam. So with a shiver of anticipation I slip back again as I have so many times before to that faraway day, that terrible day, when in the delightful green wooded hills of my birthplace, Tennessee, I first encountered Davy Crockett—to my considerable chagrin . . .

Chapter 1

Ordinarily, a bear's life tends to be pretty uneventful, and up until what I guess was about my fifth year mine was, too. Like most bears, I kept pretty much to myself. I spent my time alone in the great gothic wilderness, rambling over the hills that bumped along in every direction and made up so far as I was concerned the whole of the known world. Food was plentiful and lay, so to speak, ready to hand. I munched as I rambled, and thought about how fortunate it was to be a bear in a world in which everything seemed expressly designed for a bear's happiness. If I were hungry, I had only to reach out: food literally grew on trees. If I were thirsty, all I had to do was go a short ways to where the cleanest, most delicious water actually flowed in streams over the ground, and likely teemed with fish besides—no doubt, as I thought at the time, in case a bear got hungry while he was drinking.

But there was a canker in these otherwise unexceptionable arrangements—or rather, in me. I just couldn't seem to leave well enough alone. Maybe it was only the other side of my enjoying life more keenly, or at any rate more critically, than other bears, but the fact was that the more I thought about how nicely things were set up for bears and how just about everything seemed to fit, the more I became obsessed by the things that *didn't* obviously fit.

Boulders, for instance. I couldn't eat them at all, or mate with them very plausibly; they became what you might call stumbling blocks to my peace of mind. Boulders and other things that didn't fit forced me to realize that even a fish could entertain the kind of ideas I did about how things were set up, only putting fish at the center instead of bears. For instance, there he'd be in a stream that might seem put there just for him to swim in, with plants to eat growing on the bottom, tasty bugs dropping in on top, and females waggling their tails at him at just the season of the year that he found himself feeling randy: what else could he think? He'd be wrong, of course, and I could prove it by catching and eating him; but until I actually did—until I showed him how bears didn't fit in his scheme of things—he'd have as much to say for his theory as I for mine.

This is why boulders bothered me. As long as I couldn't see what use they were to bears, I couldn't help worry maybe I wasn't any closer to the truth than the fish was. And I didn't want to be browsing along one of these days woolgathering and find myself suddenly flipped into the air, say, in some so-far unimaginable fashion, to finish up steaks or filets. The prospect, even the bare possibility, preyed on my mind and cast a cloud over my existence.

So I made a study of boulders. I began to notice things that reassured me. For instance, I noticed that lichen grows on boulders. Now, lichen isn't much use to bears either, in itself; I had, in fact, filed it previously in the same category with boulders. But let the generations of lichen grow thick enough and moss will take to it. Moss is marginal: sometimes you can find bugs in it. The important thing, though, is that seeds will root in moss and become trees. Trees are clearly useful to bears. Things to eat grow on them, their bark is often good, when they're old and rotten they tend to be full of fat grubs, and they're nice to lean against. Was it maybe that boulders were useful for having trees?

Pleased with myself as I was over this hypothesis, I was worried it might be too pat. Still, it fascinated me. It amounted to a whole new way of looking at things. The world was made up of items that were useful to bears. But these things were like clocks, in other words (not that I knew anything about clocks, of course: that came later), and some things were sort of like the *works* in clocks.

I set out to see if I couldn't confirm this. Things did tend to fall into place on this way of looking at them, and my worries eased accordingly. Ground, for example, is good to walk on. Hills keep you from having to look at the same thing all the time and vary the going. Fallen leaves were a bit of a problem till I noticed how small animals like to scurry around and nest in them, and where they get wet and rotten they're good for bugs. Wind is good for carrying scent, birds are good to look at and for laying eggs. Bees, of course, are good for honey. Their stingers I wasn't sure about till it struck me that they're good for keeping the honey safe from animals that don't have fur like a bear's—a necessary evil, in other words. Maybe a little *ad hoc* but beneficial on the whole. Rain keeps the streams full and night is good for sleeping.

My hypothesis seemed to check out. Just about everything turned out to have some point of usefulness to bears, direct or indirect, if only I had the ingenuity to find it. There were still some difficult cases—black flies, for instance—so I always had something to think about. But at least I didn't discover anything (black flies excepted) that looked like it might stand in relation to bears the way bears do to fish.

In the meantime—for I wouldn't have you think this was *all* I thought about—there was something else on my mind. It was a vastly pleasanter something, and it wasn't so much on my mind as in my blood, making me dreamy and restless and interfering generally with my concentration on profounder subjects. Spring was in the air, and something else, too, I was almost certain of it. Again and again I found myself rising up on my hind legs, thinking I'd caught a whiff of it. Possums already earmarked for supper resurrected themselves from playing dead in that obliging way they have and scampered off while I stood sniffing. Fish swam with impunity between my ankles. I lost weight.

But I was on the scent of the willing female, if you haven't already guessed, and that was worth a few missed suppers. I've since learned that even human females aren't always willing. In fact, they have an arsenal of excuses for not being willing that ranges from the simple headache to introducing such anti-aphrodisiac subjects as the offspring's bed wetting or the male's bad breath. Even so, the human male lives in a voluptuary's paradise by bear standards. The female bear is willing on the average only once in *two years*. All of them are like that. So when the fortunate male gets wind of one who is, it's a red-letter day indeed. And I'd just got wind of one who was.

This event knocked my metaphysical worries clean out of my head. I've since found out I'm not the first this has happened to, by the way. It seems to be a common experience with philosophers the world over. When the fit passes off they even make it the subject of philosophical reflection, some of them; but whether they do this on its merits or more as an apology for having taken time off from really important work, I couldn't say. Anyway, the fit was on me now, and I quite abruptly left off worrying about black flies and headed upwind.

I don't remember much of anything about the trip except that it took me deep into new territory and that I traveled the whole way in a pleasurable haze. Details are vague, and insofar as they struck me at all at the time, seemed laughably mundane. I was anxious to be the first suitor, knowing as I already did the fickleness of a woman's heart, and I pressed on without even stopping for lunch.

When I could tell I was almost there, though, something jarred me unpleasantly back to my old fretful self. It was a sound, a yipping, barking, baying sound I'd never heard before, and somehow it put me in mind of black flies.

My metaphysical anxieties were instantly revived and hit me with the sobering effect of a cold bath. The sounds were growing louder, coming closer. I hunkered down in a clump of bushes to await developments.

I didn't have to await them long. Bursting into view came the bear whose scent I'd followed. She was a magnificent creature of Junoesque proportions, plump, her coat sleekly shining. My heart went out to her immediately. The rest of me, however, stayed in the bushes, and a good thing, too. For hard on her heels, slavering and howling, came the hounds.

Never had I seen or imagined anything half so ferocious as these dogs, or of so patently little use to bears. The reassuring edifice of speculation I'd built up crumbled away right then, once and for all, and it took with it whatever I owned in the way of optimistic tendencies.

The dogs meanwhile had ringed the female and stopped her. Gamely, she flung herself this way and that, but without much effect. The dogs in front only gave way, staying just out of reach, while those behind closed in and took the opportunity to snap at her hams. I saw that their strategy was to bring her down, after which they could tear her to pieces in a fairly leisurely fashion and with less inconvenience.

This didn't sit very well with me. I'd had something else in mind entirely when I traveled all day on a largely empty stomach to get here, and formidable as they seemed, I thought the two of us could deal with these dog creatures. I meant to give it a try anyway. I wasn't going to let go a prospective mate without a fight. Anyway, both my metaphysics and now my nerves were a shambles, and I figured I owed them one for that.

Shaking, then, with rage, outrage, and injured self-esteem, I arose from my thicket.

Well, I still think the impulse does me credit, but it was as far as I got. A new sound—"Hold her, Dodger, Whippet! Hold her boys!"—sent me ducking again for cover.

The dogs redoubled their attacks, throwing themselves at the poor bear from all sides now. Some of them, I was pleased to see, came to regret it. One whose jaws snapped a hair's breadth from her nose she disemboweled with a graceful swipe of her paw. Another went off nursing a broken snout where she'd managed, largely accidentally, I think, to kick him. I applauded inwardly: what a mother she'd make! But then she bent low to clear two others from her legs, and one that sprang at her from the side came away with an ear.

I was in an agony of mind, but that voice had petrified me.

Its owner appeared. I trembled. You can't imagine how strange men look to someone who's never seen them before. I took this one for a monster. He seemed to have the skin of a deer, pinkish, well-articulated paws like a mole's, and a double head—the body of a raccoon on top, complete with tail, and underneath, a set of pinched white features overgrown from the eyes down with a curious dark stubble.

His eyes held me especially. Like his voice, they had a certain supple liveliness that terrified me worse than the fangs of the dogs.

Under those eyes the dogs began to show off. It wasn't pretty to watch. But my bear still stood.

The owner of the voice raised the slender stick he carried and pointed it at her. He called out something and to my surprise the dogs drew back. It was inspiring to see how heroically she faced this new threat. At the same time I was embarrassed, too. She obviously didn't have the faintest idea what she was up against.

Neither did I, of course, but I did have the sense to realize that, whatever this new creature was, he was out of our class. This never crossed her mind. Her blood was up; all she was thinking about, if you want to call it thinking, was how best to set about rending him limb from limb. Though attractive, she was, I saw, entirely a creature of instinct. That was too bad. I wasn't, I already knew, and it likely meant we could never have been really close. Still, I envied her for it, in a way. Her instincts had undoubedly led her a happy life to date, free of the metaphysical conundrums that clouded mine, and that was something. It may be that—like a fish—she'd spent that life in a kind of tacit philosophical error, but barring only the present sort of rude awakening, I thought there was something to be said for that way of spending it.

Curling her lip, she lurched forward to the attack. The owner of the voice took this hostile demonstration in good part, and standing his ground, squeezed his stick.

There was a flash and a thunderous explosion that flung me over backwards. When, shaking, I'd crawled back into position, I saw blood welling from a hole in the soft fur near the center of the other bear's breast.

She and I both gaped at this. Then she gave a last wondering look around at the dogs panting their satisfaction, and fell in a heap.

In a moment the dogs were on the carcass, worrying it. The owner of the voice finished fussing with his stick and shooed them away. I was just beginning to entertain a better opinion of him for this when with difficulty he turned her over and slit open her belly!

I lost my head. Thinking back on things, it occurs to me that it's only times like this when I've lost my head that I've ever acted very much like a bear. Read what you will into this—I suppose I'll have to concede that using our heads isn't what most bears do best—the result was very satisfying and went a long way toward restoring some of my self-esteem, rather sunk in the ruckus. It also brought me as close as anyone ever gets, I think, to changing his fate.

Be that as it may, I rose up from my thicket a second time like an avenging spirit. My fur bristled so that twigs flew from it. Three strides brought me to the creature's side.

The dogs saw me. That they hadn't noticed me before I presumably owed to my scent's having been submerged in that of the bear they'd just killed, as well as my being downwind of them. Now

I stood practically in their midst, my arm raised to splash their master's brains liberally about the surrounding area. They noticed me then, I can tell you. It's not too much to say that all hell broke loose.

The creature spun around as I'd hoped he would. We found ourselves face to face. I gave him my most savage snarl—it came from the heart—and started my downswing, already visualizing how much better his shoulders would look unencumbered with his ridiculous double head. The dogs swarmed around me and attached themselves to whatever purchase offered. I didn't feel a thing. The creature's face changed. From blank astonishment it went in an instant to murderous purposefulness. I seemed to have all the time in the world, though. I searched the face for fear, found none, and registered this with an icy prickle somewhere in the back of my mind. And then my paw connected.

Unfortunately, it didn't connect with the face. A dog flung itself up in the way and went down again just as fast with either a broken or a very sore neck. But he broke the force of my swing and threw off my timing. I followed through, but the cuff I was able to administer was flimsy stuff next to what I'd intended. Except for my expression, the creature might have thought I was just giving him a good-natured push. Even this he managed to block partially with his stick. But the stick banged him on the side of the head, knocking the top half, the part with the tail, off, and sent him sprawling. I looked to see if this had finished him, but no: he sat up and glared at me. I had the horrible sensation that I'd only now made him mad.

Then the dogs intervened in a serious way. I began to realize I was getting pretty well chewed to bits and had better wind things up before my legs became too tenderized to carry me away. I took a wobbly, somewhat halfhearted step forward. The dogs hit me with everything they had. They seemed utterly careless what happened to them, which put them in a very different frame of mind from me and maybe gave them something of an edge. I damaged one or two more of them and retired a pace. They followed, but kept a distance now. We ground our teeth at each other, but mostly for appearance's sake. My valor was wearing off, and they evidently didn't feel like pressing their luck either. On that understanding we suspended hostilities.

I took time for a glance at the creature. He had been playing with his stick but had thrown it aside and was studying me, half headless, with unnerving intensity. I shivered. It was the last im-petus I needed. Mindful of the proverb about he who runs away, though less than keen about finding opportunities to fight another day, I backed off some more. The mutilated corpse of the once-desirable female I'd come to court drew a sigh from me, but under the circumstances didn't seem to warrant a more elaborate cere-mony. I was a changed bear from the innocent creature who'd come traipsing so blithely to answer her summons. Growling, as I hoped, impressively, I took myself off.

That was the first time I met Davy Crockett. As you can see, our relationship couldn't have gotten off to a worse start. What's more, I didn't look for much cordiality in the future, and subsequent events were to prove me right. Though I could make a case for saying I'd come away with the honors this time, I didn't kid myself into thinking I'd necessarily be so lucky again. I began to give urgent thought to how to avoid there being a second time. One idea that recommended itself very highly was to visit another part of the state, and that's what I decided to do.

I came to this decision one day about two weeks after the run-in with Crockett. I'd been laying up in my old territory, licking my wounds. Believe me, they took a lot of licking. Besides being fairly thoroughly perforated from the hips down by the dogs, who seemed to have been acting on the plan of reducing me to their size by chewing off segments from the bottom up, I'd been severely traumatized. Gone was the dreamy, trusting bear who so short a time ago had sallied complacently forth on his romantic adven-ture. In his place was a grizzled cynic whose paws shook uncon-trollably for hours at a stretch, who slept fitfully if at all, and who suffered under a depression that seemed in a fair way to becoming chronic.

My whole life was upside down. I was back in my own terri-tory—and felt lost. My old haunts looked unfamiliar. It was as though they were translucent and I saw through them. My sur-roundings seemed to have been artfully stage-managed to put me at ease. I felt it was all a lie. There was no more comfort in the world for bears than there was for fish in a barrel. And I'd thought I had something to worry about before! Now everything seemed ominous. It was all intended to lull me into a false sense of secu-rity. The truth was, I was on a reservation.

Then one day, off in the distance in the direction where I'd fought Crockett, I heard dogs. I stood still and listened. It came again, on the wind. I looked round for the last time on what had been the scene of my, in retrospect, happy juvenile rambles, and back at what was left of the fish I'd been in the middle of devouring with a certain amount of self-directed viciousness. On my face was a knowing sneer; on his a look of stunned surprise. I felt that I understood that look now and that I only now properly appreciated why all the fish I caught wore it. But I was wiser than he was. Life had tried to dupe me, too, but had failed. My dying expression, if it came to that, would be one of world-weary disdain.

Pausing only to finish the fish, I struck out north, away from the dogs, for parts unknown. I might be a fish in a barrel, I thought, but I could still hope with a little caginess to be one of the last ones caught.

I traveled as fast as I could and still keep an eye out for the threats I was pretty certain could be counted on to liven up the trip. It turned out to be a good thing I did. Once I saw some bushes move in a way my experience of bushes led me to believe they had no business to. I veered off. A slender shaft of wood hissed through the air and stuck into a nearby tree, just missing me. I spun around and the bushes disgorged another man creature similar to Crockett except that the top of his head ended in feathers instead of a tail. I reared up on my hind legs, keeping an eye out for dogs, and he scurried up a tree. We looked at each other. He began chanting something I didn't fully understand but which had a placatory flavor and the gist of which seemed to be that it was all a misunderstanding. I was more interested to discover that these new creatures could climb trees.

The dogs I left behind, but never for long. No sooner would I begin to relax a bit than I'd hear them again, faintly, in the distance, back the way I'd come. I developed the nervous habit of constant listening. It didn't take any great perspicacity to guess whose dogs they were or how they got there. The human the top of whose head I'd knocked off, Crockett, had it in for me. He'd made it a vendetta and wanted a rematch.

Acting on the principle that what was good for Crockett was apt to be bad for me, I pushed on in earnest. Staying ahead of him wasn't getting me anywhere. I set out to see if I couldn't lose him.

And lose him I did. Three days went by and I didn't hear any dogs. I began to think I'd *really* lost him. What's more, I hadn't run into any other dogs besides the few isolated ones I met by farms along the way, and they were easy enough to stay clear of. Humans themselves were generally easy to avoid, too, on account of their smell. I began to think I might have overrated the danger. If I could only stay away from Crockett and maintain an otherwise manageable level of precaution, I might yet have the last laugh on life. It seemed a smart bear could beat the system. Buoyed up by my success in eluding Crockett, I was certain I must be a very smart bear.

Either I was wrong about that, or it just goes to show how even a smart bear can be lulled into a false sense of security. What happened was, I started to take time off to investigate some of the new sights I ran across, and Crockett began to slip to the back of my mind. That's a very poor strategy when you're dealing with someone like Crockett, who on the whole is rather proud of his bear-hunting prowess and whose vanity was injured maybe more than any of the rest of him when I whacked him up the side of his head and ran off. That also made me the big one who got away. A true-blue sportsman like Crockett, who I later learned had been known to account for upwards of fifty bears in a month, wasn't going to throw in the sponge just because I was maybe a little hard to locate. A complication like that just whetted his appetite for slaughter.

I didn't know any of this, though, and began behaving more like a tourist than a fugitive. The world was so much wider than I'd ever imagined, and with my penchant for finding out about things, it was more than I could do not to indulge my curiosity when I thought I had the chance. I nosed around farms, was shot at a time or two, tasted my first chicken. It was all very interesting. I could see how puerile my earlier speculations were, and I held off making any more for the time being. But one thing was clear enough: the world belonged to men. There seemed to be more and more of them as I went—more of their farms, more of their roads, and more of them on the roads. Their smell hung about everywhere. As a matter of fact, though I didn't know it, I was coming to a village.

Then one day, the third of my irresponsible holiday from worrying about Crockett, I met with a smell that stopped me in my tracks. I had been following one of those pairs of ruts that passed for a road through the woods, watching the carts and men and the reactions of the horses when they winded me and the way the drivers reached for their guns and glanced around while they wrestled with the teams. Cocky as I was getting to be, I found this very entertaining.

But the smell was what held me. It wasn't a man smell, and it wasn't a horse smell either, but a smell I hadn't looked to find keeping company with these other two: another bear. And unless I was wrong, not just the smells, but the owners, too, were approaching together down the road.

This I had to see. So far my experience had been that men either shot at you if you were a bear, or, failing that, ran in the other direction. The second of these wasn't so bad, but the first I didn't care for at all. I couldn't imagine sauntering down one of their roads with them. If indeed this bear was, then maybe my experience to date had been somehow one-sided. Maybe you could get along with men, and I'd just been putting out the wrong signals. Even the Crockett business could conceivably be explained that way. I had, after all, made what he might consider an unprovoked attack. I had no idea what that female bear might have done to him, and it was true that female bears are notoriously difficult to get along with.

So I lay in wait by the side of the road to watch. Eventually, I heard the rumble of a wagon, and a little more eventually saw the whole ensemble come round the bend. There were two men up front on the seat, one, the driver, dressed in homespuns like a farmer and wearing a broad-brimmed, otherwise shapeless hat (yes, I'd deduced by then that these topmost appendages were something of the sort), and the other sporting a cap, a short embroidered jacket unlike any I'd seen so far, and enormous flowing moustaches which he vigorously wiped, tugged and twisted round his finger each time he finished drinking from the earthen jug he and the driver were passing back and forth. Following along, and attached to the back of the wagon by a chain ending in a strap about his neck, shambled a sorry-looking bear.

If these were the terms of peaceful coexistence, I wasn't impressed. Not only did he walk while the others rode, but fur was missing from the bear's lean shanks in great clumps. Where it should have been was ulcerous hide. Dust covered him from head to foot, and more was continually thrown in his face by the wheels. If he lagged, the chain brought him stumbling forward again. All in all, I saw little to envy in his situation. As a last cruel touch he'd been made to wear a short embroidered vest similar to the jacket on the man with the moustaches. It didn't suit him at all.

I shrank down in my bushes and remained there after the company had gone by. The sight took some digesting. By comparison with the bear I'd just seen, I had nothing to complain about. The life of a bear hunted by men seemed infinitely preferable to the life of a bear who theoretically had nothing to fear from them. It might be a bit precarious socially, but getting along with men began to strike me as a dubious achievement anyhow.

Having made up my mind about that, I should have faded back into the woods and got on with my life as a fugitive. I couldn't. I was still curious. That silly outfit they'd made him wear haunted me. Why had they done such a thing? What was the point of keeping him at all?

I ended up tagging along to find out. I've done more intelligent things, I admit, but it wasn't in me to let the matter lie.

I came to a clearing. The road continued past, but there was a cart, drawn off to the side of a rough plank building, while maybe a dozen men lounged about on the low porch and in a semicircle in the dust of the yard. In the center of this was the man with the cap and moustaches from the wagon, and with him the bear.

I drew as close as I dared and watched along with everyone else. Something was clearly about to begin. Then the man with the cap gave his moustaches a final adjustment and raised a stick. The bear, rather wearily, I thought, reared up on his hind legs and held the pose, meanwhile looking around at his audience in a bored way that suggested he considered he'd played for better. The men spat, whether appreciatively or not I couldn't decide.

Then, "Shit," drawled one, as I reconstruct it—for I only caught the gist of things at the time, "my old hound Buller can make a bear do that, and livelier, too."

"Wait, gentlemen," said the man with the cap, in what I later learned to recognize as a foreign accent. "My Hans has not started. Come, Hans. Come to me!"

He backed off, twitching his stick. Hans lurched after him, still standing, rolling his eyes in what I took to be understandable disgust. Backwards, the man with the cap led him round in a circle, to ironical applause.

"Hee, hee, I bet a real American bear out of them woods there what's never had a lick of training'd make the little feller backpedal a sight quicker," said one.

The man with the cap, who wasn't very big, in fact, except for his moustaches, quivered. Up went the stick again; he called out a new command.

I'll give the bear this much: he knew a lot of tricks. I'd never seen anything like it, though of course that wasn't saying much at the time. He somersaulted, backward and forward. He balanced on stumps. When the little man played an accordion, he danced; then *he* played, though not so well. I was impressed.

But what sort of work was this for a grown bear? Discounting the glamour—for I can't deny that playing for an audience was a novel and somewhat alluring idea to me—but, as I say, discounting that, it all seemed so frivolous. Then there was the fact he didn't seem to eat very regularly—an important point when you're weighing a vocation. And his audience, except maybe for me, was anything but appreciative. No, I don't deny I was attracted, but it still seemed to me that the life of a fugitive beat that of an artist hands down.

Finally satisfied, I was about to leave when a dog came streaking down the road behind me, ran into the yard and fastened his jaws in the bear's calf.

"Whoo-eee!" said the men, perking up. They capered and slapped their thighs. The man with the moustaches shrieked and ran at the dog with his stick. More dogs appeared and swarmed over the bear, egged on by the men, whose interest, at last awakened, couldn't have been livelier.

The bear's antics were lively, too, if shortlived. When the first dog hit he'd been rather languidly balancing a red ball on his nose. The ball went flying and bounded over by me. The bear hopped back on one foot and tried to shake off the dog, looking like a Cossack with something stuck to his boot. When this didn't work he took a swipe at it. By the time the dogs overwhelmed him, he was receiving applause that, in slightly different circumstances, must have warmed a trouper's heart.

Meanwhile the little man was still flailing away with the broken end of his stick. An onlooker reached him and dragged him away. Then up galloped a man on horseback.

To my horror, I recognized Crockett.

Crockett took in the situation with a dispatch I was later to learn characterized everything he did. He flung himself off his horse and waded into the heap of dogs, kicking them and pulling them off. But the bear was down, and even after Crockett and the other men had hauled away all the dogs, he stayed down. He was a mess.

"Why, Davy," said a burly man, stepping down off the porch, "you're just in time to join us in a right interesting piece of entertainment. This here little feller what owns the bear was just showing us some tricks. We was thinking it a pretty poor show, but that last one beat all, I reckon." He grinned and the others laughed, all except the little man, who broke free and ran up to the side of his wounded protege, where he carried on to himself and tore his hair. "What brings you to these parts, Davy?"

Crockett's face set in a way that sent a shiver through me.

"I'm hunting me a bear," he said, pronouncing it "bar."

"Well, I reckon you got him, Davy," said one of the men, delighted. The others guffawed.

"Davy's death on bars," said someone else. "He don't even wait for them to get outside of town."

"This here's a special bar I'm after," insisted Davy against the hilarity. "He laid me out flat and killed two of my best dogs. Fiercest fighting bar I ever seen, and the slickest. The way he snuck up on me, I expect he must be part snake. But I mean to have him. Dodger, you stay put. Can't you see when you've caused a man enough trouble?"

This last was directed at the dog he held, a nasty-looking spotted hound. This dog had been the first to attack Hans and now was making a vigorous demonstration in my direction. I told myself he just wanted to get back to mauling Hans, but if so he certainly seemed prepared to take a roundabout route. I imagined I could see his moronic little eyes boring straight into mine. But I didn't dare move. I cursed my curiosity. Why couldn't I have been born a normally phlegmatic bear? Not for the first time it struck me that those who are most blessed often have least occasion to know it.

Crockett had just been properly warming to his subject when the depraved Dodger had interrupted. The break was prolonged while he took a swig from a jug someone waggishly passed him "to cool him off after the hunt." The little man came tearing up to him, his moustaches at their most threatening angle.

"You have ruined my Hans! Never will he again perform. Never!

He is meat, a carcass. Your dogs have torn him piecemeal! He is a worthless thing. I have trained him from a baby, a cub bear. All the way from Europe he came with me. Never was there such a bear. Such talent! I have performed him for the proudest nobles in Europe. Kings and princes showered gold on us. Yes! And now he is done—no good! He is finished in this land of red Indians, of bumpkins." He whirled about. "You are all bumpkins!" he cried, sobbing.

Crockett seemed embarrassed. The others did a certain amount of shuffling their feet. The burly one chewed his beard, spat.

"The little feller's kind of all het up," he said, halfway between a laugh and a mutter.

Crockett stuck out the jug. "Here, now, mister, no need to take on so. Have a pull of this. Seems like your outlook could use some brightening. Now, I admit as how I seem to have got you in an unhandsome fix here, and no mistake. But if I don't make it up to you, sir, my name ain't Davy Crockett."

The little man bared his teeth. *"Ach,* I have heard of the brave Davy Crockett. I have heard how he kills the bears, bang! Never did I know he killed them so! It is a shameful thing. Drink? Hah! How will I eat, Mr. Crockett, tell me that? How will I eat? Your *verdammter* dogs have stolen the food from my mouth!"

And he aimed a kick at Dodger

This wasn't a bad idea in itself. I could have watched any number of kicks being rained on Dodger and not turned a hair. And indeed, this kick caught him squarely in the ribs and was all I could have wished in a kick, for openers. But Dodger, with the maniacal singleness of purpose of the truly simple, merely yelped, staggered, and finding himself unexpectedly free of Crockett, made a beeline for me in the trees, whence he'd never for one moment removed his eyes.

I believe you could say I acted quicker than thought. Maybe all along I'd been casting up the odds if I were discovered, and in advance had made a considered choice of the alternatives. If so, I don't remember it.

What I do remember is leaping into the open, as it were, spontaneously. That other ill-fated bear's ball lay at my feet. I scooped it up, plotted my trajectory, and hurled it at the lunatic Dodger. Happily, it beaned him right between the eyes. Happily, too, it bounced high in the air and fell back into my arms, where I neatly caught it, rather to my own surprise.

Dodger skidded to a halt and stared at me. Never was there a more astonished dog. I took advantage of his incapacity. Feverishly, I put the ball on my nose and hoped it would stay there. It did, long enough at any rate. I plucked it down before it could fall and tucked it under my arm. I balanced on one foot. Dodger cocked his head and shook it. I gave a hop and balanced on the other foot. I hopped on both feet. Taking a deep breath and letting go the ball, I somersaulted. The world spun around and I found myself on my feet again. I was disoriented. Where was Dodger? I located him behind me, white showing all around his eyes. The crowd of men stood petrified. I knew this couldn't last. I essayed a cartwheel that brought me closer to them. It wasn't much for style, but I didn't actually fall over. I stopped.

Crockett was the first to recover. In one fluid motion he'd fetched his gun from his saddle and was pointing it at me.

The little fellow threw himself between us, arms spread, and backed up against me. That was fine by me; I only wished he were taller. *"Nein, nein, nein!"* he said.

"Davy!" said the burly one. "Are you gone crazy?"

"That's the particular bar I've been trailing these weeks," said Crockett, with a face like a stone.

"But Davy, man . . ."

"He's mine! He's mine! You must not touch him!" said my rather inadequate shield.

"Wait a minute, Davy," sang out a voice to the side. "We'll hold him for you!"

"Aye, we'll hold him!" "He's likely too fierce to go alone." "We won't let him hurt you, Davy!" chimed in the rest.

Crockett's eyes flickered. His face reddened. He lowered the gun.

Ignoring the boisterous carryings-on of his friends, some of whom were rolling on the ground and none of whom could have kept a straight face to save his life, Crockett stalked over and looked me up and down. Our eyes met. I knew then that even chaperoned I still wasn't through with Crockett.

"I guess this bar's full of tricks, right enough," he said to the little man—or to me, actually, over the little man's head. "And I'd surely admire to have caught up to him before this so I could have had his tricks and him to myself a while. But I told you I'd make it right what I done to that bar of yours there, and I never went back on my word yet. Though I'll say this: I never was so sore tempted, either. So you best just keep this new bar of yours out of my way,

that's all I can say, or else I can't rightly answer for the consequences."

And that's how I came to trade the sleepy, retired life of a bear
for the chancy, adventurous life of an artist. It's also how I came to
take the first step on the path that was to lead me first to Sam, and
eventually—inevitably?—to this pen.

Chapter 2

My savior's name turned out to be Karl Hofstedtler, and we hit it off right from the start. During the nine months or so we were together, Karl and I traveled all over the South, with me taking Hans' place, and I found that the only reason Hans had been so thin was that Karl didn't eat too regularly himself. But what he had he shared with me, and he treated me as well as he was able. He thought I was a great artist, the greatest performing bear ever, he used to say, and he was sure someday I'd make his fortune.

Unhappily, the people we played for usually had tastes little more refined than those of the bunch who witnessed my *ex tempore* debut. Eventually even Karl began to get discouraged. "They do not appreciate art here," he used to say gloomily of the country in general. I agreed. I'd had enough of being bitten about the legs and ankles by carping critics. I soon found, too, that it didn't do to lower myself by responding on their level.

"You must not bite back," Karl told me finally, grimacing as he wiped the blood from his nose, where my late critic's owner had punched him. "The audiences do not like it."

That was true enough. But I didn't like being bitten, either. It was something I was inclined to be touchy about.

One day, after a hasty exit from a village where I'd squashed a dog belonging to the leading citizen (a big, strapping fellow: I thought he was going to come at me with his bare hands), Karl sighed and said to me:

"Bruin"—for that was the name he'd given me— "you have too much the artist's temperament. You are too sensitive. Also, you play over the head of your audience. Nuance is wasted on these bumpkins. Why don't you be more comical, as I have told you? But you are right, you are right, there is danger there, too. When you are comical, they don't respect you, and they are likely to sic the dogs on you then, too. *Ach,* I don't know what to tell you. It will put gray hairs on my head to work with such a bear. So brilliant, but so sly, too. You think to make it look like an accident today, hah? No, no, I know. But I cannot be mad. You were magnificent, how you pound up that dog with your feet. But where you learn such a thing, the *entrechat?* You tell me, where?"

The upshot was that we decided to try our luck in the city—a "center of more culture," as Karl put it. He'd worked these before with Hans and hadn't done all that well. But my skill already surpassed Hans', and given my way of meeting criticism, he thought we might be marginally safer.

Pittsburgh, when we got there, looked like it had arrived itself only just ahead of us. Trees pressed up close on all sides and it was impossible to go more than ten feet without having to detour around one of the stumps that had been left behind when the forest was pushed back. The wooden buildings floated in a sea of mud. The spaces between, humorously called streets, swarmed with dogs, children, and hogs, which last roamed freely everywhere and disposed of the municipal garbage. Sunk to their bellies in the mud, they looked like huge fat globules in some unimaginable stew.

The children loved us. Unfortunately, they were likely to throw anything but money. Karl was worried I'd get hold of one and deal with him as I had the dogs, but I knew better than to do that, and every once in a while they inadvertently threw something good to eat.

The hogs looked at me askance and kept their distance. The dogs, most of them having no masters to impress, barked furiously and sensibly left it at that.

After I got used to it, I liked the city. It was exciting, what with all the activity on the streets, and Karl was right about its being safer. I think I came in for no more harassment from dogs, urchins, and drunken passersby than the average citizen did. In fact, if I'd had a coat to wear, I could probably have passed for one of them. Some were better dressed, but there were a lot of frontiersmen who came and went, and many of these, besides being wilder-looking and shaggier than I, also smelled worse.

I ate well, too. There was enough just lying in the streets to keep body and soul together, if you could beat the hogs to it, and the dogs. But also, I could generally count on getting slops from the taverns we visited. Karl would ask for these for me. Sometimes we got them without his asking, if the tavern keeper was a humorist. I didn't mind, but when I saw how it upset Karl to have to let me lick my supper off his jacket, I made it a point to try to stand in front.

Our reception in the taverns depended heavily on what mood the men were in. Sometimes they'd have us inside and buy us drinks. In fact, they were apt to want to stand me a round more than they cared about Karl. "Belly up, mister, and be sociable," they'd say, making room at the bar. Up I'd go, and get handed a beer. They never tired of watching me drink from a bottle—not the hardest trick I ever mastered, but one of the messiest. They especially liked it when it fizzed up my nose. That was pretty much the level of their humor.

I saw that Karl was right: the best way to please was by clowning. I worked a little shuffle into my act, meanwhile putting up my paws to mime drinking, and emitting a piteous howl. It got so we were known all over town and I could get us drinks anyplace we went. This trick had the added advantage that, once they'd bought us drinks, they were in a better frame of mind to part with some money for Karl, who would wait for the right moment and then put me through some of the rest of my repertoire. The men were less interested in this than in watching me wrestle with a bottle, but they always anted up something for politeness' sake. I think it graveled Karl that that was so obviously their only reason, but I'd never been able to attach the importance he did to my "art" from the beginning.

Eventually, after a period of circulating pretty impartially among the different saloons and taverns in town, we wound up making one called the Black Bear Tavern our headquarters. There were several reasons for this. One was that it was big enough. Half the doors in town were grogshops, from barbershops to groceries, and any number of mechanics, clerks, even schoolteachers, were part-time bartenders on the side. But in a lot of these establishments there wasn't room for me.

Another reason was that the Black Bear had a slightly more subdued clientele. Once someplace else I was slipped a bottle of whiskey. Karl would never have permitted this ordinarily, but they'd taken the precaution to get him more than ordinarily drunk first and he was in no condition to protect anybody else's virtue. I drank it off like a trouper, thinking it wasn't bad stuff. In fact, it began to warm me from head to toe in a way no amount of beer ever had, and I began to think it was quite good stuff indeed. I remember wondering why Karl had always kept it from me. Hurt and a little piqued on the subject, I decided to show Karl the bottle and take the matter up with him.

I smacked my lips. Karl lay slumped over a table in the corner. Already in a very forgiving mood, I set out in that direction. As everyone seemed to be watching, I gave them all a roguish smile and led off with an amusing two-step. Somehow, as I recall, my choreography got a little complex. I remember finding more irregularities in the terrain than I'd counted on. Anyhow, I tripped and fell over a table, smashing it to flinders. Everybody thought this was a great joke. I was a little embarrassed, but pleased they weren't going to hold the table against me. Karl meanwhile had jumped to his feet and was staring around in some alarm. Tears came to my eyes to think how I must have frightened him. I was suddenly overcome by a sort of soupy fondness for the man. I got up and lumbered toward him, my arms outstretched affectionately.

"Bruin! *Mein Gott!*" he shouted muzzily, mistaking my intention. I rumbled something supposed to be soothing, but I think the general perception was there were too many teeth in it. A chair bounced off the back of my head. Everyone was suddenly shouting. Karl ducked away and joined the crush at the door. I followed, wondering what the matter was and having a good deal of trouble with intervening tables and chairs. By the time I got outside, the party had scattered in all directions, still shouting, and I couldn't find Karl.

He came for me after dark. I was in a tree at the edge of town, surrounded by onlookers, crooning to myself and thinking of home. It was something of a turning point in my career.

"Bruin," he said, "you must come down."

I looked down at him and sniffed.

"I'll bring him down for you, mister, if you like," volunteered a bystander in a leather tunic, leaning on his gun.

"Bruin, you see what will happen. You must come down."

I lifted my muzzle. The moon shone down on me unwinkingly. It looked just as it had in Tennessee. It would shine just that way if the helpful bystander shot me out of the tree. It would make a difference to no one but me what happened to me.

"Bruin! I beg of you! Have pity on your poor Karl!" he said, wringing his hands.

Well, it would also make some slight difference to Karl, whose bread and butter I was. The thought of bread and butter vaguely reminded me I was hungry.

"Bruin," pleaded Karl, who I think must have heard my stomach, "I have money. It is for you. I buy you a steak when you come down, hah? It will be all right again, Bruin. Also, I have a plan. I will tell you about it if you come down."

Thus a tug on another line that tied me to the living: besides being hungry, I was curious. I looked again at the moon. It looked back as blandly as ever. I envied it its detachment. Ejected from my comfortable bear-centered universe in which everything existed only for me, I found myself now in a world in which bears played at best a marginal role; in which everything, including bears, existed for the sake of something else, if for anything. It would be nice to float serenely through this new blooming, buzzing confusion aloof, like the moon, borne up by an air-filled bubble of philosophical detachment—but I didn't seem to have it in me. I could only achieve the requisite buoyancy on a full stomach. My detachment never lasted longer than the time between properly regulated meals. Miss one of these and I grew hungry, and when I was hungry, my stoicism slipped. It might very well be, I thought, perched in my tree, that I was in some sense insignificant; that Karl was, too—that nothing mattered or made any difference. The fact remained: I was hungry. I felt obligated to Karl. I was curious.

It seemed to make no difference that I made no difference.

With a sigh for my bearish frailty that prevented me from aspiring to true enlightenment, I clambered down out of my tree, back into the perplexing world of men, and over to Karl for supper.

Karl's plan was to set up shop at the Black Bear on a permanent basis.

"I have spoken to the landlord, Herr Grund. We are, you know, celebrities, my dear Bruin. We are known everywhere in the town. We will be a great attraction, you see—a jewel in his crown. His tavern is called the Black Bear, is it not? Hah! And now he has a black bear! And he will feed us—both of us. And we will pay nothing to sleep there, and he has a nice shed for you, too. What do you think of that, my friend?" And he rubbed his hands as he hurried me along.

I soon came to suspect there was more to Karl's plan than he was telling me.

At first the change was pleasant enough, if a little boring. To tell the truth, I'd rather liked spending the day on the streets. But cold weather was coming on and it was a hand-to-mouth existence for Karl; settling in at the Black Bear meant an effective promotion of a social stratum or two and easier living besides. In no time, in fact, he filled out so that his embroidered jacket began to sit on him the way the absurd little vest had fitted Hans, and even his moustaches prospered remarkably.

I put on weight, too. It would have been hard not to. Most of the time I just sat on a bench they'd placed for me in one corner and drank beer. I even had my own table. Sometimes a stranger would come in and not see me for a second or two, or even until he'd been served. The regulars thought it was a fine joke when that happened. I don't know how many unfortunates half died choking on their drinks as a result, but when they recovered they always allowed, too, as how it was a capital joke to see me sitting there like a customer. It became a tradition of the place that the newcomer then had to buy me a beer—never anything stronger: a sign behind me on the wall adjured them in Karl's English: BEAR HAS NO SPIRITS.

As a joke there's no denying I was good for business. There was little call for my skills as a performer, though.

"No, no, no! Why paw you at me so? You will make me spill the tray," complained Karl once when I lowed and tried to stop him as he bustled past. Later he came back, laid down the empty tray and sat next to me on my bench. He picked at his nails.

"Bruin," he said finally, glancing nervously around, "it is true, we have not been so much together. And I am sorry. But you must understand. Things are not as they were. No, no, let me talk! Be a good bear. You must behave for your Karl. It is very important. Very, very important."

I subsided, unhappily. Karl's eyes, I noticed, were fixed on the door to the Grunds' living quarters. He actually mopped his brow.

"I have been good to you, no? Yes! Never have you eaten so well. You drink beer all day, you sleep in a nice shed, you never have to worry about the dogs. You have a good life now, no? Yes, yes, I come to that," he said as I tried to interrupt. "You listen. I know you have not much chance to perform here. I know how you feel. Your talent will not rest, you want audience, applause . . ." He waved his hand, sat up straighter and for the first time looked at me. "I, too. I chafe at this idleness, my friend. A part of me, inside, it may be my best part, it tells me to run, to fly!—while there is yet time. It even brings dreams at night. 'Take your art to the world!' it says. I toss and turn on my comfortable bed. It speaks to me: 'You have a gift, it is your specialness. You must not deny it!' It is true!" he said, and his eyes flashed. He thumped his chest. "I am a great impresario. No one knows the animals as I do. No one understands them, can work with them so. See how I have trained you. Yes, as a trainer, I am unique."

I woofed noncommittally and shifted on the bench.

His eyes lost their fire. He slumped.

"As a waiter," he shrugged, "I am not unique. So-so. I admit that. But Bruin, this you must understand, too. I am no longer so young. The travel is hard for me now, especially in the winter. And the people in this rough land do not value my art. Our art, my dear Bruin. It is hard for you, too. I know that. That is why I have stopped here, my friend. Only for a while, though, I promise. We will rest and get fat and then we will plan, yes? Then when warm weather comes again we will go North maybe, hah? Soon, my dear friend. You must only be patient a little while. Be a good bear, not make such a fuss like you do and scare the good customers, hah? I know you do that much for Karl, and then soon—Ah, Gertrude, *liebchen!*"

He stood up so fast the table rocked, and plucked at his jacket in an unsuccessful effort to bring the front closed. Gertrude, Herr Grund's lean and rather antiquated daughter, glared at the two of us, then focused on Karl and tittered unconvincingly. Closing behind her the door to the family apartments, she tripped like a stringy sprite into the room. Karl scampered to meet her.

He turned to me first, though. "Bruin," he said hoarsely, pleading, "I bring you a nice beer, hah?"

Gertrude was the fly in the ointment, the part of Karl's plan he hadn't been altogether forthcoming with me about. Not that I'd been slow to see his interest in her: that was transparent from the first, even to a bear. And I didn't hold it against him, though there were times, by and large coinciding with Gertrude's alarming flights of coquetry, when I found his passion rather hard to understand. But I didn't feel threatened by it. It never occurred to me that it had anything to do with me. Karl, I thought, was simply availing himself of what offered, much in the way bears do. If his taste seemed a little peculiar, I chalked that up to my inexperience in judging of the charms of human females. If Gertrude's charms seemed dubious to me, or even nonexistent, I reminded myself that after all she wasn't a bear and the same standards mightn't apply. Another point I thought may have been in her favor as far as Karl was concerned was that he didn't have to fight for her.

So I wasn't concerned when Karl no longer spent so much time with me. These things, I knew, do take a certain amount of time. But then I noticed it was worse than that; he was avoiding me.

Gertrude didn't like me, was the problem. When I wasn't "that bear," I was "that ugly bear" and what I presume were even more eloquently uncomplimentary things in German.

And she wasn't taking any chances. Her stock had sunk too low for her to overlook any source of possible competition. It's a sad commentary that she was jealous of me: I am handsome, no matter what Gertrude said; but I'm also male and a bear.

But jealous she was, and I began to worry. Herr Grund, a large man with moustaches even more imposing than Karl's, was a traditionalist at heart. He had only taken the both of us in in the hopes of netting a mate for his daughter. I understood that now. I had never figured as a principal in these calculations, but Karl wouldn't come without me. Granted, I'd subsequently paid off well enough in my own right, but increasingly I found Herr Grund, whose small, matter-of-fact eyes reminded me of those of the hogs in the street outside, staring at me with something like speculation. Partly he resented the quantities of beer I drank, but I sensed a more general objection as well. I think he always regarded having a bear at one of his tables as a newfangled innovation, something not quite respectable, just the sort of thing he'd criticize in one of his peers. I imagined I could see him weighing this against the fact that I was so good for business. I was a conundrum that must have caused untold ripples on his glutinous soul.

What worried me was the prospect of losing Karl. I was the

more famous of the pair of us, but two things I'd already learned: one was not to rely unduly on a fickle public, and the other was that at the best of times I needed an agent. The world simply wasn't safe for a bear alone.

The situation continued to deteriorate over the next few months. Then I met Meleager.

One morning I was roused from my beery reveries by the arrival of what for the Black Bear was an unusually distinguished-looking visitor. A black frock coat descended little short of his knees and, looking well-worn but fairly clean, gave him a clerical air. But his stock, about his high collar, fell in too voluptuous folds for these prim gentlemen, and the collar itself was too high and stylish. His head, with its lofty forehead and ascetically thin, finely drawn features, would have been the glory of any clergyman, but the features lacked the proper fanatical cast. Instead they seemed to radiate a cold, very worldly cunning. Completing his attire were two pigeons, evidently meant for dinner, stuffed head downward and still struggling, in the outer pockets of his coat. All in all he cut an interesting figure.

Herr Grund hurried forward to greet him.

"Come in, sir, come in. Welcome to my house. You will like some breakfast, perhaps? We have a nice beefsteak, my daughter she will heat it up for you. Or some bratwurst and potatoes? Yes? Or a glass? What will you?"

"I have breakfasted, landlord, thank you, though I will accept a glass of brandy, if you will be so kind," said the newcomer, surveying the room and stroking and pinching his bare fingertips like someone removing a pair of tight-fitting gloves.

Herr Grund sent Gertrude for the brandy. The stranger's eyes flicked over me as if I were part of the furnishings.

"A fine establishment, sir. The finest in town, by all report. And most capacious, too, I see."

"Danke, danke," said Herr Grund, beaming and executing a frenzied series of short bows, though I don't know what he can have made of the word "capacious." "I am honored. You will please feel at home."

"Thank you, I shall."

He strolled over to my table, where I sat nursing a beer. We studied each other for a time.

"And this, I presume, is the famous Bruin?" he said over his shoulder to Herr Grund, who still hovered nearby. "He's quite tame, I suppose?"

"Oh, sir!" guffawed Herr Grund with proprietary pride. "Would I have a wild bear here, a danger to my customers? Ho, ho! He is tame as a baby. There is no tamer bear in the state, maybe anywhere. He is tame like a cat, this bear. Yes, like a great cat who likes cream." He laughed heartily and clutched his belly. "Even too much, he likes it. Someday he will make a beggar of me. But you will see. You fill up his glass, sir. It is very funny."

"I don't think that will be necessary. Thank you, my dear. You may set that down here."

The thanks were for Gertrude, who had arrived with the brandy. She set the glass on my table and left, impatiently dismissed by her father, who chewed his moustache and momentarily scowled at the stranger, then at me.

"Won't you join me in a glass, landlord?" said the stranger, rather reluctantly, I thought, laying down a quarter to cover the two drinks. I guessed he had caught the expression on Herr Grund's face.

Herr Grund called to Gertrude to bring him a schnapps and sat down with the stranger at my table, all affability again. He sipped and leaned forward attentively, watching the stranger and smacking his lips. Again he reminded me of one of the hogs.

"Good sir, allow me to present you with my card," said the stranger, producing a square of white from his waistcoat and placing it on the table in front of Herr Grund, who gaped at it. The card, which I have seen often enough since, said:

Jason X. Meleager

A.A., A.B., B.A., M.A., B.S., S.B.,
M.S., S.M., Sc.D., Litt. D., Ph.D.

PHRENOLOGICAL PRACTITIONER

Lectures   Nostrums   Demonstrations

"And you, sir?" said Meleager. "Whom have I the honor of addressing?"

"Grund," said Herr Grund. "Just Jakob Grund."

"Excellent," said Meleager. "Delighted." He seized Herr Grund's flaccid paw and wrung it, meanwhile, I noticed, with his other hand deftly retrieving his card.

"Now, Mr. Grund, we may get down to business. I won't keep you in suspense. I arrived in town last night and have been inquiring as to a suitable hall in which to hold a phrenological demonstration this evening. Your place here will do admirably, I'm pleased to say. It is large, of good reputation, and not least of all, is home to this fellow here," and he indicated me with an elegant turn of his wrist, "who could be very useful in my presentation. Now, of course, you would have to suspend serving while I speak, but afterward, Mr. Grund, you will more than make up for the loss. You will have a house full of excited customers, all wishing to stay and talk. What do you say?"

Herr Grund didn't know what to say, and neither did I. There was something about Prof. Meleager that didn't inspire confidence. At the same time he was certainly impressive and had a way of sweeping you along despite your reservations. Even without the evidence of his card, which Herr Grund was now unsuccessfully patting his pockets in search of, Prof. Meleager seemed such a superior sort that you tended to be embarrassed to have reservations and would do anything he asked rather than have him find out about them. Such, I was to learn, was the effect he invariably had. Certainly Herr Grund was no match for him. As for me, I didn't have Herr Grund's habit of suspicion, or anything to lose, either, so far as I could see, and already tingled at the thought of a little excitement. How did he purpose to make me useful? I wondered. And what, by the way, was a phrenological demonstration?

Herr Grund gave up looking for the card. He tucked his head between his shoulders and, with a smile of unspeakable cunning, said:

"But what is this thing, Herr Doktor, this phrenobobical demonstration?"

Meleager laughed. "My dear fellow, I'm terribly sorry. I might have guessed . . . A phrenological demonstration, as the phrase implies, is a demonstration of phrenology. What is phrenology, you ask? Ah, well! Nothing but the most astonishing scientific development of the age. A breakthrough, I tell you. Its teachings are unanimously acclaimed in the highest intellectual circles of Europe. Now, by means of such disinterested prophets as myself, these teachings are being disseminated for the first time in this country, where I don't mind telling you, sir, they are creating a regular furor. Here," said Meleager, impatiently seating one of the struggling pigeons more firmly in his pocket and reaching into his coat. He produced a sheaf of papers, one of which he handed to Herr Grund. "What do you think of this?"

I waited with bated breath while Herr Grund laboriously deciphered the handbill, which read in part:

The lecturer pledges himself to demonstrate the truth of phrenology in any, and in every honourable way which the ingenuity of the incredulous may devise or propose. He throws out the challenge to disbelievers and opponents boldly, and without condition or reservation. He will meet opposition publicly, and on any ground—either by fair argument, or by application of the principles of the science to the heads and skulls of animals, or to the heads of individuals selected by the audience—either with or without his eyes covered—and let phrenology stand or fall by this test.

Herr Grund's eyebrows climbed. He squirmed on his seat. Rather breathlessly, he said:

"Yes, but what is it you do to the skulls of the animals and to the heads of my customers?"

"Of course, of course," said Meleager. "Listen. Let me put it to you like this. Wouldn't it be worth something to you to know all about yourself, Mr. Grund—your strengths, your weaknesses, your talents and tendencies? You can spend a lifetime painfully learning these things by making costly mistakes you wouldn't have made if you knew yourself better. For instance, are you timid? Do you let opportunities slip away which, if you knew your timidity and could compensate for it, you would have seized? Are you overconfident? What wouldn't it be worth to you to have that demonstrated, to *know* that, so you could impose a regimen of restraint on yourself in *advance* of suffering the failures and losses into which your overconfidence will otherwise lead you?

"What of love, Mr. Grund? I'll wager you're quite the ladies' man. Are you too easily infatuated? Too easily taken advantage of? Or must you make allowances for yourself and be not so demanding or critical if you are to awaken that tender offering? What sort of mate is best for you?

"What of others? Is this man intelligent or a dullard? Is he honest? Will he serve you well or will he cheat you? What wouldn't you give to know?

"I," said Meleager grandly, "I, or rather the science of phrenology, can tell you all these things."

Herr Grund blinked. He licked his lips.

"You can tell all this?"

"I can."

"How?"

"By the simple and painless expedient of feeling the head, sir. Do you wish a demonstration?"

Herr Grund wished that very much.

Meleager rose and with a graceful flourish laid his hands on Herr Grund's head. Herr Grund stared straight in front of him and chewed his moustache with a rare expression of concentration. His eyes were blank, his attention focused on the gentle pressure of Meleager's fingertips. Meleager, too, seemed to have no thought for anything but the messages he received from these sensitive organs. Slightly frowning, he gazed into space. His hands traveled over Herr Grund's round head, exploring, exploring, feeling out the innermost secrets of Herr Grund's psyche—that is, if it had any secrets, which I was inclined to doubt. It seemed to me you could read what little there likely was to know with one glance at Herr Grund's unappealing face, and if you still had questions, five minutes' talk with the man ought to more than do. But I considered there might be something to the method even if you didn't absolutely need to use it every time.

At last Herr Grund could stand the suspense no longer.

"Herr Doktor, please! What do you find?"

Meleager sighed. Sadly he looked over Herr Grund at the circle of onlookers who had gathered from other tables.

"My poor fellow. Who would have suspected?"

"Suspected what? What?"

"Calm yourself, my friend. I'm still conducting my examination. That's better," Meleager said, twisting Herr Grund's head forward and away from him again.

"What's he got, doc?" asked one of the men, first spitting a stream of tobacco juice on the floor and politely wiping his mouth. Gertrude, who had come up too, stared from her father to Meleager and pressed her apron to her mouth.

"What's he got? Oh, no sickness of the body, gentlemen—at least none that I discover. You may set your minds at rest on that point. Yet I tell you he's a troubled man—troubled in spirit, you might say. He is a man at war with himself, fighting a never-ending battle against his baser nature; struggling to improve, to become a better man. Am I not right, Mr. Grund?"

Herr Grund's eyes bulged.

"*Ja!*"

"Yes, I thought so. How did I know? I read it here, gentlemen," said Meleager, spreading his hands to indicate the now rather tousled head of Herr Grund like a farmer showing off a prize cabbage, "as plainly written as words on a printed page—at least to one such as myself, initiated in the principles of the new phrenological science.

"For instance, you see these bumps here," and he massaged respectively two spots about an inch above the tops of Herr Grund's hairy ears. "This is the location of your faculties of secretiveness, Mr. Grund. These organs are very large. The evidence is plain: you are a secretive man, Mr. Grund—to a fault, I dare say. For look here." Meleager's hands flattened, only the tips meeting Herr Grund's head half an inch above the temples. "Your acquisitiveness, too, is positively enormous. On the strength of the size of these organs I should have to call you greedy, Mr. Grund; greedy and secretive. And these vices appear to be complemented by yet another. For here," and he pressed now a spot to the back of Herr Grund's ears and slightly higher, "we find a perhaps too well developed faculty of combativeness."

Meleager looked up. His auditors, all of whom had been palpating their own heads, hastily dropped their hands.

"If this were the whole picture, gentlemen, and my dear," he added with a nod to Gertrude, "the man before us would be a sad representative of humanity, indeed. We should have to say he displayed many of the worst attributes of the species and none of the better. But that," and he grasped Herr Grund by the ears and thus enjoined him rather too forcibly for comfort, I imagine, to stay seated, "is fortunately not the case. I have given you only one side of the ledger. Let me read you the other.

"Here is his organ of amativeness—love of the other sex, gentlemen. It is not large, but it is not small either; and here above it is the organ of conjugality. It is of a generous proportion. Mr.

Grund, I deduce that you love or loved your wife very much and are a fine husband. Is that not true?"

"Hah? What? Oh, yes, that is true. That is very true."

"Indeed, I knew it. And here," said Meleager, his fingers now deftly skipping all over Herr Grund's head, "is your philoprogenitiveness—your love for your daughter, Mr. Grund. I presume, at any rate, that that is the identity of the charming young lady?"

Gertrude simpered, startled and pleased to be called young, let alone charming, or perhaps even a lady.

"My dear girl, you are fortunate indeed to be blessed with so caring a father. Yes, and I do not say this lightly, nor only because of his regard for his family. This man, gentlemen, however unlikely it doubtless seems, is a very paragon of virtue. Perhaps not natively, I grant you. He was not born good. But which of us does not have his baser impulses, urges which it is the true test of character to put down? This man has them aplenty. Precisely for this reason it is immensely to his credit that he should master them so completely as to keep them secret from all but the all-seeing hands of the trained phrenologist."

Meleager paternally placed his all-seeing hands on Herr Grund's shoulders.

"I am moved, gentlemen, moved almost to tears by the courage and uprightness of this man in the face of the rather massive handicaps with which he was apparently born. Did I but now call him greedy? Nay, no more generous soul ever drew breath. For that is the true generosity, my friends—to overcome those unworthy impulses which occasionally plague us all, and some of us more than others. See here, his benevolence. I tremble to touch it. Such a monument to self-mastery. Even as I do touch it I feel it pulse—it grows! Yes, it grows, gentlemen. This man improves himself even as he sits here. Gentlemen, I cannot go on."

Meleager sank down on the bench. With infinite grace he brought up his hand to just brush his brow, hiding his eyes.

For the space of six heartbeats nobody moved. Then there was a shuffling of feet and a sound as of gutters overflowing as the tobacco chewers awakened as one man to the fact that their mouths were full and severally emitted brown streams onto the floor. All, even I, looked at Herr Grund with a new, if still somewhat doubtful, respect.

With the cry "Poppa!" Gertrude flung herself on her knees at her father's feet and embraced him.

Already interestingly mottled, Herr Grund's face changed color a few more times. Tears started from his eyes and wobbled down his fat cheeks.

Thoughtfully, I drained off my beer, which had gone flat.

Herr Grund stood. He thrust out his chest till it almost outdistanced his belly, and he grasped Meleager's limp hand.

"Herr Doktor!" he said with emotion.

"Mighty fine speech," said the others, beginning to mill about.

Meleager recovered his composure as gracefully as he'd lost it. Modestly, he declined Herr Grund's thanks.

"It is not I you should thank, Mr. Grund, but the phrenological science. I merely apply its methods. I take it, then, that you are convinced of the worthiness of these methods?"

"Oh, ja, ja!"

"Then I may count on having the use of your establishment for a demonstration this evening?"

Still beaming, Herr Grund acceded to this as well.

Meleager turned to the others and raised his voice.

"You hear, gentlemen? Mr. Grund has kindly lent me the use of the Black Bear this evening for a more extended lecture and demonstration of the principles of the revolutionary new science of phrenology. What did I tell you of the benevolence of this man? Is it not wonderful that he should perform this service gratis and for the good of mankind?" He flung out his arms and led the willing patrons in a cheer for Herr Grund's generosity.

Herr Grund's grin became a shade uncertain.

"What means this 'gratis'?" he whispered hoarsely to Meleager while the others cheered.

"It means for free, Mr. Grund."

Herr Grund's grin sickened.

Meleager gave his arm an affectionate and, I thought, rather ironical squeeze.

"It's for the advancement of science, Mr. Grund," he smiled.

Chapter 3

With the exception of Davy Crockett, Prof. Meleager was the most impressive person I'd ever met. I was halfway under his spell, but not completely. No amount of respect for his science, of which besides I knew almost nothing, could convince me that Herr Grund could boast of much in the way of finer qualities. If he had them at all it seemed to me they were less masters of than mastered by his other qualities with which I was more familiar. Still, I thought, maybe that was only a quibble. Maybe he just had a skull thicker than most and that had thrown off Meleager's measurements.

I wanted to believe in the science, you see. I was excited at the thought of applying it to myself. Why, if the science were true, I should be able to read off from the contours of my head the reasons for my having such an uneasy time of it socially. I was willing to learn. I thought maybe with proper counseling I could make myself over and win acceptance. How I yearned for it! I knew I was a freak. It hadn't bothered me while I still felt vestiges of superiority in being a bear, albeit a hard-pressed one. But I knew I couldn't go back to that. That I felt like a freak shows, paradoxically, that I had come to think of myself as after all belonging in the world of men, if not yet belonging very comfortably. I think there may be a more general truth here. A man (and I include myself in this) is content only so long as he believes he cuts a respectable figure in the largest sphere of action. Let him find out his horizon is but the rim of a small pond, and he will be unhappy.

I was, anyway. I fairly ached to be able to amble down the street by myself, greet my fellow citizens as equals and pick up the choicer bits of garbage without exciting comment or having more trouble than the next man with dogs or being shot at.

So I wanted the science to be true. I made excuses for what seemed to be its literally palpable error in the case of Herr Grund. It also crossed my mind that Prof. Meleager may have had reasons of diplomacy for being less than aboveboard in his diagnosis. There was something about him that was rather shifty, as I've said.

But I wasn't the only one anxiously looking forward to the evening's entertainment. Gertrude launched on a frenzy of house-cleaning, scrubbing everything in sight and ordering everybody about, customers, Karl, even her father. Poor Karl. He was thoroughly bewildered. In a tone he'd never heard her use before, but which I'm afraid he was destined to hear often enough later in married life, she had him bustle about putting together some sort of podium for the learned professor to speak from. Karl was not built for bustling—less so recently than ever; nevertheless, he bustled. I marveled and filed away for future reference this lesson on the efficacy of flattery. In Gertrude's case it never struck me for a moment that the good professor had been aboveboard.

Herr Grund threw up his hands. He seemed torn between pride that he should be hosting such a signal event, and resentment that he should be doing it for nothing.

Me, I was too excited to drink. This worried Herr Grund and Karl for a while, until I reassured Karl at least by eating an unusually large supper. Herr Grund was only further depressed to watch. Gertrude wanted to use the occasion as an excuse to banish me to my shed out back. I think this was not so much because she disliked me anyway as it was that it outraged her renascent femininity to have to receive her important guest with a bear in her parlor. But Herr Grund reluctantly reminded her that Meleager wanted to use me in his show, and her hands were tied. She had to content herself with swatting my elbows up off the table and sponging underneath them.

Poor Gertrude. It was impossible not to feel sorry for her. Not many bees had ever been drawn to that sorry blossom, and now an offhand piece of politeness on the part of one admittedly rather prepossessing bee, uttered just in passing, had precipitated a belated and quite pathetic bloom. She appeared close to the appointed time implausibly corsetted in a fine dress that looked as though it had never been worn, her hair parted in the middle and flattened to an almost enameled smoothness across her brow. She couldn't possibly wait tables in that dress—with the skirts, she could hardly come near them—and Karl soon found she didn't intend to. She passed the time standing idly by, wringing her hands when she forgot herself, and putting them behind her when she remembered.

Finally Meleager arrived, dressed as before, minus the pigeons, his arm linked with that of a plump, rather flamboyantly dressed lady with a very regal manner. Herr Grund scampered forward to greet them. The customers already there craned their necks and stared. Meleager introduced his companion as "Molly Money, celebrated songstress, who has consented to provide an entertainment before the lecture." Miss Money bit her lip and smiled. Then her eye caught Gertrude's. The smile wavered, died. The two ladies gazed at one another. Miss Money quietly laid her other hand on Meleager's arm.

The Black Bear grew fuller than I'd ever seen it. For the first time, unless you count my debut in front of Davy Crockett, I had a touch of stage fright. In fact, I could have done with some beer, or even something stronger, but nobody had a thought for me. The crowd had come to see Meleager, who with Miss Money was being entertained by Herr Grund at a table behind Karl's podium. Karl was busy with the customers, while Gertrude, who never brought me anything anyway, hovered uncertainly near the table with her father and Meleager.

Finally Herr Grund got up and introduced Meleager, with some difficulty, as the "distinguished harbinger and prophet of the new phrenobobical science" who had kindly come to entertain and edify them all this night. He sat down, looking relieved, and Meleager rose and said a few words on the subject of phrenology and how he purposed to demonstrate its principles on the head of the celebrated bear Bruin, indicating me in my corner, and the heads of volunteers from the audience. When the shouting and clapping died down he said:

"But first, ladies and gentlemen, first, as a special favor to the fine citizens of Pittsburgh, I have brought with me all the way from Boston that renowned and much-beloved singer of Scottish and Irish ballads, the beautiful Miss Molly Money!"

The beautiful Miss Money popped to her feet, covered with blushes, and minced to a station beside the podium. Thanking them for their hoots and stompings, she begged the distinguished ladies and gentlemen to indulge her with their attention while she rendered for their delectation the touching Scottish ballad, "Wandering Willy."

My attention itself wandered a little at this point. I never have had much of an ear for music. Instead I watched Karl. Karl was watching Gertrude, who was watching Meleager, who may have been the only one in the house watching and listening, or pretending to listen, to Miss Money. I shifted uneasily on my bench and let out an "Rrrrr" of misgiving. I was astonished by a gale of laughter from Miss Money's audience. Everyone was looking at me. Miss Money was also looking at me, with an expression that didn't in the least suit the plaintive lyrics of her song.

What I'd been thinking about, though, was that there was a crisis building. Gertrude was at the center of it. I'd worried before about her taking Karl for a mate and the ramifications of this for me. But only tonight did I see how bound and determined to have a mate she was. Now she had set her cap for Meleager. If that worked out, things would still be satisfactory. Karl would never consent to be just a waiter, with no prospect of getting Gertrude and the Black Bear as part of the package, and at worst the two of us would take to the road again. But I thought it very unlikely that Gertrude would get Meleager—certainly not if Miss Money had anything to say. Failing with Meleager, Gertrude would be thrown more decisively than ever into Karl's arms—quite possibly even before the night was over.

I was distracted from these gloomy prognostications by the finish of Miss Money's set. She retired to her seat, her audience signifying their gratitude for this with generous applause. Meleager came forward.

"Thank you, ladies and gentlemen. Miss Money, another bow, please. Thank you. Isn't she wonderful? Have you ever heard such a voice, ladies and gentlemen? Such pathos? Thank you.

"And now, ladies and gentlemen, if you will compose yourselves to listen, I will address you on a subject of the most singular interest to each and every one of you. What can that be, you ask? Nothing less than this: your own self-improvement and worldly happiness."

Meleager, at least, had no trouble holding his audience. Evidently as hungry for self-improvement and worldly happiness as I was, they hung on his every word. On he went, in much the same way he had spoken with Herr Grund.

"Need I point out, ladies and gentlemen, the immense benefit that an individual in any situation of life may obtain by a correct knowledge of his own talents, capacity, and disposition? How many are there who know but little of their own failings? How many with large self-esteem think they have no failing? How many deficient in self-esteem always remain in the background for want of more confidence? Now, availing ourselves of the methods of the revolutionary new science of phrenology, each of us may learn which of his propensities and sentiments need restraint and which should be encouraged, thus promoting happiness and virtue." He finished with this wonderful claim: "Thanks to phrenology, now every individual can place his own fingers on every feature of his character."

This was the stuff. I didn't exactly have fingers, but from what I'd seen earlier, they weren't strictly required. Bumps I had aplenty, and lots of character.

Before saying how to use this equipment, though, he gave us some theory.

The brain is the organ of the mind, he said. Interesting, I thought. I guessed what brains were. They were the mushy stuff inside the skulls of animals. Evidently humans had them, too.

Second, the mind has a number of different, independent faculties—one for love, one for hatred, one for reasoning, etc. We know they're different because they do different things. All right, I thought.

Third, the brain has as many parts or organs as the mind has faculties. That just stands to reason, I thought. One to do each thing.

Fourth, how strong a person's faculty is determines the size of the corresponding organ. In other words, it works the same way as with muscles.

Now, exercise of any bodily organ increases its size. If you do a lot of thinking, for example, you increase the size of the organ of concentrativeness. That means you're going to have a bulge in your skull there—for how else could the organ get any bigger?

It all sounded so reasonable I could hardly contain myself. If I had an organ for excitement, I thought it must be rising like leavened dough.

"And now, my friends," said the professor, "a demonstration. We are fortunate to have here tonight an animal—a bear—who will admirably serve to display the generic differences between the mental powers and constitution of animals and those of humans. Will someone kindly lead the animal here, please? Miss Money, will you join us?"

Karl, looking distracted, came to fetch me. Smarting a bit at being referred to as an animal, I allowed myself to be led to the podium, where obediently I sat. Miss Money eyed me warily.

"Thank you, Mr. Hofstedtler," said Meleager. "I believe you said I can place my hands on the bear's head without, ah, exciting his organ of destructiveness? I can? Very good, sir. Thank you.

"Ladies and gentlemen, your attention, please. I have here on my left hand a most attractive young lady, and on my right, as you all can see, a bear. A beauty and a beast, as it were, ha, ha. I will now call to your attention some of the—only *some,* now, ha, ha—of the important features in which they differ.

"Miss Money, favor the good people with your profile, please."

Miss Money, standing very straight, complied, causing something of a commotion in the audience at this view of her remarkable bosom.

"Thank you, my dear. And you, sir—very good, my dear fellow!" said Meleager in surprise as I obliged him by turning to face Miss Money. If possible, she eyed me more warily than before.

"Now, notice the general configuration of the young lady's brow," said Meleager. "See how it rises vertically from the bridge of the nose and describes something like a ninety-degree arc to merge with the top of the head." He traced the outline with his hand. "Here, on the other hand," he said, turning to me and moving his hand from above my nose to the top of my head, but careful not to touch me, "we have scarcely any curve at all, but more of a slope. What difference does this make, you ask? Only the better part of the entire difference between humans and beasts, I tell you. For here, above the eyes and behind the brow, are seated the organs for the intellectual faculties—comparison, causality, language, and so forth. Without them, or with them but meagerly developed, we would be as beasts. See now the significance of the brow that bulges—yours and mine, ladies and gentlemen—versus the brow that slopes!"

I was offended. From the stir Meleager's words caused, the thigh-slapping, hearty spitting, and tide of ejaculations on the order of: "I'll be hornswoggled!" and "Blast my old shoes!"—I'd have said that, if anything, the honors lay with the slopes. My confidence in the new science was sorely shaken. Especially galling under the circumstances was my lack of words in which to protest. An "Rrrrr" escaped under my breath. This brought a laugh and earned me a raised eyebrow from Meleager, but also, I realized, was a confirmation of the charges against me. I resolved to keep my mouth shut and watch for a happier means of rebuttal.

After an inquiring glance at Karl, Meleager proceeded.

"Here, for instance," he said, turning to demonstrate on Miss Money, "we have above the brow and somewhat to the side the organs of time and tune. These enable us to judge time and follow a tune. As you'd expect from their importance to musical skill, these organs are highly developed in the lovely Miss Money.

"Let us turn now to our arboreal friend with the sloping brow," said Meleager, rather flippantly, I thought. "Because his brow slopes, we may expect to find his intellectual faculties largely undeveloped. The all-important organs enabling him to perceive causal relations, to classify and abstract, to remember events, will be present only in the most rudimentary form. As a bear—!"

Meleager broke off with a start. He had laid his hand on my brow, actually touching me this time. He jerked the hand away. Gingerly, he replaced it, staring at me hard. His fingers ran swiftly over my skull.

"Extraordinary!" he breathed.

Miss Money clapped a hand to her mouth, I think meditating a scream. Some of the audience half rose to their feet.

"As I was saying . . . ," said Meleager, feeling on, unable to take his eyes from me, "that is, being a bear, of course he, I mean to say . . . Yes. Well." He pulled himself together. "As I was saying, he's a bear, and so of course these organs are almost nonexistent."

I knew better than that. I thought he did, too.

I winked at him.

"Gah!" he said. He followed this up with much vigorous throat-clearing. "Ladies and gentlemen, you must excuse me. I seem to have a bear—a frog, a frog!—in my throat. Be right in a moment. Ahem, ahem! That's better. Where was I? Time and tune. The bear has of course only a very small organ of time—"

I yawned.

"—and next to none of tune!" said Meleager, practically shouting.

He may have been right about this last. Still, I felt I couldn't let it pass. It occurred to me to croon what I could remember of the opening bars of "Wandering Willy"—just the melody, of course. It was enough. I had my audience in stitches. I think Miss Money even recognized the tune—she went very red in the face. With the others it was mainly my timing that did the trick. But Meleager surprised me.

"I see I should have said none at all of tune," he remarked. He looked at me, shaken, but with a new glint in his eye. "Also, I would say his mirthfulness is quite large."

More laughter. But I was content. I felt I had made my point.

Meleager wound things up quickly—"I know all my talking has made you thirsty." He apologized for not publicly examining volunteers as he had indicated he would, but promised to do so next time. Tonight he pled fatigue. Working with such a celebrity as myself had quite exhausted him. He advertised another lecture for the following night and invited people to see him to schedule private examinations. Then he produced a chest and he and Miss Money distributed pamphlets and sold books and lotions "compounded under my own personal supervision" which, rubbed into the scalp, would encourage the different organs of the brain to grow. He also hawked an odd-looking pyramid-shaped hat. This, he said, would help exercise the brain organs if worn regularly.

Karl led me back to my table. He was chuckling.

"You make a fool of that Herr Professor Hokum, Bruin. You are a good bear."

If it was Gertrude Karl was worried about, he needn't have been. Meleager had taken his bow at the end hand in hand with Miss Money. The applause was generous. He had put his arm around her waist and with a simper she had melted against him. I saw Gertrude turn away, stand still a moment, then take an apron and very deliberately tie it on over her dress and go to serve the customers. If Karl missed the significance of this, I didn't.

A fight broke out. Evidently someone had set his beaver hat on the floor and the men at the next table had filled it with tobacco juice. Karl ran off to see about this, and I was left alone with my thoughts.

Gloomy enough thoughts they were, I can tell you. And as if to underscore them, I couldn't get anyone to bring me beer. I could certainly have used some, but Karl and the others were variously preoccupied with the paying customers, and none of these had any thought for me. I'd been upstaged—permanently, I feared. It was a bitter pill to swallow, especially without any beer.

Then, I don't know how much later, I found Meleager staring down at me from across the table. My earlier excitement at learning about my character was gone. It didn't appear I would have much chance to use the information if I had it, and I'd come to have doubts he could furnish me with it anyway. I glanced at him with little interest.

He set down his glass and a bottle, sat, and studied me some more. Finally, appearing to have made up his mind about something and keeping his voice low, he said:

"I think I owe you an apology, my friend. I believe I misrepresented your attainments to the people tonight. Do you accept my apology? Please nod your head if you do."

I considered the proposition. I wasn't used to anyone but Karl talking with me so familiarly, but I couldn't see any harm in it. And it was nice of him to want to apologize. I nodded.

"I thought so!" he said, half rising. He sat again, drank off his drink and poured himself another one. It seemed not to occur to him to offer me one, but I didn't say anything.

He went back to staring for a while, then he said:

"Your master tells me your name is Bruin. Is that right?"

I nodded. Meleager drained his glass again. He refilled it, spilling a certain amount. I thought what an inefficient way that was to empty a bottle.

"You were very good tonight, Bruin, do you know that?"

He looked at me expectantly. I gathered I was supposed to nod again. It seemed a sophomoric way to conduct a conversation, and a boring one besides. It surprised me to find his organ for conversation apparently so little developed. In any case, if he wasn't going to offer me a drink, I didn't see why I should go out of my way to humor him. I refused to nod.

He seemed disappointed.

"Do you understand me or don't you?" he said, after a bit.

I woofed equivocally. I was beginning to wish he'd go away. I had other things on my mind. For instance, there was Gertrude, still in her apron, making her way toward Karl. I hadn't seen her for a while, and indeed it looked as if she'd been crying. I noticed uneasily that she was ignoring the customers on her route.

Meleager babbled on.

"My dear Bruin, you seem a bear of truly unusual—even singular—intelligence. If you can satisfy me that I am not mistaken in thinking that, then I have something to say to you which it would be greatly to your advantage to hear. So, please, do you understand me?"

Gertrude reached Karl and took him by the arm. He turned, and she spoke to him. Her words I couldn't make out, but their effect was pronounced enough. Karl flung down his tray; going to one knee, he scooped up Gertrude's hand and ardently pressed it to his moustaches. I groaned.

"I will take that as an affirmative," said Meleager, somewhat flushed. He slopped more whiskey into his glass, tossed it off and glared at me. "Listen to me. I'm not in the habit of making a fool of myself, or of talking to bears at all, for that matter. But if you will give me a sign that you are as intelligent as I think you are, I could be a great friend to you. Don't think I haven't seen how they treat you here: even the customers ignore you. My dear bear, perhaps you are not as intelligent as I think you are, but let me tell you this: it is the business of a novelty to be novel. You, fellow, have lost that distinction, and if I am not mistaken you are more than halfway along to making an appearance as liniment and harness grease. I propose to rescue you from that fate, not out of the goodness of my heart, but because I believe you could be immensely useful to me. Yes, immensely useful. But only if you are as intelligent as you sometimes seem to be."

Gertrude stretched out her arm and pointed to me. Karl slowly rose and looked at me with a white face.

It began to dawn on me that Meleager was offering me an escape. Faithless Karl: I knew what his choice would be between me and Gertrude, though I did him the credit to suppose it would not be easy for him to carry through with. But it was every man for himself now. There could be no objection to my compacting with Meleager.

"If you do not immediately demonstrate that you are, I shall wash my hands of you," said Meleager, for emphasis emptying his glass again and banging it down on the table.

I thought I saw a way to satisfy him, and myself, too—four times over.

I reached out with both arms—scaring Meleager half to death—and took the bottle of whiskey away from him. No more clumsily than he'd lately done it himself, I filled his glass for him. Straightening, I raised the bottle—once to him, once to Karl across the room, a second time to Meleager—then put the neck of it in my mouth and drained it dry.

Thus all at one go I drank a farewell to Karl and a hello to Meleager, quenched my thirst, and not inaptly demonstrated my intelligence.

Chapter 4

Karl's last words to me were: "Bruin, you are a good bear. You are better than I."

We stood together in the street in front of the Black Bear. Several days had gone by, during which Meleager had given additional lectures and privately examined the heads of what seemed half of Pittsburgh. He had bought me from Karl at what I gathered was a very reasonable price. Now Meleager and Molly Money were finishing loading the wagon, to which I was already shackled by a chain from the tailgate.

It was a fresh spring day and I was excited and eager to be going, but sorry to leave Karl. I bore him no hard feelings. If anything I felt sorry for him. Gertrude, sourly watching from inside the doorway, would take some breaking in before she fit the image of the loving spouse—if indeed she had it in her. Nor would Karl have my company to fall back on. In selling me, Karl had given up his only friend and the ambition closest to his heart. It was a high price to pay for assurance of a full belly and a roof over his head. I wished him well of his bargain, but I was afraid he'd come to regret it. And I think Karl had his own misgivings on the subject. He knew my leaving closed a chapter in his life, and that what remained would scarcely repay writing about. "Let no man be counted happy till he's dead," someone has said. In stopping with

Gertrude, Karl was able to enjoy much the same advantage as the dead person of seeing the events of his life ranged complete and in their final order, and I think he hesitated to count himself happy. I saw somewhat of this in his eyes as he gazed at me. They glistened, then overflowed; with a sob he threw himself on my shoulder and wet my fur with his tears.

Gertrude's voice shrilled from the Black Bear's dusky interior: "Come now, Mr. Hofstedtler, leave you that dirty bear."

Meleager climbed up beside Miss Money on the wagon seat. I wrapped poor Karl in my arms and licked his face. Gertrude shrieked and ran down the steps, probably afraid I was going to devour him before she could. I let him go.

Meleager's whip cracked. The wagon started. My chain grew taut and jerked my collar. When I looked again Karl was gone.

My troubles with Gertrude were over, but my troubles with Miss Molly Money seemed just begun. The whole way that first day she occupied herself with twisting about on her seat to frown at me, then twisting back again to complain to Meleager about his having brought me along.

"I do wish you hadn't taken him, Jason. I don't know why you did. He wasn't at all nice to me during my performance that first night, and I was nervous the whole rest of the time that he was going to do it again. You know how I hate it when people laugh."

"Now, Molly. He behaved himself well enough overall, I think."

"Yes, but you never know. I was so embarrassed. I don't know why you bought him from that man, Jason. You could see he was only too anxious to get rid of him, although he tried to make it seem he was so attached. I don't know what we need with a bear. I thought we were getting along so well without one. Weren't we, dear?"

"Mm-hmm."

"And you must see how it lowers the tone of things. It's demeaning—Jason, dear, are you listening? It's demeaning for me to have to go on with a performing bear. Why, what will people think? The better class, I mean. Only the lowest types have bears: none of the better sort do."

"Then it will be up to us to set a precedent, my dear."

"Oh, Jason. I wish you wouldn't joke about it. I'm really very upset. He frightens me, Jason. I don't like the way he looks at me. I'm certain he knows I don't like him. I can see it in his eyes. Oh, he has such beady, penetrating eyes. Every time he looks at me, I'm sure he wants to eat me up."

In fact, the thought never so much as crossed my mind. But Molly, I don't believe, was much of a judge of character.

Actually, I was far too occupied just keeping pace with the wagon to think about eating anybody up, even if that were the sort of thing I did. Those first few days on the road again were a nightmare for me, until I finally began to recover from the effects of the past two months, during which my principal exercise had been drinking beer. If I hungered for anything when I looked at Miss Money, it was her seat.

But I did feel bad about the poor impression I'd made. She was self-conscious enough about her singing without having to put up with detractors in her own camp. And really, her singing didn't bother me too much. The second day out or thereabouts I thought I saw a chance to make amends. Molly had so far forgotten me puffing along behind as to break into song, a rather more extravagant rendition, full of sighs and pauses, than she'd given at the Black Bear. I waited till I was fairly certain it was over, then woofed and clapped my paws. She jumped and spun around.

"Oh, how can you be so cruel! You see, Jason? He's making fun!"

Meleager smiled.

"Do you accuse the good bear of sarcasm, my dear?"

Nevertheless, he turned and gave me a rather narrow glance.

If I had my troubles with Molly, I had a somewhat uneasy time of it with Meleager, too. We just didn't seem able to get along.

Part of the trouble was that Meleager just wasn't Karl. Besides missing the chitchat and confidences, I'd grown accustomed to a certain amount of solicitude from my protector. With Karl this went a long way toward compensating for bad conditions. If I had to go to sleep supperless, for instance, I felt better knowing it was because Karl couldn't help it and he was going to sleep supperless right beside me.

Meleager never went out of his way for me. Sometimes I went without supper for no better reason than that he simply forgot to give instructions to get me some. I more or less put a stop to that at least when one night after I'd been with him a month or two I helped myself in exasperation to a couple of one tavern keeper's chickens that had been foolish enough to wander past. Meleager had to pay and listen to a tongue-lashing besides. I enjoyed that very much. The tavern keeper himself didn't omit to remark that if Meleager was going to haul a bear around and stable him with honest folk, the least he might do was feed him.

The incident turned out to have unexpected ramifications. When the tavern keeper finished with him and left, Meleager reached down his whip from the wagon seat and turned to me. Molly was still indoors and the two of us had the yard to ourselves. He shook out the whip.

"You see what your chicken-thieving has brought me, Mr. Bruin. I have had to stand a dressing down from that lout and pay a pretty penny for the two chickens. You disappoint me, sir. I would never have expected such ill-considered behavior from one of your supposed intelligence. You force me to impress on you the error of your ways."

Without warning he laid the lash across my shoulders.

I was more startled than hurt. My fur pretty well kept the stroke off me. But the tip stung my side and I roared and jumped away. My chain brought me up short.

"You don't like that, do you, Mr. Bruin? Yes, the lessons of life are often painful. Believe me, I'm sorry if I have to be the one to administer some of them. But I fear you need the instruction, Mr. Bruin. You do need it, don't you, Mr. Bruin? I would like you to nod that you do, please," he said, following me and suggestively twitching the whip.

I'd backed up as far as I could and could only stare at him astonished. I hadn't intended anything against Meleager when I ate the chickens, and even their obviously fair-minded owner hadn't laid the crime to me. Meleager's rage seemed so arbitrary—not to say unjust—that I was stunned.

The lash cut the air again and beat dust from my hide in a line from shoulder to rump.

"You will learn, Mr. Bruin," Meleager said, panting slightly. "I promise you will learn. We shall begin again. Your first lesson will be either to nod or shake your head whenever I require an answer of you. Are you listening? I require one now." He drew back his arm. "Do you understand?"

I was beginning to. Karl had been good to me, which had prevented my seeing it, but evidently I was still as much under the gun as on that first day when I'd had to exercise all my charm to keep from being shot by Davy Crockett. In the process I seemed to have accomplished rather less than I'd thought. I saw now that being under somebody's protection only meant that nobody else could rightfully shoot me without at least asking first, while my so-called protector could still shoot me or abuse me anytime he pleased. Karl had never exercised this right, but Meleager, as I was rapidly finding out, was a different kettle of fish entirely. In a manner of speaking, I wasn't out of the woods yet.

In my chagrin, entirely as an emotional reaction, you understand, I believe I showed my teeth. The lash whistled down again.

This time I threw up my arm. The whip twined around it, its end spitefully flicking the back of my head. I tried to jerk free; startling both of us, the butt of the whip shot from Meleager's hand and landed at my feet.

"Jason!"

Molly stood horrified in the doorway. Dropping her things, she grabbed up her skirts and came running.

"Oh, Jason! You're not hurt? I told you, he's a vicious, bad-tempered . . . Why, Jason, what were you doing?"

Meleager waved at her, and there was something in the way he did it that shut her up. Glaring at me, but with more bafflement than fury, I thought, he bent down and cautiously retrieved his whip. Molly, who could never be silent for long, was babbling again. Not so gently, he took her arm and led her away, twice looking back.

What gnawed at him, I later found out, was that I'd acted throughout our little rencounter so much like an ordinary bear. I've already remarked I'm apt to do that when I lose my head. This time the lapse proved useful. Meleager still wasn't sure of me, you see, and by acting like a bear of average instincts and intelligence I'd worried him that maybe an average bear was all he'd gotten after all. Needless to say, I kept it up. I did this in the beginning just to irritate him—it galled him no end to think *he'd* been taken—but then I saw that I stood to gain in another way. One lesson Meleager had taught me—not the one he'd intended—was that I needed a more congenial protector. Undermining his reason for picking me up in the first place struck me as being as good a way as any to get him to fall in with the idea of letting me go. It was a risky game, but life with Meleager was no bed of roses at the best of times.

In the aftermath of this business I did eat more regularly, though still nothing to get excited about. Slops were still all I got, and I generally didn't even get enough of them. My belly grumbled all the time, and the leaner I got, the more I disliked Meleager.

It wasn't only me he treated this way. The man was a miser from the word "go." Molly suffered, too, though in her case it wasn't so easy to see the effects in her waistline.

"Oh dear, Jason," she said once when he handed her her share of the proceeds of one of our early shows as a threesome, "is this all I'm to have?"

"You find that insufficient, Miss Money?"

"Oh no! That is, it's just—"

"Indeed. Am I to understand that you wish to go back on our arrangement—?"

"Oh no, Jason, no! I want you to have the institute. I want it with all my heart. I do so want to settle down and get married and live in a house of our own—"

"Well, then, my dear, what is your difficulty?"

"It's just that there were so many people tonight, and you sold two of the skulls from ancient battlefields, and I know the books went well, because I sold quite a number myself—"

"In short, Miss Money, you think I'm cheating you."

"Oh, Jason!" gasped Miss Money, clasping her hands on her bosom.

"My dear, what else am I to conclude? You accuse me of holding out on you—"

"Not holding out, Jason, I really didn't mean that. If you say this is all we took in, then of course—"

"You relieve me immensely, my dear. I couldn't bear to think. . . . There has always been such perfect trust between us. As it happens, you're quite right: the receipts were excellent tonight. Unfortunately, the fact of the matter is that the landlord exploited his advantage of having the only suitable auditorium, and I was obliged to pay a rather exorbitant fee for the use of it." He looked at her sardonically.

"I understand, Jason." She sighed. "It's only that I did let myself get my hopes up. My dress is so worn out and mended that I'm quite ashamed to appear in it. I really don't know how much longer I can make it last, and when I saw how good the attendance was, I confess I thought you might give me enough that, with what I've already managed to save, I might be able to afford a new one. But I'll have enough soon in any case."

"My poor darling," said Meleager, unbending so far as to squeeze her hand, "you make me ashamed. Do you think it's easy for me to watch you scrimp and save and bear up so bravely under all hardship? Do you think it's easy, my dear, when I know that it is I—yes, I—who am responsible? That you do this for me? There is not an hour that I don't reproach myself and admire you the more, believe me. My darling Molly," he said, drawing her closer and soulfully gazing into her eyes, "how many times haven't I wanted with all my heart to increase your poor stipend out of my own pocket or the funds we've set aside with so much sacrifice for the institute, but that I knew you'd only refuse the offer. But dearest, let me now, just this once—"

Molly straightened, recovering from all this eloquence. She withdrew her hand. In a trembling voice, she said:

"No, Jason, I won't hear of it."

Then, unable to contain her emotion any longer, she flung herself into his arms:

"Oh, Jason, you're so good!"

All that day on the road Meleager kept up his professions of esteem and affection. Molly sang, chattered on about how well she could do without a new dress for a while yet, and periodically embraced Meleager or wriggled close to gaze at him with an expression that was pretty unmistakable. Sometimes, too, she tried out the sound of different titles for Meleager's institute-to-be, toward the founding of which she was apparently contributing her own money.

" 'The Phrenological Institute of Boston.' No, better: 'The Boston Phrenological Institute.' Or how about: 'The American Phrenological Institute, Boston'? That sounds nice, I think. Can we have it in Boston, please, Jason?"

For his part Meleager refrained from both sarcasm and reprimand, and was more discreet than usual, I noticed, in wiping off her kisses.

That night we came late to an inn. Over the barking of the dogs and assorted idlers' comments and questions about me, Meleager and Molly learned that all the rooms were taken; they would have to make do with the floor in the dining room. Molly was crestfallen. Brushing aside a child with a piece of twine for a belt, who wanted to know of me "Does he bite, mister?" Meleager snapped his fingers.

"Come, my pet. It's warm enough: we'll spend the night in the wagon."

This pleased Molly no end. Indeed, her satisfaction was such that she even had a fond glance for me.

They wasted little time over their meal. I was still licking the inside of my bucket when they came out in the yard again. They were no sooner clear of the porch than Molly took Meleager's hand and, practically skipping, drew him on to the wagon. With many whispers and giggles, all of the latter Molly's, and most of the former, too, they climbed inside.

All females are sisters. In the dusk Molly's friskiness reminded me poignantly of the regrettably few willing females of my own species I'd known. Her pretended coyness and the coquettish glances she shot at Meleager were the same. I ached with loneliness and an unrest that wasn't exactly desire, but . . .

I guess maybe it may have been desire at that.

And all males are brothers. I cursed Meleager for a lucky bastard and added his good fortune to the list of things I held against him.

But all this passed off quickly enough, and I found myself more curious than horny. For a while I watched the wagon shake, the canvas sides bulging as Molly and Meleager undressed. Then things quieted down and I was left to my speculations.

Edging closer, I put a paw to the side of the wagon. I felt it heave; it began to give out a rhythmic creaking. Then the pace of this picked up and began to be accompanied by an interesting shuffle-thump, shuffle-thump figure, almost like a ground bass, to which Molly contributed an abandoned keening. The pace and intensity of all these sounds increased until they were abruptly broken off with a loud thump that sounded like a wrong note. I heard Meleager cry:

"Damn it, woman, curb your enthusiasm!"

Allowing time for things to heat up again, I cautiously put my head over the tailboard.

They were doing it backwards! What a revolting perversion, I thought, watching them rub bellies in the dim light that also caught Meleager's buttocks circling on high and driving on the recumbent Miss Money, who had fairly immobilized the rest of him in a sickening tangle of arms and legs. Then:

"Jason! He's peeking!" Miss Money screamed.

A boot sailed past my ear. I retired precipitately, my head jangling with images.

Chapter 5

Can you wonder that I came to feel quite attached to Miss Money? Well, I did, and even before she herself began to appreciate me. She was the sweetest soul who ever lived, and she won me over completely, despite her inexplicable blindness to my own finer points. But seeing to the bottom of things was never her strong suit. Her attachment to Meleager was certainly proof of that.

But I never met anyone so prone to be taken advantage of. Meleager, of course, was a past master at it, but he could get around almost anyone. It's other people I mean. She seemed to bring it out in them, and I don't know but what she was better off with Meleager than she would have been on her own. At least if anyone else tried to cheat her, Meleager resented it as a sort of poaching.

But it didn't bother him a bit that our audiences gave her such a hard time with her singing. That didn't cost him anything, and didn't engage his professional jealousy. I think he scarcely noticed. But Miss Money suffered acutely. It wasn't so much that she liked to think of herself as a great artist, but she loved her songs and was wounded in her self-respect. What made it all the harder for her was that she was anxious to regard herself as a full partner in Meleager's work. She wanted to be important to him, and didn't want her claim to rest solely on her willingness to share his bed.

Others were equally willing in that respect, and it seemed Meleager was reluctant to frustrate any of them.

"You don't love me," she burst out one morning on the road after a show the night before. She had prefaced the remark with a long and uncharacteristic silence.

Meleager sighed.

"I was afraid you might take my absence last night uncharitably," he said at last.

"You went off with that floozy. I knew you would the moment I saw her making eyes at you. You went off with her and left me alone all night, and I know what you did with her. I hate it! I hate it, and I hate you."

"Now, my dear, you really mustn't be so hasty to judge, you know. I didn't do anything to get excited about. The lady was anxious to have a private consultation, and as we were leaving this morning—"

"But all night, Jason!"

"Hers was a particularly involved case. Yes, I don't remember meeting with such a fascinating case in some while. Her head, my dear, was simply extraordinary."

"Her head, Jason! Oh, why do you torment me so? I suppose you didn't have anything to do with the rest of her?"

"Her neck was interesting, too, I confess. It was most unusually slender. Now, now, you mustn't take on. I didn't mean to sound critical of you—quite the reverse. You know what a thin neck means. It indicates an abnormally underdeveloped organ of amativeness. If your own organ is perhaps even a little hypertrophied, I couldn't be more pleased."

Molly fumed.

"I'm not a complete fool, Jason. You had relations with the woman."

"My dear, I didn't do anything that wasn't strictly demanded of me in my professional capacity. The woman's case was desperate. Her amativeness when I found her was practically nonexistent. I judged this to be the result of a lack of any natural and healthful exercise of the organ, and I determined not to leave her, as she specially begged me not to, before I had initiated her in a proper course of therapy. I'm pleased to say her case now looks very promising."

"Oh, Jason, how could you?"

"I just told you, my dear. It was a case of professional ethics."

But Molly was sobbing.

Meleager stretched his arm across her shoulders.

"My darling Molly, sometimes duty is distasteful. But you know that in matters of the heart—"

She shrugged off his arm. This time Molly was not to be mollified.

I couldn't do much to keep Meleager from straying, but at a lecture not long afterwards, I did take a hand with Molly's audience.

It was in the middle of a particularly strenuous rendition of "Lochaber No More" that she came to grief, as I recall. She was given in general to a fairly athletic delivery—the more the song moved her, the more she moved—and "Lochaber No More" always was one of her favorites. Anyhow, as you may know, the song closes on a peculiarly heartrending sentiment, and Molly, to dramatize it full measure, had thrown her head back and flung out her arms with perhaps even more than customary vigor. She'd been doing a certain amount of this right along, and she might have gotten away with it this time, too, except that she chose to hold the note for a rather provocatively long time. What with the way her pose raised up and compressed her bosom, and the fact that she anyway more nearly surrounded the note than actually hit it, I guess she was drawing fairly heavily on her audience's patience. A fellow in front broke under the strain. I don't think he can have been much of a music lover to begin with—he'd been cracking nuts all through the set—or maybe he was, and that was the problem. But he took a filbert—we found the nut: it was a filbert—and chucked it at Molly's cleavage.

I don't know if you've ever seen a mason size up a piece of stone, pick just the right spot, and shatter the whole thing to bits with a single tap. Well, that was more or less the effect of the filbert. Aborting "Lochaber" on a high note not in the score, Molly gave over waving her arms about and brought them spasmodically down to clutch the injured part, or parts, depending how you count. The sudden strain proved more than her mended dress could stand; the back seam gave with a *scccrrrtch!* that was heard to the far end of the hall.

Pandemonium. Men stamped their feet, shouted, swallowed their tobacco. Chairs were overturned. The fellow in front who'd thrown the nut brushed off the hands of his neighbors, whose congratulations threatened to pulverize him, and delighted with

the effect of the first, readied a second missile. The target, meanwhile, had grown easier. Molly's dress had seen its last show. The
damage was wholesale, and evidently extended to the corset underneath. As the back of the dress slid forward, expanses of pink
and white flesh began to overflow from Molly's arms.

With no very clear idea how I was going to act on them, but full
of gentlemanly impulses, I loped forward from the wings to protect
her. Molly was too busy trying to hide behind what was left of her
dress to give me much attention, but I shot her an encouraging
look anyway and planted myself in front of the crowd. Not knowing
any more than I did just what I had in mind, the more nervous of
these took this as a cue to start sidling toward the exit, and by the
time Meleager arrived with a coat to cover Molly, I had them all in
a fair stew. Meleager, no doubt worried a panic would be bad for
business, tried to get me to follow him off. But he had his hands
too full with Molly to make me, and I declined the invitation.

My reason was, I was thinking about the dogs. Since I'd come
up in the world, as arguably I had, to phrenological assistant, I
didn't have so much trouble with audiences anymore. But it was
still a sensitive point with me, and when I saw one abusing another
performer, well-intended, like myself, even if maybe not so talented, it made my blood boil and brought out the bear in me. In
this instance, though, I didn't know just what to do about it. Rending and tearing were, unhappily, out, and bears are at an acute
disadvantage when it comes to delivering the cutting remark.

Then Meleager came hurrying back to fetch me, waving his
arms to calm everybody down. I still hadn't come up with anything
that didn't promise to be lethal and I had to submit to being
pacified. "There's a good bear," said Meleager, at length venturing
to pat me on the head—this for the audience's sake, not mine. I
quelled an impulse to cuff him into next week and let him gingerly
begin to lead me away.

Laughter again, and catcalls. I was surprised at the violence of
my feelings. Here I was, physically strong, more than a match for
any or all of my crowd of tormentors—and not only could I not lift
a finger in my defense, but I apparently had no other recourse
either, as humans do. I was handicapped. My exploitable abilities
were just two: my cleverness, which seemed to be letting me down,
and a certain quality of temperament or outlook the value of which
was yet to be proved. These were all I had to work with; if these
were inadequate to the task of functioning in my adopted world,

then so was I. If you are what you do, as some say, then you're even a little less than the sum of the things you *can* do, and in my case this sum struck me as being depressingly small.

Then I saw the fellow who'd thrown the nut at Molly, looking at me with a speculative gleam and cradling another nut.

Something snapped. It was as though I'd been touched by the divine finger: the dam penning my inspiration burst, and I saw in a twinkling how to pay the fellow back in his own coin.

I happened just then to be passing a table littered with Meleager's phrenological paraphernalia. Scooping up a larger than life-size plaster head complete with phrenological markings and weighing, I would guess, anywhere between five and ten pounds, I pitched it at the fellow in the best trained-bear style. It hit him, too—right on the top of *his* head, on his deficient bump of veneration—broke in two and stretched him out, nut still in the breech, on the floor.

I gloated down on him, ignoring Meleager, who was batting at me with the end of my leather leash. Then I had a thought. If phrenology was true, I'd actually improved this fellow. Not that I really expected his thanks for it, but certainly tomorrow his bump of veneration, if that was where I'd really hit him, would be nothing like so small. I'd made a better man of him. Why, it opened up a whole new method of treatment. Quick and easy as it was, I wondered Meleager hadn't thought of it.

Meleager was about fed up with me, and I sensed that matters between us were fast approaching a climax. Hardly a day went by now when he didn't badger me with the prospect of stripping my skull of its comfortable layers of flesh and removing it from its accustomed site to add to his collection of similarly naked headpieces of rare races and skulls from ancient battlefields. "Then, by God, you'd behave, wouldn't you?" he'd sneer at me.

I had made progress with Molly, though. We traveled the whole day after my gallant sortie—I think Meleager wanted to outdistance the news of it—and I was in such disgrace with him that she didn't dare approach me. But that next night, as if to punish us both, he closeted himself with another private consultation, and Molly came out to see me.

"Bruin?" she said in a low voice, searching me out in the moonlight. My eyes, better adjusted, saw how nervously she twisted the stalk of grass she'd plucked and brought along. "Bruin, that was nice what you did last night for me. I want to thank you. It was, it was nice." She sniffled. Her eyes glistened strangely. "Jason is mad at you, and I know you don't get along, but it's only because you broke the head. He'd have wanted you to help me, I know he would. You have to try to understand him. He's really very noble, and he loves me, I know he does. It's just that he's weighed down with so many problems and has to be traveling all the time to raise money for the institute. It's hard for someone sensitive like he is. I mean, he has to put up with so much. The people in the audiences are so far beneath him, it's very wearing for him to deal with them. And we never seem to have any money. I don't know where it goes. I just don't know where it goes." She dabbed at her eyes with her sleeve.

"And now he's mad at me. And he's right, it was all my fault. If I wasn't such a big—" She choked and for a moment couldn't go on. Her outline shook, and the wagon, which she was leaning up against, emitted a sympathetic creak. "He says my new dress will have to come out of my share. He thinks I did it on purpose!" she wailed, throwing the stalk away.

I felt a burning curiosity to see what Meleager's own skull would look like as a free-standing piece. On impulse, propping my forepaws on the tailboard, I stretched my neck and licked Molly's face. She started back, then collapsed on my shoulder, sobbing.

She drew away and peered at me.

"Oh Bruin, you're such a nice bear. I don't know why, but I'm not afraid of you at all anymore. I feel like you really do understand."

I woofed and licked her again. She giggled.

"Silly! What would Jason say if he saw us?" I felt a tremor pass through her, like an earthquake in a swamp. "He's with another one of his skinny ladies. I know the one, too. She made it a point to sit next to him at supper and made up to him all meal, the minx. I know it's her. Oh, if he doesn't love me, why doesn't he just say so? Only I think I'd die if he did." There was a pause. She appeared to be musing. Then she said: "Bruin, dear, if I asked you to, would you do something for me? Would you give Jason a little *poke*? Oh, just a teensy one, of course. Nothing serious. But would you?"

It's true, Meleager did seem to have a decided weakness for women with thin necks. I don't know if this was because they posed a professional challenge to him, what with their supposed phrenological handicap, or if he picked them just to spite Molly, as I think Molly believed. Or it may have been just coincidence. Certainly none of the women advertised in what way they may have been amatively impaired, and to me Meleager's exhaustion on subsequent mornings argued that they weren't entirely dysfunctional. Anyhow, he found occasion to treat enough of them that Molly was thrown more and more on my companionship.

One rainy morning I woke up from a dream that I was drowning, to find myself curled up under the wagon, three-quarters submerged in a puddle the size of a small lake. I knew there wouldn't be any traveling on a day like this. Molly and Meleager wouldn't stir from the fireside at the inn. I wouldn't have wanted to stir either if I'd had a decent place not to stir from. But it was no special treat standing out in the rain in water up to my ankles, and not being a duck, I had nothing to gain by going back under the wagon. Feeling restive, I put up with the situation till a cautious stableboy set down my breakfast bucket at the farthest reach of my chain. First the bucket almost floated away before I could grab it, and then the rain filled it up and turned my breakfast, not all that appetizing to begin with, to an even less appetizing watery gruel. That did it. I decided that, come what might, I was spending the day indoors too.

I went up to the back of the wagon and stuck my nose inside. For a minute I hesitated. A small voice told me I might do well to think twice about this. My nostrils, meanwhile, flared at the novelty of being in a dry place, and the rest of me, envious, was impatient to follow. I shrugged off my qualms and popped inside.

For a time I just sat and looked around me, savoring not being rained on. I'd never been inside before, and I had a feeling Meleager wouldn't have liked it. But it doesn't do to dwell on the unpleasant. I put him out of my mind. I was dry now, and I concentrated on that and on getting comfortable. Climbing up from the puddle that seemed to have followed me in, I began moving things around, and to pass the time, I took stock. There was Molly's trunk, with the ill-fated dress on top, saved for the fabric and buttons, I suppose, and more clothes underneath. After a cursory look I pushed it out of the way. There was Meleager's collection of skulls, which I examined thoroughly, more out of boredom than real interest. The wagon standing on a slant, the skulls all rolled conveniently to the back and out of my way when I put them down. There were

Meleager's clothes, full of his smell. A good deal of these I pitched outside where they wouldn't bother me. And there was a box full of the phrenology books and pamphlets that he sold.

I sat down by these and idly rooted through them. Most of the pages looked as though legions of very small birds with peculiar feet had marched abreast outward from the spine and then leaped off together into space. Some pages had profiles of heads, improbably shorn and decorated, like the one I'd broken, and these were also liberally tracked over by the birds.

There didn't seem to be anything very interesting in any of it, but then I happened to notice that some of the bird tracks matched some larger designs on the outside of the wagon: "P-h-r-e-n-o-l-o-g-i-c-a-l." It was a design I wasn't likely to forget in a hurry, and there it was on the page. I wondered what to make of it.

More interested, I went back to one of the drawings of a head. In a line underneath it with some other designs was "phrenological" again. Absently picking up one of the loose skulls and dandling it, I sat back to think.

I knew the books had something to do with phrenology, and I'd never seen anybody rubbing one on his head or trying to wear one. I remembered Meleager's advertisements: ". . . chart your character . . ."; ". . . record your progress . . ."; ". . . map and function of phrenological organs . . ."; ". . . summary of phrenological principles . . ."

Were the books a kind of list, maybe? An aid to the memory? If so, the bird tracks must be a sort of code. I looked at the drawing of the head.

I located the spot on the drawing where the bump of veneration ought to be. I'd attended enough lectures to pick up a pretty thorough phrenological training and could generally give a character reading of people hailed up from the audience that matched Meleager's own, when he didn't have special reasons for varnishing the truth. Where the bump ought to be on the drawing was the design "veneration." I stared at this for some minutes, none the wiser.

At the base of the neck was a section of track: "amativeness." Above it, standing on end in an area roughly egg-shaped, was: "combativeness."

Ah ha, I thought. "Amativeness" was where amativeness ought to be and "combativeness" was where combativeness ought to be. It wasn't lost on me that the designs were partially similar, and that the words somewhat rhymed. "-Ativeness," then, was likely the code for -ativeness.

This was easy enough to check out. I compared "approbativeness" and "vitativeness." "Acquisitiveness" and "inhabitiveness" gave me some trouble, but things seemed to be going so swimmingly I decided not to let two misfits worry me. And with each comparison I learned how to pronounce more of the code.

I went from "destructiveness" to "constructiveness," and applied the "con-" to "conscientiousness," "continuity," and "conjugality," whence I made rather a large leap to "spirituality" by the unlikely route of "causality." I was rapt.

Then "What are you doing!" came a squeal from behind me. I flung up the book. There was Molly, holding the hood of a cloak closed under her chin and staring at me from the front of the wagon. She looked frightened.

"You were reading!" she gasped. I retreated uneasily. I didn't see what was so bad if I were, but I didn't like her being so upset about it. I thought it wisest to act like I'd never read a word in my life.

"You were *too!*" she said, climbing in out of the rain without taking her eyes off me. She sat down, dripping and panting, filling up her end of the wagon as completely as I filled up mine. She threw back her hood. I saw her eyes widen. I guess I had made kind of a mess. "Goodness, what have you been doing? What's this?" It was one of Meleager's shirts. She held it up, aghast. "Oh lord, you haven't been into his clothes? Oh, you bad bear! You've done it now. But where are the rest of his things?"

I tried to look as if the question didn't concern me. This wasn't turning out well at all.

She gasped again and looked out into the lake. I thought I heard even more gasping. She swung back to me.

"You threw them out in the rain?"

I began to be frightened myself. I whined piteously. Molly wrung her hands, inadvertently squeezing water out of the shirt.

"Whatever got into you to make you do such a thing? What were you thinking of? Oh, you're so bad. Jason will be furious. He'll give you away. Oh! He might even kill you." A tear—I know it was a tear—trickled down her cheek.

Touched, I crawled nearer, lowing deep in my throat. It was bad, I wanted to say, but I wouldn't let him kill me. I'd run away first. If I'd been a match for Davy Crockett, Meleager certainly couldn't hurt me. There was the little matter of the chain, of course, but probably she could help me there. I hefted it suggestively in my paw.

She pushed me away with surprising authority.

"I know," she said, starting up. "We'll say it was an accident."

That was fine by me, although I didn't see exactly how calling it an accident explained how Meleager's clothes got out of the trunk by themselves, let alone out of the wagon. But she was ahead of me there. Out she jumped to gather them up.

"We'll say there was a leak in the canvas," she puffed, returning and throwing the sopping bundle down by Meleager's trunk. We both looked up. The canvas was as whole, if not as clean, as the day it came from the mill.

"Well, we'll just have to make one," she said. She began to root through a pile of loose junk. She stopped. "I don't find a knife. You do it."

Rolling back on my haunches, I picked a likely spot over Meleager's trunk, struck a claw through and made a rent. Water gushed through handsomely. I dropped down on all fours again. Molly was staring at me.

"You *were* reading, weren't you?" she breathed, with an inflection as if she'd caught me biting children instead of just looking at a book. She was acting frightened again. "You understood every word I said about making a tear. You can't fool me anymore. I know."

She seemed to pull herself together.

"It's all right, I won't tell Jason. I don't know what he'd do. I think it's best if he doesn't know. Bruin," she said, coming up and gazing at me seriously, "I think you're a very special bear. I really do. I've grown very fond of you, and I think you like me too, don't you? Yes, yes, only don't lick me. Well, I want to tell you, dear, you must be very careful. It's very difficult, being special. You might think it makes things easier, but it doesn't. I've learned that myself. People don't like you if you're not just like them and don't do what they expect. Oh, if you're very good at doing something rare and wonderful they'll let you alone because then of course you're not one of them and it's all right. But if you fall just the least little bit short in raising yourself up that way—and we can't all be in the first rank, my dear, though some of us do try so hard—well, then people can be most unkind, that's all. Far and away best to be like everyone else, dear." Sadly she smoothed the wet fur on the top of my head. "You really should try to act more like a bear, sweet," she whispered.

Nevertheless, next day she had a present for me. I was chained up now on higher ground, behind the outhouse. The skies were clear, but we were still laying over, waiting for streams to fall and the roads to dry. My new spot stank, but it was dry and private. Molly checked over her shoulder, then drew two volumes from under her shawl.

"Here you are, honey, but don't let anyone see you."

The books were *Poems and Epistles, Mostly in the Scottish Dialect; With a Glossary,* by Ebenezer Picken, and, by George Hughes, a really ancient-looking octavo, *The Art of Embalming Dead Saints.*

As for Meleager, I don't think he was fooled. "That bear's behind this," was his comment as he scowled at the damage to the wagon, then at me. But he didn't make anything of it. I think the weather had him down.

Later I found out he was waiting for news. He'd been corresponding to line up a theater in Paterson, New Jersey, for a lecture series, and apparently the bad weather had held up his receiving confirmation. The day it came he was in high spirits. He had the letter in his hand when he came to tell Molly. She was sitting beside me, helping me with the hard words in Picken. When she saw him coming, she snapped the book closed and hid it behind her.

"Molly!" he shouted, hurrying up. "Wonderful news. Here, look at this." He handed her the letter. Glancing at me, he wrinkled his nose and said, exploiting my proximity to the outhouse, "Couldn't you find company whose air was a little sweeter, my dear?"

I yawned at him and scratched my testicles.

Molly was reading.

"It's not his fault," she said, rather too ambiguously for my taste. "Oh, Jason, this is marvelous. They're letting you have the theater. And they're not asking such a terrible lot of money, are they? Why, we've paid almost as much as this to use a tavern with a dirt floor, haven't we, Jason? Many times, I remember; you've told me so. This is so exciting. Why, if we fill the theater every show as you expect, my share alone will come to—"

"Ahem, yes," said Meleager, disconcerted. He snatched back the letter. "The important thing of course is that now we can make definite plans. I must see to our itinerary directly. We need to be in Paterson on September 30, which gives us two months. I shall have to learn what are the larger towns along the way. Although really it will be like picking up pennies on the way to the golden fleece. Ho, ho, I rather like that—the golden fleece. Do you . . . ? Oh never mind. The point is that with a little luck we'll never have to descend to touring these benighted villages again. I shan't miss them."

"Oh, Jason! Do you mean we'll be able to set up the institute?"

"We shall see, my dear, we shall see." And he chuckled at the both of us with a sly air I didn't much like.

Chapter 6

We got in to Paterson around midday September 30, 1827. We'd made our way there gradually, taking our time and leisurely stopping off at towns along the way to give lectures and consultations. The weather had been good all month and the traveling easy. We were all in a good humor—largely because Meleager was. The Paterson show was to be his first fling at a somewhat cosmopolitan—read cynical—audience, but he was feeling his oats. Afterward we were to go on to New York, where Johann Spurzheim, great light of the phrenological movement, was dropping in from Europe. Meleager had it in mind to sound him for his endorsement of an American phrenological society, which Meleager would head and which would have as its centerpiece an institute for the training of practitioners like himself to take the message, as we'd been doing, into the hinterlands. It was, as Meleager these days continually proclaimed, an idea whose time had come.

"Think of it, Molly!" he would say. "Thousands of virgin craniums are out there waiting to be explored—countless bumps and dips that have never felt the intrepid fingers of the trained phrenologist. Why, it's a brave new world, Molly, a wilderness full of riches. And you'll see, Molly, I shall reap them. I'll be rich. That is, of course, we will be. I shall train up my students so that the yokel doesn't exist who will be able to resist putting his head in their hands, to say nothing of his purse. In time I shall have the citizenry so broken to the yoke that it'll be afraid to take a step without phrenological guidance. Employers will demand character readings of their employees. Ladies will run their fingers through their lovers' hair—not just out of affection, but to feel their skulls! Candidates for office will publish charts of their bumps and criticize, not their stand on issues, but the shape of their opponents' heads. It's a glorious vision, Molly, and I know how to make it a reality."

"Oh Jason, it sounds so grand. And we can afford a house then, too, can't we?"

"Of course, dear; a palace, if you like, with your own wing in which to give musical recitals—so the guests don't have to troop through the parlor, I mean. Once the proceeds start rolling in I— I mean we, of course—won't know what to do with it all anyway. I haven't told you the half of it. You see, besides training practitioners I plan to market a line of phrenological wares—books, pamphlets, skulls, plaster heads—that sort of thing. They'll go like hotcakes—a phrenologist without a full complement will be like a missionary without any Bibles. And I shall *license* my practitioners. That may be my best idea yet, I think. It gives things a certain tone, you know, and then, too, no one will want his bumps read by someone who isn't accredited, so it should be useful in stifling competition. Oh yes, I have it all figured out."

"Yes, and don't forget the good work you'll be doing, too."

"Not for a minute, my dear. No indeed. I have several new regimens I plan to introduce—quite harmless, of course—and which I shall insist our clients follow religiously, so to speak. Soon, Molly, I will bring to everyone the happiness that attaches to making efforts to improve oneself which are basically trivial but just troublesome enough to engender an emotion of virtuous well-being. Nor is this all. By imparting that sense of knowledge and power that comes with belief in the efficacy of phrenology I will also be combating the helplessness all men feel in the face of life. From this, hope may spring, and I believe we are all better for a little of that, however we come by it.

"So you see, I'm not just thinking of myself."

"No, Jason, you're not," said Molly worshipfully.

Meleager preened.

"It's not just any eye could see it, Molly, but under every hat out there lies a land of milk and honey," he said.

So Molly sang as we rolled along, and Meleager talked. I listened to the both of them, enjoyed the fine weather and exercise, and dropped into balmy reveries from time to time about my reading. Molly had uncovered a cache of books belonging to Meleager and was feeding them to me one at a time. I'd got into the habit of reading for a while every evening and found it very soothing after a hard day's walk. The selection wasn't much, but I was too new at the pastime to be critical. I devoured alike *Heberden's Commentaries on the History and Cure of Diseases* and Zachariah Allnutt's *Considerations on the Best Mode of Improving the Navigation of the River Thames from Richmond to Staines;* James Beattie's *Elements of Moral Science* and, by Anonymous, what I think was my favorite, *Salmonia: or Days of Fly-Fishing*. I remember wishing Molly would find me more by him.

As I say, we reached Paterson around midday. Meleager sat up straighter and harrumphed when we got our first sight of the place, and Molly was so excited she actually *stopped* singing. There was no reason for me to be excited, but I was. I'd caught the contagion from them, I guess, and found myself looking at the town, nestled on a river between rolling hills, as if it held as momentous promise for me as it did for them. It did, as a matter of fact, though I didn't know it.

We began to wend our way in, our iron-shod wagon wheels raising a clangor on the cobbles. In fact, we sounded louder than usual, and then I realized why: the street was deserted. Apart from a dog or two displaying the usual canine emotions at my appearance, no one came out to see us, not even children. We were the only traffic.

Meleager and Molly craned their necks, beginning to be uneasy. I thought it was a little strange myself, unless it was a hanging. I saw a hanging once with Karl in Pittsburgh. That was in the winter and even so it was well attended, and would have been better attended still, I gathered, if the judge had gone along with postponing it to warmer weather. I remember my informant thought it was specially ungracious of him not to, considering even the prisoner was so strongly for it.

Anyhow, we pulled up in front of the first hotel to find out what was going on. The landlord appeared in the door while Meleager was tying up, looked at me askance and enlightened us.

"If you mean to stop here you'll have to take out yourself, mister. Stableboy's down to the falls with the rest of the town, watching them lay Tim Crane's bridge across."

"Thank you, sir. I guessed something of the sort," said Meleager, but he seemed relieved.

The landlord gave Molly a nod and a mumble and went back to eyeing me.

"I don't know as we can rightly accommodate the bear, though, mister. Ladies might not like it."

Meleager was used to this reluctance.

"Not to worry, landlord. He'll be no trouble. You see how he's chained to the wagon there. Quite safe that way, but I could even turn him loose and he wouldn't hurt a fly, I assure you. Gentlest member of his race you ever saw. The ladies actually love him, sir. I frequently have to come out and beg them to leave him be or the poor animal would never get any rest. That's a fact, sir. We'll just park him off in a corner of your yard, landlord. I guarantee you'll never know he's there."

"He's tame, is he?" said the landlord, advancing.

"Tamer than your mother-in-law, my friend, and better educated. Up, Bruin. Show him a trick. For your supper."

I did my standard impress-the-landlord routine, which I'd evolved to meet this case with minimal expenditure of energy. Standing on my hind legs, I first clasped my paws on my head and hopped from one foot to the other for a while to build suspense. The landlord blinked. Still hopping, I began to gracefully revolve, the chain wrapping around me till I bumped up against the wagon, when I reversed field and unwound myself the same way, still dancing, till I was back where I started. Then I sat down.

The landlord scratched his head. I could see he was impressed.

"He do other things?" he said.

"Does he do other things? My good fellow, I'll have you know this is the most talented, highly trained bear in the East, West, or in-between. He can dance, as you saw; he also juggles, does acrobatics, and has been known to sing, when properly encouraged. He did all this when I acquired him, and I have since trained him to assist me in my phrenological expositions, as you will have every opportunity to witness if you care to attend the first lecture tonight. It's free, by the way. I dare say you've seen the handbills?" Meleager finished a bit anxiously.

"Ah, you must be that Mulligan fellow then. The perfesser. Yep, I seen 'em."

"Meleager, sir, please. Professor Jason X. Meleager, at your service. And this is my charming associate, Miss Molly Money, songstress of renown. Now, if you'll just be so kind as to direct me where you'd like me to leave the wagon, with bear attached, I'll attend to the horses. And you may do me the further consideration of showing Miss Money where she can refresh herself while you prepare us some lunch."

"Some lunch" turned out to be salt fish, cold ham, hot cornbread, chicken and boiled beef, and potatoes and cheese, rounded off with coffee, as I found out when Meleager came back out where I was, picking his teeth with a gold toothpick and carrying a bucket with the meager leavings of it all, complete with coffee grounds. He set the bucket down in front of me, briefly removed the toothpick and said with a burp:

"Eat up, my brutish friend. I've decided to bring you along. Our delightful host is so taken with you it's all he can talk about. Not even the flattering hints I threw out about the interesting shape of his fat head, to entice him to the show tonight, could distract him for long. If he comes, it'll be to see you, I think, and I can't have him wearing you out in the meantime and tiring of your tricks." He laughed. "Hurry up, wolf it down. I want you to advertise for me. We're going to show ourselves where they're putting up that bridge."

I cleaned out the bucket in about the time it takes to say so, and the three of us set off. We were all in a holiday spirit. Meleager hummed to himself and surveyed the houses we passed as if tallying the likely take from each one, while Molly clung to him and gazed about her in a daze of contentment. My lunch hadn't been nearly on a par with theirs, but I felt awash in the same tide of well-being. The sun was too bright and the air too crisp not to. I didn't get many holidays.

We found the falls without difficulty. They were where all the people were, as predicted. The bridge sat nearby on the bank, the center of a buzzing crowd of men some of whom appeared to be actually working on getting it ready. The other nine-tenths seemed to be chiefly contributing advice and relieving the first tenth from having to break off to go in search of liquor.

The bridge itself was a large wooden construction, fully roofed and enclosed, with openings in the sides for light and overall some forty feet long or longer. It looked completely finished and evidently needed only to be hauled into place. Ropes stretched from it across the chasm to the other side, where another handful of men busied themselves making final checks of the apparatus, in the spare moments when they weren't, like the group on our side, fortifying themselves for the coming effort from one of the jugs I saw circulating. Several clusters of picnickers were scattered around them on the grass, but most of the people were on the town side with us. The river roared along between us through a gorge that began at the falls. We could hardly see it from where we were, only the falls themselves, tumbling some seventy feet into the cloud of mist that rose up from the foot of the drop and occasionally disgorged a rainbow.

Meleager, with Molly on one arm, and me, or my chain at any rate, on the other, sauntered onto the trampled margin between the lip of the gorge and the adjacent buildings like a proud father out with his family for a stroll. People scrambled out of our way; watchers on the roofs cried out and pointed. From all sides I heard the word "bear." Drawing our throng of followers along behind like the tail on a comet, Meleager made his way straight to where the crowd was thickest, by the bridge, nodding and smiling to all and from time to time directing Molly to give out a handbill.

We stopped near the bridge, where we had a good view of the falls and the river, and where everyone around had a good view of us. I cheerfully gave back stare for stare, discountenanced one young fellow in the middle of a ribald remark at my expense by giving him a wink, and generally radiated affability. Meleager meanwhile distributed more handbills. Giving him the last of them, Molly spread a cloth on the ground to sit on and I dropped down beside her with the only half-humorous intent of landing on a noxious little dog. I missed, but got a laugh.

"That old dog, he just *bearly* missed being pancaked," said one witty fellow in a wide-awake hat that looked as though it might have been sat on a time or two itself. This also got a laugh.

"Is he part of the show, mister?" yelled an admiring urchin, pointing at me.

"Part of *my* show, young fellow," Meleager began jovially. "He—"

"I'll bet they're going to pull him over in the bridge. That won't be keen," said another urchin, indistinguishable from the first but that they were standing side by side.

"Not a bit!" agreed Urchin No. 1 enthusiastically.

"First rate!" said Urchin No. 2, summing up.

"Are you with Tim Crane, sir?" said a more mature newcomer, resplendent in a bright yellow and dark blue checkered vest under a sky blue frock coat.

Meleager turned to him gratefully.

"No, sir, we are merely spectators here, like yourself. My associate and I are newcomers to Paterson. We have consented to a week's engagement at the Liberty Theater for a phrenological lecture series. The first is tonight, sir, by the way, and it's free. *Pro bono publico,* you know. Miss Money, another handbill, please. Eh? There aren't? Well, here you are, sir, my card," said Meleager, fishing out and surrendering that article reluctantly.

"Benjamin Kitchen, professor," said the other, offering his hand, "owner of Kitchen's Cooperage, largest cooperage in town. If you see a barrel of anything, most likely the barrel's mine. 'When you think barrels, think Kitchen.' That's my motto, sir, and a better one you won't find. Just like my barrels, sir, if I may be permitted to say so. 'A barrel full of quality.' That's another motto we have, almost as good, some folks think, but I made up the first one myself."

Meleager hastily introduced him to Molly.

Mr. Kitchen bowed. "A pleasure." He turned to me. "Remarkable specimen," he observed intelligently.

"Indeed, sir, that he is," said Meleager, warming up again. "You cannot imagine fully how remarkable. Not only is he highly educated, but I believe he may have saved Miss Money's life once. Yes, sir, it's a fact. A band of rowdies set on her and were subjecting her to fearful verbal abuse, and one of them actually flung something at her. Why, who knows what might have been the result? Bruin here routed the lot of them. Ah yes, it was something to see, I can tell you that. Not that I was actually there in a position to help, you understand, but I witnessed the end of it, sir, that I did, and it was grand. Yes, he's a great help to me, and a wonderful draw. Normally, of course, he's gentle as a lamb. And highly trained. But you must attend tonight and see for yourself, Mr. Kitchen, as a personal favor to me. Miss Money will be offering a musical entertainment, and you'll also hear much to interest you, I promise, on the amazing new science of phrenology."

Mr. Kitchen huffed and blew noncomittally.

"Mr. Kitchen," broke in Molly, immediately receiving all of that gentleman's gallant attention, "where are they building the bridge *to*? I don't see anything over there."

It was true, the other side of the gorge was just a grassy field without buildings.

"Well may you ask, ma'am. As it happens, that's precisely the attraction. You see the tavern there right up by the edge behind where they're checking the ropes on the bridge? That's right. Well, that place belongs to Fyfield, and he's got some hundred steps run down from it to the bottom of the falls. You can't see them from here, but they go into the gorge. Well, he's been making out pretty good, with the falls as an attraction and all, and Tim Crane—he owns two hotels in town, the Thomas Jefferson and the American Eagle, and I don't mind telling you he's a close personal friend of mine; bright fellow, knows how to make money, he does, though he doesn't have a motto—but anyhow, like I was telling you, Tim Crane got the idea to give Fyfield a run for it and put up a place on the other side. Of course, for that he has to have a bridge so folks can get there. Then he means to build a pleasure garden all round the place and get the weekend trade and all. Fyfield hasn't just simmered much while they been building the bridge right outside his door, I can tell you that. We've had quite a bit of fun teasing him about it, in fact."

"And those men?" asked Molly, pointing to a cordon sealing off the top of the falls on both sides. "What are those men doing there?"

"Oh, them," said Mr. Kitchen dismissively. "They're there on account of this crazy fellow works in town here at the Hamilton Mill. Name of Sam Patch. Bosses the mule spinners, I hear, so I suppose he must know a thing or two. But he's just a drunken fool. I guess he's had a heavy go of it, poor devil—bad luck, you know. Came here early this year from some place in Rhode island where I guess he started his own mill up and had it going good, too, when his partner, Scotsman name of Kennedy, I believe, skipped with the funds. Kind of unhinged him, I reckon. Goes around telling everyone he's jumped the Pawtucket Falls—a hundred feet, he says. Why, Pawtucket Falls ain't even that high. But he says he used to do it regular, when he was a youngster working at Slater's Mill; jumped off the bridge there, he says, and off the roof of the Yellow Mill on the other side. Darn fool has to be lying, I reckon, but everybody laughing at him has worked him into such a lather as he keeps trying to do it here—full as a bug when he does, mostly. Guess I would be too. Couldn't tell you how many times he's tried, but they just catch him up and put him in the jug till he acts more sensible. Why, just last night they found him crawling away from folks in the street, yelling as how they was crows, trying to pick his bones. Just let him out this morning in fact—why is more than I can say, considering there was this bridge business on. Now they've got to keep an eye peeled he doesn't try it again. Don't make no sense at all.

"But look there, ma'am. They're starting her across."

A loud murmur went up from the crowd and we all looked at the bridge.

The ropes grew taut and began to strain. The end of the bridge lifted, teetering, and the whole structure began to lurch ponderously out over the chasm.

Cheers. The crowd around us melted away and others went running past. On the far side men cracked whips and tugged at the harness of the teams of horses that drew the ropes. On our side men shouted and put their backs and shoulders to the landward end of the bridge, pushing with all their might. The bridge inched out on the slender lines like an ungainly, somewhat acrophobic caterpillar hesitating to trust its weight to its own thread. Now just the nose of it pushed cautiously over the edge, then a little more; another window in the side crept past; another.

The bridge was halfway across, its weight bobbing springily on the ropes, when there was a crack like a gunshot. The men on the ropes all fell flat on their faces and the horses were dragged screaming onto their haunches. A long wooden cylinder, a rolling pin around which several of the ropes had been turned, burst from shattered moorings and shot like an arrow straight out from the falls and into the river. With a lurch the bridge tipped almost vertical and did its best to follow, swinging in the ropes and lunging at the water in a way that would have expelled anyone inside like a fly shaken out of a beer glass.

A cry went up, everyone expecting momentarily to see the bridge break free and disappear in a final spectacular plunge. But the ropes held. The bridge hung end down, precariously swaying but still suspended, though for how much longer was problematical, as were the prospects of retrieving it.

"Damn me, that's tore it!" cried Mr. Kitchen, smacking his hip. "What a terrible thing!"

The sentiment was universal. All around us the crowd surged and babbled, beside itself with excitement. "There goes Tim's bridge. She's a goner now, I reckon," they said, eyes bright. "Poor Tim Crane, he's took a bath this time, I guess," sympathized others breathlessly. Urchins One and Two, or a pair of others like them, stood on the brink in front of us, as affected by the catastrophe as anyone, pointing at the crippled bridge and jumping up and down.

Then a new commotion absorbed everyone's attention. A figure darted from behind a large dead oak at the top of the falls and, penetrating the distracted cordon of constables, ran to the very edge of the drop.

Molly's hands flew to her cheeks.

"Who's that?" she gasped, making part of a general exclamation.

"That crazy mule spinner Patch, that's who!" returned an agitated Mr. Kitchen.

"What's he going to do?" shrieked Molly.

The figure waved its arms. An abrupt hush fell over the crowd. Above the roar of the falls the figure's voice reached us. He bellowed:

"Old Tim Crane thinks he's done something great. But I can beat him!"

And with no more preliminary than that he sprang in a great leap straight out from the edge—seventy feet above the river—to vanish feet first into the spray.

Molly screamed. Everybody screamed, or shouted, or in my case, woofed. Stunned, we watched him plummet, arms close in at his sides, dropping like a defenestrated statue against the backdrop of the falls. The bridge hid him for an instant, then he reappeared, arms spread now in what seemed a pathetic effort to break his fall—and then the seething billows swallowed him up.

A moan went up from the crowd. No babbling this time. Everyone was struck dumb. The fellow was mad, of course, but still . . .

Then:

"Look!" shouted the two urchins already noticed. They capered and danced, moved beyond speech, but still capable of pointing.

I looked.

What was that round black object moving across the current in the smooth water downstream from where the jumper had disappeared? Yes, it was a head, a head and shoulders, a man swimming, strongly and cleanly and making for the shore.

"I'll be jiggered!" said Mr. Kitchen, eloquently summarizing the feelings of the throng. "It's him!"

It was indeed him. As the fact became noticed the noise of the crowd swelled from a bewildered buzz to a jubilant uproar that drowned even the din of the falls. People hugged each other, jigged and clicked their heels. Bottles were waved dangerously about; hats soared and fell to earth again, or in some cases landed in the river, like flakes of outsize confetti.

The swimmer heeded none of this, if he knew it was going on at all. Swimming like an otter, he came up to the trailing guide rope, found the end of it and clenched it in his teeth. A group of men near us detached themselves to meet him on the shore. But he wasn't coming in just yet. We watched him tread water, as if to take his bearings; suddenly he struck out. He made straight for the rolling pin, hung up in a waterlogged tree, and grasped it with one arm. Only then, with the pin under one arm and the rope in his teeth, did he finally strike out for shore.

They plucked him from the water. Triumphantly relieving him of pin and rope, which they brandished like trophies, the men hoisted the dripping hero to their shoulders and started in procession up the bank. There, scarcely able to contain itself, the rest of the crowd pressed forward impatiently, now and again precipitating one of its forwardmost members over the edge.

"By thunder, damn my eyes if I ever seen the like!" said Mr. Kitchen, mopping his face with a handkerchief and straining to keep the recovered hero in view as the crowd pressed and jostled the four of us closer. Molly squealed, as carried away as anyone and a little frightened. Even I couldn't keep from being swept along. Fortunately, I had reared up on my hind legs to see better; my arms were pinned to my sides, but the crowd supported me. A man in front, squashed against me and with his head rapping me uncomfortably under the chin, twisted his neck around to exclaim, "Burn me, weren't it grand?" and twisted back again, never realizing, I think, that he had spoken to a bear.

"There, look'ee there! That's Tim Crane himself!" cried Mr. Kitchen as a well-dressed man ran down the bank holding his hat and with his coattails streaming out, to greet the man who'd saved his bridge. "I suppose he ain't glad!"

Another cheer at sight of Crane. He reached the procession, which opened for him, and seized Sam Patch's hand. The noise this time was deafening.

Crane said something we couldn't hear. With one mind the crowd stilled to catch the hero's reply.

He grinned down at Tim Crane.

"That's mighty generous of you, Mr. Crane. But I just wanted to show folks how some things can be done as well as others." He glanced around him at the admiring faces. "Isn't that right, boys? And I reckon as now everybody knows there's no mistake in Sam Patch!"

Chapter 7

Somehow we all got sorted out. Sam Patch was installed up by the bridge, the center of a riotous celebration. Under his supervision and spiritual guidance the pin and rope were repositioned and Tim Crane's bridge went the rest of the way across without a hitch. It was an anticlimax.

Meantime I'd gotten separated from Molly and Meleager and put the time to good use wandering around enjoying the sights. Nobody seemed to care, if they noticed. I did give one fellow a bit of a shock when he stepped on my chain, but most people were too busy searching for lost children and mates or too engrossed in talking about the events of the day to pay much attention to me. As the crowd thinned out I began to be noticed more and had people running away and throwing things at me. But as what they threw tended, either from policy or because they were handiest, to be their picnic baskets, I didn't much mind. All the excitement had given me an appetite. As you may have noticed, most things give me an appetite.

I was finishing off one of these baskets when Molly caught up to me. Something in the way she bustled up, lips pursed, the outlying portions of her anatomy jouncing about as if trying to fly off into space, caused me to see my little holiday in a new light. For a blessed while I'd forgotten about Meleager; of course, it was too much to hope he'd forgotten about me.

Confirming this, Molly pounced on the loose end of my chain and, going on about how she'd been looking all over for me and how Jason was fit to be tied, gave it a yank that damn near unseated my Adam's apple and rerouted my last swallow of roast chicken down the wrong throat.

"Oh, you're *such* a bad bear!" she wailed, pounding me on the back. "Why do you do these things? You know how Jason is. I think you deliberately provoke him. You enjoy making him mad. It's so mean of you. He only takes it out on me."

Grabbing my chain again, she dragged me along back to the bridge. Meleager was waiting there for us and she hadn't exaggerated the state he was in. He snatched the chain away from Molly and immediately set the tone by giving me a rap over the head with the end of it. I will say this, it took my mind off the roast chicken.

"There you are, you wretched piece of dog meat. I'll teach you to run away from me." He raised the chain again, but thought better of hitting me with it when I gave him to understand by a look—which was all I could manage, with the chicken lodged in my throat—that he might wind up dog meat himself if he did. He spun on Molly instead. "What are you staring at, woman?"

He advanced on her and Molly shrank back. I coughed and he froze. They both looked at me, both frightened but for slightly different reasons. "Bah!" said Meleager and turned away. I saw no point in explaining, even if I could have, that the cough had actually been the chicken.

Meleager seemed to shake off the incident.

"I beg your pardon, my dear," he said to Molly, composing himself. "I was overwrought. But we have to hurry. They're toasting that Patch madman in the tavern. It's a tailor-made opportunity for us. The whole town is buzzing with that jump of his, and we can cash in on it if we're quick. Come along now. We'll use the bear to get us in."

He took Molly's arm and pulled us on.

We entered the crowd around Fyfield's tavern. On every side we heard "Sam Patch," "Sam Patch," "Did you ever . . . ?" "I never . . . ," "Damn me for a . . . ," " . . . jump . . . ," " . . . greatest thing . . . ," " . . . beat all!" Meleager forged ahead like a cutter through the waves.

Finally, and not without getting our share of dirty looks, which however tended to become noticeably cleaner when they got to me, we reached the knot outside the door. Meleager halted, caught his breath and pushed me in front.

"All right, what are you waiting for? Go on, go on, get us inside!"

Molly whimpered. I hesitated.

"Push them out of the way, you fool!" screamed Meleager.

Surveying the field of packed bodies, it wasn't easy to see where out of the way was. But Molly looked close to fainting. I laid my paws on the shoulders in front and woofed apologetically. The men made way with politeness and alacrity.

Inside we weren't much better off. Meleager pointed to a table dimly visible through the haze of pipe and cigar smoke and indicated to me to clear it. Its occupants obliged by moving before I even asked them, which I thought was nice. In fact, we could have had the tables to either side as well if we'd wanted them.

We took our places in a sudden hush in which the only sound was the scrape of our chairs. Meleager settled into his with a dignified air; Molly flopped into hers, and I lowered myself cautiously into mine. Everyone stared at us. The Sam Patch fellow, himself obviously the center of attention before we came in, sat on the bar, a small puddle under his boots and a bottle beside him, and stared as hard as any.

"Keeper," said Meleager, rising to the occasion nicely, "beer for myself and my friends."

There came a slight relaxation of the tension. A tall, gangly fellow behind the bar began to bustle. He stopped, partly straightened again and looked over at us uncertainly, evidently struck by Meleager's use of the plural.

"Yes, yes," said Meleager with an elegant flick of his wrist that took in both Molly and me, "you heard right: beer for both my friends." He fished out a quarter and tossed it on the table as further earnest of his meaning.

In the murmur that followed, the tavern keeper bent over again to emerge finally with a tray bearing three frothy glasses. These he set down, one in front of Molly, one in front of Meleager—and then his heart failed him. The third glass he left in the center of the table, recovered his tray and stepped back.

Meleager shoved it over to me, raised his and drained half of it, setting it down with a sigh. Molly sipped at hers. Meleager looked at me.

Believe it or not I hesitated. I had half a mind to leave the drink untouched, just to make a fool of him. On the other hand it was awfully inviting sitting there with that big frothy head, little drops of condensation running down the sides. I hadn't tasted any in so long (he never gave me any) and I still felt like I didn't have all of that chicken out of my throat. I don't know what you would have done, but I put it to you, it was more than a fellow could bear.

With a groan I reached out, caught up the glass and downed the contents manfully.

Meleager had wanted a sensation and he got one. It took me back to my later days with Karl. I smacked my lips, getting into the spirit of the thing, and before Meleager could interfere, thrust my glass at the gangly fellow for a refill. Meleager blinked, then laughed and sent him off with a nod.

"Well, I'll be. How'd you teach him that, mister?"

"Very easily, my friend. You'd be surprised. He has as much natural aptitude as yourself. But drink up, drink up, everybody. It's no intention of mine to keep a man from his liquor. I must apologize for the commotion. It's often the way, where we go. But my associate, the beautiful Miss Molly Money, songstress of renown, whom by the way I invite you all to hear tonight at eight o'clock at the Liberty Theater absolutely free of charge, where you'll also see more of this thirsty fellow, ho, ho—Miss Money, as I say, would not hear of leaving before I introduced her to the hero of the hour, that bold gentleman on the bar, you, sir. I believe the name is Patch. Mine's Meleager, sir, Jason X. Meleager, doctor, professor and practitioner extraordinaire of the miraculous new science of phrenology, a demonstration of the wonders of which you are all, as I say, invited to witness tonight at eight o'clock at the Liberty Theater. I believe that's on Washington Street. A marvelous feat, sir, that jump of yours. I salute you and drink your health and continued good fortune." And he emptied his glass.

Sam started to puff up when Meleager called him a hero, and he pursed his lips and sent a very gallant look at Molly, plainly meditating a courtly acknowledgment. As the chance for it didn't come and didn't come, he sagged, and by the time Meleager finally did wrap things up, Sam was looking rather quizzical. He burst out with a laugh that rang off the walls and somewhat disconcerted Meleager.

"Blast my old britches if you ain't just the windiest talker I have met up with this year and more. I expect you could talk the bark off a tree if you was to set your mind to it. But that's meaning no offense, Mr. Meleager, as I think you said you was. I've been known to talk a mite myself. Why, next to drinking and, I should say, jumping, it's one of the things I like best to do in this world, and no mistake. Except till today there was a regular shortage of people willing to listen, and a man can't talk proper without people around being in a right frame of mind to hear him, no more than he can on a dry throat." Sam seized his bottle with a loud laugh and looked around merrily as he poured himself a tumblerful. This sentiment, or his way of expressing it, was roundly endorsed by the company.

"Indeed he cannot," said Meleager, smiling thinly, I think a little miffed in his turn. His eye shifted, fell on my empty glass. He pulled himself together and said with an air of bonhomie, "Ho there, Bruin, don't you join in the gentleman's toast? Why, your glass is empty. Landlord, another round for the table here. My friend," he said humorously to Sam, "is a most polite bear. It would grieve him deeply not to be able to show his agreement with so congenial an opinion, especially when it is advanced by so notable a champion. Ah, thank you, landlord," he said, hailing the return of our three glasses and giving me one. "In fact, let me on his behalf propose a toast in return. To Mr. Patch," he said, lifting his glass; "may he hereafter always have the audience he deserves!"

This ambiguous salute was greeted with a roar, at least some of which I take credit for, as the toast was offered in my name, after all. I'd never proposed a toast before, but I can tell you I took to the practice right away and sent my third beer to join its predecessors all in a gulp, so that in case I or somebody else proposed another, Meleager would have to start me on a fresh drink.

Meanwhile Sam had to hurry to pour and get that one down, but he laid on with a will. Then, blinking and plainly moved by my thoughtfulness, he refilled and raised his glass to me, though a little wryly.

"Thank you kindly, mister. I didn't just get your name there, but here's one for you: to as fine a gent as ever wore fur."

Somehow I had a full glass again. I think in my excitement I must have appropriated Meleager's. I tossed it off, rapidly warming to this Patch fellow. He maybe had a screw loose to be jumping off waterfalls, but catch him in a lucid moment and he was as fine company as anyone could wish.

Sam banged down his glass with a laugh and wiped his mouth.

"Why, takes me back to Pawtucket, it does. There was this fellow Jenks Maxwell I worked with, though actually he was a little older than me at the time, and Jenks and me did jumps would make your hair stand up, and that's a fact. This little business today is just nothing compared to it. Why, there was this old stone mill, you see, and it had a flat roof that was just about a hundred feet up in the air over the water, and the only way you could jump it was if you got way back and took a good running start or you'd land smack dab on the bank and then you'd make a splash, I can tell you. We was always kind of careful how the wind was blowing when we made that jump, I recollect. But anyways, like I was saying, old Jenks had this pet fox as was sharp as a tack and trained up to beat the band."

"Like Bruin here himself," broke in Meleager with much joviality. "Do you know," he said, swinging around just as if he hadn't cut Sam off, "this bear once outfoxed Davy Crockett, speaking of foxes. It's a fact. I had it from his previous owner. He was there and witnessed the entire incident. Said it left him a shaken man. Crockett came *this close* to meeting his maker prematurely, gentlemen, at the hands of this very bear, the same that he'd pursued for days. And what saved him? I can scarcely bring myself to say, gents. It's too incredible. But the fellow swore on the Bible it was so, and from what I've seen since, I believe him. He said Bruin here knocked Crockett down and stood over him, and Crockett was lying there defenseless and at his mercy but putting a good face on it like the brave man he is—and what did Bruin do? Stepped back and helped him to his feet. Threw his gun away first and then helped him up. The fellow swore it. He said Crockett dusted himself off and went up to Bruin, looked at him a while and said: 'I reckon I can't fight a fellow who holds his hand, even if he is a bear, or I'd take my knife and wrassle it out with him here and now. But he's too smart by half and I won't have him running around loose either, so you take him and train him up and show him to folks, for there's none like him and he's a credit to his kind.' That's what Crockett said, the fellow swore it. And the fellow did just what Crockett told him, and then I bought him off him, gentlemen, trained him some more, and now have brought him on here to Paterson at considerable expense to assist me in demonstrating the principles of the astounding new science of phrenology—on Crockett's instructions, you might almost say.

"Ah yes," he sighed, with exquisite timing—for I was onto his game now and saw how he waited on purpose till Sam, who you can imagine sat through all this rather restlessly, was just opening his mouth to speak again—"Ah yes," said Meleager reverently in the awed silence that followed his tale, "Davy Crockett: now there's a *real* hero for you."

Murmurs of assent. Sam, whose mouth had been open, closed it.

"Well, gentlemen," said Meleager brightly, standing, "time presses. I wanted to pay my respects to the gallant gentleman who saved the bridge today, but now we have preparations to make for our show tonight. I shall look forward to seeing you all there, and you especially, sir," to Patch. "Eight o'clock, mind—at the Liberty Theater. I expect you all know where it is. Now then, Miss Money. My dear Bruin." He extended his hands.

Molly pushed back her beer, scarcely tasted, and stood up, more than ready to leave. I started up too, my eyes on her beer. It seemed a shame to let it go to waste. I scooped it up and poured it down. The room rang with laughter.

"I declare," chortled Meleager, "he could almost pass for human, couldn't he? But just you gents look in tonight if you've got a taste for something remarkable. We've got a show that'll top the limit."

Cheers. I plunked the glass down, to more applause. Amid the ruckus Sam Patch watched stonily from his seat on the bar. I felt a pang. Meleager had sure stolen his thunder, and at his own party, too. I didn't blame Patch for giving me a kind of sullen Crockett look, as if he thought the world had too many bears. I could sympathize, at least to the extent that it didn't seem fair that downing a few beers should be put in the scales with jumping off a waterfall. Not taking his eyes off me he raised his bottle to his lips for a consoling slug. I threw him a wink. The bottle slipped from his fingers and broke on the edge of the bar. The puddle of river water under his boots became flavored with rum.

Chapter 8

"Blast that fellow Patch! I've never seen them like this."

Meleager peeped again through the curtain. A sound very like that of the Paterson Falls, only rowdier, flooded the stage where we waited in the wings for eight o'clock. Meleager flinched. He seemed more anxious than I'd ever seen him. Molly was no better off; in fact she was terrified. She habitually got attacks of stage fright before going on, and her nerves had never entirely recovered from the incident with the filbert. I sat by myself in a corner, feeling far and away the most seasoned professional of the three of us, and waited philosophically for things to start.

"There isn't a soul out there who hasn't been drinking since this afternoon. Why couldn't the fool have drowned as he deserved? This is all his fault, damn him. Molly, cut back to one or two songs tonight—jolly ones, for God's sake, if you know any. None of those blasted interminable laments you specialize in. And in English, if you can. You have to try not to provoke them. Don't look at me like that, just listen. I'll come on with the bear as soon as you're done. Let's see. I know, I'll give him some of the skulls to juggle—get them out: the ones we dug up last week will do. They're in the 'ancient battlefields' trunk."

Not happily, Molly did as she was told. She came back with three skulls cradled in one arm on her bosom and a fourth dangling from a finger by an eye socket. A blast from out front rocked us as Meleager parted the curtain again and she dropped them all, costing one its lower jaw and variously concussing the others. She rushed to Meleager's side.

"Oh Jason, I can't sing for people like this. You know I can't. They're horrible. They'll throw things, like that other time. You know they won't like my songs, and I'm too afraid to sing anyway. Oh, please say you won't make me. Please!"

Meleager brushed her away with some half-intelligible remark about the advancement of science requiring sacrifices, and chewed a fingernail.

She came back by me and sat down, trembling so much the uneven legs of her chair were rattling on the floor. I thought inviting her to think of her performance as a sacrifice wasn't the best reassurance Meleager could have given her, and I put my paw on her knee to try to cheer her up. Nothing. Thinking to try a stronger dose of animal comfort, I stretched up and licked her ear. Possibly this would have gone over better if I hadn't had fish heads for dinner, but the vigorous scrubbing it precipitated did take her mind off having to sing.

Then it was eight o'clock. Our high-spirited audience marked the hour with foot stamping and a huge cheer. They began chanting: "We want the bear! We want the bear!"

"Damn that Patch!" said Meleager, closing his watch with a snap. He took a breath, gave his coat a tug that must have tried the seams sorely, threw back his head and marched out onto the stage to introduce Miss Money.

Her set was of course a disaster and probably the less said about it the better. It wasn't long in any case, though it was memorable enough in its way. Molly was petrified and sang in a choked whisper that would have been largely inaudible under the best of conditions. As conditions were nowhere near that, almost no one could hear her. This by itself might not have been such a bad thing, considering, but it had its provoking side. When an audience expects and has every right to hear a person sing, you can't blame them for becoming restive when the person appears, represents that he is singing—and they still can't hear him. Depending whether they sat in back or in front the audience retaliated by calling for her to sing louder and to go away, respectively, either of which might have saved her and neither of which she had the courage to do. Others meanwhile indulged in a certain amount of cruel humor at Molly's expense, taking off from her having appeared just as the "We want the bear!" chant became more or less universal, and from certain superficial points of resemblance between Molly and myself. How she held out as long as she did I don't know. The end came when some of those up front, who couldn't hear any better than anyone else by this time and possibly found additional grounds for resentment in what they had heard already, stormed the stage. While some set out to teach Molly some "real American music" by planting themselves in front of her and bellowing out songs of a more approved sort, others were more in a mood for dancing and took to pawing at her. Meleager spirited her away before I could take a hand. Dumping Molly in the arms of a stagehand, he intercepted me, loaded me down with the skulls and dragged me on.

We were greeted with a shout that shook the building and rippled my fur like a wind. What a clamor! I'm ashamed to say it wiped Molly clean out of my mind. My trouper's instincts pricked up and took over like an old war-horse that hears the bugle sound the charge. My arms were full of skulls. Without conscious thought I took a tuck and a tumble onto the stage with them, rose to my hind legs and lofted one skull after the other into the air till I had all four going and the crowd carrying on so I thought it was going to hurt itself.

Meleager meanwhile was waving his arms around and making grand gestures as if the whole thing were his idea and I only performed under direction. The skulls' grimaces looked happier than his did, though, and rather relishing the situation, I kept going till the uproar diminished to the merely deafening, then flipped the skulls to him one at a time over my shoulder.

He caught them, too—an unexpected feat which impressed both me and the audience no end. All in all, and though I didn't doubt he'd pay me back for that last innocent flourish, the net effect was that we made a rather stylish entrance. Meleager was quick to capitalize on it, too. Holding up the last skull, he bowed and waved for silence. In time they gave it to him, more or less.

"Ladies and gentlemen," he began optimistically, "good citizens of Paterson . . ." And he was off and running.

Trust Meleager. If he can lay a finger on an audience, he'll soon have them in the palm of his hand. Even this one began to show signs of tractability under his touch. Some I saw cling to their neighbors in an effort to sit up; others removed their hats, the better to feel their bumps as he talked; still others paused in their singing, or their shouting and fighting, and the ones who didn't were shouted at and fought. Something very like a hush began to settle over the hall.

Meleager took heart. His voice rang out with more of his old confidence; his gestures took on more masterfulness. He swept away the cobwebs of time and described in minute detail a misspent life of such poignancy and sorrow for the skull he was brandishing that a man in front offered him ten dollars for the thing on the spot and was only with difficulty dissuaded from trying to take it from him forcibly. And how did he know all that he pretended to? How did he seem to know the very names of the skull's family, of its invalid mother, who perished in want and despair, attended only by a lone aged servant who had been with the family for years and indeed had dandled the profligate scion on her knee in better days? Of the bereaved young widow, a veritable goddess, her silken tresses untidy now in her grief; and, yes, of her three pathetic babes? Well, perhaps the exact names were something speculative, and the exact circumstances of their owners only probable. But there could be no doubt of the propensities indelibly recorded in the skull, which could be read in this ancient carapace as readily by those with the skill as if the unfortunate man yet lived and breathed. See here, perhaps the man had no mother. But if he had, this innocuous-seeming low spot at the back of the head indicts him for an ungrateful child. Not intentionally, perhaps, for his benevolence and friendship or adhesiveness are good; but his conscientiousness is small. How many of you have put off—too long— that visit to your mothers dear? And so on, and so on.

Yes, he was reaching them, all right. They listened spellbound as he described the benefits to be gained and the pitfalls to be avoided by a timely recourse to the insights of phrenology. Save for the continuous spatter of tobacco juice on the floor and the occasional clunk and roll of a bottle, the audience listened like they were in church.

In fact, it was the subject of church, or religion anyhow, that caused the first ripple of trouble.

Away in the back a lean, inquisitorial figure in a black hat and closely buttoned black surtout stood up and leveled at Meleager a lean, inquisitorial finger.

"Stay, sir, I beg of you. Nay, I command it! Cease you this instant the spread of your vile and pernicious doctrine!" he said, or words to that effect.

The fellow's problem turned out to be that Meleager left no room in a person's head for a soul. Every square inch of space was otherwise accounted for. This, the man said, was the sort of talk that got folks thinking people were no better than animals; it was downright atheistical, he said, and shouldn't be tolerated in a God-fearing land.

Meleager tried to reassure him there was nothing irreligious about phrenology—"For if God does not exist, my worthy friend, tell me what is the organ of veneration for?"—but it didn't look like the reverend was having any. He began to turn rather black in the face and seemed to be working up to another outburst when some-body behind him knocked his hat over his eyes. This caused him to lose his train of thought and delighted the crowd, who didn't see why in a democracy the whole bunch of them should be quiet just to let one man speak. Finally he gave it up as a bad job and stalked out shaking his fist.

Meleager hastened on; they were getting out of hand again.

"Gentlemen, gentlemen! I wish to proceed now with what I am certain many of you will find the most vitally interesting part of the lecture. May I have your undivided attention, please? Yes, thank you. Yes, I am trying to speak up. I wish they would stop singing, too. Yes. Gentlemen, if you will listen, we are come to that point in the lecture where I customarily demonstrate a concrete applica-tion of the principles of phrenology on the heads of persons from the audience. What's that? No, I'm not going to hit anybody. I simply want to examine their heads. Gentlemen, please! Now, who will step forward first for a free phrenological examination? Who, I say, will be the first to receive a roadmap of his character, to learn his strengths, his weaknesses—to know, in the words of the old philosophers, *himself,* and that more surely than his mother ever did?"

I sat watching from my position at the end of the stage. Ordi-narily we never had to ask twice for volunteers: it was free, and whoever we used became a celebrity without the onus of having to do much of anything for it. So I was a little puzzled when no one came forward right away. There was lots of commotion, though. It was like the mass of them was meditating a selection. And then there began to be a consensus in the direction heads were turn-ing—namely toward the very center of the noisiest group in the hall—and out popped a familiar face: it was Sam.

"Mr. Patch," said Meleager, recognizing him, too. He rubbed his hands. "Of course, I should have guessed . . . This is an honor, Mr. Patch. I suppose you've come to see if I can tell you why you jump into waterfalls?"

"I reckon I'm clear on that already, professor," said Sam, "but you can try and spy it out if you've a mind to. I guess a fellow as ain't afraid to jump off them in the first place got no business to be afraid of somebody wants to tell him why he done it, does he, boys? Ha, see there? Do your blamedest, professor. You was good enough to come see my stunt, now I reckon I'll just let you alone to do yours."

Meleager bowed. Everybody else cheered. Sam began to make his way to the stage, a time-consuming process that required him to shake hands with everyone in reach, wave repeatedly at everyone who wasn't, and take a polite sip from every bottle offered. In this last regard particularly, he was punctilious, I noticed.

Meleager meanwhile was readying the stage. He fetched out a chair, positioned it front and center, and beckoned me over beside it. I was evidently to be subjected again to that insulting disquisition on the inferiority of sloping brows to fat ones; only this time, what with Meleager's trace of jealousy of Sam, I suspected I wouldn't fare as badly as I usually did.

Scorning the steps, Sam swung himself up on the stage, gracefully acknowledging the cheers with a bow and a rustic shuffle. He faced me and gave an exaggerated start:

"Ho, seems like I'm to have the treatment proper. Well, I won't run away, professor. Squeeze my head all you like. Reckon you can't get blood out of a stone." He clutched his head and gave the audience a very comical wink, which they heartily appreciated.

Rather overdoing the courtesy, Meleager motioned him into the chair.

"Now, Mr. Patch, if you'll kindly face the audience, I will stand surety for the bear's good behavior."

"If you mean you'll give me your head if your friend goes off with mine, I don't just reckon I like the terms. Ow, easy on the handles, professor. They's but lightly attached."

"Now, ladies and gentlemen," said Meleager, smiling rather tensely, I thought, "we have here before us representative specimens of *Homo sapiens* and *Euarctos americanus,* better known to you all, I'm sure, as man and bear, respectively. This one, I feel fairly certain, is the bear, and this one is the man, in case of doubt."

"Don't this professor know his stuff, though?" marveled Sam.

"Quite. Now, notice the different—well, marginally different anyway, in this instance—configuration of the foreheads. The bear's slopes. The man's—well, to be candid, the man's slopes too, in this case, but I believe you can still see, at least those of you in the front, that it doesn't appear to slope as much. Well, not quite as much. If you can't see, I'm afraid you'll just have to take my word for it. As a rule anyway, a bear's will slope quite a bit more."

"Best come to the point, professor, before that bear gets impatient of being slandered," remarked Sam, not smiling very much just as he said it.

"Yes, well, the only point I'm trying to make is that the higher faculties, the functions that distinguish man from the beasts, are located here, behind the forehead, and that the beasts, having sloping foreheads, are consequently able to accommodate far less development of these faculties."

"If that's the only point you're trying to make, I reckon that's all right then," said Sam.

"But let us move along now to a brief general consideration of what these faculties of the mind, or brain, are and where they are located," said Meleager, evidently taking Sam's point.

He started in then on his survey of the thirty-seven different organs of the brain, and I turned my head to look at Sam, who by this time rather piqued my curiosity. It wasn't often that somebody stood up this well to Meleager, and I wondered if there wasn't more to him than met the eye. Any fool can jump off a waterfall. The more fool he is, likely the easier he finds it, I'd guess. Sam Patch didn't seem a fool, though, and that made him interesting. Just what he was instead I wasn't sure, as persons given to jumping off waterfalls, fools or no, were pretty completely outside my experience. But he had a nice face, I decided. Just now it was a little flushed, to be sure, but it didn't look ordinarily loose or dissolute. If anything there was a more than ordinary firmness in the mouth and jaw, and contrary to Meleager's report, the brow was high and full, till I lost sight of it under locks of hair so dark as almost to match mine. The cheekbones were good; the rather stubbly cheeks flushed, as I say, but not puffy. It wasn't what I'd call a handsome face, but there was something likeable in it, and something, I don't know, that somehow garnered my respect.

I had plenty of leisure to study it, because as soon as Meleager took off on the general stuff Sam folded his arms on his chest, slid down in the chair and closed his eyes. In a minute his head began to nod, and Meleager had to hold it straight with one hand and point with the other, which he didn't appear to find amusing, although everybody else did.

"Mr. Patch's alimentiveness," he finally interrupted himself to say, "has overcome his concentrativeness, it seems"—meaning Sam was too drunk to sit straight. He sneered: "It's a pity that on this public occasion at least, he couldn't manage to give a less equivocal showing of his supposed superiority to the beasts"— meaning me, or so I took it.

Sam's eyes popped open. He rolled them about and brought them to rest on me. They were blue, I noticed, and unexpectedly piercing. He looked at me speculatively with them for a minute, then closed one in a wink.

"Why, burn me if he ain't at it again, bad-mouthing the poor bear. If it was me, I reckon I'd be getting kind of wrathy." He shook off Meleager's hands and sat up. "Tell you what, professsor, let's just skip the in-between stuff and jump direct to what I come up here for, which is to have my head examined. You can read all the rest of it off that fellow there," he said, indicating the skull Meleager had set down on the podium, "and not have to worry about waking him up, neither."

"Very well, sir," said Meleager. He hesitated. "I trust you will take it in good part if in the course of my examination I have occasion to make observations you may not regard as altogether flattering. You must allow me the privilege of my profession, to state the truth as it is revealed to me. If you will object to everything that doesn't suit you, I tell you right now it will be hopeless to proceed."

"Just you call 'em as you see 'em, professor, and I'll do the same."

Meleager still looked put out, but he shot back his cuffs with an elegant undulation of his arms and once more rested his hands lightly on Sam's head. Sam gazed out over the audience. He was more serious than I'd yet seen him. Even the audience quieted down some.

"You're father is no longer living, am I right, sir?" said Meleager after some initial exploration. Patch gave a start and Meleager nodded. "I'll wager he was taken from you at an early age. I have often observed that to have the effect of augmenting the philoprogenitiveness, or love of parents, when the child is raised by the mother." His fingers traveled over Sam's head, pressing, examining. Patch held his breath. His eyes had that inward-seeing look people tended to get when Meleager felt their heads.

"Your self-esteem has lately suffered, hasn't it?" Meleager continued. "Perhaps you are not happy in your work, or have undergone some personal setbacks. I detect a restlessness, a dissatisfaction with your life. The configuration is quite decisive. On the one hand we have a somewhat stunted self-esteem, on the other a very full approbativeness, or love of approbation. I would say you crave recognition and standing in the world, perhaps even fame. Am I correct, sir?"

"I reckon I like to be well thought of as much as the next fellow," said Sam. Meleager smiled.

"Yes, at least as much, or why do we jump over waterfalls, eh? No, no, don't turn around. I speak only from what I feel here, written on your own head. If you had not already jumped over a waterfall I should have said you were about to, or do something else equally quixotic. One's bumps don't lie, my friend."

"Well, maybe not, professor. But I been telling folks straight along I could do it and not a one of them believed me or thought I could until I showed them the very thing today. I'm thinking them bumps is a whole lot easier to hear now I've gone and done it."

"You doubt me, sir? You think I would stoop to chicanery?" said Meleager, resenting this slight to his art.

"Now, just cool your pipes, professor, before you busts a boiler. I don't accuse you of any such thing. I was only just remarking it's a sight easier to predict things what's already happened than the other kind and reminding you as how I had a hand in it, too."

Meleager seethed for a moment in silence. Then he said:

"My friend, there are some things I could tell you about yourself you wouldn't find so easy to make light of. I could even venture a prediction or two, if you'd like. I only hesitate for fear of giving offense. Reassure me on that score and I think I can promise you a character reading that will give every satisfaction."

"Whatever you want's okay by me, professor. You're in charge."

Meleager stepped from behind Sam and stared down at him with a look that reminded me of the one I'd gotten when Meleager found his trunk full of wet clothes. Sam withstood it placidly. Meleager gave him a chill smile.

"To begin with then, you're a worthless layabout, Mr. Patch. Shall I go on? All right. You have a job, I understand. You hate it though, don't you? It doesn't matter, at the rate you drink you won't have it long. You're a malcontent, Mr. Patch; nothing's ever good enough for you. You'll never advance yourself in your work yet you cherish the most fantastic notions of preening yourself in the adulation of your fellows. They like you but only suffer your absurd fancies because you amuse them—do you know that? They find you congenial because they misunderstand you. They think you're just another windbag like themselves. But you're not. Unlike them you're not content with your swinish life. No, my friend, you're vastly more pathetic than they are. You're genuinely unhappy. You see your life slipping by and you still haven't discovered anything to make it worth living. Oh, drink you have; you like that well enough, and many another man is content with as little. But not you. Try as you will, you can't make drink serve for that reason-for-being that you feel the want of, that foil for care and trouble that enables a man to persevere in the face of bad fortune. You're lost, Mr. Patch. You have no more idea where you are and where you're going than the ox who must ever pick his way obedient to the drover's call. You have no more say in choosing your path than he, and no more opportunity to answer the questions which, though you can scarcely articulate them better than an ox, haunt you every waking moment: 'Is this all there is? What am I doing here? What's the point of it all?'

"Am I right, Mr. Patch?"

"It's your show, professor. Only I don't know as I've heard much predicting," said Sam calmly enough, but in a somewhat strange-sounding voice.

"All right, you shall have some of that. I'm not a fortune teller, sir, but I believe that in your case your destiny is so plainly fixed by your character that I may hazard to read it for you. But by all means stop me again if you think my analysis too superficial.

"Yes, I believe it's quite clear what will become of you. You hope for an opportunity to leave your present life for one more meaningful to you. But as I've said, you yourself are at a loss to specify the route, even if you had only to name it and everything you want should be yours.

"My prediction, sir, is this. You have no prospects *but* to be a driven ox; you will not find that opportunity you yearn for so. It will elude you for the simple reason that there is nothing in you which might enable it to exist. There is nothing you intensely enjoy, save perhaps drinking, and apart from that you excel in nothing. You have no talent or gifts; your work, as I say, does not engage you, there aren't any wars presently in which to lose yourself and perhaps look for distinction, and you haven't the wit or capacity to be a leader if there were. Nevertheless you will not give over looking and yearning, and this fruitless dissatisfaction will sour your existence. You will sink into misanthropy, resenting everything and everyone. You'll stagnate, wallow in self-pity, and cease to amuse these uproarious fellows of yours. In time, and probably not such a very long time, you'll drink yourself to death or throw yourself away in some other trivial fashion and die never having lived.

"There, is that a reading more nearly after your heart, my friend?"

Chapter 9

Sam sat still. I think everyone held his breath, expecting to see Sam jump up and repudiate Meleager's charges and deal appropriately, if not kindly, with their author. Only Meleager himself seemed insensible of his danger. He stood, arms folded, watching like everybody else, but with a sardonic smile that grew as Sam remained silent. If the rest of us waited more and more anxiously, Meleager himself was as confident as a doctor who, having administered a drug he knows, sees signs that the dose is taking effect.

Then someone in the crowd broke the spell.

"Make him eat them words, Sam!"

"Thrash him, Sam!" said somebody else.

Meleager went white. He took a step back.

"Mr. Patch, remind them of the terms of . . . of my reading. Mr. Patch?"

Sam didn't stir. His eyes rested vacantly on the footlights. An unhealthy-looking slackness had crept into his features. I had a horrible feeling that if anyone had nudged him, he'd have tumbled out of his chair and lain where he fell, still staring.

"Mr. Patch?"

"He's done for Sam!"

"Gentlemen, please," said Meleager. He collected himself and appealed to them. "Gentlemen, I regret it intensely if the bitter truths I have been unwillingly forced to divulge—"

"Git up and git him, Sam, consarn it!"

"—That is, I regret that in my zeal to defend the integrity of the new science of phrenology—"

"Wake up, Sam!"

"Golly, what'd he do to Sam?"

"—Still you can all bear witness, gentlemen, it was a—"

"Let's fix him!"

"—Fair fight!"

The crowd was on its feet, those in front already swarming over the edge of the stage, brandishing fists and bottles and clearly meditating no good to Meleager. Sam was still in a trance and everyone seemed to have forgotten about me, so after weighing for a minute where my loyalties lay I went back behind the podium where I wouldn't be a damper on the proceedings and settled down to watch and let matters take what I hoped would be their course.

I was just getting comfortable when Molly charged out from backstage shrilling one of her higher notes. Bowling over two or three men in her path, she took the bottle away from another and creased his hat with it for him. Down he went. Taken unexpectedly in their flank this way, the men fell back in confusion. Hair wild, and a large whiskey stain down her front from the upended bottle, Molly placed herself between Meleager and the crowd like a brave she-bear defending her cub. It brought tears to my eyes to see so much sheer womanliness expended on such an unworthy object. What a bear she'd have made! Meleager meanwhile cowered behind her, cravenly letting her stand between himself and the danger. I felt a growl building deep in my throat. Molly whirled this way and that with her bottle, shrieking warnings and imprecations at the men who tried, like a pack of dogs, to sidle around and take her in the rear. Laughter began to sound beyond the footlights, and ribald shouts egging the men on. Somebody got his hands on Molly's bottle and tried to take it away from her. Up came her knee and down went her attacker, his plug of tobacco shooting from his mouth like a bullet and taking a bearded fellow who was reaching for Molly from behind, smack in the eye. A squawk and she spun around. Two men had caught Meleager, who thus far had managed to evade their clutching hands. Molly aimed a blow with her bottle and they let go, but somebody else grabbed the bottle from behind and in a minute others had pinioned her arms. Meleager made a dash for backstage but was intercepted. Everybody roared.

"Let's git out the tar and feathers, boys!"

"Let's pitch him over the falls!"

I saw I was going to have to take a hand, if only for Molly's sake. Personally, I'd have liked nothing better than to see Meleager trussed up, dipped in tar and bundled over the falls—it was an idea whose time had come, as Meleager was so fond of saying. Its aptness more than made up for anything it may have lacked in originality. But I couldn't just leave Molly in the lurch like that. How could I face her again if I stood by while they mauled her and chucked her lover in the river? That would not be the act of a friend, even granting Meleager was all I knew him to be.

"Bruin, oh dear Bruin, save us!" cried Molly, seeing me. With a sigh for the good work I was undoing I reared up on my hind legs—I look quite formidable when I do that—and waded out. The group recoiled but still clung to their prisoners. I bared my teeth and made menacing gestures. Even when you're really mad, a lot of the initial overtures in this fighting business are mostly theater, and I wasn't really mad. Meleager they could keep, and I hoped they would, so long as I was able to acquit myself of not having tried to help him and could make them let go of Molly. But they were either too scared to think of this last or not scared enough. I lumbered closer, slavering ferociously and throwing my shoulders around. Several men toppled backwards off the stage, others jumped, and one man pinned in the forefront of the group fainted dead away. They all scrambled back. The shouting and Molly's shrieks rose to an earsplitting pitch. Still they hung on to her. Quite a few of them now were actually hiding behind her, in fact.

Then I saw something that took the nerve clean out of me and turned the whole affair serious. Out of the corner of my eye I caught a glimpse of a coonskin cap. It brought me up in mid-slobber. I turned and stared. The face was still a blur, but below it was a deerskin jersey belted over leather leggings. I knew if I could see them the feet would be shod in moccasins.

The newcomer made his way forward from the back of the theater, holding his long rifle delicately aloft and parting the men in front of him like a cougar going through tall grass. It wasn't Crockett, I saw finally, and began breathing again. But it hardly mattered who it was. All those frontiersmen were just as bad.

The men cheered him on and thronged after him. He approached the stage and stopped. We stared at each other. I saw the unholy light burning in his eyes, flinty eyes like Crockett's that only kindled at the chance to shoot a bear. I shivered. I was falling into those eyes. He smiled.

"Now just hold it there, boys. Rein in a sec."

It was Sam Patch, looking as bright as a new-minted penny and not downcast at all. In fact, there was a gleam in his eye I hadn't seen there before, and a new springiness in his step.

He put himself between me and the others and stretched out his hands.

"Don't turn your back on him, Sam! He's a mean one."

"Simmer down, boys," was all he said.

"Stand aside, mister," said the Kentuckian, never taking his eyes off me. "I'll pop him for you."

"I don't reckon as that'll be required, friend, though it's kind of you to offer. But I think this old bear here," and he turned his head and looked at me, "isn't so fierce as he makes out."

It struck me the man was trying to do me a favor. I dropped down off my hind legs, rolled onto my back and gave a wriggle. I saw the Kentuckian, upside down, turn away in disgust.

"What'd I tell you? Yessirree, gents, this whole ruckus is a misfortunate misunderstanding. Now where's that professor fellow? I owe him an apology."

It was giving me a headache, seeing everything upside down. Cautiously I rolled over on my belly, still making sure to keep a low profile. There was Molly, still under restraint, but Meleager was nowhere in sight.

The skull on the podium clacked its teeth. It toppled off its perch and hit the stage with a crack. Sam strode over. He reached down and produced Meleager by the scruff of the neck, like a rabbit out of a hat.

"There you are, professor. I was wondering where you'd wandered off to," said Sam. He thumped Meleager on the back in a friendly way that made him cough and dusted him off. "That's better, ain't it? You look right as rain now."

Meleager goggled at him, for once at a loss for words.

"Now don't get going again, boys," said Sam as several of them started forward.

"He bit my thumb, burn him!" said one, displaying the evidence.

"Well, your intentions to him weren't just kindly neither, I reckon," said Sam. "Listen, you boys got this professor all wrong. I allow he took me in too, but he ain't half the rascal he looks, boys, so you just let him be. Nope, the gent knows his stuff and no mistake. Professor, put her there," said Sam, shoving out his hand. Feebly, Meleager took it. "I done you wrong and I admit it. But there, we're all square and aboveboard now, ain't we?"

Meleager freed his hand and nodded, blowing on his fingers.

"That's good. I own as how I had some hard feelings for a while there, when I thought you was just going all out to take me down a peg. But then I got to thinking it weren't your fault if a lot of them things you was saying was true, and like you told the boys, I asked for it. And then I was thinking how mortified I'd be if I was to let the fellows wrap you up like a parcel and bung you over the falls. It would be downright spiteful of me, I thought, and I'm glad I was able to catch them in time. But you gave me so much else to think about I reckon for a while there I was in kind of a maze.

"But you was wrong in one particular, professor, and it's one as makes all the difference." Sam paused, inciting Meleager to nod furiously, with rare humility.

"You said I got no gift. Well, there's one gift I got, and it was you as made me see it. I got a gift of jumping, professor. I'm just the best jumper there ever was."

This was the stuff, and the audience loved it. Sam looked up and smiled.

"So from now on I got me a new career. I done my last spinning, professor. You was right, that ain't for me. I got more in me than that. I'm going out and do the thing I'm best at. Nobody ever jumped like me, and so long as there's folks will come to watch, I reckon I'll have work. It can't kill me no quicker than drink, you was right about that too, and anyways, you know what they say: if a man was born to be hanged, he'll never drown."

Meleager coughed.

"I'm glad if I was able to be of service," he said, "in helping to point out your true destiny."

"That you was, professor, and I'm feeling that grateful I've a mind to shake your hand again to show it."

Meleager hastened to assure Sam that this was by no means necessary.

"Your bare testimonial is enough, sir. Yes, ahem. And for my part I apologize for the somewhat severe treatment you received at my hands. I can only offer the poor excuse that I heard the wonderful science of phrenology maligned, the science to which I have devoted my life, sir, and the effect was instantaneous and involuntary. I threw myself into its defense heedless of consequence, even at risk of serious bodily harm to myself, sir, as you saw. It is a failing of which I am aware, but my cautiousness is not large enough to restrain me when the cause of phrenology is at stake."

"Yes, sir, I noticed you was a regular wild man in the fracas we had," said Sam. "Well, sir," he went on, I think not seeing the suspicious glance Meleager shot him, "that's all water under the bridge now, and we must let bygones be bygones. Boys, the professor here is the real Simon Pure and I recommend his treatment to any one of you who thinks maybe his life ain't just on the right road. You seen what he done for me. I feel a new man already, gents, and no mistake."

"Hooray for Sam!" said one of the group. The rest chimed in, retrieving and waving the bottles that still had anything in them. Several were pressed on Sam. He took one and drained a third of it, looking every inch the hero again.

Still on my belly, I stared up at Sam with the intensity of a bear torn by conflicting emotions. I'd never seen anybody get the better of Meleager before, so there was that; but sweeping this clean out of mind was the realization that I'd just seen a man break at one stroke with his old life when that life had seemed to have him hopelessly fettered. The old Sam was flown and a new one hatched before our very eyes, though I doubt many there had the wit to see it. The implications for me made my head swim. So I looked up at the changeling still somewhat skeptically, but awed, too, and with yet a third emotion which grew by leaps and bounds till it outpaced the other two: envy.

Yes, envy. Not since my days with Karl, when I still aspired to someday cut loose from the umbilical of a patron, had I felt so keenly my difference from men. Sam could cut the knot that tied him to the old meaningless round. It was a bit startling that he had, but still he could do it. For me it was not even a possibility. Yet my malaise was essentially the same as Sam's, though I probably thought about it more philosophically. But I needed a better vantage on life's vicissitudes as much as ever Sam did. Ever since Crockett winkled me out of my cozy place in the scheme of things the way I might shuck a turtle out of his shell, vicissitudes for me were all there were. Now Sam in finding a way to give his life purpose had shown there was a way out—or maybe I should say *back*—and I was balked from following his example by an exasperating and otherwise trivial accident of birth. From where I stood, and must stand it seemed, the only "purpose" in my life was to try to keep body and soul sufficiently together that the question could still come up. No wonder my life felt aimless, unsatisfying: it was. Not that there weren't diverting moments: you could hardly travel with Molly and Meleager without your share of those, and the whole world I was in was new enough to me that, even though I didn't see it from the best angle, it was still a pretty constant entertainment. But I saw now how the lack of a larger purpose than simply to stay alive contributed more even than Meleager's personality to making me bitter and unhappy.

But if indeed I was bitter and unhappy, I was the only one in the room who was. Everybody else appeared to be rather emphatically the reverse. Sam, his good humor entirely restored, was again the center of a rollicking group while if anything an even larger group, though more subdued, had formed around Meleager, who was scribbling appointments for personal readings as fast as he could write. Cautiously disentangling myself from the stupefied celebrants who had pillowed themselves on my body, I got up and went over to join the men around Sam. They made way tolerantly, I think accepting me as a friendly hallucination. I hunkered down to watch Sam. He was drinking out of a different bottle now, a fuller one—for the time being at least—and I think he must have drunk twice what anyone else had. Beyond stoking his flush and making his eyes bright it didn't seem to affect him. I studied him as intently as if he were a coded prescription for my own deliverance. Everything about him was newly absorbing, significant. I took in his stocky build, his wavy black hair—how like mine, I thought.

Then a man on my right who had already spoken to me several times and clapped me on the back once suddenly handed me his jug.

"Here, hold this for me, will you, mister?" he said, blinking. His eyes seemed to be trying to cross. Next thing I knew he stretched out on the stage and, having made himself comfortable with his head on my foot, took to emitting the loudest snores I'd heard since coming on Herr Grund once asleep with his head in a washtub.

Sam and the others looked over and noticed me.

"Easy, boys," said Sam, as the plug-swallowing and bottle-dropping threatened to start all over again. "Me and this bear here is already something acquainted and he's not such a bad cuss. Judging from that jug he's hanging onto, I'd say the fact is he just means to be sociable."

That helped, and suggested a congenial way for me to help some more. I hoisted the jug, stuck the neck in my mouth and did my best to allay all doubts of my sociability.

"Whooee!" they said as I dropped the empty jug. At the sound its owner groped in his sleep, found his property and clutched it to him with a seraphic smile.

"What'd I tell you, gents?" said Sam with some pride. I saw I'd made him look good and he liked it. That was nice, I thought, feeling very friendly towards him. The warmth of the liquor spread out from my stomach and I burped happily. This Patch lunatic was all right, I decided.

Then I had an inspiration so heady that the drink I'd just taken was weak stuff in comparison. I squinted, keenly interested of a sudden in bringing Sam into sharper focus.

He was studying me, too.

"And burn me," he said slowly as we gazed into each other's eyes, "if he don't give me an idea.

"Professor!" he called out. "Wasn't you saying your helper here had some run-in with Davy Crockett and bested him at his own game? Well sir, I'm thinking a bear all trained up to appear before the public like this one would be mighty useful to a fellow in my new line of work, and it kind of tickles my fancy to think of him having such a famous pedigree. How much will you take for him?"

Meleager had evidently bowed to pleas that he do some more readings on the spot. His hands were each on a different unkempt head. Sam's question stopped both readings cold. I held my breath.

"Here," said Sam, digging in his pockets and producing a gold piece, "Tim Crane gave me twenty dollars for what I done this afternoon. It seems to be all I got on me just at present, but you can have it. Have we got a deal?"

Meleager's face lost some of the look of tortured sensibility he was working up at the thought of parting from me. Rather curtly he said:

"My dear sir, the bear is worth easily four times that. What do you take me for?"

Our audience murmured. "Eighty dollars!" they said. They sized me up and shook their heads. Now that I was on the block they seemed to have lost all fear, or even respect. One of them reached out and grabbed a handful of my fur at a spot that had been itching me for the last few weeks. He pulled and it came out. More shaking of heads.

"He ain't worth no eighty dollars," said a little man with bulging eyes, just as if he'd been buying and selling bears all his life and I had no feelings at all. Everyone nodded and muttered assent except the two stiffly holding their heads straight under Meleager's hands. These followed the negotiations out of the corners of their eyes.

"Fifty's more like," asseverated another officious fellow, pinching my lips and pulling them apart to peer at my teeth. "Tops."

Sam scratched his chin.

"Eighty dollars do seem a mite steep, professor," he said. "This old bear may have manhandled Crockett in his salad days, but I'm doubting he could do the trick a second time on what you've been feeding him. What do you say to fifty? I might raise fifty."

"I could hardly settle for less than sixty," said Meleager. The crowd hissed. He drew himself up. "Sixty is the least I could let him go for." His eye happened to light on me.

I curled my lip at him, all around, showing every tooth. Then I tipped him a very meaning wink.

Convulsively he slammed the heads under his hands together.

"But since it's you," he stammered, "I'll sell him for fifty dollars."

Cheers.

"Well, that's right nice of you," said Sam. "You can take this here twenty on deposit till I can raise the balance. I reckon I can get that amount together in a few days' time." But I thought he looked sad and I wondered if he could.

"I reckon you can raise it right here, Sam," said a short man in a tall hat, who looked less damp and disheveled than most of the rest. He pushed his way forward. I recognized Tim Crane. "Boys, I'd make it up myself except I'm betting the rest of you'd like to pitch in too. What do you say? It's for the hero of the Paterson Falls here, Samuel Patch. Who'll help show what we think of him? Step up, boys. Two bits apiece will more than do."

"By thunder, I will!" came a voice offstage. I recognized Mr. Kitchen. "Here's ten dollars of it, Sam. That jump of yours was the dad-blamedest sight I ever seen!"

The rest was speedily collected. Sam came up to me, turned

around and surveyed his supporters. There was moisture in his eye.

"I thank you, friends," he managed at length. "This *here's* the dad-blamedest thing *I* ever did see."

Then, just as he made to lead me away, there was a commotion backstage. I tracked its approach by the train of bodies being strewn to either side, and Miss Molly Money flung herself sobbing on my neck.

Chapter 10

Ah, Sam, I think back now on the six months or so of our travels after that and I see them as the happiest days of my life. I would have been startled at the time by the suggestion that someday they would appear this way to me, but it's true: I was blissfully happy. How it was possible for me to be so happy and not know it, I can't say. Perhaps happiness isn't so much a feeling, though, as a pitch of feeling—an uncommon vitality coupled with a sense of having matters in hand. We did feel that way, both of us. Cold sometimes and sometimes hungry, we never took our hardships to heart. We knew what we were about and endured such petty discomforts as came our way, indulgently. I think the closest either of us approached to our angst of former days was during the period of enforced idleness in the dead of winter, when Sam chafed so at having to wait for warm weather again to continue to stun the world with his jumping qualities. True suffering, I've learned, is spiritual, and Sam's confidence of purpose and my contentment in his company buffered us against it.

Yes, let me tell you something about true suffering. I sit here in this foul pen and I don't feel my hunger or the cold now either. These things aren't even flyspecks on the towering gray numbness that envelops me. Poor stomach, I can almost feel sorry for it, as for something separate from me. It can't compete; there's no contest between it and my misery of missing Sam, of knowing that I'll always miss him, that the world must somehow pretend to make do without him.

It's my penmate who gets me started on these thoughts. She has come close again, drawn by her craving to be comforted and probably, too, by a female curiosity to find out what could inspire a despair so profound as possibly to seem disproportionate even here. I haven't anything to give her. She looks at me with her great golden eyes—remarkable eyes, really—pleading, wanting to help and be helped, to give me what she's quite confident I need: to nuzzle and drug pain with animal closeness, hugs, and wet furry warmth. She rouses me from thinking of Sam in the same way a steamboat whistle can jar you out of a dream, and she brings me back again for a moment to the present. I take in our pen, my aggrieved stomach, her poor ankle, her eyes. Still she doesn't know the half of it, I think. Almost the worst she feels is puzzlement— puzzlement at finding herself here, puzzlement at my strange immovability. Her thoughts still run largely in their accustomed channels—mate, food, and family. Nothing diverts them for long. Already she's enough used to being here that I'm becoming an object of a new kind of interest. There's a new speculation in her efforts to get my attention now—sidelong looks from those eyes of hers: appraising looks, looks full of life . . .

Oh, unbearable looks, unbearable eyes . . . !

But enough.

The time I speak of now was October and the leaves were changing. The nights were cold but the days were often still warm. Sam, flexing his shoulders in the sailor jacket he always wore and breathing deeply of the morning chill, said it was "prime weather for jumping."

"Although I do wish I could have met up with that Meleager fellow a mite sooner. In this jumping game sometimes it don't hurt to get yourself a good running start."

That day we crossed the Hudson, aiming for Connecticut and the mills of Massachusetts, but taking our time. Sam was savoring his new freedom—glorifying in it, I should say. He talked and talked, rehearsing his boasts and dreams till I knew them by heart and they had lost some of their initial charm. But he refused to make plans.

"What's the use of working for yourself if you can't do what you want once in a while?" he said. "Anyways, all I need in this new line I'm in is some water to jump into and a good high place to jump into it from. I got the rest right here with me."

I had no comment to make to this. To tell the truth, I was getting a little fed up with all this talk of the romance of the independent life and of a fellow just doing what he liked. Molly and Karl had both effused all the time, too, about the grand things they were going to do someday, and I'd never grown impatient with hearing them. But there was the difference that Karl and Molly were still dependable (in Karl's case, only fairly dependable) providers. When they began to spout what even I, a relatively unsophisticated bear, could tell was utter balderdash, I could indulge them in it and no one would starve.

My worry was that Sam was up to somewhat the same thing, but less productively; that where Karl and Molly duped themselves out of dread of the reality, Sam deluded himself because he liked it. I worried he liked the idea of spending the rest of his days drinking and loafing; that the only thing he didn't like was admitting it to himself and having no more prepossessing image to show others. I worried that Meleager's reading was correct after all and I had pegged my fortunes to those of an amiable good-for-nothing.

But meanwhile, as I say, Sam talked.

"Who'd have ever thought a thing like jumping, what I did just for the fun of it, was the answer all along? It fair amazes me to think of all them times the work was getting me down and I was looking forward to doing a little jumping just to pick up my spirits, and it never once hit me that that right there was what I was good at and should have been doing straight along. And then when me and Kennedy was killing ourselves starting up our own mill, and it was going good, too, I was too dignified to go jumping, of course. And I thought I was going to make it big someday and felt pretty good about myself. But even then it was like the world went and got smaller of a sudden, and all serious somehow. Like I was getting paid for what I was doing, and I was going to get paid good someday, but part of what I was getting paid for was for getting so serious and forgetting about jumping. I'm telling you, Mr. Bear, this old life is a hard thing to read. Why, when Kennedy went and skipped with our capital, I got to feeling about as low as a man can feel. Now I think if I was to meet him, I'd go right up and shake his hand."

He paused.

"After I wrung his neck, I mean," he said and laughed.

I'm afraid I didn't pay much attention. It was beginning to occur to me that even if he turned out not to be a drunken layabout I wasn't much better off. This jumping business was bound to be dangerous. Besides promising an uncertain income at best, there was the possibility Sam would try it on once too often, and then where would I be? You can see how benighted my outlook still was. In my defense I can only plead long association with Karl and Meleager. I still didn't understand Sam or what we were about.

Even so, I was already beginning to like him, though my doubts about the future kept me from showing it much. Meleager had given me a lesson in caution, and I didn't care to make myself too attractive a commodity while there was still the possibility I might want to jump ship. In other words, I didn't let on how much of his talk I followed. I adoped a certain reserve. But Sam soon maneuvered me out of it.

"You sure don't say much, do you, old feller?" he spoke up at one point, casually glancing at me over his shoulder. "I been feeling your eyes boring into me like a pair of yellow jackets all day and not a peep out of you. I'd sure take it kindly if you was to just kind of grunt once in a while to break the monotony. Make you worlds more fun to be with."

I pricked up my ears but said nothing.

"Well, I reckon there's no law says a fellow's got to talk if he don't feel like it," he said, apparently to himself. He slowed to inspect a thicket of raspberry bushes and I was reminded we hadn't had lunch, which didn't improve my mood any. "Yep, you're probably figuring I talk enough for the both of us anyhow, and I won't deny it's so. It do help pass the time though, and there's no telling how long it's going to be till we get just exactly wherever it turns out we're going. Seems like we might as well take the chance to get better acquainted along the way." He looked at me inquiringly. "Course I reckon a man would have to be a fool to sign on a bear for his powers of conversation, so if you calculate talking's not just in your line that's all right by me, so long as you don't mind if I take the liberty to run on a bit now and again same as if you was a-hanging on every word. Hand me the end of that there chain of yours, will you? It seems to have sort of slipped out of my belt."

I handed it to him, wondering if he was so scatterbrained he didn't realize he wasn't wearing a belt. He took it with a nod, stuffed it into the back of his pants again and stepped out jauntily whistling "Molly Malone."

He whistled it through twice before I realized I'd been had.

In a couple of days we reached a town with a mill. This was where Sam meant to launch his tour, and by way of preparation he went so far as to wait outside till he could hitch a ride in on a wagon to make a more impressive entrance. I trudged along behind, as usual, in deference to the farmer's reservations about what my five hundred pounds might do to his horses and what I might do to him. But my heart was lighter than on such occasions in the past with Meleager, notwithstanding my stomach may have been lighter, too. They say a kind heart butters no parsnips, but I think my feelings that day were, if not a counterinstance to the rule, at least a strong indication that the parsnip test was misconceived. I doubt there *were* enough parsnips to make me feel as good with Meleager as Sam made me feel with his friendliness, his outgoing ways, and such acts of kindness as his efforts to make the farmer let me ride. It may be my mind still dwelt on his possible shortcomings as a breadwinner, but he was daily winning my heart.

There was the usual stir when we reached the town. Horses bucked, women gave demure little shrieks and some less demure big ones, pigs squealed and scattered in all directions and dogs and children converged at such a rate to replace them that it was as if every pig was no sooner out of sight than he metamorphosed into two or three dogs and urchins, wheeled about and charged back again. Sam was in seventh heaven. This reception was the stuff of his dreams. He beamed and waved, and even the farmer sat straighter and carried himself, I thought, with a conscious air of importance. I was used to it all, of course, but even so there was a freshness about it for me, too. Seeing the excitement through Sam's eyes made it all new again. I toyed with the dogs that came snapping at my ankles, roguishly flipping them on their backs or sending them flying short distances through the air to land in mud puddles rather than doing them any serious injury. I felt I had a special responsibility to see that Sam's debut went well.

As for Sam, he couldn't wait to begin, and if there had been anything there in the street worth jumping off of, I think he would have jumped off it. Failing that, he waved his arms and tried to get people's attention, but the snarling and yelling defeated this project too. In fact, I think that, happy as he was, he was a little confused by the uproar and the crowd and wouldn't have known what to say to them even if they'd been able to listen. I thought of Meleager and his painted wagon, which all by itself would have turned the event of our arrival to better account, and I confess I felt again a certain superiority to Sam in virtue of my past associations.

But Sam recovered quickly. He shook hands with our driver, jumped down, came back and fetched me.

"Boys," he said to the men who gradually had begun to displace the boys and dogs and were gathering into a curious, spitting circle around us, "if any of you wants to follow us on down to the Independence Tavern, I reckon you just might hear something or other to your advantage."

He'd gotten the name of the Independence Tavern from the farmer. Where he'd picked up that phrase, "hear something to your advantage," I don't know, unless from the Public Notices column in the newspapers, but it served the purpose. We trooped down the street in a body.

When we reached the tavern, the loungers in front parted for us with more respect than I think they were accustomed to showing to strangers. Sam took it as his due. With the aplomb of Napoleon occupying a captured citadel, Sam marched us up to the bar, turned around and surveyed the place with satisfaction. It wasn't much, but Sam seemed to be seeing more than the sawdust floor, rude benches and greasy walls. Now I know he was looking at the bottom rung of his ladder to destiny.

One of the loungers finally succeeded in fighting his way through our entourage and took up a position behind the bar. Sam ordered a bottle of St. Croix rum for himself, slapped down a dollar he must have been saving and glanced at me. His eyebrow gave an inquiring twitch and I waggled both of mine vigorously back at him in the hope we were talking about the same thing.

"And a lager for my friend here," he said gratifyingly.

This our bartender also produced, but more slowly, as if uncertain of the establishment's policy on serving bears. I hastened to down it like a model customer.

"Step up, boys," said Sam over the hubbub. "Don't be bashful. Me and Bruin have had us a hard tramp today and now we're here we could use some company to relax in. That's it, come on up. Ain't no part of our plan to put this poor fellow out of business on our account. Who'll buy Bruin another?"

There was a chorus of offers. The bartender, who couldn't keep up with the orders now, shot me a look that was markedly warmer. Soon glasses were being thrust under my nose from all sides, knocking into each other and slopping down my front. I drained them as fast as I could and still couldn't keep up. It all went down on an empty stomach, too, and that old glow began to spread. I felt an impulse to sing, but suppressed it. My singing wasn't always received much better than Molly's, and I didn't want to upset Sam's program, if he had one.

I looked over to see how he was making out and found he was regaling the bar with a version of my bout with Crockett even more bizarre than Meleager's. In the snatches I heard, it appeared that after Crockett and I had wrassled to a standstill, giving and receiving much punishment, I'd been struck with remorse at the treatment I was dishing out to so renowned a hero, and Crockett and I had fallen into each other's arms with mutual tearful expressions of esteem. Then, concerned that the woods should be safe for other hunters and desirous of giving so deserving a bear a leg up in life, he had referred me to friends who had trained me up in various departments of learning and turned me loose on the world in the company of a distinguished professor, who in turn had surrendered me to Sam, reluctantly, and only in the belief that Sam stood a better chance than he himself of achieving that Crockett-like fame that a bear like me was entitled to look for in his nearest associate.

"No," they said, looking at me with new eyes.

"Yep," said Sam.

I emptied another glass to counteract the chill of hearing Crockett's name.

"But who's going to make you famous?" asked someone evidently possessed of a more analytical bent than the others.

"I am," said Sam. "Maybe you boys have heard of me already somewhat. Does anybody recollect the name Sam Patch?"

Nobody did.

"You him?" they said, wanting to be sure they understood.

"Big as life," said Sam, nothing dismayed.

"I might have heard of you once. I can't remember," offered someone. The others, including Sam, turned to him expectantly. "I ain't just sure, but wasn't you run out of someplace for something?"

Sam leaned back. He took a drink.

"I expect that must have been some other gent," he said kindly.

"Could have been," admitted the speaker. "It was a long time back. Transpired in my pappy's day. Reckon it's nothing you're that proud of anyways."

Sam assured him again it was a "different gent."

" 'Sides that, friend, I'm thinking I'd have had to be one hell of a rip-roaring urchin to get myself run out of town at such a tender age as you imply."

This shot having struck home, Sam hastened to move things along.

"But listen here, boys, what's just the gol-darnedest stunt you ever did see?"

They scratched their heads.

"You mean like what somebody did?" they asked.

"That's what I mean," said Sam, and took a drink.

"I saw a blind man cut his foot off once," ventured a grizzled fellow in red suspenders. "Was back in '01, I believe. Luke Jeffries had a dog named Toby then, and Toby had ahold of this fellow's boot and was annoying him something fierce, what with making him hop all over and him not able to see nothing. And the fellow whanged up against the cabin and lighted on this adze, see, and he took a swipe at Toby with it, only he missed and lopped his foot off instead." He spat. "Sure did surprise him—Toby, I mean—when the fellow's foot come off. He just sat there screeching and carrying on—the fellow, I mean—and Toby he up and run off with the boot with the fellow's foot still in it and nobody ever did see hide nor hair of either one of them again. The boot and the foot, I mean. Toby come back that night right as rain, though I recollect he wouldn't eat no supper. But we never did find what he done with the poor fellow's foot."

"Don't that beat all," they said.

"I reckon the dog must have buried it somewhere," said one. "Dogs are always burying things."

"It sure must have been a sight."

Red Suspenders preened himself and took a drink. Everybody took a drink.

"That minds me of the time my old dog Rascal—" began someone else.

"Now pull up a sec, boys," broke in Sam. He gave Red Suspenders a nod. "That was a mighty fine tale, mister, but it wasn't just exactly the kind of stunt I had in mind. I meant more like a dangerous, death-defying sort of stunt a fellow does like on a dare or a bet maybe. The kind of thing as takes real grit to do and ain't just everybody's cup of tea."

"I guess I got a stunt for you, mister," said a burly fellow with a bushy black beard I rather envied. He went over to the fire and snatched up a small iron shovel that had been left lying with its scoop in the coals. He brought it back and spat on the hot part. The spittle hit with a *crack* and was gone in an instant. The man held up the shovel and grinned evilly at Sam over the end of it.

"Here's a stunt for you, mister," he said again.

Then he opened his mouth, winked at Sam, and pressed the length of his tongue to the shovel.

There was a horrible hissing. A thick cloud of steam gouted up, mixed with smoke from his beard where the hairs came in contact with the glowing iron, glowed red themselves, curled and fell off. An acrid stink filled the air.

"Whoo-ee, that was a good one, Zeb!" they yelled. Zeb jerked his tongue—well done by now, I guessed—off the shovel and grabbed his glass. He took a hasty mouthful, sloshed the contents from cheek to cheek, spat, and with a malodorous "Hah!" stuck his tongue out again for inspection. It looked good as new.

"How's that for a stunt?" he crowed. The others clapped him on the back. He thrust his still-smoking beard under Sam's nose, cackled, and demanded with more wit than I'd have given him credit for if that stunt was "more to your taste."

"It's a first-rate stunt and no mistake," Sam told him generously, putting a little more distance between his nose and the reeking remains of Zeb's beard.

"First-rate? I should say so. Why, I guess it was, all right," said Zeb with a leer. He exchanged this suddenly for a look of guileless simplicity. "All the same it ain't half so hard as it looks. You could do it yourself, mister. Care to try?" He held out the shovel.

"I expect I could if I knew the trick," said Sam. "But I figure I can match it my own way." He stood up a little straighter and said casually, "I hear tell there's a mill hereabouts. About how high up would you say it is over the water? Eighty feet? That's fine. That's real fine. Well, what would you give to see a fellow jump off it?"

"Jump off it!" they echoed, taken aback.

Forgotten, I helped myself to another glass from the bar and sipped quietly, watching. Zeb was forgotten, too, but didn't take it so well. He brandished the shovel.

"I want to see him lick it!" he said, still smoking a bit.

"Mister," said Sam, "that stunt, though it's a fine one, ain't my specialty. However, I'm offering to match it in my own style if the other gents here will kick in to help with my traveling expenses, since it's what I come here for. But just so's there's no hard feelings between us, I'll make you a deal. You keep me company in my little jump off of Jaeger's Mill and when we get dry I'll try me a bite of your shovel. How's that for fair?"

Regardless of what Zeb thought, this proposal struck the others, who weren't being called on either to jump or lick, as eminently reasonable. They urged it on Zeb enthusiastically.

"You can do it, Zeb," they said. "If he can do it, you can!"

I felt sorry for Zeb. His rise and fall had been truly meteoric. He combed his fingers through his beard, precipitating a fine shower of ash, and looked from face to face as if seeing each for the first time.

"Why, yes, I reckon I could," he said slowly, "if I was fool enough." With a nod to Sam he replaced the shovel and left with something like dignity.

Chapter 11

After Zeb left we got down to brass tacks and set the jump for the following day. Some were all for having him do it right then, but Sam said he wanted to "get in shape first," by which he mostly meant catch up on his drinking. But also he wanted to allow time for publicity, with which his sponsors willingly undertook to help. This mainly involved spreading the word in the other taverns and saloons in town, and everybody found it congenial work. At one of these we ran into a wagoner from Paterson who recognized Sam right off and gave everyone an account of the Paterson jump that was almost as bloated as Sam's story of my meeting with Crockett. This did nothing to lessen the interest and the next day practically the whole town turned out to watch.

Sam was magnificent. What Meleager would have tried to effect with showmanship, Sam brought off just by the force of his personality. He was so full of confidence and good spirits, to say nothing of rum, that the crowd took him to their hearts right away. And I did the same. It felt like a knot in my chest suddenly loosened and fell away. It was impossible to doubt him anymore. Oh, it was still true that he was as different as could be from Meleager and that there was every chance that I'd have to get used to eating somewhat irregularly. Somehow that didn't matter so much anymore. As I watched him caper up there on top of the mill, the way

I saw him changed. I realized it was a mistake to measure him by Meleagerean standards. What his skills were, what he could reliably be depended on to do, mattered next to nothing beside his qualities as a man. Maybe the best way I can put it is this: no amount of jumping could make a hero of Meleager; or anyway, he would be a hero only because he jumped. But Sam was a man who jumped because he was a hero.

Zeb, who stood beside me, was won over too. We'd run into him again on our rounds and Sam had gone out of his way to conciliate him, telling everyone that it was plain he and Zeb were "made in the same mold" and giving Zeb charge of me for the event. Now Sam had no more loyal supporter. Zeb was craning his neck, savaging his already mutilated beard with his teeth. He held the end of my chain clenched in his fist, his knuckles white with an intensity of feeling that I knew had nothing to do with me.

Then Sam jumped. He sprang straight out from the roof, brought his feet together and down he sped. He hit feet-first with hardly a splash and the crowd gasped as if they'd been dropped in cold water themselves. A woman shrieked.

I'd seen it all before. I *knew* he'd come up. He had hit the water perfectly poised, in an exact reprise of his Paterson leap. There was no trusting to luck here, I told myself. He had technique. Still, my breath came short till I saw his dark head reappear, saw him shake the water from his eyes, and knew that he was all right.

Hats filled the air. The jump was a huge success and Zeb and I were among the first to congratulate him.

Chapter 12

"Whoo-oop!"

Early morning, the day after the jump. We were on the road and Sam had broken out in a jig again.

"Waa-hoo!"

He grabbed my arm and we dosey-doed in the middle of the road.

"Weren't that just the most splendiferous jump you ever did see, and didn't they just eat it up though?" he shouted. I woofed and tried to lick his ear.

"Wa-a-hoo-oo!"

But we were not alone. An ambiguous figure all in black had come up behind us on the road and stood eyeing us from a respectful distance.

"Ho, there, mister," said Sam, "I reckon we're blocking your right of way. Well, don't be shy. Come on up. I ain't half so crazy as I look. Just feeling good, is all, and not afraid to own it. There now, howdy do."

"Greetings, brother," said the newcomer, with a mixture of condescension and unction that, together with his rusty black suit, made me take him for a preacher. He eyed me askance. "And thank you. I take it your companion is peaceable minded, too?"

"If you mean is Bruin here going to bite your head off, you can set your mind at ease. Bruin here never bit nobody in his whole life except one fellow as deserved it, so he don't count. A preacher fellow, as I recollect. Hold on now, don't go off like that. Can't you tell when a fellow's joking? Come here and let me introduce you. Bruin'll be fine so long as you don't try and convert him."

He fetched the man up by the arm.

"This here's Bruin. Me, I'm Samuel Patch, who you may have heard of. And now, sir, I reckon it's your turn."

"The Reverend Flexible Grummet, at your service," said Sam's captive, freeing his arm.

Saying his name seemed to give him courage. He straightened his coat and we looked at each other. Somewhat shifty goggle-eyes peered at me from under an overhanging gray thatch of eyebrow.

"Fine figure of a bear," he said.

"He is that."

"I would not have you think I was afraid of him, brother. We laborers in the Lord's fields scorn such dangers as would keep us from our work. It's said Mohammed used to tell his followers that if any fell on the field of battle their groans would be exchanged for shouts of glory and their lost wounded limbs for angel wings—that the greatest fighter would get nearest the seventh heaven. Well, we spreaders of righteousness know it's the same with us: a reward awaits us in Paradise. For it is written, 'And they that be wise shall shine as the brightness of the firmament, and they that turn many to righteousness as stars forever and ever. Amen.' Yes indeed. But it is not the part of humility to seek the martyr's crown, and I was swayed in my initial resolve steadfastly to confront the brute— begging your pardon, brother—only by the reflection that there are sadly too many souls that still need turning to righteousness for me to risk a premature assumption of my reward."

"Ain't that the truth, sir. Why, I'm pretty close acquainted with one of the very same myself."

"If it's of yourself you speak, brother," said the Reverend Grummet severely, "I can only say I feared as much when I saw you. You are crapulous, are you not, brother?"

"What?"

"Inebriated. Intoxicated. A slave to the demon rum. Drunk, brother, in a word," said the reverend, breaking off and dabbing nervously at his lips with a handkerchief.

"Oh, that. Nope, you got me dead wrong, Reverend. But I'm going to be," Sam added generously, on seeing Mr. Grummet's evident disappointment. "Just as soon as I can. Me and Bruin just made us better than twenty dollars, and as it's the first we've made in what's a new line of work for us, I figure to lay off some of it on some celebrating, next town we come to. And I'd be proud if you was to come along and see I go about it right."

"It's possible I might be able to save you from yourself," allowed Mr. Grummet, and I noticed his eye grew brighter again at the prospect.

The three of us traveled together for the rest of the day, sometimes walking, sometimes riding (Sam and the reverend, I mean). Naturally, Sam told the reverend all about his jump.

"Burn me, I wish I could have seen it, brother!" said Mr. Grummet. Hastily he added, "Though of course you were likely tempting Satan."

This sort of pious afterthought turned out to be typical of Mr. Grummet's style of conversation. The parts before the afterthoughts, however, partook of such a different character and were so at variance with what might have been expected from a man of his profession that the effect was much like talking to two persons sharing a single suit of clothes. Sam noticed the same thing.

"Well, it's this way, brother," Mr. Grummet explained readily enough. "If you were one of the sanctified, I'd have to be a mite more particular in my sentiments so as not to offend or seem to be setting a bad example. But seeing as you're one of the wicked who refuses to be saved, well, I reckon it can't do any harm."

Soon after this he wondered aloud how far it might be to the town where Sam intended to commence his celebrating, as he, Mr. Grummet, though a teetotaler by ordinary, thought the occasion might warrant just a single friendly nip.

I don't know how it was, but there was something about Mr. Grummet I didn't trust. Maybe his extreme flexibility reminded me a little too much of Meleager, but whatever it was, I wasn't inclined to take all his affability at face value.

And even an affable man can be pressed too hard.

"Tell me, Reverend," said Sam earnestly at one point, "course I'm just a poor sinner—but do you really believe how that Jonah fellow swallowed the whale?"

"I sure do, brother, " said Mr. Grummet, putting on his business face. "It's in the Scripture."

"Well, it's a bit more than I can swallow, Reverend. Ain't no man could eat a whale."

The look Mr. Grummet gave him smelled of brimstone.

Then we reached the town and Sam hauled the reverend, protesting feebly, into a saloon.

"Well, I ain't no cold-water drinker like some, brother," said Mr. Grummet when Sam had him ensconced finally at the bar. "I figure the Lord wouldn't have afflicted us with something that was totally bad, and it's a widely known fact that alcohol has numerous medicinal and restorative properties. It ain't the drink as turns a man into a sot, brothers," he said to the crowd around us, "it's the man who don't know when to stop."

"Ain't it the truth, Reverend," agreed Sam. "Moderation's the very thing. That's why there's just two occasions I'll have a drink myself. One is if I feel real good, the other is if I don't."

"I make it my firm policy never to have but one drink, brothers," went on Mr. Grummet fervently, not hearing this, I think. "One drink is all I ever take. Wild horses couldn't make me pour a second. It's a test of character, brothers, an exaltation of spirit over flesh, to have one drink and then retire the glass. And I don't mean go drinking out of the bottle then neither. I mean face it down square and know you've beat it and can still call your soul your own. One brandy, bartender. The last you shall hear me call for."

Sam called for the same. The man set down their glasses and filled them in what amounted to a religious hush. Mr. Grummet folded his hands, closed his eyes and turned his face heavenward. He began to pray.

It was, as Sam might have said, considerable of a prayer. Reverend Grummet called on the Lord to bless this potation which he in his divine wisdom and goodness had sent us to comfort the comfortless, warm the cold and cool the overheated; to heal the sick and brace the weak. But it was a medicament to be used sparingly and with care. God made man in his image in giving man free will, but there too lay the possibility of sin. Poor finite creature that he was, man must ever prove himself against the temptations and evils of this world, not the least of which was intemperance. The victim of intemperance is as stupid as an ass, as ferocious as a tiger, as savage as a bear, as poisonous as the asp, as filthy as the swine, as fetid as a goat, and as malignant as a fiend. Thus it ever behooved a man to be on guard against the devil in the bottle lest it summon up a worse devil in himself. After some more of the same the Reverend Grummet said Amen.

He opened his eyes, gazed about him with a very spiritual expression, and reached with a sigh for his glass. It was empty.

"Brother," said Sam, smacking his lips, "I reckon this just goes to show, you must watch as well as pray."

I mention this passage because it had important consequences. It turned out I was right to mistrust the latitudinarian little preacher. Events proved him to have a decidedly unchristian streak.

There was a bridge in the town, and when people heard about Sam's other jumps they pressed him to jump off it. A mere sixty feet high, it scarcely struck Sam as worth the effort, or so he said, but his new cronies wouldn't take that for an answer.

Word spread of what he was to do and once again a sizeable crowd assembled—as much to see Sam, I think, this time, as to see him make this jump. Around noon, after Sam had had a little breakfast and I'd had quite a lot (my initial worries notwithstanding, actually I ate like a king in those days), he fetched me from a shed out back and we sauntered together with our drinking companions from last night through town to the river. Some along the way looked at us askance, but many more, I noticed, at least of the men, called out and waved if they didn't fall in with us. Sam led the group with the easy stride of a man perfectly confident of his powers and who finds life entirely to his liking.

At the bridge they greeted us with a cheer. Sam and I and the crowd from the saloon marched out over the water from one end, while from the other a mixed crowd of boys, men and dogs set out to meet us in the middle. Much cheering and commotion. Sam and I both had our backs slapped and several jugs were going round.

"Well, boys," said Sam to one and all, "I'm glad to see you, mighty glad. There's nothing in the world I like better than jumping and having a chance to show folks how some things can be done as well as others."

He handed my chain to one bystander and his jacket to another (who clearly felt himself the more fortunate of the two), climbed over the rail and positioned himself. The crowd quieted. Then off he jumped. All of that went the same as last time. There was also the usual sensation when he reappeared in the water, and the usual hullabaloo when they fished him out. Then, since the fellow holding my chain would neither move from the spot nor surrender me up to anyone else, the crowd brought Sam back on their shoulders to me.

He was taking turns drinking and waving when a voice I thought I recognized sang out:

"Let's see the bear jump!"

The cry caught on. It was picked up and echoed from shore. "The bear! The bear! Let's see him jump!"

Sure enough, there was Flexible Grummet with the group from the other end of the bridge, waving his hat and stirring up the crowd.

Sam looked nonplussed. In vain he temporized.

"Boys, this ain't a bear as jumps. He can hold his own drinking with any three men, he can dance up a storm, and I even hear tell he sings. But jumping just ain't in his repertory."

But no one could hear him but a few up front and they weren't listening. The idea of seeing me follow Sam had captivated them all. I started giving thought to how I was going to negotiate a way for us through Sam's disappointed admirers.

Then somehow it dawned on me we weren't going to disappoint them. I don't know how I knew it; I wasn't even looking at Sam when it hit me. I think I just realized that, though Grummet had his own reasons for proposing it, the idea of my jumping was too natural not to come up again. And in the long run there was just one way to deal with it if I meant to be true to Sam.

I wouldn't have you think my decision to jump was made as quickly and simply as that. In fact, it wasn't so much a decision at all as just a strong suspicion that was how things were going to fall out. Mine was like the case of the poor devil tied to a stake who has a premonition that, without consulting his own feelings in the matter, the Indians have him tapped to provide the evening's entertainment. Except I was also going to be expected to light the fire myself.

So I watched Sam apprehensively, but I already knew the outcome.

"Well, of course he can jump," Sam was saying. "Ain't he the same as faced down Crockett? Do you think I'd lug around a bear as wouldn't do me proud?" He turned and glowered at me, dripping.

I went up to the rail, moving like a sleepwalker. The river below rippled and scintillated like the gleaming hide of a snake. So high, I thought! It had looked high when Sam jumped; now it looked twice as high. The breeze flattened my fur. I felt a tingling in my palms.

I didn't have to jump; no one could make me. Why was I going to, then? What had he done to me that I knew that even jumping was not the limit of what I would do for Sam?

"Get on up there, blame you!" he said, and gave me a push. But it was the first and only time I ever saw him look anxious. I licked his face.

"Go on and get it over with, you rascal," he growled.

Somehow I clambered over the rail without falling. With a last, I fear piteous, look at Sam and the world I knew, I let go.

Water and sky wheeled before my eyes. I remember my astonishment at seeing the underside of the bridge and the rail lined with faces. Then, after what seemed ages of breathless tumbling, I hit the water with a splash that reached shore.

Soon after, I reached shore myself, physically none the worse for my experience, but with my mind still spinning somewhere in space. Then Sam was there. He dashed into the water to lead me out. The clench of his strong fingers on my shoulder bit through the numbness I felt all along my back from the river's slap and partially revived me. But I still couldn't connect my emergence from the river with my plunge into it. There was a gap—not in my recollection, but in my understanding. What I recalled of the interval between bridge and shore was no link at all, but a transit through another plane. I had seen too much and too little. In one sense, the smallest child on the bank knew more of my fall than I did; on the other hand, I could not forget I had seen the whole nominally friendly world of appearance stripped away like an old rug, to pitch me headlong through the patchwork flooring beneath into a boiler room in which I was vouchsafed, all unwilling, a glimpse of life's engines. Like the criminal on the scaffold who feels the trap spring under him, I had known the utterest solitude for a time not adequately to be measured by clocks, and for a brief while still I saw everything about me with a terrible perspicacity.

At least for the time it took Sam to lead me back to dry land, I was in truth no ordinary bear.

But then, not even waiting for me to shake myself off, he squeezed the life back into me with a hug that crunched my bones.

Chapter 13

Fall and the last of the jumping weather passed all too quickly—
for Sam, at any rate. I wasn't nearly so enamored of this activity
myself, notwithstanding that after that first time I got as much
practice at it as he did. But even though we kept performing so
far into the cold weather that each jump was a plain invitation
to a case of pneumonia, and even though people came to see us
now as much because we were throwing ourselves into water at
all as because we were doing it from a height—even so, the best
things come to an end, and eventually, with ice all but forming
on the rivers, even Sam had to admit the jumping season was
closed.

The difficulty was deciding what to do with ourselves now that
we were unemployed.

Actually, I didn't mind that so much. After all that flying through
the air (not something bears are specially suited for) and splashing
about in freezing water, I had vividly before me at least one worse
way to pass the time than to spend it nodding over a toddy in the
quiet corner of some tavern, comfortably close to a cozy fire. Not
so Sam. The man was fretful as a caged . . . well, bear. He resented
the enforced hiatus in his jumping campaign as though it were a
personal affront.

"Burn me, Bruin, it galls a man to no sooner find what's his proper work than to have something come along as jerks it right out of his hands and leaves him a-setting there like some old toothless hound dog as knows he ought to be chomping somebody's leg but ain't got the wherewithal to do it!"

These bitter reflections even seemed to steal the fun out of drinking for him. I don't mean he drank any less, but I'd certainly seen him enjoy it more.

Part of the problem was the elections. That December saw a landslide victory for the Jacksonians, sweeping into the 20th Congress a host of people whose chief claim to fame was that they were very models of the common man.

"Why, I'm as common as the best of them," grumbled Sam over his newspaper.

We'd run into a number of the new congressmen in the course of their campaigning and it was true, they were no better fitted for their new eminence than Sam would have been.

"I can out-talk them, out-drink them, and out-jump them," said Sam on this subject. "And I reckon I could out-lie them and out-steal them too, if I was willing to work on it."

Not that Sam had any special leanings toward politics. About the tariff he was indifferent. About national improvement, the other major election topic, he was all but indifferent, except insofar as he considered that if the government did build more bridges, there would be that many more opportunities for him to jump. The only social issue I ever saw him get much worked up about was temperance, which affected him personally. On principle, too, I believe he had a constitutional aversion to being browbeaten into doing something "for his own good."

"If I was the sort of man as listened to that pabulum, why, I guess I wouldn't jump," he said, and as far as he was concerned, this was unanswerable.

I think he just didn't see anywhere that politics and the issues of the parties fitted very closely into his life.

"Sure, I guess that politics stuff is okay if you care about it," I heard him say once to someone trying to embroil him in a wrangle. "But somehow it don't seem to me to touch on what's important. I mean, is politics going to help you if you're sad? Is it going to keep you from getting your heart broke? Can it make a low-down bad man turn good, or fix it so folks is nicer than what they are?

What if a fellow don't know what to do with his life? Can politics help him there?"

"Sounds like you're talking about religion, to me," said the other.

"Well, maybe I am at that, in a way. I guess that's what religion's for, ain't it?—helping folks with death and dying and the other ways life grinds you down that you can't do anything about. Only, religion's only good for them as believes in it. So I figure every man's got to go his own way and face things square and just be as true as he knows how to be and not peg his hopes on anything else. That's what I think," said Sam.

But even if his interest in politics was distinctly limited, it irritated him to see others no better favored than he, using their time to better advantage while he had to sit idly by, waiting for good weather again and letting precious days slip by when he was in his jumping prime.

One day there was a piece about Crockett in the paper. Sam thought I might be interested and read it aloud to me. The piece referred to the early story of Crockett's dinner with President Adams when Crockett was newly arrived in Washington, and how the newspapers had printed that the backwoodsman helped himself from the serving dishes with his hands, ate with his fingers and the aid of an enormous knife, and tried to take a bottle of wine away from the serving man for his own. The piece told how Crockett had subsequently gotten three of the other guests to write letters repudiating the slander, and how after a year on the job he was one of the most popular and promising members of Congress.

"That Crockett," said Sam, "there's a man for you , I guess. Just a plain fellow, but not a mistake in him. Set him down anywhere there's a spot of trouble and burn me if he don't have it sorted out in two shakes. Just a fellow as goes his own way and gets appreciated for it, too, on account of the stuff that's in him. I'd sure admire to shake his hand.

"And to think you and him is friends," he said, looking at me as if he thought my acquaintance with Crockett made me a pretty lucky fellow. "Maybe someday you can introduce us. 'This here's Sam Patch, Davy,' you'll tell him, 'the fellow as you've been hearing so much about. He's been hoping for a chance to meet you.' And Davy'll say, 'Why, thank you, Bruin, old friend, the only bear what ever fought me to a standstill. I hope you've been well. And it's mighty pleased I am to meet you, Sam. I've heard such a whopping lot about you that if the half of it is true, why, I reckon you must be near as great as me. I just wish I had you by me here in Washington,' he'll say. 'I reckon the pair of us could whip this old country into shape in about no time.' " And he laughed heartily.

I took a too-hasty swallow of beer.

"Course I keep forgetting you can't talk," said Sam, thumping me on the back. "Well, then I guess I'll just have to introduce myself. But I'll be sure you're there, old fellow. I owe you a lot, and I wouldn't miss being the one to bring you and Crockett back together for anything. Meantime, it's like you keep me in mind of him, and if I wasn't restless enough already, seeing you makes me specially want to stir my stumps. Every time I look at you, I keep thinking how much catching up I've got to do if I'm to show as I mean to how some things can be done as well as others."

The aftermath of this conversation was that Sam's restlessness would no longer let us keep to our snug quarters and wait the season out. So we said good-bye to our new friends and off we went again, tramping the frozen roads, me comfortable enough in my winter fur, but thinking how much more sensible it would have been just to hibernate; and Sam in his flimsy sailor jacket, warmed by his ambition.

On one of our jaunts we fell in with a peddler, still making his rounds even in this weather, a tin box full of his wares strapped to his back and bending him nearly double.

"Here, old son, let Bruin lug that for you," volunteered Sam when we'd been introduced.

"Thank you kindly for the offer, but I reckon not," said the other, whose name was Jacob Siler. "There's most everything I'm worth in here and I couldn't rest easy without I feel the weight of it. Besides, I've been carrying it so long now I reckon I'd clean pitch over backward if I was to try to walk without it. I'd sure let him carry these, though, if he could," he said, freeing a hand long enough to produce a pair of chestnuts from a bulging pocket. "I ain't used to the shape of them and they're chafing up my thighs something fierce."

"Whyn't you stow them somewheres else?" suggested Sam.

"I couldn't do that," said Jacob, with a sigh that froze more vapor onto his already pretty well iced-up beard. "Then they wouldn't work."

It turned out he'd heard that filling his pockets with chestnuts would help cure his hemorrhoids.

"Ah," said Sam, "now you mention it, I've heard the same,

although so far I've been lucky enough never to just want to put it to the test. A mighty sorry complaint, though, by all accounts," he said, unable to repress a sympathetic glance at the sufferer's behind.

"Well may you say so, friend. But it's like an occupational hazard. Comes of resting on my box."

"I don't wonder," said Sam. "I've also heard tell sweet potatoes will ease the discomfort, same as chestnuts."

"I've heard that, too. I only went with the chestnuts as they're smaller. But by all reports I figure they likely work as good."

Sam asked what brought him out in such weather. Jacob Siler replied, rather defensively, I thought:

"Well, I guess folks need pins and needles and such just as much in the winter as any other time."

"Well, I don't doubt that a minute," said Sam, "but ain't you putting yourself to pretty considerable of an inconvenience to save them a little ride into town? I recollect when I was just a tad there wasn't so many stores about and the roads was full of you gents. But now folks can pretty near buy whatever they want to in town. Don't that kind of cut into your trade?"

"There's folks are glad enough to see me," said Mr. Siler, his ice-bound chin going up. I didn't know how it was, but I could see Sam had somehow touched him on the raw. "And anyways, where do you think all them stores come from? Folks as own them used to tramp just like me, that's where, till they got the capital together to settle down. I don't mind saying that's my aim, too, and I bought this very box off a man who did it. So it's a good luck piece, like, besides what it's got in it."

"Well, I reckon I can understand that," said Sam.

Mr. Siler thawed—figuratively, at least.

"Sure, there's lots of folks would say I'm behind the times, but I know what I want and I mean to get it. It's slow, it's real slow, but I'm saving up, and meantime thinking about my store and how I'll fix her up keeps the heart in me. Sometimes, walking along, I get to picturing it all so clear I clean forget where I am. Do you want I should tell you about it?"

Sam signed his willingness to hear.

"Well, I most generally imagine I'm coming to her from the street," said Mr. Siler, "so the first thing I see is the big window in front, with 'Siler's General Store' printed on it in them fancy gilt letters. That's how she looks on the outside and she's pretty as a picture, I can tell you. I never can go in without I stop there in the street and admire how sweet she looks, all so warm and bright, making me feel so good, and like she's beckoning me inside. I ain't lying when I tell you it's like she's saying to me, 'Come on in, Jacob. Let me show you all the nice things I got.' Well sir, so then I step in the doorway and the smells of all them good things hit me like a blast of perfume. Fact is, some of it is perfume. I mean to stock a bit of everything, I do. But it all smells that fine to me—the hats and shirts, the flour and beans and molasses, salt fish maybe, medicines and liniments, books . . . You name it, I'll have it for you when I get my store. Won't nobody go away unsatisified.

"So then I go inside. There's a stove there in the middle and some chairs for them as wants to set and pass the time, and counters along both sides for waiting on the customers. I figure I'll need the pair of them and a clerk or two to help out, once folks see the kind of things I got. Why, I'll have clocks and spectacles, tin-ware, hooks, eyes, buttons, razors, combs, spoons, knives, lace and ribbon and every kind of fabric—and everything of the finest. There'll be pots and pans and shoes and boots and some dresses ready made, and just generally so much of everything I won't know where to put it all. I'll have it stacked up on the counters and sitting out on display and crowding my shelves on the wall to busting. I'll have jewelry and such in some glass cases down to the end, and jars of candy for the little ones, and pickles and crackers in big barrels you can just help yourself out of, and a regular post office at the back for folks' mail, and—"

A violent sneeze interrupted Mr. Siler's recitation. We all paused there in the road, the frigid wind licking and plucking at my fur and every loose flap of clothing, while Mr. Siler clumsily dug out an enormous soiled handkerchief and blew his nose.

"She sounds like a mighty handsome store, friend, and no mistake," said Sam.

Mr. Siler blinked. He gazed around him at the barren country-side, pulled up his collar and gave his box a hitch.

"And I mean to have her, too."

We parted ways. Sam and I walked on in silence, each thinking his own thoughts, till supper and a warm fire began to edge out Mr. Siler from mine.

Somehow we got through that winter, but I think if it had lasted a month longer Sam would have had us jumping through holes in the ice. As it was, ice was still to be met with in shaded hollows and under the bridges when we did take up again in April, but you'd have thought the water was bath water, to see Sam's evident pleasure in plunging into it. But after the day Sam declared the jumping season open, even nature hadn't a prayer of holding him back.

This was just as well, from the point of our finances. These had sunk as low as finances very well could during our months of idleness. For while Sam might have found work to tide us over, this he flatly refused to do.

"I got work, thank you, sir," he told one well-wishing prospective employer. "Jumping is my work. It's what I do full-time. If I was to go and work for you, now, then I reckon the most I could jump is part-time, on account of I'd be doing two things instead of one. And I don't allow nothing to cut into my jumping."

This paradoxical remark was spread around and became as celebrated as that other dark saying of Sam's, "Some things can be done as well as others," so that Sam found himself with a reputation for wit as well as for profundity. But when our fellow-drinkers taxed him with having a unique style of "jumping full-time," Sam never cracked a smile. I believe he meant every word of what he'd said.

So all in all it was a good thing for both of us that I wasn't without resources of my own. Not only was I an attraction by my reputation, but unlike Sam, I was an attraction people would buy drinks for just to see me drink them. And I could eke out these gratuities by various other slight forms of entertainment that brought in cash. But Sam, even though he was the principal beneficiary of this income, didn't really approve of my means of earning it. Again, my tricks were too far removed from jumping. I had to be careful not to overstep. But as long as the income wasn't too great, or the exertions I made to gain it too notable, Sam was tolerant. I think he considered me only a part-time jumper and so would forgive much, as long as nothing else I did threatened to eclipse the primacy of jumping. How he thought we would eat if *somebody* didn't bring in some money, I don't know; but then I'd already learned that artists can be extremely unpractical. I was really the practical member of the partnership.

So off we went, jumping our way through Connecticut, Massachusetts, and upstate New York when the buds were scarcely formed on the trees. And people began to hear of us. Now when they turned out to greet us in a new town, everybody knew who we were. Sam no longer had to drum up a crowd or concern himself with publicity. If anything, we had the opposite problem. We couldn't pass through a town without meeting with invitations to jump, and if Sam didn't accept, the citizenry took it as an affront to their civic pride. And some of these towns didn't have any water.

Sam took this attention as his due. He never became particularly excited about getting it, and I never saw him worry about not getting it—for all that he enjoyed it when he had it, of course. Oh yes, he wanted recognition as much as anybody else, but I began to see how profoundly serious he was when he said jumping was his work. The recognition pleased him, all right, but it wasn't to gain recognition that he jumped. No, he jumped because jumping was what he did.

So it didn't bother Sam that his renown at this point had less the character of fame than of notoriety. Certainly people turned out in droves to see us, but they did so more the way they might have turned out to see a two-headed calf than a famous war hero, say. Wonder there was aplenty, but their admiration, except on the part of the less reputable elements, had overtones of contempt.

Sam forgave them for it, if he noticed at all. Let people think he was crack-brained. As long as they came to watch him jump, he was satisfied. And each time they did, more of them were captivated by the patent, unconquerable vitality of the man; were thrilled to see a kind of nobility in his braving destruction to pit himself, for no other reason than to show that "some things can be done as well as others," against such elemental champions of nature as swift-flowing rivers and waterfalls. Each time, more spectators went away unexpectedly touched and proud of their kinship with such a man. And the blindness of those obdurate ones who didn't, troubled Sam not a bit, who jumped, after all, not to please anybody, but because jumping was what he did.

But then one day in June came a letter that shook even Sam's equilibrium.

"Burn me, Bruin, listen to this."

The letter, addressed to "Sam Patch, the Jersey Jumper," was from Tim Crane, back in Paterson, inviting Sam to return and repeat his celebrated feat of jumping the Paterson Falls. The town was holding a Fourth of July extravaganza, also to feature fireworks and a parade, and they wanted their own hero, Sam Patch, for its centerpiece.

"Why, don't that beat all. It sure is mighty thoughtful of old

Tim. Who'd have thought when they was trying to lock me up a year ago to keep me from jumping that they'd be wanting to fetch me round again someday just to do the very same? It sure is a curious thing, Bruin, the way a fellow can make out sometimes, just going his own way. Well, I reckon we'd best study on how we're going to get down there in time."

Chapter 14

I'd never been on a steamboat before, and what I'd heard about their habit of blowing up didn't dispose me to look forward very eagerly to the experience. I thought it was bad enough to have to be jumping *into* the water all the time without having to worry now about being blown out of it. But this jump was special and Sam wanted to arrive for it in a style befitting a guest of honor. So instead of just going overland by shank's mare as we usually traveled, we headed west to Albany, jumping at a town or two on the way to raise passage money, and boarded a night boat to take us down the Hudson.

In one way the boat was no different from the little towns so many of which we'd passed through. Sam and I were recognized and right away became the center of attention, and if it hadn't been too dark, there's no question but that Sam wouldn't have been much longer aboard before he found some fancy way to jump off again.

Even without that treat to look forward to, though, the group around us seemed in peculiarly high spirits.

"Anyhow, there's more ways of having fun than jumping, ain't there, Sam?" leered one of our fellow passengers.

"And more things to jump than waterfalls, too, I reckon," said another, whose hat was on at a precariously rakish angle and whose breath alone, could it have been bottled, could have made three men drunk.

"I guess you boys know best," said Sam in the wake of the hilarity following this remark, "but me," he said, accepting a friendly nip from a proffered flask, "I'm partial to waterfalls."

This touched off a new wave of hilarity, laced with commentary cryptic to me, but incapacitatingly funny to everybody else. I accepted a friendly nip of my own from Sam and turned away to wonder some more what it felt like to be blown up and to watch the other passengers, some of whom were still boarding by means of a gangplank from the pier. I noticed that the better-dressed ones of these tended to go up the stairs to the second level, where some of them reappeared on a narrow balcony that ringed the upper deck. The more rambunctious ones, on the other hand, all seemed to stay back to mill about where we were, on the deck below.

But I wasn't the only one watching the boarders. A cry went up from one of the men:

"Here they come, boys. They're here!"

What seemed the whole population of the lower deck hurried to the rail and set up a clamor of shouts and gunshots intended, I gathered, to welcome aboard a party of rather fantastically dressed women just arrived at the pier. These curtsied and waved, bawled ribald rejoinders, and set out across the gangplank with in many cases a gait so exaggeratedly feminine that I wondered none of them fell into the river.

"Ain't you coming, Sam?" cried the wit with the raked hat. "It's the whoores!" He pronounced it to rhyme with "boors." Not waiting for an answer, he lurched off, making what speed he could.

"Best step along, Sam," said the one who had offered the flask, "or you'll have to take Ma Cluppins. Last one always does."

"That's mighty kind of you to say, friend, but you go ahead. I reckon I'll sit this one out."

The friend hesitated. Then he brightened.

"I guess you're likely saving yourself up for the jump, huh, Sam? 'Cause if you was feeling poorly, there's things these whoores know . . ."

"You go along. I feel just grand."

Worriedly pressing his flask on Sam "for a tonic," the friend left with a haste that was far from flattering to Mrs. Cluppins. Sam leaned back against the rail.

"You know, it's a funny thing, Bruin," he said, helping himself to a meditative swallow and passing the flask to me. "Time was not so long ago there's no way a chance like this here would have found me behindhand. Fact is, I'd have been leading the pack and there ain't a soul would have to worry about me drawing Mrs. Cluppins. Now, I don't know. It ain't that I don't feel the need. But somehow that just ain't my game anymore."

I was glad. To see the others yipping and swarming around that flaunting group of lubricious females put me in mind of nothing so much as the manners of a pack of dogs—easily the lowest form of animal life. Clearly Sam's devotion to jumping had had at least one salutary effect.

But then he stiffened, stood away from the rail staring at the women, and abruptly made off toward them with every appearance of meaning to make up for his late start. It was too sudden to be backsliding: something was wrong. As soon as I finished the flask, I hurried after him.

He was making a beeline for the thick of the group, removing astonished stragglers from his path without even turning his head. Behind him, I discouraged any who felt entitled to an apology from asking for one and followed him up to what resolved itself into a knot of men competing for the favors of one woman.

Sam paused on the outskirts of this group. He peered uncertainly for a moment past the bobbing heads and shoulders, then reached out and parted them like so many bushes.

We pushed through the circle. The yips all around went to barks, then to whimpers and growls as I exercised my diplomacy. Then they died altogether as the men saw who we were and remarked the strangeness of Sam's behavior. They stared at Sam, and Sam, unconscious of anyone or anything save only the feminine object of his fascination, who could not have drawn him to her side more surely if she'd had a hook in his jaw—Sam, as I say, stared at the woman.

Slightly built, but with a very large self-possession, she had turned her head to discover the cause of the commotion among her admirers. Her glance brushed by me as lightly as if she found bears in her retinue all the time and was quite accustomed to it. She gazed at Sam.

"Jenny?'" he said, his eyes shining in the ruddy glow of the lamps.

She contemplated him in silence. At last her lips parted. With a note of the pleasure one feels at finding something missed which, though of little value, one would have been somewhat sorry to lose, and finding it just where it might have been expected to turn up if anyone had had the sense to look for it there, she said softly:

"Sam."

The miniature flames in Sam's eyes seemed to leap . . .

Then "Hooray!" yelled an onlooker I recognized as our solicitous friend with the flask. He gleefully rubbed his hands. "Didn't I tell you, boys? I knowed there was no mistake in Sam Patch!"

Chapter 15

I was perplexed. I'd never been ignored before; it was outside my experience. I'd had everything else done to me, but not that. Particularly I'd never been ignored by Sam. And that was not merely outside my experience: I didn't like it. I felt quite definite on the point. Nevertheless, there I was, padding along after the pair of them more like a lost puppy than like a favorite bear, and without the faintest idea what to do about the situation. If I didn't actually throw myself overboard on account, as I considered doing, it wasn't that I didn't feel moved to, believe me, but only that I wasn't sure Sam would notice I was gone.

Not altogether giving up on the idea still, I followed at a discreet distance as they made their way to the stern. The whole while, I kept my eyes on the female, trying to gauge the threat. She was shapely enough, I had to admit, though nothing like on a scale with Molly, of course. But I'd seen figures as shapely—and with more buxom fronts, to boot—on various of the ladies before this who found a man who jumped waterfalls hard to resist, and Sam had never been more than understandably attracted to any of them. No, clearly there was more going on here than a matter of avoirdupois.

By the same token I was inclined to rule out her hair. She was blonde, and while it was a most unbearlike color, I had to admit her hair appeared to good advantage in the light. Even I noticed how every strand of it glowed whenever we neared one of the lamps, and whenever we passed one the whole mass of the stuff blazed up so it seemed to light up the night—not to wax too poetic on a subject that caused me considerable uneasiness at the time.

But I'd seen blondes before and so had Sam. I didn't think it was that.

Well, her features were good—flawless, I suppose, if you go for the "finely chiseled" sort. I didn't, myself. I much preferred features like Molly's—modest and matronly, always on the lookout to make laughter or tears at home on short notice and with about equal readiness. This one's were anything but so hospitable. I sensed they were more accustomed to showing—or hiding—more complicated emotions. Laughter, for instance, would never be entirely easy in them. There would always be some qualifying sadness, or detachment, or sympathy—or who knows what all—to make the laughter uncomfortable and keep it from really settling in. And tears, tears would have just as uncertain a time of it. A bird with a broken wing might make her cry, I thought. A play or a beautiful piece of music. But little that was human could. And it struck me that if ever something did, her tears would be terrifying. On so sublime a face, tears would seem anomalies of nature; I wouldn't care to see them. It would be like seeing a statue weep.

But what I came to think it really was was something harder to localize. There was a kind of stillness about her, and a remoteness, as if she viewed you from a great distance off. All five hundred pounds of me felt small up too close, which had as much as discretion to do with my keeping my distance. She was like an abyss a person could fall into if he didn't watch his step.

So it was a very uneasy bear who laid himself down grumbling outside the circle of lamplight where they stopped at the stern. The huge paddle wheel churned stolidly at the river, dampening the breeze that carried the smell of water and wood smoke and most becomingly, I couldn't help noticing, stirred tendrils of the female's hair. Forward I could glimpse now and again the glow of naked fire in the engines, like a balefully winking red eye. I found myself wishing for an explosion.

For a while the pair of them just stood there like ninnies. Then Sam said:

"It sure is good seeing you again, Jenny."

She smiled. It was a smile that gave me the chills, but it seemed to have just the opposite effect on Sam. He turned almost as red as the fire in the engines.

"Burn me," he said, "you're just as pretty as, well, as I remembered you was. Jenny Hansom! To think of that! And here all this time I thought you was back in Pawtucket and many's the time I was that near coming back to see you and Ma, but seemed like something always come up. How's old Jenks? You seen him? And Gardner and the other boys?"

She said they were fine, last she knew. Sam nodded, looking her up and down. He went right on nodding, too, as I think he would have if she'd started talking about the wars of Assurbanipal, and he might have kept it up till we docked if he hadn't suddenly felt her smiling at him. He pulled up with a start.

"So they're doing all right then? Well, that's good. I'm right glad to hear that, right glad. And how about yourself, Jenny? I ain't seen you in so long, why, I don't just exactly remember how long it is. I expect it's two, no, better than three and a half years if it's a day. You been doing okay?"

She laughed.

"I've been fine too, Sam. Thank you."

This information, however suspect, triggered another spate of vigorous nodding. Sam managed to halt it, but the effort only seemed to build up pressure inside.

"And that Jeffers fellow," he blurted out finally, "you still sparking with him?"

"He went off to Boston," said Jenny.

The breeze gusted, whipping sparks from the stacks and hurling them high like a handful of blazing confetti. Sam and Jenny looked, then both turned to watch a large moth fling itself at the heartless glass of the lamp, as if the creature's attempts at self-immolation were of the most absorbing interest.

Sam blew out his breath. Jenny looked at him, a little shyly this time, I thought.

"Ah," said Sam, evidently feeling obliged to say something. But this expression of sympathy, if that's what it was, seemed to exhaust his conversational resources. He stared and began to grow red again.

"And what about you, Sam? How have you been?" she said, coming to his rescue. "I've heard about your jumping."

"Oh, that." He swelled up and glanced at me for the first time, with a kind of sheepish apology for which I was inclined to forgive him much. "Yep, I've been doing some of that, I guess," he said. He began to nod again, but checked himself. "You've heard, have you?"

"Oh yes."

"Well," said Sam, "I don't mind if you have. Not a bit. Fact is, I'm on my way to Paterson now to do more of the same. They wanted me back, they did. It's where I got my start."

"Yes," said Jenny, with an inexplicable gentleness.

"Say, you can come too. Burn me, why didn't I think of that already? Seeing you here knocked jumping clean out of my head, I reckon. First thing as has, too, and only thing as could have, Jenny. You'll do it, won't you? You're not off to somewheres else?"

"I was going to Paterson."

"Well, that's settled then. That's just fine."

Sam missed the look she gave him. It was fond enough, and still shy, and so far everything it would have warmed him to see. But her eyes crinkled at the corners and I sensed that the shyness was what she might have felt yoked to an ox, say, which, however good-natured, could take her wherever an ox chose to go, and so merited handling with some circumspection. And the fondness was like the fondness a mother has for a child, who is never dearer to a mother's heart than when most seriously engaged in some particularly childish piece of business.

"Yes indeed," said Sam, turning back from admiring the night as if he'd never found one so much to his liking, "you could say I've been doing some jumping. But don't think I've been playing, Jenny. Oh, no! You don't think so now, do you?"

"No, Sam. Not if you say not."

"Well, I haven't, and I wouldn't have you think it. The fact is, I've growed up a lot, Jenny. I mean, I know you always thought of me as a kid . . ."—she was kind enough not to nod; Sam hurried on—"and them jumps you saw, it's true, they was just kid stuff. Me and Jenks and Gardner were always trying to outdo each other and them jumps was for fun. It's different now, Jenny. I wish I could tell you."

Her smile was tolerant, as much as to say "If you say so" again. It seemed more to goad him than otherwise.

"What I mean is, it's serious now. It's what I do." He looked at her anxiously to see if she registered the force of this pregnant phrase. "All them years in the mill weren't more serious. Why, they was play, by comparison, if they'd been any fun. Wasn't none of it meant anything. Why, you know what it was like. I don't have to tell you about that part. You was doing it, too. Coming to work at the peep of day and settling in with them pulleys a-whirring and them belts a-slapping and them gears a-clashing so a person couldn't think straight; a-baking in the summer and a-freezing in the wintertime, six days a week, working on for twelve hours till 7:30 when the bell said we could quit and go home. And not a bit of point to any of it except to get up and do it again tomorrow.

"Well, Jenny, I'm through with all that. Just going along and going along, not caring a hang about anything—it was wearing me down and making me reckless, it was. It was like I didn't have a stake in nothing and just didn't care. That's all different now. Why, I've growed up so much I don't hardly recognize myself. I'm a regular solid citizen now, inside. And it's jumping what's done it. The very thing I was doing before just for fun. Well, I'm good at it, Jenny, better at it than anybody, and that makes me feel special. And burn me if I don't take it serious, too. That's a good one, I know, and you're probably laughing to think of me taking anything serious. But jumping ain't like just anything, Jenny. It speaks to me a special way somehow. There's something about it as draws me on and just makes me want to do better and better. It's the one thing I care about now and yet in a funny way it makes me care about other things too.

"I'm a changed fellow, Jenny, and jumping's what's done it. I ain't just a harebrained kid anymore and I . . . I just want you to know."

She listened with her head to one side and seemed waiting for an opportunity to laugh off his seriousness. When he finished without giving her one, she seemed caught off balance.

"We all change, Sam," she said, laughing anyway. It was not a success. Sam looked at her, puzzled. Her face shone. She turned away.

"Not you, Jenny."

She made a pettish move with her hand and turned back. Whatever she was about to say was no match though for the earnest attention with which Sam waited to hear it. I saw the thought melt away. Her face softened and smoothed.

"You always were sweet."

"Sweet on you, Jenny, and you always knowed it," said Sam, with the beginnings of a grin. "But listen here, Jenny. Now we're back together again we can get new acquainted. I've come along considerable and when you see me jump you'll know what I'm talking about. And afterwards maybe, well, maybe we might want to travel together a while, seeing as we're both kind of free in our schedules."

This was the closest he came to referring to her new line of work. I think she saw that it was the closest he ever would come, too. She smiled again, this time as if the smile escaped from a secret place and surprised her.

Then a sudden volley of cheers and gunshots broke in on the conversation and livened up the night. Another boat appeared to our left, glittering with lights and working past us upstream like a huge floating birthday cake. As she approached, answering flashes of gunfire speckled her lower deck, the reports reaching us a second later across the dark water.

That brief salute marked the closest we came. The newcomer passed on astern and the cheering died. The figures lining her rails grew still and dwindled with the rest of her, watching as we slid silently apart on the river. Soon she rounded a bend and was lost from sight and the night closed in again.

Chapter 16

Reaching Paterson in the small hours of the morning, we clambered ashore over the darkened decks of other boats and Sam led us off to the American Eagle, one of Tim Crane's two hotels in town. Jenny, wraithlike and composed, accompanied us, her silence making Sam's boisterous attempts at conversation ring loud and foolish on the night air. I brought up the rear, feeling less threatened now, but sorry for Sam.

The hotel was full; we had to pick our way to the desk over men lying everywhere like snoring cordwood. A dried-up old clerk, corpselike but for the regular motion of his jaws as he worked a plug in his sleep, dozed in a chair. Sam shook him, though at first without visible effect except to make him chew faster. But eventually we roused him, and after copious spitting he found us all places—Sam a corner of the floor; Jenny, whom he knew, a corner of a bed upstairs "with a couple of your lady friends"; and me a corner of a small shed out back that smelled like it used to be a smokehouse and gave me dreams all night long.

Sam took leave of Jenny with a slightly anxious pressure of his hand.

"You'll see tomorrow what I've been telling you about, Jenny. How I'm a changed feller and all. You just rest up now. Tomorrow we'll talk some more."

"Good night, Sam," she said, gently extricating her hand, and followed the old clerk upstairs.

Sam watched her out of sight.

"You know, Bruin," he said, "that's a powerful lot of woman there."

I thought he was probably right about that, but wrong if he thought she was going to surrender herself lightly into his keeping.

Drums brought me to in the morning, and a squealing that chimed musically with my confused dreams of venison and stuck pigs. I peered out the door and was treated to the sight of some twenty men dressed peculiarly, with a significance that escaped me, in what appeared to be castoff parts of various uniforms—here a cocked hat, there a coat or belt or high boots of a military description—which taken together might have completely outfitted two or three men, but which under no circumstances could have made them seem members of the same branch of service. Those without any other claim to a military affiliation had stuck feathers in their hats, or hair, and all were milling about punishing drums of different sizes and timbres, or, with considerable spirit but not much coordination of effort, blowing into fifes and producing the high-pitched sounds that had made me think of distressed pork. As I looked on, a musician more fortunate than his colleagues in the possession of a uniform complete down to the boots, for which he had substituted a pair of moccasins that looked remarkably like bedroom slippers, and with a feather in his hat besides, waved his fife in the air and rallied the group into a stirring, not to say earthshaking and earsplitting, rendition of "Yankee Doodle." To this accompaniment they variously marched, walked or shuffled down the street, beaming or frowning as if they were doing something really fine.

Sam came out with my breakfast.

"A tune like that sure puts the heart into a fellow, don't it, Bruin?" he said, setting down the bucket.

He stood back as I applied myself to the contents with an appetite none the worse for a whole night's insubstantial visions of food. But before my field of vision was swallowed up by the bucket, I saw him absently rub his chin and I noticed he was clean-shaven. He was still standing there like that, his hand exploring the unusual smoothness, when I came up for air some minutes later. I thought he looked in need of an even stronger dose of "Yankee Doodle."

"Well, anyways," he said, catching my eye on him and throwing off his musing look, "it's a fine day for it." I took him to mean jumping, not having the heart put into him, much as he seemed ripe for the operation.

But there were other events to be gotten through before the jumping. There were parades of militia and veterans to witness, toasts to be drunk, speeches to be heard, cheers to be cheered and more toasts to be drunk, meals to be eaten with various toasts to be drunk, and more speeches to be heard while a variety of toasts were drunk. As the drinking of toasts made up such an inordinate portion of the agenda, it was felt by many that it would be well not to put off starting too late if the drinkers were to get through them all; and when I went back in with Sam, I saw many who seemed, if anything, already so far along that they were in some danger of having nothing to do by midday but cheer and listen to speeches. Some of these hailed Sam and me and invited us to join them. It was only patriotic to accept and we each drank a bumper to George Washington. But Sam, I noticed, kept looking at the stairs.

"If you're waiting for Handsome Jenny," cackled our shriveled host of the night before, who was one of our number and looked in a fair way to being thoroughly rehydrated before the day was through, "she was up and out hours ago."

"Who?"

"Handsome Jenny, what you come in with."

Sam, looking dazed, drank off a toast to Lafayette without, I believe, one reverent thought of that hero crossing his mind. He stood up.

"Sam, my friend. There you are."

It was Tim Crane, dapper as ever and beaming a welcome. He grabbed Sam's hand and wrung it, his fresh-looking coat giving off a strong odor of turpentine, courtesy the cleaners, while his breath intimated he was not lacking the patriotic spirit.

"Delighted to have you back with us. You're getting quite famous, you know. The *Inquirer* carries the news of all your jumps. The whole town's proud of you, Sam. I guess we feel like you sort of belong to us. But no one's prouder than I am, Sam. No sir, I won't forget in a hurry how you saved my bridge, and I want you to know that if I ever hear of your trying to pay so much as a cent at any of my establishments, we're no longer friends. All set for the big event this afternoon, are you, Sam?"

"If it's the jumping you mean," said Sam with a slow smile, "I reckon I'm always set for that. But listen here, Tim, there's a thing I've got to take care of first—"

"Nonsense, Sam. You've got hours for that, whatever it is. What could be more pressing than renewing old friendships, I ask? What do you say, boys? Are we going to let him get away so easy?"

"No!" chorused the drinkers who heard the question, closely seconded by those who hadn't but whom drink had rendered unusually agreeable to any popular proposal. There was only one abstention, from under the table.

"There now, what did I tell you, Sam? Your friends won't give you up. A toast, boys," Tim Crane said, appropriating a glass for himself and handing Sam's back to him. "To the Thirteen Colonies: New Jersey!"

"New Jersey!" they shouted, happily going off on this new tack. Perhaps they had run out of patriots.

Sam drained his glass with the rest of them, but Tim Crane still clutched his arm and jovially signed to the man with the jug to refill the glasses.

"Massachusetts!" he cried.

"Massachusetts!"

There's no telling how long they might have kept at it. After Massachusetts came Boston and I realized that the proposed theme was meant more as a rough guideline than as a curb to invention. I guessed there was probably no hard and fast rule against repetitions, either. But a sudden thumping and squeaking from outside broke things up just as we were lapsing into patriots again.

"The parade!" they all shouted, and outside they ran.

Sam waited till they had gone.

"Come on, Bruin," he said in a voice I was relieved to hear still sounded unsoused, "them fellows is a mite too sociable for comfort, and we've got to find Jenny. I can't figure why she'd run off like that."

We left by the back way and circled around to the street. There the whole town was ranged, cheering in the dust stirred up by the marchers. The excitement was terrific. Dogs barked and ran back and forth in a patriotic frenzy, packs of children did the same, and even the pigs, suspending their rooting to eye the proceedings mistrustfully, seemed at least aware that something out of the ordinary was going on.

The flag bearer was just passing. A somewhat portly gentleman, he looked grim and determined enough to make up for a far
worse handicap in any time of national peril. Following him was a
ragtag assortment of warriors on whom time had inflicted more
serious wounds now than shot and shell ever had, and all wearing
the scraps of uniform that seemed to be the uniform of the day.
This body passed, with its stragglers slowed by dogs, pigs, and
rheumatism, to thunderous appreciation, and there was a brief
interval when there was nothing much to stare at and the crowd
raised all its jugs in step; and then the drums and shrilling fifes
grew louder and ushered the militia onto the scene, complete with
feathers and guns that presumably worked. The appearance of this
irregular-looking body of irregulars, who at least had comparative
youth on their side, was more martial than its predecessor's, and
indeed, these men looked robust enough to give pause to any
enemy no less drunk than themselves.

"You don't see her anywhere, do you, Bruin?" said Sam, on
whom the pageant seemed to be wasted. I dutifully looked too, but
wasn't surprised not to spy her.

"Burn me if I understand it," he said, the words just reaching
me over the racket of the band I'd seen warming up earlier, now
passing in front of us. "Unless she figured to be back before now
and got stuck in the crowd."

I thought that was too remote a contingency to be worth com-
menting on. Poor Sam. Even a bear could see that she didn't like
him the way he wanted to be liked, and while women are apt to
change their minds often enough about other things, I'd never
heard of one deciding about a man that she loved him on second
thought. Oh, that she might soften and reward his perseverance
and good taste wasn't unheard of, or that she might get hungry and
lower her standards. But as far as agreeing in her heart to open his
case again, once disposed of, that was entirely without precedent,
I believed. And I was glad of it, too, in this instance. The Jenny
woman was a threat of no mean proportions. I shuddered to think
how things might have turned out if Sam had met her on one of her
earlier business trips and talked her into retirement. Where would
I have been then? The same place as Tim Crane's bridge, more or
less—up a crick. Instead of following a rewarding career with me,
Sam would have found his reason for existence in a woman, as
others have done before him. I'd have been deprived of his com-

pany and my own reason for being—and not least of all, the world would have lost its greatest jumper.

The parade was winding down now. It had degenerated, in fact, to a miscellaneous troop of underage noncombatants filing by with their arms swinging harder, their knees lifting higher and their voices sounding shriller than the arms, knees, voices of the keenest militiamen. Following these was an even more miscellaneous assemblage brandishing sticks and poles at the bystanders and looking rather like a nondescript but belligerent sports team. "Old Hickory Forever" said one of their banners, explaining the sticks, and "Paterson Committee for Jackson" said another.

I caught the word "barbecue" from one of this group and pricked up my ears.

Just then a leathery-faced man with a sprig of something that looked like poison ivy in his hat came up from behind and plucked at Sam's sleeve.

"There you be, Sam. We was looking all over for you, hee, hee. Come on along this way," he said, tugging Sam into the street.

"Hooray for Sam Patch!" yelled the men with the sticks, waving them about. "Hooray!" said the crowd, not unwillingly, as Sam was pulled into view.

"Hooray for the hero of Paterson!" shouted the leader of the sticks, a bearded man in what looked like a borrowed black coat worn over a pair of rumpled dungarees and most of a shirt.

"Hooray!"

"And hooray for the hero of New Orleans!" the man shouted next, "the nation's great defender of liberty, who drove the tyrant's army from American soil!"

I stared at Sam uncertainly.

"Hooray!"

The sticks paused in the street to greet their hero.

"Welcome back, Sam," said the leader. "We're honored to have you among us, sir. A hero is a fine thing to have and we reckon we know how to treat one, especially when he's our very own, don't we, boys?"

"Hooray for Sam Patch!"

"And you being a hero and all yourself, and a man of the people, I reckon you understand how we feel about that other great hero the whole nation can lay claim to, that other great man of the people, who fought to preserve our precious freedom from being ground 'neath a foreign heel. A cheer for Andrew Jackson!"

"Hooray!"

"Sam," said the man in the borrowed coat, clapping him on the shoulder emotionally, "I'd be proud if you'd carry this here hickory pole of mine as a kind of pledge of one hero's regard for another on this great day in our young nation's history." And he tried to thrust the pole into Sam's hands.

Greatly to the other's surprise, Sam refused to take it.

"Well, I reckon not," said Sam. "It ain't that I ain't honored by your intentions, gents," he said to the group of them, "but, well, this here is a mighty big stick and I'd be afeared it just might get in the way of a fellow's jumping."

Borrowed Coat laughed as if this were a great joke.

"The truth is," said Sam, going on to explain more conscientiously than the other seemed to expect or want, "there's things as are bigger than politics and don't rightly mix with them, and jumping's one. So I'll just thank you kindly, mister, and hope you don't take no offense, but when it comes to my jumping, I'm strictly nonsectarian."

"Hurrah for Sam Patch!" said a man in the crowd, better dressed than the Jackson supporters. "Adams forever!"

With a strained something meant to be a smile, the Jacksonian produced a hickory sprig from his pocket.

"Well, here, Sam, you'll wear this anyhow." He tried to stick the sprig in Sam's buttonhole, Sam not having a hat, but Sam intercepted his hand, whether to fix the sprig himself or push it away I couldn't tell. Neither could the Jacksonian, evidently.

"You'll need this to get into the barbecue," he hissed.

He little knew Sam if he thought Sam would sell out his jumping for a pound or so of flesh, however nicely roasted. To be safe I took the sprig myself.

"Hooray!" they all said again as I put it between my teeth, flamenco style, for ease of carrying. The leader in the coat was delighted. From the sidelines I heard the gentleman who had cheered Sam and Adams say something about my not being politically very astute, and add that the Jacksonians must have scraped the bottom of the barrel clean, to judge from the way they were starting in now to recruit outright brutes. But somebody else knocked his hat off for this remark and our leader professed not to hear it.

"Onward!" he cried, waving his pole. "To the green! And after the speechifying, ladies and gents, and Mr. Sam Patch's jump, put some hickory in your hats and bonnets and come on across to the barbecue. Only them as fear to grease their fingers with a barbecued pig, or twist their mouths away at whiskey grog—or find the company overnice—" he said with a glare at the heckler, "need stay away."

"Hooray!"

Up went the banners, up the sticks, and up the voices in a song that lumped Adams and Clay with Indians and Spaniards as being alike scourges that the saintly, peace-loving Andrew Jackson could be counted on to eradicate, given opportunity. And off we marched, me chewing my hickory sprig but already tasting roast pig, and Sam turning his head this way and that, scanning the faces for Jenny.

Chapter 17

The green where the "speechifying" was to take place was the same place by the falls where Meleager, Molly and I had watched Sam's first jump. Set back where the noise of the falls would not drown out the noise of the speakers, a platform had been erected and draped in bunting, and on it were ranged all the dignitaries Paterson had been able to entice or been unable to turn away, whose patriotic sentiments were to edify us this day. The crowd, twice the size of the one I remembered, thronged the area to the water's edge. That the singing, shouting, shooting, lighting of fire-crackers, and general mayhem quite prevented anyone from hearing more than scattered fragments of these sentiments, and that the loss seemed to grieve no one at all, showed what an amiable mood everyone was in.

We were greeted with a cheer that went up from the people nearest and quickly spread through the whole crowd. "Sam Patch! Sam Patch! Patch!" they cried, finally even silencing the speaker, who at first had redoubled his activity under the impression that the cheering was for him.

Our escort of hickory sticks raised Sam up on their shoulders and bore him along in triumph. An effort to honor me similarly not succeeding, they left their two comrades injured in the attempt in the care of well-wishers and conducted me to the platform more sedately in Sam's train.

Sam waved, bowed, and capered when finally set down at the top of the steps. The dignitaries pressed forward to shake his hand and take him to a seat, and nothing would do but that they had to shake my hand too, at his urging, which they all eagerly did after the precedent was once established by the most dignified-looking of their number. And then Sam raised my arm to the crowd and grinned round like a devil, and I went up on my hind legs and waved too, and everyone went wild past belief, even the dignitaries, and I realized they thought I'd saluted the flag.

Well, eventually we were allowed to take our places and the speaker we had interrupted backed up fifteen minutes' worth to the beginning of his last sentence and made another run at it. I settled in to dreaming about the barbecue again and Sam went back to searching faces. But before any of the three of us made any real headway, Sam and I were joined by a newcomer.

"Mr. Patch, sir?" he said, bending low to make himself heard and giving us a close-up view of his hat, which was scuffed. I recognized him as the heckler of the Hickory Club. "Benjamin Kitchen, Mr. Patch," he said, and suddenly I recognized him all over again, "owner and founder of Kitchen's Cooperage, largest cooperage in town, sir. Very likely you've heard my motto: 'When you think barrels, think Kitchen.'" He confidently took out and twirled a thumb-size miniature barrel on the end of his watch chain as a possible aid to the memory. "No? Well, no matter, no matter. I would like to shake your hand, sir, anyway."

Sam having no objection, Mr. Kitchen proceeded to satisfy this desire.

"Indeed, sir," said Mr. Kitchen, having found a chair and squeezed in beside us, "I have so many reasons for wishing to shake your hand I hardly know which one to start with. A remarkable feat, sir, that jump of yours last year. I had the good fortune to witness it and damn my eyes if I ever saw the like. Extraordinary, quite extraordinary. I remember I was standing with your associate's former associate and *his* associate at the time. They're back in town, by the way. I saw them just yesterday."

I felt a chill.

"Jiggers! What's wrong with the bear? He looks like he bit an unripe persimmon. There, that's better. I was just going to remark how jumping seems to agree with him, he's filled out so since last year. But then so have I, so have I," he chuckled, looking complacently at his rather barrel-like paunch, "and I haven't so much as jumped out of bed in longer than I care to say." He chuckled again, his eyes twinkling so in the process that he looked like a lively barrel set with rhinestones. "But seriously, my friend, I take an uncommon interest in your career. Having been present at so many of its critical junctures I feel quite like a partner—a silent partner, to be sure, sir, ho, ho, but a partner for all that. I wish you the greatest success this afternoon when you repeat the feat, sir, as I have no doubt you shall to perfection."

Sam thanked him and said he reckoned folks as was curious to see how some things could be done as well as others wouldn't go home disappointed. Mr. Kitchen slapped his knee.

"Jiggers! That's another thing. What a motto, my friend! A man should always have a motto, I believe, even if he keeps it to himself. A motto is a banner to fly in prosperity, a support in adversity, and something to live up to between times. Yours may be the most remarkable I've encounterd, Mr. Patch. What does it mean?"

"Why, it means what it says, I guess, same as yours," said Sam, rather neatly, I thought.

"Why, so it does, ho, ho, so it does. I only meant . . . well, never mind. A delightful motto, my friend, as I say. Quite thought-provoking. Yes, quite. And now let me shake your hand again, sir."

Sam let him.

"That's for the way you stood up to those rascally Jackson men. There was a sight! You might have improved it if you'd broken the fellow's stick on his head, as I would have done, but I'm content, I'm content. The rapscallions have had it all their own way for too long, marching and shouting and planting their infernal hickory bushes everywhere. It's got so I can't stand the sight of the wood anymore. Won't use it. Pity, too. It's good wood. But to see it puts me in mind of that scalawag and his rabble of flag-waving rowdies, whose chief objections to the President, so far as I can tell, are that he stands for something and is 'too much of a gentleman.' Did you ever hear such nonsense in your life? They'll bring the country to its knees, sir, to its knees. You're for Adams, I take it?"

"Well, that depends," said Sam. "If you're asking me in my professional, jumping capacity, I ain't for neither of them, as I said to the boys. If you're asking it of me as just a private feller, why, I don't know as I've rightly made up my mind."

Mr. Kitchen digested this information. He looked as though Sam's answer, even carefully thought out as it obviously was, fell short of giving him satisfaction.

"Well, sir, I suppose I must leave the matter to your own good judgment and conscience," he said, but as if he had doubts as to the wisdom of this. Meanwhile a wave of cheering came and went. I gathered the speaker had successfully completed his sentence and started on new material. "And now, sir, there is another matter I would take up with you. I would choose a better time, but it pertains to your jumping."

"You can always talk to me about jumping," said Sam. "I don't care if it's Sunday."

"Very well then, I shall. Have you ever considered endorsements?" said Mr. Kitchen, giving his hands a brisk rub, as if to limber them up for counting money. "Yes, endorsements, my friend. There could be a gold mine in it for you, properly handled. I myself could put you in the way of a client or two, and I've no doubt others would flock to your door quick enough once they heard it was open for business."

"Maybe you ought to just spell that out a mite more, Mr. Kitchen," said Sam slowly, "always keeping in mind as how jumping's my trade, and not mining."

"Naturally, Mr. Patch, I'd be glad to," said Mr. Kitchen with another preparatory rub. "My proposal is this. You're becoming well-known, Mr. Patch. I have every confidence you will soon be famous. Be that as it may, yours is a line of work in which the remuneration is apt to be spotty and the fame fleeting. Not only that, it's a trade in which your earning power is subject to certain natural physical limitations. You will hardly wish to continue pitching off bridges into your dotage, Mr. Patch. Should you try, those golden years, assuming you manage to reach them, will be short-lived indeed." Mr. Kitchen chuckled, rhinestones merrily twinkling. "The thing for you to do, sir, is to look ahead. You must put your affairs now, while you are still young, on such a footing that you are able to provide for a comfortable early retirement with capital to start you on a new venture making more moderate demands of your declining powers. For instance, you might found a canal transport line, or open a store."

I stared at Sam, fascinated. His expression, as he listened to Mr. Kitchen describe how he could make something of himself, was very like the one he'd worn when Meleager had explained why he would never amount to anything. But Mr. Kitchen, thoroughly warmed to his subject, seemed gratified by the fixity of Sam's attention, and likely would have been on any terms. He pursued his theme, his eyes sparkling now more like diamonds.

"To start doing endorsements now, Mr. Patch, would put all this within easy reach. You would simply make a point of tying in whatever product you happen to be endorsing with your jump. Anything in the bath line would be a natural, for instance. Soaps, scrub brushes. Think of the impact if you were to jump with, say, a MacPherson brush. Simply wave it about a little first and do a few amusing scrubs while you're still in the water, and there's not a man, woman, or child, sir, who saw you who could rest till he owned a MacPherson brush. The men would buy them to feel like heroes too. The ladies would probably not even use theirs, but put them on display or in a place of safekeeping, and children would take them to school. Can you doubt that MacPherson would pay anything for an endorsement worth that?"

Sam expressing no doubt, and indeed, the question being rhetorical, Mr. Kitchen pressed on, closely attended by the whole row of dignitaries, who had leaned toward us to hear.

"Even clothes," said Mr. Kitchen with a wave of his hands. "You jump in the clothes you stand up in. What's to prevent your saying whose clothes they are—who made them, I mean? Extoll their warmth and freedom of movement, praise how quickly they dry. Is there a soul who ever saw or heard tell of your jumps who wouldn't want clothes of the same make, to feel like Sam Patch? Sell your name! Let a label go in with your name on it. 'Clothiers to Sam Patch.' Damn my eyes, what a motto! Show me a tradesman who wouldn't kill for it and I'll show you a man dead to commercial initiative!"

A murmur went up from the dignitaries. Not that I heard it, but I could see their lips move. From the way they began edging closer I guessed it to be a murmur of excitement. Indeed, they were already packed so densely that, suddenly leaning back to assess the effect of the pictures he painted, Mr. Kitchen bruised the nose of his neighbor, who bruised his neighbor's nose the same way, and so on to the end of the row, causing the whole line of dignitaries to hike back in their chairs, where they sat staring at Sam and thoughtfully rubbing their noses.

"Now, Mr. Patch," said Mr. Kitchen, leaning in again in a manner more cautiously followed by the dignitaries, "you are scheduled to jump this afternoon. Let me make this the first step on your road to riches. I know today is the Fourth of July. Well, patriotism and glory are all very well, and I hope I'm as patriotic as the next. But is that any reason to pauperize yourself in the service? I should say not. Why, what could be more patriotic, in fact, than to merge your interests with those of your country, sir? You have the example of the Founding Fathers for that. If some few of them were out-of-pocket when we won independence, it was only because they miscalculated the return on their investment. Why, for what else was the glorious Revolution fought, my good sir? Economics! The right to found our own industries! 'No taxation without representation.' You see? A blind man couldn't miss it!

"Now, Mr. Patch," said Mr. Kitchen, wiping his hands, which, though there still had been no money for them to count, seemed to grow sweaty in anticipation, "in my warehouse I have a cask all made up of the soundest oak, that would accommodate you, sir, in comfort and style and keep you dry as a bone through a hundred jumps—"

"And I, sir, I notice you don't wear a hat," broke in the nearest dignitary. "I have a hat for you, sir, absolutely guaranteed crushproof that will hold its shape through any number of wettings—"

"My boots, sir—" broke in another.

"My trousers—!"

"—Tobacco—!"

"—Harness—!"

"—Home furnishings—!"

"Stop!"

All stopped. Even the speaker stopped and, after a woebegone look at his script to see how far back lay the beginning of his interrupted sentence, turned to see what the fuss was about this time.

"Gents," said Sam, "I came here to jump, you're right about that. And seeing as jumping's what I do full-time I'd be a fool worse than anybody's accused me of if I didn't take what folks is ready to give for the show. But you're mistook if you think that's how come I jump. Sadly mistook." He shook his head in pity of their limited understanding. "No sirs, I jump because jumping's what I do and to show folks how some things can be done as well as others. That there's more than my motto. It's the whole works. And if I was to take on to promote all you gents' products, why, folks wouldn't know if they was seeing a jump or a medicine show. And meantime I'd feel so weighted down with all these here extra responsibilities I reckon as even if one of you gents made a patent life preserver it couldn't keep me from going straight to the bottom.

"A fellow as jumps," said Sam, "needs to keep clear just what he's about. He can't have a lot else on his mind. Let him start doing things on the side and before you know it he ain't the jumper he was."

Such was the earnestness with which Sam said this that when he broke off to stare at each dignitary to see how his point was being taken, not one ventured to start up again.

Sam sat back.

"But to keep from there being hard feelings," he said with a certain gleam stealing into his eye, "you can feel free by me to take up the business with Bruin here. Bruin only jumps part-time. And if he goes along, well, burn me if I can find fault with it."

Which is how it happened that, in tight-fitting new boots, pants, shirt, and uncrushable hat, I was far and away the more magnificent jumper that day, though my sartorial splendor was brought to nothing by my jump taking place in a barrel.

Chapter 18

After the jump came the fireworks. The Hickory Club did their best to give the impression that the fireworks were theirs, in honor of Jackson, which was not true, but I didn't care. Having no strong political sentiments either way, I was more than ready to forgive them this piece of opportunism for their generously forgiving my having lost my hickory sprig somewhere. Indeed, they went further. Not only bringing me choice bits of haunch and all I could eat of it, they boasted to everyone who came by how I had rallied to the cry of Jackson and Reform and how proud they were of our connection. People listened and shook their heads, amazed. I think that between this story and my spanking new outfit I was as much a marvel for political sagacity and sharp business sense as Sam was for jumping.

But all good things must end. Finally I was as full of roast pork and beer as a bear could well be, and one bite more would have been one bite too much. So, tugging off my new boots and leaving them for the first person to come by in bear feet, so to speak, I gave a stretch (cautious) and a burp (very satisfying) and struck out with my shirt open and my hat over my ear to find Sam.

What a picnic that was! The fireworks were over by this time and the grounds were lit up with torchlight. Faces that would have been red and sweaty anyway at this point in the proceedings, shone like lamps. Men shouted and offered me drinks, and many times—sweetest of all—just took me for one of themselves. I brimmed with good fellowship and gladly would have hugged someone if I'd thought anyone would take it in the right spirit.

Well, finally I enjoyed my solitary saunter to the extent that my new trousers would permit, and I decided that before the inseam did me a permanent injury I'd go look up Sam and lie down. I found him flushed, happy, and outwardly dry in the midst of a collection of empty bottles of St. Croix and a crowd of men who seemed as full as the bottles were empty. Everybody hailed my arrival, made admiring remarks on my outfit, and generously offered me bottles with something still in them; but I went straight up to Sam. We'd only been separated a little over an hour, but I felt as glad to be back as if it were months. I gazed at him with a full heart and then took off my hat to him with an eloquence that I don't think even my weaving a bit entirely spoiled.

"So there you are, old son. I was wondering where you'd gotten to. Boys, this here's my new business manager. I want you all to meet him. Got an eye for a dollar keen as a lizard's, he does. I trust him implicit. Come here, Bruin, and sit down before you fall over and crush a body. Careful of them duds, too."

I lowered myself into a place by his side. Sam looked on approvingly, but my caution had more to do with what my trousers might do to me than with what I might do to my trousers.

"I don't suppose you've seen Jenny anywhere about?" he asked me quietly when I was settled. I woofed a negative and he sighed. "I can't figure where she would have took off to."

To cheer him up and remind him that I at least would always be true, I licked him from his chin to his eyebrows, catching him unawares. He flung away, sputtering.

"Burn me, Bruin," he said, wiping his face on his sleeve, "if I don't stay drier doing a jump than when you start cozying up to me."

The others were laughing and Sam went on to say something unnecessary about my breath being bad enough on top of that to make water run uphill. I didn't hold it against him, of course, even as I smarted under the injustice—his breath would have made a wolverine blanch—but he caught my eye and gave me his bottle, and I found after that that there was really nothing to forgive.

Feeling drowsy after I'd finished with the bottle, most likely on account of all the excitement, I tucked my legs under me and laid my head in Sam's lap for a little nap. No sooner had I done so, though, than the talking and laughing died and I had the sensation, as terrible to bears as to anyone, that I was missing something. I opened one eye a crack, then both eyes wide, and had just time to lift my head a bit when further preparations were precluded by my being suddenly engulfed in an embrace more passionate and possibly stronger than my mother's best, and I found myself licking away Molly Money's salt tears.

"Bruin!" she sobbed, not complaining a bit.

Another figure loomed. Actually, I suspect he was there all along, but I only gradually became aware of him, and then only as the source of a vague chill. I turned my head. Jason Meleager, looking even more diabolical than usual in the flickering glare of the torches, smiled into my eyes.

"My dear Mr. Patch," he said, though still looking at me, "what a pleasure. Allow me to compliment you on your magnificent performance this afternoon. Truly a spectacle. I was quite ravished. The stolid courage with which you subdue nature's most implacable works is a wonder to behold, Mr. Patch. I don't know how you make it look so easy. My congratulations, sir, both on your success and on your happy invention of such a field of endeavor in the first place."

"I thank you for them," said Sam, not the least flustered, "and I'll just treasure them up as if they was worth something valuable. And how goes the head-squeezing trade, Mr. Meleager?"

"Very well, sir," said Meleager, with a smile that threatened to slice off his ears. "Miss Money and I have been to New York and visited with the great Spurzheim, who expressed unqualified interest in my proposed institute, I am happy to say, and now Miss Money and I are touring again for a brief while to gather additional funds while certain final arrangements are made overseas. I must say, I miss the services of my former assistant," he said, his glance sliding back to me. "He was a considerable asset in drawing attention and providing the demonstrations with a lighter side. But I gather from his decidedly striking appearance that you've hit on that discovery yourself."

"Old Bruin pulls his weight, I reckon," said Sam.

I meanwhile had released Molly—which is not to say she released me—and was making a largely futile effort to button my shirt, not so much to render my appearance any less decidedly striking, but to put something, even a layer of cotton, between me and the hateful, probing gaze of Meleager.

"Oh, he looks so—happy!" said Molly, standing off at arm's length to study me, her eyes glistening wetly; but still not letting go for a minute. "And so, well, *plump*," she added, much to my embarrassment. "I never saw you so well, my dear, despite these silly clothes. I'm so glad for you." The tears that had been waiting just such an occasion let go their hold and ran down her cheeks. "Mr. Patch must be a very nice man."

Meleager, who had opened his mouth undoubtedly to make some snide remark, seemed taken by surprise by this tacit comparison. He blinked at Molly and, either forgetting the snide remark or, more likely, filing it away for the future, closed his mouth again and said nothing.

Meanwhile Molly chattered on to me about how excitedly she had followed any news of our jumps, and how even Jason had always been interested in anything that came their way on the subject, although he professed not to be, but she could tell, and how things just hadn't been the same since I left—so dreary, you know—and how even though now she had learned a new repertoire that the audiences seemed to like much better and had dropped "Lochaber No More" and "Wandering Willy," two of her favorites really, which was such a shame, and that as a result she wasn't in nearly such terror of her audiences as she used to be, still she thought of me every time before she went on, and many other times too, of course, and dreamed of me sometimes, and often turned in her seat in the wagon to look out the back to where I had always used to follow, except that now, of course, I wasn't there anymore, and not seeing me always made her sad.

I hugged her again. When we drew apart she exclaimed:

"Oh Bruin, you sweet thing, you're crying!" And for all I know it was true.

General conversation resumed, by which I mean drinking, and Sam and Meleager ever so casually allowed their attention to be drawn into different channels. Sam went back to talking and laughing with the men beside him and Meleager became smilingly engrossed with what was being said in his own different vicinity. But I could tell that neither one of them missed a move of the other's.

Eventually Meleager ingratiated himself to the extent of a few remarks and accepted a bottle, which he drank from with a showy if indescribable swagger that communicated as clearly as words that, for all his superior accomplishments, he was nothing if not a regular fellow. Then he said to Molly:

"Come, my dear, it's time we were going." And to Sam:

"I believe we are sharing a hotel. The American Eagle? Yes, I thought so. We shall meet again, then. Good night. Good night, gentlemen."

Molly clutched me to her heroic bosom.

"You be careful," she told me. "Don't take chances." Then, dabbing at her eye with a handkerchief, and with a shy smile for Sam, she joined Meleager.

We did meet again, sooner than I'd hoped. Sam was anxious to find Jenny, and so instead of seeing the carouse through to the end as we doubtless would have otherwise, we returned to the hotel ourselves not long after Meleager.

The lobby was crowded and full of smoke and racket, with those guests who were still unsteadily ambulatory making navigation difficult enough without the additional hazard of trampling those with less stamina, numbers of whom were dispersed about the floor wherever the urge for repose had overtaken them. I didn't see Jenny, but Meleager had a table to himself in a corner. There he appeared to be silently communing with a brandy bottle as if he hoped to learn secrets of moment by staring at it intently in the same way he might read the bumps on a shiny bald head.

Sam made directly for the shriveled clerk at the counter.

"Handsome Jenny?" said this indestructible functionary, his jaws working tirelessly. "No, I ain't seen her."

Sam turned away.

Meleager beckoned, catching Sam's eye. He raised his brandy bottle a few inches invitingly, as if to show Sam its label.

"Well. Back so soon?" he said as Sam drew up a chair and I settled down beside it, as close as I could get. Sam fetched a pair of glasses off a neighboring table and Meleager poured us both drinks.

"I've been trying to locate a friend of mine. I reckon she must have lost track of me in the ruckus."

"Indeed? 'She'?" said Meleager, eyes alert behind his polite smile. Sam looked down at his drink. Meleager cleared his throat. "I did see a party of . . . ladies . . . come in a while back. They were all accompanied by gentlemen, however, and retired directly to their rooms. I don't suppose your friend might have been among them."

After a pause, Sam said:

"I reckon not."

"No, of course not," said Meleager good-humoredly. He refilled the glass Sam had rather abruptly emptied. "Ah, the ladies," he expatiated, leaning back very much at his ease. "Such delightful creatures. So ornamental to the scheme of things, so filled with the finer feelings and softer sentiments, and with such natural propensities to virtue that I believe it is scarcely going too far to say they must have invented it. Such brutes we should all be without their improving influence, don't you agree? Of course you do. Yes, they were born to be cherished, the ladies; to furnish that light without which a man's soul would be a gloomy thing indeed, and really insufferable company. Yet there's no denying, and I say this as a man with some experience of what I describe—as which of us has not, to his sorrow—there's no denying they are sometimes just a trifle arbitrary, just a trifle cruel, oh, all inadvertently, no doubt, but still with the same effect, namely, that all of us have been wounded by them at some time or other and can look forward with confidence to more of the same, and that all of us now and again find them just the slightest bit trying."

As Sam made no response to this beyond refilling his glass, there's no telling how long Meleager might have drawn out a theme which he could see caused his listener pain. But just then someone else came in from outside. Meleager looked up and was sufficiently impressed with what he saw to lose his thread. It was Jenny.

I gave Sam a nudge. He jumped up saying her name.

I doubt that she heard him, or could have in all that pandemonium. But perhaps she was looking for him, or possibly he caught her eye by suddenly jumping up the way he did. Anyway, she came over smiling. Meleager uncoiled himself and stood, too.

"Dear Sam. There you are. I'm sorry I lost you."

"Lost me? Why, Jenny, I was looking all over for you. Did you see my jump?"

"I, I wanted to, Sam," she stammered, her composure, which had handily survived seeing me in hat and shirt (I'd shucked the pants), slipping a bit. She shot him a look at once guilty, sorry, and resentful and seemed for a moment more human—by which I mean more animal—than I'd yet seen her.

Sam seemed to soften under this look, as if partly consoled for his disappointment by having provoked it.

"Well," he said awkwardly, with a smile that showed he could hold nothing against her, "it don't matter. There's plenty more jumps where that one came from, I reckon."

Meleager had been hopping from one foot to the other with another ear-endangering smile.

"My dear Patch. Introduce me."

Sam, who had clearly forgotten Meleager, gave him a look now that strongly intimated he'd have preferred having no occasion to remember him. But Jenny had already recovered herself and turned politely, so Sam with a sigh did the needful.

"Delighted," said Meleager, looking as if he meant what he said for a change.

"Will you sit a while, Jenny?" asked Sam. "I reckon it's late and you're tired, but I'd sure like it if you did."

"Yes, do," said Meleager. Bolder than Sam, he took her arm.

So they sat and talked, and Jenny thawed. Soon she was smiling and at ease, laughing as Sam told the story of Bruin's new clothes, and at Meleager's sallies, many of which hovered playfully on the verge of being at Sam's expense; and looking at Sam with a fondness and amusement he seemed to find more heady than drink.

"Jenny and me," he told Meleager at one point, "we go way back."

Meleager smiled and nodded. He glanced at Jenny. His smile grew wider.

Not once while they sat together did Sam ask where she had been. Not once did she offer to tell him. Always he joked and spoke only on light topics, only one time casually referring to her seeing him jump "some other time." Meleager's eyes darted again to Jenny, but Sam had already gone on to say in the same easy voice that before he was done he reckoned there wouldn't be so much as a half-dead old zany as hadn't seen him jump "some time or other." I saw Meleager look at Sam with new respect.

At last Jenny got up to retire. She laughed as Sam and Meleager protested. They bantered with her and she stood smiling, absently smoothing her dress; but her purpose was firm. She thanked them, but now she really was tired. Meleager was desolated; would she at least let him see her to her room?

"No, thank you," she said, with a smile that threw even him into confusion. "I can manage.

"Sam," she said gently, turning to us, "good night, Sam. And thank you."

Sam started to speak, choked, managed a wave. When she'd gone I heard him mutter hoarsely to no one in particular: ". . . talk in the morning."

Chapter 19

In the morning, Jenny was gone.

"She left this for you, Sam," said the old clerk, who seemed to work a twenty-four-hour shift. He handed Sam a note.

"Dear Sam," said the note (I read it over Sam's shoulder).

I know you will forgive my leaving like this when you understand why I have done it. Last night was so wonderful and you were so sweet that I could not bear to see things spoiled. Our ways do not lie together, Sam. You must go where your jumping takes you, and I have my own path to follow. Pawtucket was a long time ago, and neither one of us can go back. I will always be fond of you and think of you often. I wish you good fortune in your jumping and I know you will be famous someday. I will read faithfully about all your jumps in the newspapers, and someday I am sure I will see one, as last night you predicted. In the meantime I know you will think kindly of me, though I have disappointed you, and will remember me always as

Your dearest well-wisher & friend,
Jenny Hansom

Sam continued to pore over the note long after I had finished rereading it a second time. Again and again he read it through. At length, he folded the note gently along its original creases, held it a moment as if he might tear it in half, then gave it one last deliberate fold of his own and tucked it inside his jacket.

"Well, Bruin," he said, looking up and finding the clerk's and my eyes on him, "let's find us a bite to eat. I ain't as hungry as I was, but a fellow's got to eat pretty much no matter what."

Meleager came down with Molly and joined us where we waited outside the dining room doors with those other guests who were so far up and about. Sam was listening with an abstracted air to a tall, cadaverous fellow who, having said how he himself admired Sam's jump more than he could say, was in the process of introducing a plump, smiling wife and a really astonishing number of plump, smiling daughters who took after their father so little in appearance that they might all have been produced by the plump, smiling wife unaided—and who all, according to their cadaverous father, admired Sam's jump more than they could say. Meleager broke into this somewhat inarticulate orgy of admiration and dispersed the severally plump and cadaverous participants.

"Good morning, Mr. Patch. I do not see our charming companion of last night. Is Miss Hansom late abed this morning? I hope she's not indisposed," he said, with his usual sure instinct for causing pain.

"She's stole a march on us all this morning, I reckon," said Sam. "She's already up and gone."

"Ah," said Meleager, surprised. "And when you say gone . . . ?"

"I mean gone," said Sam, in a way that closed the subject.

For the next half hour, breakfast preoccupied everyone to the exclusion of conversation. Sam shoveled away meditatively; Meleager, now and again shooting a glance in Sam's direction, followed suit; and Molly, notwithstanding stiff competition from the contingent of plump and still-smiling females, managed anyhow to garner enough of the comestibles to feed five. Two of these shares came to my portion; three she encompassed herself.

"And what are your plans, if I might ask?" said Meleager afterwards, lighting a cigar with a coal preparatory to accompanying Sam for a stroll outside. There was something in his tone, intended to be casual, that caused me to look at him sharply, and he dropped his eyes.

"I reckon I'll just take some time and study on that question, Mr. Meleager," said Sam. "Just at present I don't seem able to come up with an answer to it. I'm thinking maybe I'll rest up a bit before anything."

"So much derring-do takes its toll, eh?" said Meleager, discarding the coal and puffing away.

"It ain't that so much. Things is changed now, is all," said Sam.

He declined to elaborate, but I thought I knew what he meant. I remembered that first time I ran into Crockett and how all my troubles had begun with a certain scent on a breeze. Before that, everything had been going swimmingly for me, too. A little more time and I'd have been convinced past any disillusioning that bears were the end of creation and that I was one hell of a bear. Then came that scent, like an itch that needed scratching, and I was off on my adventure.

Sam had caught the scent now. I knew he had to go after it—have you ever tried to just forget about an itch? But there was no more telling with him than with me just where the pursuit would take us.

So we stayed on in Paterson while Sam worked out his next move. These cogitations took the form of a restless ambling about the town in the daytime, a restless and interminable consumption of St. Croix in the nighttime, and—notwithstanding his own dictum—a certain forgetfulness of mealtimes that I found more troublesome than either of the other two signs of cerebration.

"I don't know, Bruin," he confided to me one night. He shook his head. "I don't know if going after her is the right thing or not. But I can't seem to let it lie. It ain't as I just won't take no for an answer. But Bruin," he said, his fingers tightening around his forgotten glass, "it's eating at me as Jenny plumb don't know me."

I licked his hand, wondering how well Sam knew her.

So days passed while we prowled the town and Sam tried to sort things out. Often he took out Jenny's note and read it through again, as if he suspected it of being in a code which, if worried at sufficiently, would turn out to mean just the opposite of what it seemed to mean. Perhaps anticipating this result, Sam took me with him one night to meet the boat from Albany.

" 'Scuse me, ma'am," he said, approaching a large harridan of remarkable ugliness, "but I reckon you'll be Mrs. Cluppins?"

The woman, not for a minute slackening her hold on a sadly demoralized-looking man three-quarters of whose shirt she held bunched up in one enormous hand, smiled vacuously and tottered around in search of the source of the voice. Her gaze lighted on Sam. Perhaps I should say: one of her gazes. For while the eye delegated to inspect Sam sized him up and widened with pleasure, the other eye, either from congenital defect or by dint of arduous training, maintained an independent surveillance of her captive.

"Who calls for Ma Cluppins? Is it you, young feller? Well! Ain't you the good-looking piece of goods, though, I'll be bound. I'm more or less spoke for just now, Sonny, but—damn me if I don't like your looks, though—what I can see of them. Tell you what. If you ain't in a hurry, or too much of a hurry, it'll just take me a minute to satisfy this gent here"—lifting said gent off the ground by his shirt—"or maybe less," she interpolated, giving her victim a meditative shake, "and then I'll be yours. Can you wait?"

"Well, ma'am—"

"No, no. No need to explain. You *are* in a hurry. Seems like young folks always are, these days, I'll be bound. Any time I catch one he's usually hurried himself along so he isn't even young anymore, but some broken-down old winded thing who couldn't run any faster. Well, listen, Sonny, I'll tell you what. What do you say I do you both together? And I'll knock four bits off the price. Couldn't say fairer than that, now, could I? Course not!" And she reached with her free hand, which had been clenching and unclenching as if it itched to fasten its fingers in Sam's shirt.

Sam sidestepped as politely as he very well could.

"Ma'am, I believe you have slightly mistook my meaning," he said. He explained that it was Jenny Hansom he was after, better known to Ma perhaps as Handsome Jenny.

"Oh, that one," Ma said, slumping enough that her captive was encouraged to make a brief but futile bid for freedom. Absently, she gave him a shake. "I might have knowed. It's all I've been hearing since she met that feller on the boat. 'Where's Miss Jenny, Ma?' 'When's Handsome Jenny coming back?' I declare, it's a sight more than I can understand what all you young fellers see in that skinny icicle. I was twice as good-looking when I was her age—not that I'm so terrible old now, mind—and the boys never flocked about me so. And I was willing, too. That Jenny, now, she's a cool one. I don't know as I seen the man yet she cared a hang about unless maybe that feller as caused her to pull stakes. She'll as soon take a fat one as a thin one, an old one as a young—just so's his money's good and he's polite. But I never seen her once let on a man pleasured her.

"Now me, I believe in giving fair value, I do. A feller comes along as is ready to pay for a little honest pleasuring, it ain't professional to send him off less than happy with the service, which he won't be if he don't leave thinking he's as good as the best there ever was. You take this feller here," she said, producing her captive, who momentarily brightened as if he thought there was a chance Sam might actually do just that. "I can tell just by looking at him that he won't do nothing for me. But will he ever find that out? Not from me, he won't. I know fellers has feelings too—even this one does. He'll think there never was such a man as him when I'm through with him, he will. That's how I treat them and always have. And what's the end of it? They flock to that icicle and old Ma has to make shift with the ones too drunk to appreciate me proper. I tell you, Sonny, it's a sorry thing when a real professional has to take a backseat to a little chit like Handsome Jenny, and all on account of I don't have the heart to treat them mean and play hard to get like some. But then I always was too kindhearted by half." She scowled at her captive, as if she suspected him of wishing to desert her, too, given the chance.

"I've no doubt there's a world of truth in what you say, ma'am," said Sam, "and there's no accounting for tastes. But it may be my situation's something different from the run. I ain't looking for Jenny in what you might call her professional capacity, you see. No, ma'am, Jenny and me was kids together and I always did admire her, but from afar, as you might say. And to make a long tale short, I was hoping you could help me find her again, seeing as you know her lately some ways better than me."

Mrs. Cluppins rallied her forces and surveyed Sam intently with each eye in turn. The effect was a bit like watching someone run back and forth with a lamp behind two windows. At length she settled which eye she favored and transfixed him with it, the other careering off and disconcertingly coming to rest on me.

"You're sweet on that blonde baggage, ain't you, Sonny?" she rasped, not unkindly and with a certain sadness.

"I'd take it as a favor, ma'am, if you was to go in for a more respectful turn of phrase," said Sam a little stiffly.

"Well, well. No disrespect intended, I'm sure." She sighed. I couldn't tell if it was in pity for Sam or for herself. She unquestionably had an air of feeling sorry for someone. "And it may be I do have a notion where she might be found. Course, having it and sharing it's two different things." A shade of calculation crept into her expression. "Just how much might the sharing be worth to you, would you say?"

Sam's hand went to his jacket pocket, but money was not what she had in mind. It was strange to think of Ma as bearing out the old saw that there are some things money can't buy, but she did, and it was one of these things for which money is sometimes useless that she wanted Sam.

"Listen, Sonny. I always did like good-looking fellers, dark ones specially, and it's been so long since I've had me a real good-looking cuss as was in his right senses that I've near clean forgot what the feeling's like.

"So my terms is these, Sonny, and there's many," she said with a horrible simper, "as wouldn't call them hard. Before I tell you how to find this here Handsome Jenny, who can have her pick of all the fine fellers there are, I want you to be nice to Ma."

I don't know if anyone's love has ever been put to a severer trial than Ma was proposing here for Sam's. But he never wavered. If he turned pale, that certainly can't be held against him; and if he hesitated, I knew him too well to think he considered backing away. No, he was only thinking the matter over. And when I saw his head go down and his lip curl up, saw those blue eyes of his crinkle and that gleam come into them the way it had the afternoon I wound up going over the falls in a barrel, wearing pants—I guessed he'd hit on an idea for getting himself out of his difficulties.

"It wouldn't be polite, I reckon, to say you drive a hard bargain, ma'am. But I'm tempted to say it anyhow, meaning it as a compliment. Yep, you seem to have me over a barrel, and no mistake. It's a fortunate thing the barrel ain't all that hard, like you say. Now ma'am, I'd oblige you myself in a minute, I would, if I was free to. Indeed, it'd be entirely my pleasure. But I'd only be thinking of her all the while and that would plumb take the fun out of it for both of us, I know. So I'm wondering if you'd consider letting a good friend of mine who's as dark and good-looking as I am and whose affections ain't spoke for stand in for me in this. I know you're too kindhearted to say you won't."

"Well," said Ma broad-mindedly, "let's see your friend."

It was a reasonable request and the weak spot in Sam's plan. Doubtless he'd hoped to get her agreement first and then insist that a bargain was a bargain. He temporized.

Ma growled that she wasn't born yesterday—a truth I'd have thought too obvious to mention—and demanded to "see the gent" first.

I shambled into the light.

Ma gazed at me uncertainly. She didn't seem to know what to make of me with either eye.

"I don't suppose you'd be the gent yourself as run into Jenny that last night on the boat?" she asked Sam.

Sam allowed as how he was. Ma Cluppins sighed.

"I had sort of a feeling. There was talk of that gent having a bear along for a friend." Absently she rubbed her nose with the head of the man she still held prisoner. Reminded thus of her prior engagement, she set him on his feet and suggested he "run along"— a suggestion that he didn't even wait to hear out to act on, and one I wouldn't have been slow to follow either, given the chance.

Ma turned back to me. She looked me up and down and gave herself another scratch while I tried desperately to look unappealing.

She spat.

"Well, I will say this, he ain't just my usual line of customer. But I always was a game one, I was, and it has been a spell since I've had me a real challenge. I reckon I'll take him on.

"Buck up, dearie," she said cheerfully, seeing my distress. "We've all got to lose it sometime." Then, advancing on me with a chuckle that seemed to disconcert even Sam: "Be easy, Mr. Bruin. It'll make a man of you. I reckon Ma can do it if anybody can."

Chapter 20

Jenny Hansom was in New York City. At least, she had always professed a desire to go there, according to Ma, and that was where she always threatened to go whenever the routine on the night boat got too much for her—as I suspected it must have often enough, if my own bout with Ma was at all representative. On those occasions, fed up with her usual clientele, she would speak of New York as a place where she might meet "somebody different." Sam tried but could get no more information from Ma, either on the subject of where in New York Jenny might go, or on what Jenny might have meant by "different." To the best of Ma's recollection, Jenny had never elaborated on either topic, though it was true that Ma's recollections were perhaps more disordered than usual just at the moment by her recent tumble with me. For that matter, my own head had been clearer: I kept catching myself thinking that in the dim, romantic shadows, Ma didn't really look half bad.

Anyway, Ma only happened to remember as much as she did because, in the first place, Jenny had mentioned New York so often, and in the second, the notion of any man's being "different" had struck Ma as so quaint.

("Until I met you, dearie," she said, reverently scratching my ear.)

The information worked an immediate change in Sam. His

listlessness evaporated. Now he was all activity and impatience and wanted to leave Paterson that very night. I was glad for the change, regardless of what it had cost me. After missing them for so long, his grinning at me, rumpling my fur and calling me an old fussbudget were like rain on parched ground.

Before we could leave Paterson, however, Sam had to say his good-byes. In the circle of Sam's admirers, this tended to be a time-consuming and even physically debilitating process. Anticipating as much, Sam got an early start on it, but as word spread that we were leaving, the ranks of his admirers swelled at a rate that outpaced Sam's best efforts to have a last drink with everyone. People who had grown so blasé about having the hero in their midst as to pass him on the street with only a nod now converged on the hotel to make as much of us as if we'd only just got into town. In fact, we met with so much good feeling that Sam and I wound up having to put off our departure for another day just to recuperate from the effects of having announced it.

Finally, though, we tore ourselves away and left for the city.

My first thought when we got there was that I'd never seen so many pigs in all my life. Rooting everywhere in the streets, they were underfoot of everything that had feet, and in their single-minded pursuit of their own business at whatever inconvenience to others, I thought they were striking models of republican initiative. Ready to hobnob or dispute the way with anyone, regardless of his inclinations or condition in life, they must have been a constant source of inspiration to the more egalitarian citizenry. I had no doubt but every last porker was solid for Jackson—whole hog, so to speak.

There were also more people about than I was accustomed to seeing, for that matter, and more traffic. Every sort of gig, cart, coach, wagon and carriage rumbled and racketed over the cobbles, all tearing along at top speed, scattering pigs and persons with an evenhanded disdain, as if contending in a race in which everyone had a different idea concerning the location of the finish line.

Nor were those on foot behindhand in this regard. Eating and jabbering, or grim-faced and solitary, all classes of pedestrian hurried along, jostling one another when necessary, deftly sidestepping the halt, the lame and the pigs, and pursued their way at a rate that would have permitted no uncertainty as to the supreme importance of their affairs had not all alike been going at the same rapid clip, and had it not been plain that they always did no matter what.

Sam and I, too, were caught up in this mad rush and swept along by it all day without so much as a break for meals. Considering that we didn't even know where we wanted to go, I thought we might have eased the pace a bit, but there's no denying we made excellent time getting wherever we did get and saw quite a bit of the city on the way. Finally, though, shortly after what I thought should have been supper time—a circumstance that seemed lost on those around us—Sam grabbed a handful of my fur and pulled me into a doorway. When he caught his breath he said:

"Bruin, it strikes me we need a better plan. I'm thinking it'll take a mite too long to look just everywhere for her, and it would be easy to miss her besides. What we need to do is figure where she might likely head and go look for her there."

I hadn't realized we had a plan, but this new one sounded eminently logical to me. But for the fact that it presupposed our knowing just what we'd come to find out, I didn't see how it could go wrong.

You'll gather I was feeling out of sorts.

"Now where," said Sam slowly, "might the ladies in Jenny's present misfortunate line of employ tend to set up shop, I wonder?"

That was the nub of it, of course, and from what I'd seen of the city so far, I thought the answer might be: almost anywhere. Hardly a block seemed entirely free of their telltale ostentation of dress, vamping looks and beckoning fingers. And while maybe none of them looked quite so enterprising as Ma Cluppins, they were more versatile in another way. Several I saw seemed to have a sideline selling hot corn, to see them through slack periods, I gathered, and it seemed unlikely that any group as resourceful and diverse as this would let itself be shunted into any one precinct.

"Maybe the best we could do is go back by the river. I recollect seeing a number of likely-looking ladies there, and as Jenny must have come in by there, maybe we could strike on someone as actually saw her."

Except to recommend that we stop for a bite to eat first, I had no objection. Sam promising we'd break for a rest at the first opportunity, we each drew a deep breath and pitched back into the tide.

For all Sam's promising, it was growing dark by the time we

reached a place called Duane Street and we still hadn't stopped for that meal. I supposed Sam wanted to get back to familiar surroundings first, but I could have waited. We'd been lost all day, were lost now, and seemed likely to be lost for the foreseeable future, given that, as I say, we didn't even really know where we wanted to go. And the crowd, willing enough to take us anywhere else, gave no sign of being about to take us wherever that was. Anyway, we now found ourselves on Duane Street, where I had no recollection of being before or of wanting to be, when a bell atop an adjacent building set up an urgent clamor. Then another bell started in an instant later somewhere nearby, and for a heady while I thought the city at large was called to supper. Indeed, all pedestrian traffic immediately halted and people began excitedly to group themselves about the building where the first bell had rung. Beyond that, though, they didn't act much like people waiting to be fed, and my hopes fell. What they actually were waiting for I couldn't imagine.

Suddenly they made way with cheers and a man pushed through to the building at top speed. If he was on his way to his supper, I thought, his table manners must have been something to see. For not content with disencumbering himself of his coat, which he carried wadded up under one arm, he had stripped off his shirt too, with a fine disregard for the buttons, before he vanished inside, as if he meant to throw himself bodily on his victuals and take them in through his pores. Then hard on his heels came another fellow in a similar state of undress, and after him two more. In a minute they were flocking inside. Then the double doors burst open onto the street and the whole company reemerged newly and uniformly attired in red flannel shirts, boots, and odd-looking leather hats each displaying a large shield bearing the number 13. Bystanders' hats soared into the air at the sight. An avenue opened for them and, at the urging of a leader flourishing and sometimes blowing into a trumpet, the men came trotting out into the street in two lines, each man grasping one of two long parallel poles attached to a gleaming contraption like an ornately decorated hay wagon with a modest-size silver tree stump upright in its center.

"Bla-a-a-t!" said the leader's trumpet.

"Hooray!" said the spectators, once again making way.

The red-shirts swung their engine around and took off after their leader at a run. A number of onlookers followed, as did a noisy troop of small boys, several of whom were resplendent in red

shirts of their own, and one of whom was even the proud pos-
sessor of one of the queer leather hats, which, however, rather
hampered his ability to see or keep up.

Just as the excitement seemed to have peaked, a new cry was
wrung from the crowd. Looking where every second man was
gleefully pointing, I saw another troop of red-shirts swing into the
street a block away and go tearing off in the lead as if the devil
were at their heels. The leader of our group blew into his trumpet
till I thought his eyes would pop, and the men redoubled their
efforts, as did the boys theirs and the onlookers theirs, and all alike
went clattering over the cobbles in hot pursuit.

"Come along, Bruin," said Sam, slapping my shoulder. "This
here looks too good to pass up."

Off we ran. New recruits swelled our ranks every minute, ban-
tering, shouting, red-faced with running, and cried out encouragement to our team of red-shirts. These strained at their engine with
a grim purposefulness that was wonderful to see and that couldn't
have been a starker contrast to our own festive air. I even forgot
how hungry I was and woofed happily as we pounded along, though
I hadn't the faintest idea what all the fuss was about. "Where is it?"
newcomers would shout. "A house in Roosevelt Street!" someone
would shout back. But just *what* was waiting for us at a house in
Roosevelt Street, and just why it was so important that we reach it
before the similarly garbed troop in the lead, were two gaps in my
knowledge.

That troop was not in the lead by much, in fact. We had
approached so close that our troop of Number 13s was nosing into
the crowd that had attached itself to the other company. Our
captain was blowing his trumpet almost all the time now, so that
it was a wonder where he found the breath to run with, and the
captain of the forward troop—whose hats were emblazoned with a
"12," as I saw when heads were anxiously turned to monitor our
progress—seemed to have lungs of comparable fortitude. Indeed,
we never would have caught up at all, I'm certain, if it weren't that
the 12s' engine was bigger and bulkier than ours.

But catch up we did. First it was only our captain who passed
the back end of the 12s' engine, turning as we did so to wind
another blast on his trumpet and beckon the 13s on. Then he was
even with the rear elements of the 12s themselves, who glanced at
him expressionlessly and threw themselves even harder into their
struggle to stay ahead. But the lighter weight of our engine told.

Soon the forwardmost 13s were neck and neck with the rearmost 12s and still gaining. Man after man pulled past. Now the two captains were even, blowing without pause, as if the contest were not only to see who should arrive first but who should announce himself the loudest.

It was a dead heat on both counts, as it happened, for the race ended just then so suddenly that I went tumbling head over heels some yards past the finish line and was only brought up by a lamppost. I righted myself in time to see the two troops of red-shirts furiously unspooling long, snakey articles from their engines and running with the ends of these to a stubby protuberance of a sort I'd already remarked as receiving much singular attention from male dogs. But I was distracted before I saw what the men had it in mind to do with the snakey articles. I had just noticed that a house across the street was burning down.

When I turned back to look, the men in red shirts were heat-edly trying to settle which troop had won the foot race and were much too engrossed in their argument to pay any attention to the fire. I didn't see Sam anywhere. The crowd, meanwhile, had di-vided its energies pretty evenly between complacently watching the flames lick out of the windows of the burning building and complacently watching the progress of the feud between the men in red shirts. I began to have an inkling what all the excitement had been about.

Finally, one of the 13s pushed a 12 out of the way and coupled his snake to the protuberance. A valve was turned and the snake, which I now saw was a leather hose, filled with water and, leaking spectacularly, delivered a flow to the Number 13 engine. A cheer went up from the other 13s. They fell to on a pair of long rails, one on either side of their engine, and began to work these up and down. Water spurted from the ends, joints and seams of several more hoses. Then blood spurted from the nose of the 13 who had pushed the 12 and general battle was joined, to the great delight of the onlookers, whose happiness was now complete.

Suddenly Sam appeared at my side.

"Come along, Bruin, and be quick. There's some funny busi-ness on as might be worth looking into."

Feeling markedly less enthusiasm than I'd followed him with before, I hauled myself to my feet and hurried after him. He was heading for the crowd in front of the burning house, which by this time was blazing up pretty impressively. The flames that had only been timidly peeping from the windows when we arrived were now brazenly leaning out and reaching for the shutters. Their light flickered and danced with ever wilder energy as the night grew darker, and even the sound of the fire, spitting and roaring as it gathered itself in the upper story—for the moment not far hence when it would bound up and onto the roof—was sufficiently fearsome that I didn't much care to go any closer. But Sam, skirting the crowd in front of the house where the show was most spectacular, seemed intent on going right up to the burning building, albeit from an angle that promised at least a little more safety than a frontal approach. Indeed, we were soon stumbling through shadows in a lot to the side on a course that would take us right to the house's back door.

Just what business we might have with this door, or with the house at all except in its capacity as a rather forlorn spectacle, I couldn't imagine. I doubted very much that Sam had designs on the larder, and for the life of me I couldn't in my present state think of anything else about the place likely to interest me.

But Sam's interest only seemed to intensify as we drew closer. Suddenly he stopped. I peered through the darkness. Sure enough, darker patches of shadow were flitting about the yard. As my eyes grew more accustomed to the light, or lack of it, I saw that these flitting shadows were uniformly larger and slower leaving than on the approach.

"Bruin, old feller," Sam said to me in a low voice, "if someone was to tell me I've done smarter things, I don't know as I could make him out a liar. But I've a suspicion them fellers there toting off the movables can give us a line on Jenny if anybody can. Now, you just keep kind of in the background. I expect their nerves are something sensitive, and I don't want you giving anybody a turn."

With that he slipped away, giving me such a turn at being left so unexpectedly that my own nerves suffered more than a bit. When next I caught sight of him, he had insinuated himself into the group of shadows, and either they had accepted him or, what I was afraid was more likely, simply hadn't noticed yet that they had extra help. But have it they did. First a chair, then a mirror, then a chest passed into Sam's hands from the hands of the shadows in the house. All of these articles he dutifully relayed to other shadows who came up and relieved him of them without comment. In fact, so intent on their business were these shadows, and so little anticipating this sort of interference, that I think I could have joined Sam in handing out booty and, except perhaps for a vague and probably not unpleasant sense that the work was going uncommonly well, no one would have noticed anything out of the ordinary.

Of course, this couldn't last. If nothing else there were only a limited number of articles to be shifted. But in particular, the house was burning down. This fact was forcibly brought home to us again by a crash from upstairs where the fire raged and by a sudden access of illumination that bathed the shadows—and Sam—in an uncertain glare.

Two of these lurid shadows, looking much more substantial now, boiled out of the house after the crash. A third, who had just handed Sam a large portrait of a disapproving-looking old gentleman with his hair all on end, was practically tumbled out of the doorway into Sam's and the portrait's arms. He gaped at both faces, seeming rather taken aback to recognize neither one.

"Hop it, Snooks. The joint's caving in," growled a companion in passing.

Speechless (a condition I feared was not to last long), Snooks flung off Sam's steadying arm and fled after his fellows, evidently not reassured by the patent friendliness of Sam's smile. Sam grinned and handed me the portrait, which I believe could not possibly have looked half so disapproving at any other time in its history or no one could have borne to have it around.

"Well, Bruin, here's where the fun starts. Best stick close now, I reckon. Only try not to scare the fellers too bad. Be best if we can take them on their good side."

He dashed off after Snooks, chuckling as if this whole mess were a capital joke. I communed with the portrait for an astonished second or two, during which it was likely a toss-up who looked least happy with the other or the way things were going or life in general just at the moment—then dropped him on his ear and took off after Sam.

Mindful of Sam's admonition not to put the erstwhile shadows out of sorts, I satisfied myself with keeping Sam in sight and tried to keep myself out of it. Snooks meanwhile had overtaken his colleagues and to all appearances was giving an alarm. They stood irresolute in a group of ten or twelve about a heavy wagon parked in a deserted street and piled high with mysterious cargo only just covered by a carefully secured tarp. They seemed to be making up their minds whether to fight or fly. Their leader, a tall, brawny man in a soft-crowned felt hat, spat disgustedly, though without relaxing from his posture of vigilance.

"He ain't no bull," he said, scowling at Sam.

"And what if he is?" sniggered a lean, stoop-shouldered man with a shape like a broken wagon spring. "There's only the one of him."

Sam came up to them as if his strongest apprehension was that he might have kept them waiting. Stopping a little short, he grinned round.

"Howdy, fellows," he said.

The leader spat, looking as much like a man of stone as a person very well can and still chew tobacco. The others fanned out to surround Sam without being told, the thin man like a broken spring loping to take up his position just at Sam's back.

Sam grinned at them all in the friendliest way imaginable.

"I sure am glad to have caught up with you boys. You see, I'm a stranger hereabouts and I've heard so much about all the ways a fellow as don't know the ropes can come to grief in this town that I just thought I couldn't do better than to throw in with some hardworking folks as seemed to know their way around. I hope you don't mind."

The leader spat ambiguously and the circle around Sam tightened.

"That's good," said Sam, seeming immensely relieved—by what, I couldn't imagine. "That sure is first-rate of you to take it that way. I thought from the start you was a friendly-looking bunch, that I did. Which brings me to my special reason for imposing on your good graces at such short notice like I've done. And that is, I've a sort of favor to ask and you folks seem particular likely to be able to help me out with it, if you've a mind to."

The leader had not altered his stance in any perceptible way, but somehow he and the rest of them, too, gave the impression of listening intently and of being more than a little at a loss what to make of Sam. Snooks spoke for all of them when he scratched his head, perplexedly pushing his hat over one ear. Only the thin man at Sam's back didn't seem particularly interested in what Sam was saying. I made it a point to keep my eye on him.

"Now I know you fellows are likely pressed for time just at the moment, and I don't want to hold you up," said Sam, pouring more oil on the waters. "But I was thinking if you'd just let me tag along and maybe pitch in again with disposing of this here merchandise, we could set down over a friendly bottle any time you found it convenient and have a talk."

Sam made this sound so reasonable that I can only guess it was that that provoked the thin man. Probably he was worried he was about to lose his chance to keep his hand in with a little refreshing skulduggery. That hand, in any event, had been buried throughout deep in a pocket of his shabby coat; now it came suddenly clear and flashed in the light of a street lamp.

I was on him like a five-hundred-pound thunderbolt. His hands splayed out on the cobbles, as did a gratifying number of his teeth. A long, wicked knife flew from his grasp and clattered to rest at the feet of his leader, who more nearly resembled a figure of stone now than at any time in the proceedings.

The circle of men around us rippled and fell back. My dander properly up, I straddled the man I'd flattened and snarled at the others indiscriminately while I assessed whether I had time to rip my first victim's head off. Plainly I did. Very likely I could have opened him up and played cat's cradle with his innards, too, if I'd wanted to, so dumbfounded were his associates. In fact, they seemed more dumbfounded than terrified. I think they were affected less by what I'd actually done than by my inexplicably having shown up to do it wearing a bear suit.

It was all one to me. I dropped down and, attending to the first item on my agenda, took the unconscious man's head in my paws. I felt a tug at my collar and reared back. It was Sam.

He stroked me, saying my name again and again, and as nobody seemed inclined to take me up where I'd left off, I hunkered down and licked Sam's hand. He hugged my head to his chest.

"This here's Bruin," he said, looking at the men. I showed them my teeth. "I forgot to mention he's along, too."

Snooks snapped his fingers.

"Say, ain't you"—he snapped his fingers again and took off his hat—"ain't you the feller as jumps?"

"I've done some jumping, I won't deny," allowed Sam, beginning to smile.

Snooks slapped his leg with his hat and said to the tall, grim-looking man:

"Why, he's all right, Wideawake. This here's Sam Patch!"

Chapter 21

Back at our new-found friends' lair we sat down together in the dingy back room where they received visitors and improved our acquaintance over some St. Croix. As this was the favorite tipple of the tall man styled Wideawake, too, the acquaintance, as you can imagine, prospered famously. Nor was I left out of account. Sharing with Sam the place of honor at the only table, I was made at least as much of as he was. After all, they hadn't actually seen Sam in action; I'd impressed them firsthand. Snooks, saying he'd never particularly cared for Dogs Meat anyway—the man I'd "done for," as Snooks put it, and whose groans could be heard now and again from the closet where he'd been carried—ran out himself to fetch dinner for me and wouldn't let anyone else but Wideawake, and Sam, of course, share the table while I ate it. Snooks, as the one who had discovered Sam's imposture and later been the one to identify us, seemed to take a proprietary interest in the pair of us. But I was his clear favorite and my least little mannerism made his bright red face even brighter under its white stubble till it looked like a brilliant sunset on a partially cloudy day.

Collectively, our new friends were known as the Shirt Tails. Roosevelt Street was not strictly a part of their territory, but neither did it belong unequivocally to anybody else, the nearest neighbors on that side being the Daybreak Boys, who had come out worst in more than one fray with the Shirt Tails, and whose permission to conduct business in that neighborhood the Shirt Tails consequently did not feel obliged to solicit. The Shirt Tails did lord it over quite a large area, in fact, and regarded themselves and were generally regarded, or so they proudly told us, as one of the premier gangs in the city.

"Oh, the Plug Uglies won't be green when they hear we've got Sam Patch—*and* Bruin—staying with us! Oh, no, not a bit!" chortled Snooks, hugging himself and turning very red indeed.

Even Wideawake almost smiled.

"It's a fact, Sam," said a sprightly junior associate who went by the name of Cutaway. "This is a real honor for us. We follow all of your jumps in the papers. All the boys do. Why, I reckon if there was a falls anywhere as could be carried off, we'd have lifted it before this and asked you by to jump off it!"

It was a while before our friends got sufficiently used to having us by that they could take up their customary pastimes and give Sam a chance to say what was on his mind. But such is human nature that eventually even the sight of my drinking beer from a bottle ceased to edify anyone but Snooks, and cards and dice made their appearance and were pressed into service in corners of the room. Wideawake filled Sam's glass with unusual gravity, then raised his own and looked at Sam over the rim of it.

"You said there was a particular business as brought you to our neck of the woods, Sam. I reckon you know you can count on us to help you in it if we can."

Sam had been waiting for this moment. Now that it had come, though, I thought he looked less gratified than might have been expected.

"That's mighty handsome of you to offer, Wideawake. And yes, there is a little matter as you and the boys might be able to do me a service in," said Sam. He hesitated. "The fact is, I'm looking for a person, a certain lady friend of mine. I heard tell in Paterson as she was bound this way. If she's here at all, she would have come a couple of weeks ago. Now, I've a notion you keep pretty close tabs on anybody passing through as is in what you might call a related line of work, and I was thinking maybe the boys could give me some lead to her whereabouts."

Wideawake nodded, evidently finding nothing in this to tax either his conscience, his capabilities, or even his curiosity very much. Sam fiddled with his glass. I guessed he was torn between wanting Wideawake's help on the one hand, and being reluctant to learn that Wideawake actually could help, on the other. If the Shirt Tails could tell him nothing of Jenny, I sensed that Sam would not feel entirely let down.

"All right. I guess I might as well come right out with it. Last I saw her she was in a trade where she meets a certain amount of men, if you catch my meaning. Now don't take me wrong. She's as fine a woman as you could ever meet, and I won't hear no different about that. It's just she fell on some hard times and got sort of turned around. I know how that can happen to a body, as it's happened to me. But I expect this is none of it to the purpose. No. Well, let's see, she's a real looker, too, I can tell you that. Prettiest blonde hair you ever did see, and the nicest figure, without being the kind as looks like it's going to bust right out of its duds at you. Nothing splashy about her, in fact, but makes a real strong impression somehow. I reckon it has something to do with this kind of quiet way she has. Why, I guess she's more ladylike in her own natural right than many as could plumb weary you with their pedigree. Her name's Jenny Hansom, though nowadays folks pretty much call her Handsome Jenny."

Snooks jumped. He had been about to pass me another bottle of beer, having just watched in a kind of ecstasy as I disposed of the last one. Now, with the bottle poised aloft he said:

"Handsome Jenny? Did you say Handsome Jenny? Is that who you're after?"

"You know her?" said Sam.

"Why, sure," said Snooks. "We know Handsome Jenny. You know her too, Wideawake. She's that one as Raskin's been making so much fuss about. I reckon we do know her, all right," he said again, coming back to Sam. "There's been two fellers killed on her account already, and there'll be more, if I don't miss my guess."

The other Shirt Tails had perked up on hearing Jenny's name. They left off their cards and drinking to agree with Snooks. Sam looked from face to face, winding up with Wideawake. Wideawake looked troubled. He glanced sharply at Snooks, who fell silent.

"Raskin," said Wideawake slowly, answering Sam's unspoken question, "is a bad character."

Snooks could not leave this unembellished.

"You don't want to mess with Raskin," he said very rapidly. "No sirree. Raskin's a mean one."

Wideawake glanced at him rather more sharply than before and Snooks turned very red.

"What's he got to do with Jenny?" demanded Sam. "She ain't in no danger?"

"No, it ain't like that," said Wideawake, his eye glinting ominously at Snooks. "It's more like he's took her under his protection, in fact."

"Hah!" snorted Snooks, feebly but unmistakably.

Wideawake brought his fist up and set it down on the table with a soft thump. The hint was wasted, though, for just at that moment Snooks was seized with a tremendous coughing fit which by itself seemed to drive Jenny from his thoughts. Certainly when he recovered he sat back gazing into space and picking his nose for all the world like a man with nothing on his mind.

It was not lost on Sam that no one, not even Wideawake, seemed to want to meet his eye. When one after another they had all coincidentally found some other object demanding their attention—a die that needed moving half an inch, a deck of cards that needed straightening—just as Sam looked their way, Sam said quietly:

"I reckon you boys better tell me more about this Raskin feller, as it seems as one way or another him and me are due to get better acquainted."

As no one else seemed to relish the job, it was Snooks who spoke up finally, receiving tacit permission from Wideawake.

"Flavius Raskin's the one as heads up the Dead Rabbits," he said and stopped, as if this information alone should suffice to deter any sensible person from wishing to pursue a closer acquaintance. Seeing that Sam plainly expected more, though, Snooks was nonplused. He appealed to his friends.

"The Dead Rabbits are a bad lot," said a melancholy string bean of a man named Old Gooseberry, swallowing rapidly several times so that his prominent Adam's apple went up and down like a yo-yo.

"They're a bunch of murdering, thieving rascals," put in Cutaway, looking angry and frightened.

"Bad," summarized a squat man with a large mouth named Bellows (the man, I mean).

After this exercise in calling the kettle black, everyone waited breathlessly to see what Sam would say. We were not kept long in suspense. He frowned at Wideawake.

"These gents don't sound a bit like the right sort of company for Jenny, and I find it hard to swallow she'd have chose them for herself. They ain't keeping hold of her against her will, I don't suppose? 'Cause if she's with them at all, I'm guessing that's the terms of it."

"No, no," said Wideawake uncomfortably, perhaps envisioning a request that the Shirt Tails add their influence to an invitation to the Dead Rabbits to release their prisoner, "it ain't like that at all. No, she was there, all right, on account of Raskin saw her and took a shine to her—"

"A thing which he ain't never been known to do to anybody, man or woman, in living memory," put in Snooks with a shudder.

"But she wouldn't have none of him, not after a day or two," resumed Wideawake reluctantly. "I reckon it's so, like you say: she must have a way about her. Anyhow, the story's told that she said she wasn't staying and then just up and left, and Raskin didn't lift a hand to stop her."

"Only thing is," said Old Gooseberry mournfully, shaking his head, "he swore to do for anybody else as tries to have a thing to do with her till she comes back to him."

"And there's two already as knows he means it," said Cutaway. "Both of them found still wearing their watches and carrying their pocket money—not as if either one of them was likely to be spending or wanting the time where they was sent to."

"Aye, and there's Kendrick, too," put in a fellow known as the Brick, who was in all respects a younger, less battered version of Wideawake, even to his hat.

"What about Kendrick?" said Sam. The men had lapsed into a meditative silence at the name.

"He's a swell as took in Handsome Jenny and didn't take serious Raskin's warning," said Snooks.

"Well? What happened to him?"

"Burned out," said Snooks.

"Aye," said the Brick. "Burned out and damned near burned up, too. Would have been if Raskin had had his druthers. And he almost did, only Kendrick slipped out through the cellar, a way Raskin didn't know about."

"The Rabbits was all around to keep him in," explained Cutaway. "Others of them held off the fire companies till the house was gone. They plumb meant to roast him, all right." He spat moodily.

"What about Jenny?" said Sam.

"Oh, she was all right. She wasn't there at the time."

This account of the recent activities of Mr. Raskin and his Dead Rabbits seemed to do nothing to raise either one in Sam's good opinion. I didn't remember ever seeing him look so grim. He even began to scare me, and then I realized why: his expression had changed as he listened until it looked unnervingly like Davy Crockett's on the occasion of our last encounter.

"And just how might a feller get to meet this Raskin gent?" said Sam in a tone whose carelessness assorted so ill with the look on his face that I started to be frightened in earnest.

The question took them all by surprise. It was as if someone just told that in a certain place people were dying of the Black Death had asked directions how to get there.

"Sam," said Wideawake, who had been brooding the while, "let me talk you out of this here that you're proposing to do. This Raskin's even worser than you've been told. He's pure poison. There ain't nothing he won't stoop to. Why, he ain't even American."

It soon emerged that Wideawake did not mean to call Raskin a foreigner, but only to charge that the man was not an admirer of Jackson. All the Shirt Tails were foursquare for Jackson—Jackson and Reform.

"He's full of crazy ideas nobody can make head or tail of, and the long and the short of it is there's no telling what he'll do next. None of the boys—and I don't just mean the Shirt Tails—will have anything to do with him and them Dead Rabbits. They don't play by no rules, that bunch. They'd as soon burn a feller out as look at him, and maybe not take nothing either. Do it just for wickedness. They roam about here and there, not paying any mind to whose turf they're on, doing what they please and getting us in trouble with folks as think it's us, and then melting away when we come looking for them, so as we can never have it out with them proper and settle things. Or else maybe they'll jump us on our home ground—for no reason—just to say they don't care two pins for nothing. Why, they've got no respect for law and order, that's what. They're just the indecentest bunch you'd ever want to mess with, and if you're smart you'll leave this Handsome Jenny to handle them herself. She seems to be doing all right, by all reports, and it's a cinch that what Raskin lets her get away with he sure as I'm born won't take from you. I hope you don't take me wrong. I'm telling you this, Sam, entirely for your own good."

I think there may have been just a smidgeon of self-interest involved as well, for all the look of almost tearful sincerity Wideawake bent on Sam; for I had had the impression from the start that Wideawake didn't want any trouble with the Dead Rabbits and their unorthodox leader if he could avoid it. But if Wideawake's motives were complex, there was nothing but solicitude behind the urgings of the others, who fervently seconded him. More and more it was sounding to me as though, in point of dangerousness, the Paterson Falls itself was a piker next to Raskin.

But Sam's mind was clearly made up, and as usual when he was in that condition, there was no budging him.

"It ain't so much I'm dying to meet Mr. Raskin for his own sake, boys. No, I calculate I could go quite a ways without missing that honor. But I do mean to find Jenny if I can, and it strikes me he's just the gent to give me a line on her. So if you'll just inform me where he hangs his hat so me and Bruin can pay him a little call, I'd be mighty obliged."

It turned out that this was a more difficult request than might have been supposed. Raskin and his Rabbits, perhaps owing to some consciousness of their general unpopularity, had no single fixed abode. People didn't visit Raskin. He visited them—to their sorrow, vastly more often than not.

"Well," said Sam cheerfully, "how do I get word to the gent that he's got a standing invitation to drop by any time?"

The Shirt Tails shuddered to a man. At length Old Gooseberry suggested sadly that spreading news of Sam's interest in Jenny ought to bring Raskin around if anything could.

"Well, that's settled then. We'll do her. That is, I'll leave the word-spreading to you boys, if you'll be so good. Meanwhile, so as not to get you fellers too mixed up in my affairs, you can tell anyone who's interested that me and Bruin will be taking the air regular by that house where we fell in with you boys, in case anybody wants to look us up."

Chapter 22

So it was that we spent the better part of next week ostentatiously loitering about Roosevelt Street, waiting to be accosted. It was dreary work, I can tell you, and not especially relieved by the company of small boys and dogs who surrounded us the better part of the time. These were well-disposed, of course, the dogs even going so far after a few days as to fight other dogs from the next street until it was clearly established whose bear I was; but I had an intuition that the Dead Rabbits, however fearsome their reputation, would be kept off by this escort of ours perhaps more effectively than if we were accompanied by a personal bodyguard of New York's finest.

In time Sam came to share my misgivings.

"You know, Bruin, I wonder if we're going about this in quite the right way. The kind of attention we mean to invite ain't the kind of thing you can expect a fellow to come right out and do in the open. He'd be too embarrassed, I reckon. Now, I've seen a whole passel of prime suspicious characters since we've been here, though it might just be the neighborhood. But any one of them I reckon the Dead Rabbits would be proud to count as one of their own. Whichever they are, though, being a naturally retiring lot these fellows seem to be shrinking from advertising themselves in front of our friends here. I'm thinking we should maybe set things up more intimate-like. What say we come back after the boys here"—and this time he *meant* boys—"have turned in for the night? I'm thinking these Dead Rabbits, from all we know about them, might find it more congenial doing business after dark."

This plan, it emerged that evening, had the drawback, however, that the parents of our young friends evidently allowed their offspring considerable latitude in setting their own bedtimes. We were no better off—i.e., no more exposed to attack—than we had been during the day. Finally Sam had to speak to our following, who had grown so accustomed to being with us by this time that they had even adopted Sam's manner of peering hard and curiously at every shifty face that offered—a practice which put to flight more than one promising skulker. Sam told them he was looking to meet a fellow who was a "particular shy customer," and that he was afraid the fellow wouldn't show with all "you men" around. Thus flattered, our admirers took themselves off, but only after extracting promises that Sam and I would be all right in their absence. Somehow they had divined that the shy customer was not an altogether sterling character, and I believe that if the Rabbits had tried to do us an injury any time that night, they would have found themselves beset without warning from every quarter by squads of determined juveniles.

We were doing our promenading in the small, quiet street where the Shirt Tails had parked their wagon the night of the fire. Now that our young friends had left us, the street seemed doubly close and still. The houses themselves seemed to stir and lean against one another surreptitiously, whispering that we were at last alone. Though to all appearances the street had never been emptier, I had never felt so strongly that we were the focus of numerous sharp eyes.

Then, after we'd been at it alone for a couple of hours, finally a shadow rippled out of a darkened doorway and confronted us. So well did the figure match his dirty, decrepit background that it would have been possible to look right at him and not see him, had he not sidled up to us showing his ratlike teeth in a sneer and blocked our way. Sam looked him up and down with interest and said to me:

"Bruin, I'm thinking this is the gent we've been expecting as was sent to meet us. There's no doubt about one thing: he does look considerable like a dead rabbit."

The man showed his teeth some more, possibly taking this as a compliment.

"You Sam Patch?" he said, looking back and forth at Sam and

me as if an affirmative answer from either of us would have satisfied him.

"The very same," said Sam. "This here's Bruin," he added politely, to remove all possible grounds of confusion.

The man sneered—on principle, I think—and told us to follow him then, turning back to look at us and seeming to find it vastly amusing when we did so. He turned off the street at the first alleyway that offered, and five or six more shadows that had been waiting detached themselves from the sides of the buildings and closed in around us. One of them gave a short nasty laugh and prodded Sam with something in the back, making him stumble. I gave a short nasty swipe that hurled the fellow into a brick wall. When his friends had picked him up and shown him how to work his legs again, we proceeded with more decorum.

Through backyards and alleys we went, over, under, around, and sometimes through fences, ducking clotheslines and sidestepping every imaginable sort of litter and filth. Even had we known the city, we could not have kept our bearings, I think—which consideration, together with a desire not to be seen, doubtless had much to do with our friends' bringing us along by such a route.

Our journey ended abruptly with our being ushered through a doorway, down a narrow passageway, and into a room even darker than some of the culverts we'd crawled through. Our shadowy escort melted away again, and except for a spate of hoarse whispering and a stifled groan I took to proceed from the man I'd hurt, we might have been alone in a pit underground.

Then a square of light materialized as someone drew back the shutter on a dark lantern and played its beam on Sam and me. By its glow I could make out sundry indistinct figures ranged watchfully around us. Sam never stirred. He did not seem to see the figures, did not even pay any particular attention to the lantern, except as his eye happened to rest on it as he gazed idly about. He might have been dreaming the time away at a coach stop. I half expected him to break out whistling under his breath.

More lanterns were opened. Matches were struck and candles lighted to the accompaniment of spitting and a shuffling of feet. Our hosts emerged from the shadows—and I wished immediately that it rested with me to send them speedily back again. Never had I seen such an obnoxious crew. With all their shortcomings in point of respectability the Shirt Tails might have passed for pillars of the community by comparison. Flushed or pale, the unhealthy-looking faces of the Dead Rabbits gloated at us from all sides with the same knowing leer, each face showing enough depravity to have furnished out the Shirt Tails on generous terms for six months as a body, leaving a handsome surplus. From every quarter the same bleary red eyes burned at us from behind the same filth and stubble and with the same ratlike fixity. So strong was the family resemblance among the Dead Rabbits that they might all have had the same mother. In fact, if they had, I don't know that that would have been much more wonderful than the fact that they each presumably had some mother or other.

But Sam only glanced about him as if just becoming aware we had company, and he even managed to look pleasantly surprised to see who it was. He distributed a number of friendly nods and then went back to gazing at nothing in particular as if he had just done with greeting a party of pleasant-looking strangers who'd joined him to wait for his coach. I followed his lead, treating myself first to an elaborate scratch and then licking my crotch. The Dead Rabbits seemed a little crestfallen.

One of them was finally forced to break the stalemate.

"You're Sam Patch?" said a man standing beside the leering villain who had opened the first lantern.

"I am," said Sam.

The other tried to stare him down and failed.

"I'm Flavius Raskin," he said at last in a dry, rasping voice.

The two of them sized each other up. Raskin was a thin, sharp-faced man with deep-set, haunted-looking eyes and a mouth whose long, carious teeth were prominent in outline even when his lips were closed. What with this and his sunken cheeks and lank, wispy hair, he reminded me of one of Meleager's skulls from ancient battlefields. There was no heaviness to his looks, none of that thickness about the jowls or puffiness about the eyes that so distinguished the Dead Rabbits' rank and file. There was hardly an ounce of flesh on him anywhere. He seemed as near entirely made up of nerves as any man I'd ever seen. He looked, in fact, as if he resented being saddled with a body at all and found it a constant temptation to give it the slip.

Once again Raskin spoke first, his voice hissing into the room like air escaping from an inflated bladder.

"I've heard of you, Mr. Patch. I won't pretend I haven't. You're quite the celebrity, aren't you?" He looked Sam up and down as if he thought Sam's being a celebrity was a pretty good joke. "I hope you don't hold it against us that we had to bring you here in such secrecy, Mr. Patch. I know you must be used to finding adoring crowds wherever you go. But the fact is that I'm something of a celebrity too, in my small way, and I thought it best to be discreet. But perhaps we can still find some way to honor you and show how glad we are to see you."

The Dead Rabbits chortled and carried on as if they could hardly wait to start. Raskin silenced them with a chop of his hand. Sam gave a slight nod, which might have been gracious or not, as it pleased the beholder.

"And this then is the equally famous Bruin," said Raskin, clasping his hands behind him and sauntering over to me. "They say he's as talented as his master. Jumps like him, drinks like him, and juggles besides. A most impressive list of accomplishments—for a bear. And for that very reason perhaps a little less impressive when owned by his master—wouldn't you say, Mr. Patch?"

"I don't know as it's any worse than a lot of work I've seen grown men do, Mr. Raskin," said Sam equably. "I can think of some doubtfuller lines of endeavor."

"Meaning mine, I suppose, Mr. Patch? No, no," Raskin said to some of his Rabbits who seemed eager to avenge the slight, "I'm sure Mr. Patch meant no offense. We simply have an honest disagreement here, don't we, Mr. Patch? You find it more admirable to make a spectacle of yourself for the least enlightened masses than to labor tirelessly (as I do, and at constant risk of my life, too, Mr. Patch) for their emancipation from ignorance and oppression.

"And you're not alone in thinking so, I must say. You have the newspapers and all upright citizens on your side," he said, nodding and smiling nastily. "Small blame if you hold the opinions you do. Who wouldn't, under the circumstances? Your actions are universally acclaimed and you meet with a hero's welcome everywhere you go (well, perhaps not *quite* everywhere; I'm so sorry, Mr. Patch), whereas I'm regularly denounced as an enemy of society. What would you say, Mr. Patch," he asked suddenly, dropping his genial manner for a fierce one he wore much more naturally, "if I told you our places should rightfully be reversed: that I'm the one who ought to be honored, and that the real enemy of society is you?"

"Why, I reckon I'd find that pretty hard to swallow—meaning the part about me, anyhow," said Sam. "For the rest I ain't all that well acquainted with you that I'd be comfortable saying whether folks have you pegged right or not. The little bit I know about has a kind of doubtful look to it, but then the papers tend to paint me out a fellow as jumps just to make a fine show, which ain't entirely on the money either. So I'm ready to allow as how it may be we're both a trifle misunderstood."

Raskin laughed, apparently surprised at Sam's reasonableness. A lot of people underestimated Sam.

"Very good! I never thought of that. So you feel misunderstood, too." The idea seemed to tickle him. "I must say, it never occurred to me we might have so much in common. Yes, and you have courage, too; I can see that. There are many," he said with a sly grimace that made him look more like a death's-head than ever, "who would find it easier to throw themselves off a waterfall than to stand up to me here as you're doing. I respect you for that. Yes, I can see you doubtless have many good qualities.

"Unfortunately," he said, suddenly picking up steam, "when good qualities are perverted by the uses to which they are put, when they are used to dazzle and beguile the hapless worker, distracting him from the realization of his oppression by dangling before him the illusion of a freedom and independence which, as long as the wealthy are allowed to enslave with their riches, he can never possess—*then,* Mr. Patch, virtue is no longer virtue, but vice; what in itself would be good becomes evil, and the bearer of these false qualities deserves—nay, requires—to be extirpated!

Raskin brought up quivering and glared at Sam with a concentrated malevolence that all by itself would have appalled a lesser man. The Dead Rabbits heaved a collective sigh. They had evidently been holding their breath, though whether out of awe of the rhetoric or from an understandable reluctance to draw Raskin's attention to themselves, I couldn't tell. I was put in mind of the speakers at Paterson. Raskin was all by himself a sort of devil's Fourth of July, I thought. I wondered if he'd ever considered taking up politics.

"I wouldn't know about any of that," said Sam after a while, finding that he was evidently expected to comment, "except to say it seems a mite hard on a fellow as is just going his own way minding his own affairs. But being that as it may, it don't have much to do with what I actually came to see you about."

"What you came to see me about?" repeated Raskin, surprised again. He laughed and the Dead Rabbits chimed in with a suitable chorus of growls and sniggers.

"Well," Sam amended, seeing his error, "what I was hoping we'd meet so we could take up together. And that is the whereabouts of Jenny Hansom. Jenny and me go way back, you see. Now, I hear tell you seen her and I thought you might just be able to fill me in on where she's to be found."

At mention of Jenny's name the Dead Rabbits all sucked in their breath again. Raskin himself was struck dumb. Then the bones in his face seemed to swell and stretch the skin to the thinness and color of parchment.

"So I've seen her, have I?" he said, having trouble getting the words out. He choked and his head sank down between his shoulders. "Did the Shirt Tails put you up to this? Did they send you here? By heaven, if they did . . ."

"Well, not just exactly," said Sam. "No, it was mostly all my idea. Fact is, they sort of tried pretty hard to talk me out of it."

"They told you then about Kendrick? About what happened to those others who tried to take up with her? About Vanderbilt? But no, Vanderbilt is still to come," he mused. His lips curled back from his teeth.

"They did say something about a couple of gents as cashed in kind of mysterious. But I didn't figure I ought to just take their word for it, seeing as I knew the boys and you ain't always seen eye to eye about everything."

Raskin laughed again in amazement. The Dead Rabbits sniggered uncertainly.

"You're a man in a thousand, Mr. Patch," said Raskin when he'd done staring at Sam like a man waiting to hear a punchline. If he was disappointed when Sam didn't deliver one, he didn't show it. Probably he consoled himself with remembering what he meant to do to this Vanderbilt. "More than that: a one of a kind. I begin to believe you: you are misunderstood. The papers don't know you. No, you're not the simple lout I took you for. I can even see," he said, tilting his death's-head on one side, "how such a man might take to jumping waterfalls. Indeed I can. Why, it's a thing I might have done myself if I'd ever thought of it and had less sense. But really, I'm impressed. I see your jumping now in an entirely new light."

He stepped forward again, looking almost friendly.

"You know, we're not really so different, you and I, Mr. Patch. Oh, on the surface, of course. But what I mean is that we're both outcasts, Mr. Patch. Society has failed to absorb either of us. Why?

I'll tell you. Because neither of us will rest content with the position he's been assigned, that's why. So you spend yourself out jumping over waterfalls—a highly symbolic activity, Mr. Patch; my compliments on your instincts—while I go beyond empty gestures and work directly to change the society that would keep us down and deny us our rightful places.

"Mr. Patch," said Raskin, stroking his chin as if struck by an idea, "I have a proposition for you. We could help each other, you and I. Yes," he said, becoming excited, "you must join me, Mr. Patch. Join me! Together we would be an irresistible force for change. That absurdly straightforward way you have about you and your other patent good qualities would win recruits by the score. I wouldn't need this scum," he said, carelessly indicating the rather astonished Dead Rabbits, "and could take my proper station behind the scenes, where I would be most effective. My personal qualities put good people off. I'm too corrosive for them, too hard. I have no patience for their sentimental illusions. But you they could rally to. I would stay in the background and chart our course. And I could explain to you more fully why you really jump, Mr. Patch, and help free you from this last shackle that prevents you from fully realizing yourself. What do you say, Mr. Patch? Will you join me?"

Sam scratched his cheek. The Dead Rabbits were holding their breath again; it was a wonder to me they didn't all turn blue in the face. And I was holding mine right along with them. Not that I was much worried about Sam joining Raskin. Raskin wasn't Sam's type and Sam wasn't a joiner anyway. And then of course there was Jenny. No, what worried me was that by all accounts Raskin was the sensitive type and felt slights keenly. He was almost bound to have his feelings hurt if Sam turned him down, and when he did have his feelings hurt he seemed to have a habit of doing things that no doubt he regretted as much as anyone the following day. And then, as I say, there was Jenny. Raskin was already on record as having a short way with rivals, and Sam must look to him like a more serious rival than any to date.

"Mr. Raskin, I thank you kindly for the offer," said Sam when he'd done giving his cheek a very thorough scratching. "It's flattering to a fellow to have his services put so high. The fact is, though, that the work I'm doing suits me pretty good. So meaning no disrespect I reckon I'll just decline to join up with you and the boys here, some of whose doings I don't entirely go along with anyways, and I'll stick to doing what I understand and what I'm pretty sure there's no mistake in, and what if there is, don't hurt nobody but myself."

This he dismayed me by saying with a downright insulting finality. I thought that under the circumstances he might at least have put on a small show of reluctance, of having a hard time making up his mind. But no, Sam was plainspoken to a fault and jumping was a subject only to be approached with the greatest gravity and candor. He would sooner be a martyr to it than show it one whit less honor than it was due.

Well, that was what had drawn me to him in the first place. Just this once, though, I wouldn't have minded a little prevarication. The Dead Rabbits, with renewed confidence now in their continued employment, crowded around us, evincing a lively desire to help Sam along to martyrdom on whatever grounds he chose. I jostled a few of them none too gently, and that helped, but I could see the situation was deteriorating fast.

Raskin meanwhile seemed to grow smaller and more concentratedly poisonous. He restrained the Dead Rabbits with a chop of his hand, but I had a feeling he did so less because there was anything much left to talk about than simply because he wanted to save the last word for himself.

"You disapprove of me, I gather, Mr. Patch," he said in a muffled voice. Even the Dead Rabbits flinched when he chuckled. "Well, I suppose I might have expected it. 'Decent folk' have never had much use for me—nor I for them! Bah, you don't see beyond the ends of your noses," he said, evidently lumping Sam with decent folk generally. "You let squeamishness keep you slaves. But what's the taking of a few insignificant lives against the gain of initiating all mankind into true humanity? Sometimes it's necessary to do unpleasant things—even to shed blood—for the greater good. But it's not your fault you don't understand. Beautiful, sublime ideas— the kind worth killing for—and any idea worth dying for is worth killing for—are lost on you. You have no true sensitivity, no finer appreciation; no philosophical acumen," he said, glaring at Sam now. I thought he was probably right, too, but I didn't see that Sam suffered for it. "You're just another good man, a plodder after all. You're not to be blamed that these aren't the times for good men, that good men nowadays only serve the existing evil. What the times need," he said, swelling dangerously, "are evil men, men without scruples or squeamishness, or men who, like myself, have the intellect and will to cauterize these virtues become vices—root them out, deny them—in order to do what must be done.

"Things aren't as they seem to the good man. Aren't there times when to save the life of a patient a surgeon must cut off the man's arm? Doesn't all surgery require the scalpel and the infliction of pain, Mr. Patch?"

"Mr. Raskin," said Sam, and I could tell he was getting impatient. Even the Rabbits registered the change and drew back. "I expect we'll get on a whole lot friendlier if you and me just drop this talk here. It ain't bringing me round a bit and to tell you the truth it's making me kind of wrathy. Now, I'm looking to find Jenny Hansom. I believe you know where she is, and I'd take it as a considerable favor if you was to tell me."

"Fool!" said Raskin, very much as if he meant it.

"Well, that's about what I expected you'd say," said Sam, in no way moved. "And that brings me to the second thing I've been wanting to tell you. And that's just this." He glanced round at the Dead Rabbits, as if to apprise them that this concerned them, too. "If you lay a finger on Jenny or make out to keep her anywheres against her will, not all the dead critters in Creation will keep me from hunting you down, Mr. Raskin. And I think you know me well enough already to know I ain't easily turned from what I set my mind on."

The Dead Rabbits wanted to close with us so badly after this speech that I felt almost sorry for them. But Raskin still kept them in check, and it was a measure of his hold over them that he could do it. What puzzled me a bit was why he bothered. Maybe he thought that haranguing a live person was more rewarding than haranguing a dead one, or maybe he wasn't sure who would be doing the haranguing and who the dying if it came to a falling out. I snarled and did my best to impress him with the weight of this latter consideration. At the same time, I wished Sam hadn't found it necessary to figuratively spit in his eye.

"Do you really think you'd make out better if you found her than those others who defied me? Better than Kendrick?" rasped Raskin, panting and showing his yellow teeth.

"I'll take my chances," said Sam. "And if you do do for me," he added dryly with the air of a man delivering a parting shot, "I reckon I'll anyway have the consolation of knowing it was nothing personal, but just to make the world a better place."

Raskin gaped. Sam turned to me.

"Come on, Bruin. I reckon me and the gents here understand each other as well as we're likely to. We might as well be going."

That suited me to perfection. Plainly matters were approaching a crisis, and I couldn't see that Sam's handling of them was improving things any.

Meanwhile our way was blocked by one of the Dead Rabbits—the one who blended so well with the filthy alleyway and had guided us here, I think, though they all looked so much alike in that respect that it was hard to be sure. At any rate, whichever Rabbit he was, he was hopping mad, so to speak, as were the others. They clustered around us, baring their teeth and darting glances at Raskin, only awaiting a signal from him to have a go at ripping us to shreds—certainly not about to let us pass.

"You taunt me with Kendrick. Kendrick was rich!" cried Raskin as we confronted this barrier. "Damn you, what right has he to own one penny more than me or the meanest of my men?" He flung his arm out at the Rabbits, all of whom looked pretty mean, I thought.

"None, maybe," said Sam, surveying the Rabbits with equanimity while I kept a particular eye on the lively one in front, who had thrust his hands in his pockets in a way that expressed anything but careless indolence.

Raskin stood quivering outside the circle of Dead Rabbits, who had begun to press up around us. Now he flung himself on their backs and clawed his way through.

"I see what you're trying to do," he gasped, thrusting his face at Sam's. "I see it now." He laughed. It was a ghastly sound. "You're trying to make me doubt myself, to make out I'm filled with spite and envy; that I misuse my power. It's very clever, but it won't work. It won't work," he repeated shakily. A Rabbit grabbed his arm and supported him. "You're right, I want the woman. And I'll have her, too. But no, don't worry, not against her will. Why do you think I let her go when I could have kept her? I don't want her against her will. I want her to come to me freely—and she will in time. I know she will. But she must have time." He glared. He was looking at Sam, but I sensed he saw not only Sam but a whole host of enemies, some perhaps wearing his own face.

"I'm not like other men. I'm no good at the things most women like. I know that. I can't be warm and tender. It's not in me. I only know heat—heat and passion—and I frighten women. Yes, and men, too," he laughed, though not as if he was enjoying himself very much. "Even when I was a schoolteacher I frightened people and they shunned me. And then I realized the true reason they despised me and laughed at me. I realized that they hated me not because I was small and odd-looking and had no social graces, but because I was weak and powerless and wouldn't act the part; because I didn't care a damn for their money and fine airs. Yes, I spat at their grand carriages and horses, I made their fine ladies walk in the dust to pass me and laughed in their faces. They'd never seen a really free man before and they hated and feared me, all of them did. And when I realized that it wasn't me they hated but the fact I was free, *free* of envy of their riches, free of the power they had over other men; and when I realized that what they feared was that I would rouse up other men and open their eyes to their slavery—then I came here." He cast an overheated look at the Rabbits. "And ever since, I've carried on my war to free other men from the twin tyrannies of privilege and riches and to make all men truly equal. I've worked selflessly. But you can't know how lonely it's been—you, with your adoring crowds and mindless swilling. To be always reviled, always misunderstood . . . I'd given up on meeting another human being who could truly understand me. And Jenny," he said in an altered voice, "Jenny Hansom wasn't afraid. She didn't despise me. Jenny Hansom carried a loneliness as deep as mine and a hunger as strong. We lived in the same world. We knew each other at once. We were brother and sister— twins. We didn't even need words between us. We were one spirit."

He drew a shuddering breath. It wheezed out of him like the exhalation from a freshly breached tomb. The Rabbit supporting him administered a deferential jab with his elbow. He was straying from the business at hand.

"Yes, but what's all that to you? What can you know of the inner life of a man like me or of a woman like Jenny? What can you know of inner life at all? You're no better than an animal. You eat when you're hungry, sleep when you're tired, and devil take the question that doesn't fill your belly. You think no more about the forces that impel you than the waterfall thinks about gravity. I'd say you were more waterfall than man if I hadn't already called you an animal. Bah! You are like a waterfall: powerful and stupid."

"If it ain't asking too much," said Sam, with the deadly, satiny calm I'd seen on water about to plunge over the lip of a falls, "I'd be curious to know why she left if you two were getting on so famous as you say."

Raskin turned his head away. A shock of his lank hair fell

forward and screened his eyes. The effect, though unintended, was as if he had drawn a cowl up to cover his face. He looked more like a specter than ever. It was startling to realize how much the life that was in him was concentrated in his eyes.

"She pitied me," he said at last, more as if the recollection would give him no peace than as if he actually meant to answer Sam's question.

I don't know how long we stood there, Sam and I, Raskin and the Dead Rabbits. It can't have been as long as it seemed. But only our shadows moved the whole time, shivering uneasily in the suspense. The room was filled with shadows. They hovered around us on all sides, clogging the air and stifling us. Raskin brooded in this cobwebby murk, while the Rabbits snarled and grimaced but seemed to have no more initiative to act than so many cast-off puppets.

Quietly, without a look back and with no one moving to stop us, Sam and I left.

Chapter 23

It was still dark when we emerged into the deserted streets. I filled my lungs gratefully with the night air and looked round at the huddled buildings with as much delight as if they were old friends. In fact, of course, they were anything but, and we hadn't the faintest idea where we were or how to get back to the Shirt Tails. But the bare circumstance of the street's being a byway of this world and not of the next strongly disposed me in its favor.

We wandered aimlessly for a while. Indeed, Sam was so preoccupied that I won't guarantee we wouldn't have strayed from our course if we'd had one. As we didn't, not much was lost, and I was just glad to be putting some distance, in whatever direction, between us and that madman Raskin.

Then, after yet another random turning that failed to show us a landmark, I made out a figure at the end of the block who seemed to stiffen at sight of us and then came on at a half-trot. It was Snooks.

He ran up puffing, stopped, and gazed at us uncertainly, as if not yet sure he had the right man and bear. Then his face lit up like a piece of stained glass with a candle behind it.

"You escaped!" he exclaimed after Sam had slapped him on the back and called him an old son of a gun and a sight for sore eyes and I'd given his face a lick that made it redder than ever.

"Well, I reckon you could say that," said Sam.

"I thought sure you was goners," said Snooks, keeping me off with one arm and wiping his eyes—where I don't remember to have reached—with the other. "I never yet knowed Raskin to let a man off with a warning. He's generally more minded to do for a feller on suspicion than give him a second chance."

Sam grunted.

"I reckon," said Snooks more slowly, seeming to have a hard time getting the words out, "I reckon then this means you won't be staying around long?"

"Depends," said Sam.

"I mean, I reckon you won't be trying to see Handsome Jenny then? On account of it's like Wideawake said, I mean: she's being took care of all right?" He finished this speech staring resolutely at Sam's feet.

"Well, I don't know as I'd say that," said Sam. "No, I don't know as I'd say that at all."

Snooks darted a look at Sam's face. He went back right away to staring at his feet, but seemed to find them marginally more genial subjects now than a moment ago.

"You mean you're still going after her even now you've seen Raskin?"

"Mr. Raskin's a persuasive gent, but I already had my mind made up about Jenny before I went," said Sam.

Snooks gave an ambiguous shiver. He shook his head.

"That Raskin's a mighty bad character," he warned—with considerable relish, I thought. "You know it don't do to cross him. No sirree! Smartest thing would be to push on quick before he gets to feeling sorry how he went so easy on you."

"Well, I don't imagine I can go much lower in the man's esteem, that's a fact," said Sam. "And I won't say I'm exactly looking forward to meeting him again. But that's as may be. So what say we head back. I've a craving to get something as will wash out the taste of talking with him. And then I've a deal of thinking to do."

"About catching up with Handsome Jenny?"

"The very same."

Snooks dashed his hat against his leg.

"Burn me, I knowed it!" We looked at him inquiringly. He was glowing like a lamp. "I never thought no different," he said. "I knowed there was no mistake in Sam Patch!"

Similar self-congratulatory remarks spilling out of him at every step, Snooks led off at a pace that forced even Sam, with his longer legs, to trot now and again to keep up. I lumbered along in my usual place at the rear, looking forward every bit as much as Sam to washing away the taste of the encounter with Raskin—and maybe to tamping it down after with some stew or chicken—and smiling to myself at how little it bothered Snooks that Sam's being mistake-free should conflict with his being smart.

Back at the hide-out we found the rest of the Shirt Tails anxiously waiting up. It must have been a singularly quiet night in the city, in fact, what with Sam and me holding down the Dead Rabbits and the Shirt Tails immobilized while they waited for news. Now they gathered around us exclaiming. Someone thrust on Sam a fresh bottle of St. Croix, which he wasn't long in opening, and Snooks disappeared for a moment, only to return to me, eyes shining, with his arms full of bottles of beer.

"We thought you was done for," swore Cutaway when things had quieted a bit. Old Gooseberry, on one side of him, was dabbing at his eyes with an enormous red bandanna. Bellows, on the other, smacked his lips emotionally. "One of them young-uns as was hanging about said he saw the both of you go off with a bad character. I don't know, somehow the minute we heard that we all of us felt so low we couldn't none of us look another in the eye. Ain't that right, boys? And we was just now figuring how we was going to pay Raskin out for what he done to you, no matter what it took." He thumped the table with his fist.

"It's a fact."

"We was, too."

They exchanged looks, as proud as if it were their post-mortem resolution that had brought us back to life.

"How *did* you get clear, for the matter of that?" asked the Brick.

The hubbub faded. They turned to Sam for the answer. I saw the excitement die from some of the faces as the possibility struck them that had struck Snooks: that their jumping hero had feet of clay.

But Snooks, though himself the first to play host to such a suspicion, could not tolerate that anyone else should entertain it.

"Why, he faced them down, that's how!" he sputtered.

"No!"

The light rekindled in their faces.

"'Course he did! You don't think that rat Raskin and them skunks as call themselves Rabbits could buffalo Sam?" he demanded, rhetorically and somewhat zoologically. "There's no snakes if they could. Why, he just bellied up to Raskin and said, 'Bruin and me has come to pay you a call and straighten out a particular matter as stands between us,' he says. Then he says, 'I reckon you heard about Bruin here, who licked Davy Crockett himself once and wouldn't need but a word of mine to make luck charms of the lot of you,' he says. And he says, 'I reckon you'll want to stay on Bruin's good side, so I'll take it kindly if you'll just hand over Handsome Jenny,' he says. And old Raskin says, he says . . ."

Here Snooks was brought up by the predicament that he didn't in fact know what Raskin had said. Not that he knew what Sam had said either, of course, but at this point a misstep threatened dire consequences to his credibility.

"Why, tell them what he said, Sam," said Snooks offhandedly, turning away to open me another bottle of beer.

Sam gazed moodily into his St. Croix.

"What did he say, Sam?" said Wideawake, speaking for all of them.

Sam took a nip. Thoughtfully, he sloshed the liquor from side to side. The hush of expectancy was so complete that I actually saw men start when he swallowed.

"Does the name Vanderbilt mean anything to you gents?" he said finally.

Vanderbilt. Maybe it did and maybe it didn't.

"'Cause there's a gent by that name as Raskin kept talking about in the same breath with Kendrick, and whoever he is, seems like he's due to get the same treatment someday soon."

Wideawake blanched.

"Not *Cornelius* Vanderbilt? Not him they call the Commodore, as was running Thomas Gibbons' steamship line for him and has just come to town to start up one of his own?"

Sam couldn't rightly say.

Wideawake was appalled.

"Why, him and the mayor's thick as thieves. If Raskin cuts up with him, there won't none of us be safe. A man won't be able to do a lick of business in this town. Them constables will come down on us as if we was all mad dogs like Raskin, and it won't matter a fart in a bag all the favors we done them and what we've worked out. It'd clean be the end of things, is what."

Sam, expressionless, took a swallow of St. Croix. The others, infected with Wideawake's alarm, denounced Raskin as a spoiler and a menace to free trade.

"This time he's gone too far," said the Brick.

"Too far, too far," they said. Cutaway banged the table again with his fist. "We've got to do something," he said. All agreed; but do what?

Here Wideawake displayed the activity and decisiveness that made him such a successful executive. In a commanding voice he detailed Snooks to seek out the Plug Uglies and sent a quiet, watchful fellow named Mops on an embassy to the Daybreak Boys to alert them to the danger and coordinate an arrangement for putting the Vanderbilt house under constant surveillance. The Brick he dispatched to the constabulary on a mission of peculiar sensitivity.

"It's hard," he said, with an anguish that did him credit, "to turn on one of your own, no matter what kind of louse he is. Live and let live is my motto and I hope it always will be. But when a fellow ain't got no more consideration than Raskin to go and do a thing like this as takes away the livelihood of hardworking folks and sets a bad example all round, well, I reckon that for the good of everyone he just has to be stopped, that's all, no matter how it hurts."

So affected was Old Gooseberry by this homily that the red bandanna made another appearance. The others by and large bore up more manfully, braced perhaps by the rare prospect of performing an act of civic virtue.

"While you're about watching the Vanderbilt place," put in Sam, who had taken a keen interest in Wideawake's disposition of forces, "I'd take it kindly if you'd sort of keep an eye peeled for Jenny, too. It's my best guess she'll show up there along with Vanderbilt one of these days."

The Shirt Tails were only too glad to oblige.

Thus began a tense week of waiting. Wideawake, with his new allies the Plug Uglies and the Daybreak Boys, set up an immediate twenty-four-hour vigil. Not so much as a dog was allowed to approach the house without undergoing the closest scrutiny—for the Dead Rabbits were known to be masters of disguise. At the same time, the watchers were discreet. The comings and goings of servants, deliverymen and other occasional callers were monitored with unremitting attention, and these visitors were studied and examined down to their shoe buckles, but all without giving suspicion. The watchers kept to the shadows or patrolled the street, dressed and equipped as icemen, junk dealers, fishmongers, fruit sellers and the like. In fact, a cover operation that vended fancy preserves and imported delicacies did such a brisk trade there and in the surrounding neighborhood that Wideawake—who was not averse to making a dollar however honestly—made plans to continue the business beyond the term of the present need.

"It ain't for nothing his name is Wideawake," Snooks confided to me with a wink, seeming to think this fling at "going legit" one of Wideawake's boldest strokes so far.

But all this care not to be seen puzzled me. Why, I wondered, if he wanted to guard the house, didn't he make as much as possible of its being under his protection?

I found out one evening a few days into the week. Dogs Meat, whom evidently I hadn't smashed up as badly as I'd intended, was back on his feet again, albeit marginally, and had been sent to loiter in the role of a feebleminded person in the vicinity of Vanderbilt's mansion, Wideawake judging that assignment sufficiently sedentary to be within Dogs Meat's still diminished capacities. Dogs Meat returned, boasting of having tripped and beaten with his crutch an urchin who had jostled and picked the pocket of one of the Vanderbilt maids.

"You blamed fool!" Wideawake shouted at him, kicking Dogs Meat's crutch across the room so he fell in a heap. "Do you want them Rabbits to know as something's fishy? Let everybody start doing good deeds and what'll folks think? They'll tumble that things ain't natural, that's what! Then what's the good of the trap? Burn me if I want to play nursemaid to that Vanderbilt for the rest of my days," he said, giving Dogs Meat another kick for emphasis as he tried to crawl to his crutch. "For years that Raskin's been a thorn in my side and we never could catch him because we never knew where he'd show next. Now we've got us a chance to spike him for fair and let the coppers have all the credit, which they won't mind a bit, and you go doing your best to queer it. Why, I ought to knock the rest of your teeth out," he said, "and I would, too, if they wasn't so few and hard to find."

And so the week dragged on. I didn't much care what happened to Vanderbilt or whether they caught Raskin or even whether Jenny ever turned up again (in fact, I wouldn't have minded if she didn't), so I was perhaps the only one who passed the time in anything like a placid frame of mind. But the Shirt Tails were on tenterhooks about Vanderbilt's house and nabbing Raskin, and Sam of course, though maybe no one who didn't know him would have seen it, was anxious for news of Jenny, so the overall mood in our hide-out was decidedly strained. All other activities having been suspended for the duration, nobody had much to do but to await developments, and there really weren't any of these. Each shift of Shirt Tails returning from duty in their various disguises made the same report: no change. Still no sign of Vanderbilt, Jenny, or, so far as anyone could tell, Raskin or the Dead Rabbits either.

Actually, this last was hard to be sure about, considering what a secretive bunch the Rabbits were as a group and the fact that the individual Rabbits didn't tend to mix socially. But at least it was certain that there weren't any new faces about or any obvious skulking going on, and so the Shirt Tails' reports tended to be taken up with the details of the growing ill feeling between them and the inordinately large company of vendors who were already servicing the neighborhood when the Shirt Tails arrived and who seemed to resent the Shirt Tails' presence with a fierceness that even the new competition they represented was hard put to explain.

As for Sam, as I say, he was anxious but didn't show it in any obvious way. Mostly he kept to himself, brooding alone or with Wideawake over a succession of bottles of St. Croix, and except for the fact that he brushed his clothes regularly and took to shaving every other day, there was little sign but his quietness of his disturbed state of mind. I knew him, though, and guessed what he was going through. And one evening late in the week I got confirmation I was right.

"Bruin, you old fussbudget," he said, plumping down with his current bottle in the chair Snooks had just vacated to bring back more beer after losing to me at cribbage for the third game running (which galled him no end, as he'd just taught me the game himself), "you've got some sense and I reckon you know me as well as anybody does. Am I making a damned fool of myself, chasing after a woman as not only said she wouldn't have me but cleared out once when maybe it looked like I was going to make a serious play? Should I just put her behind me—though I'm blamed if I see how to do it!—and get on with my business of jumping, which she has sorely compromised what with all my fretting on her account? I don't know, Bruin. I can't seem to see my way clear to nothing. It's hard to let her go without another try when I figure she don't really know me."

He had out her Paterson note and now he unfolded it as carefully as if it were a dried flower whose petals would crumble away to dust at the least rough handling. He smoothed the paper on the table and stared at it with the old perplexity.

What could I do? It seemed I lost either way. He might never find her, but I had a suspicion that he'd never forget her either, which boded ill, I thought, for his jumping. That was one activity that took a certain singleness of concentration. And if he did find her, what then? I still smarted over the treatment I'd received at Karl's hands on account of Gertrude. If even Gertrude could exercise such power over a man, what was to be expected when a looker like Jenny said, "It's either that bear or me"?

You'll gather I put no great trust in the gentler sex. In my present estate, we were natural enemies.

Still, there seemed only one course to follow, and that was dictated by both policy and love. We had to find her. Sam's hunger for her was eating him alive. I could only hope that if we did find her, she herself would do something to dispel the rose-colored mist that made her loom as large as jumping.

Oh, Sam, poor Sam, carrying such a weight about like a peddler's box, odd words and remembered smiles in this tiny bin, old secret longings in this one. What an irony that you and Raskin, of all people, should be in some ways so much alike. You both sensed in Jenny the very same thing—a spiritual kinship, a gift for understanding. Ah, perhaps it's as you once said: it's the ordinary ones who are luckiest, the ones who find a mate and all the understanding they need in whoever will agree to have them.

My pretty penmate here is doubtless like that. The strange thing is that that doesn't keep her from attracting—attracting me, I mean. Yes, I feel stirrings that embarrass me, stirrings even harder to put down than the querulous rumblings of my stomach. Nature is a cunning adversary that undermines from within. Like responds to like, and my penmate herself being little more than a piece of unimproved nature, she speaks strongly to whatever of the animal remains in me—to my stomach, for instance; to the part of me that would like to come in out of the wet; to those curious stirrings.

Yes, do I seek understanding? whispers a voice. Touch her damp cheek and you touch timeless truth and reality, to say nothing of all the oldest, surest specifics for loneliness. Comfort and solace? She offers me these now on easy terms—a simple exchange for same. If she only knew how I begin to be tempted. What matter really that in some recondite ways she could never understand me? I steal a glance at her as she sits next to me in the drizzle like the helpmate she would like to be. No longer whining for attention, she marks time by my side, allying herself to me by imitation, facing as I face, trying to move no more than I move. And her weapons are not without effect: the warmth of her has gained a foothold in my thoughts.

But that foothold will mark the extent of her advance: no one can build a fire from ashes.

Well, you can probably imagine how it made me feel to hear Sam go on like this. Suffice it to say that I now awaited developments in nearly as distracted a condition as the others. And Snooks, fetching out the cribbage board, played unscrupulously on my weakness. It may give you some idea of the shape I was in if I tell you that I even let him peg my points.

But as it turned out, we never finished the game anyway. Sweating and dredged in the coal dust that was part of his persona as a coal dealer, Old Gooseberry ran in with news that caused everyone to forget everything else.

"He's back! The Commodore's back! I saw him," Old Gooseberry announced breathlessly, clearing a horizontal white stripe on his forehead with a swipe of his sleeve. Consternation. "Yep, he rolled up in a carriage just a bit ago, big as life. I come right away. Run the whole distance."

Interpreting this correctly, someone handed him a bottle and he chugged gratefully.

"Was there any Rabbits about? Anyone else see?" demanded Wideawake, approaching from a corner where in fact he'd been sleeping.

Old Gooseberry wiped his lips.

"Nary a one. Nope, the whole street was empty except for this other coal dealer feller as has been giving me such a rough time, and I don't know what he was doing there at such an hour."

Very likely wondering the same about you, I thought. Then something began to dawn on me.

"Coal dealer feller?" repeated Wideawake, startled. He swore. "These other hucksters as has been about. You ever see if they sell much of anything?"

Old Gooseberry scratched his head.

"About as much as we do is all, I reckon," he said, clearly not seeing the pertinence of the question.

This time Wideawake swore in earnest.

"Brick! Mops! Get the others. Send somebody off to the Plug Uglies and the Daybreak Boys. Tell them Raskin will be making his move tonight or I'm a lizard. Gooseberry!"

Old Gooseberry looked up from spitting in his red bandanna, which he'd brought out for a more systematic wash-up.

"Who's left at the house?"

"Just Cutaway, of ours," said Old Gooseberry.

"Tell him we're coming. And tell him to watch out for them other venders. They's all Rabbits, hang them!"

"Gooseberry!" It was Sam. He'd risen to his feet on hearing Vanderbilt was back. He turned the small folded square that was Jenny's note over and over in his fingers.

"When this Vanderbilt came back, was he—was there anybody with him?"

Old Gooseberry snapped his fingers.

"It clean slipped my mind! I meant to tell you, Sam, honest I did. There was this woman he had with him all right and I thought at first she looked a bit like Jenny, only she was maybe twice as handsome as I ever seen Jenny be and all rigged out in silks and velvet with a fur muff like a bass drum, and the way she moved when the Commodore helped her out of the carriage was sort of like silk and velvet itself, that's how smooth and pretty it was, and I said to myself right away, No, I said, that ain't Sam's Jenny. And then she saw me standing there and looked up"—Old Gooseberry's voice dropped and there crept into it an echo of his original wonder—"and sure enough it was Jenny."

"All right, get along with you," said Wideawake, but not without first shooting Sam a sidelong glance of sympathy.

"We'll fetch her back for you, Sam," he said as Old Gooseberry made posthaste for the door. "We've got her now, so first we'll square Raskin and then we'll nab her for you. Have things right as rain in no time."

But before Sam could reply, there was a commotion at the door and Old Gooseberry came staggering back, supporting Cutaway.

"Hurry!" Cutaway gasped, flailing the arm that wasn't around Old Gooseberry. He brought it back down for a minute to wipe the blood that streamed into his eye from a nasty gash in his scalp. "Raskin! Him and the Rabbits is firing the house!"

Chapter 24

We ran like the devil. Horses reared as we dashed in front of them, but we ran on, as deaf to the curses of the drivers as to the outraged complaints of the dogs and pigs we scattered or sent flying as we raced along. Wideawake and Sam set the pace, bowling over anyone and anything too slow to get out of the way. The rest of us followed, streaming by under the noses of astonished horses and drivers and leaping over prostrate bodies. I brought up the rear, as usual, with Snooks puffing away at my side, his legs pumping and his bright face glowing redder than ever.

I was the first to smell it—an acrid odor, ominously different from the smoke from chimneys. I wrinkled my nose and woofed, and in a minute the others caught the scent and redoubled their efforts. We fairly flew along. More joined us. The streets began to fill with people running to the fire. Smoke was heavy in the air now and the night resounded to shouts and alarms.

Then we turned a corner and saw an orange glow pulsing wickedly at the end of the street. A last burst of speed brought us gasping to the edge of the gathering crowd.

I saw in a minute that there was no hope of saving the house. Standing alone, a stately but strangely regimented-looking edifice of dark stone, it was built narrow in front and with sides extending far back free of porches or other projections—like a soldier with his arms at his sides, expecting to be joined soon by his fellows. It was a rendezvous he was not destined to keep. The whole bottom story was filled with flames. The Rabbits had done their work well. The upper two stories sat on a cushion of flame, like a pot on a stove. The ground floor windows must have been broken in all at once, from the look of things, and bottles of kerosene or some such thrown through into the rooms.

Then I saw figures milling about close in, surrounding the house, whom at first I took for fire fighters. But no: they were Rabbits. Even as I watched, one then another flung through the gaping windows objects that gleamed in the light like glass. Loud muffled "crumps" sounded from inside the stricken house and new gouts of oily smoke and flame burst from its broken sides.

Wideawake saw, too, and cursed the Rabbits with a fury that would have singed the fur on any of them within earshot.

"The house is a goner. But where in hell and tarnation is the companies? They ought to be here by now. And where in hell is the other boys?"

He scanned the crowd anxiously. Some few scuffles there were as here and there an outraged bystander threw himself on the Rabbits in isolated attempts to halt the destruction. These good citizens were dealt with summarily by the defending Rabbits, who I saw now wielded bats and pipes, and more than one of the attackers were swiftly struck down and didn't get up while I watched. But there seemed no organized resistance. The Rabbits maintained their perimeter about the house almost unchallenged, the menace of the clubs holding the crowd at bay.

I glanced at Sam. The firelight gleamed on the brass buttons of his sailor jacket and turned his face into a drawn mask of planes and shadows. He had no eyes for the Rabbits, but gazed above the choker of fire ringing the bottom story to the darker windows higher up. These, I saw to my horror, were filled with frantically waving people, their cries lost in the general tumult and the roar of the fire.

"There's nothing for it," said Wideawake, taking in the panic-stricken figures without surprise and returning his attention to the Rabbits. "We're going to have to go on in there and bust up them Rabbits so the companies can follow." I heard the distant blast of a trumpet; then another, closer. Wideawake lifted his head. "That's them, boys," he said as we clustered around him. "And I expect the Plug Uglies and the rest will be along too, soon enough. All right," he shouted, his eyes flashing at everyone who might hear the sound of his voice. He pointed dramatically. "Grab what's handy and let's smash them Rabbits!"

Bellows broke a stave from the side of a nearby cart. The others followed suit or pried up stones from the street and the little group advanced. Some of the crowd joined in, so that Wideawake soon had a tidy following.

But Sam hung back, and so I hung back with him.

"Do you see her, Bruin? Burn me, if I just knew what room she was in . . . !" He dashed off, searching first one side of the house, then the other, and I followed.

But none of the faces we saw looked like Jenny's. Though most of the figures I could make out in the windows were women, most of them seemed to be servants. As I watched, one of these, a large woman in mobcap and apron whose shrieks had been audible even above the rest of the noise, began clawing her way out of the second-story window where she and three other women were clustered. The others tried to restrain her, but she shook them off and threw over the sill a meaty leg encased in white drawers. As the crowd cried out, she followed with the other leg and hung shrieking from the sill, the flames licking her feet, her face red as an apple in the firelight. A few moments she hung there screaming and kicking as the other women tried to drag her back inside. Then with a last wail of terror she lost her hold and dropped like a sack of potatoes to the ground, where she lay senseless.

Her fall wrung a great cry from the crowd, which surged forward. But they were stopped first by the wrought-iron fence about the yard and second by the watchful Rabbits behind, whose truncheons were not idle when there were arms and heads to be bashed.

I began to have a decided itch to rend and tear. A growl built in my throat and welled up of its own accord. I glanced hopefully at Sam, but he only gave a cry and flung off again around the front of the house. I lumbered after, suppressing my impatience and dribbling saliva where my lip was curled.

Wideawake meanwhile had had no better success than the crowd at large in forcing the front gate. Already the conflagration had grown so that a dull light began to be visible behind the heads of the increasingly frantic occupants of the house. Figures were now to be seen at windows on the third floor, having fled there from the growing heat on the second. Their cries were even more pitiable than before, but the swelling roar of the fire still all but swallowed them up, and the heat was now so intense that I guessed it must be making even the Rabbits uncomfortable inside the gate. If something were not done soon, I thought, there would be only the Rabbits to attend to.

Thrown back from the gate, the exhausted Shirt Tails flung themselves on the ground near where Sam and I stopped. Wideawake's face was smudged with soot from the great flakes of it that were flying about, and he wore a large smear of blood on one cheekbone. He looked up and saw Sam.

Just then there was a stir in the crowd. It parted with a shout to admit a group of perhaps thirty men in leather hats and red flannel shirts.

"Make way! Make way!" they cried. Another group, similarly attired, arrived. This time, though, there was no nonsense. While men from the first company tapped a hydrant across the street, the two captains conferred briefly. Then the second group broke away and hauled their engine around to the side.

Wideawake loomed next to us.

"It's no good," he panted wearily, watching the firemen. "Them Rabbits will never let them in close enough." Wincing, he removed his hat. The crown was crushed in. As he meditatively pushed it out again, a trickle of blood ran down from under his hair.

Fireman shouldered past us bearing a hose. Other firemen and helpers from the crowd manned the two arms of the fire engine pump and water began to inflate the hose and to spray from the joints as the men ran. They were headed for the front gate.

"Damn them Rabbits to hell!" said Wideawake, foreseeing the result. "Come on, boys, let's lend a hand! We'll do her this time! You coming, Sam?"

"I'll be along in a bit," said Sam, still searching the windows. Two more groups of firemen ran by with ladders.

Wideawake clapped his hat on again.

"Well, you'd best not keep off too long."

The men with the hose had indeed been halted at the gate as Wideawake had foreseen. I saw the man in the lead struck down and the heavy brass nozzle of the hose knocked from his grasp. Fists flew, and then Wideawake and the Shirt Tails struck, their impetus driving the Rabbits back for the first time inside the gate. Quickly the firemen followed. Leaving the fighting to the Shirt Tails and their helpers, the firemen played the hose on the lower windows. One of the groups with a ladder followed, but the Rabbits wrested the ladder away from them and soon the firemen had their hands full just defending themselves. The other ladder party came at the fence from the side. They managed to pull down a section, but as often as they tried to push through the breach, the Rabbits beat them back. Similar battles raged at other points around the house as additional incoming fire companies tried to fight their way to the fire. Meanwhile, over the cursing and shouting, the blast of trumpets and the roar of the blaze, came a constant high-pitched keening—the despairing cries of those inside.

Suddenly I saw Sam stiffen. He ran up to the fence.

"Raskin!" he cried. "Have you gone plumb crazy?"

There, a short ways across the fence, was Flavius Raskin, directing the battle from inside a small knot of vigilant Rabbits.

There came a thunderous crash from the house. We turned in time to see huge tongues of flame leap from first and second floor windows at the front corner of the house. People at windows immediately above on the third floor fled with cries of dismay. The floor below in that corner had collapsed.

But we saw something else. Everyone in the house had sought safety on the third floor by now, and people waved and cried out from every window. But now at the other front corner appeared a face that struck a chill in me despite the heat of the fire: it was Jenny.

Sam reeled as if he'd been clubbed. His arms flew up. He shouted. But smoke billowed from the window, half obscuring her. She coughed into a handkerchief she held over her nose and mouth. I knew she couldn't see us.

Face contorted, Sam turned back to Raskin. He struggled to speak but could not. The most he could do was point.

As if he couldn't help himself, Raskin followed the line of Sam's arm to the house, his handiwork. I even think he saw it for a moment through Sam's eyes. He seemed to blanch.

But then a new face joined Jenny's at the window, a scowling face with a high forehead and framed with bushy whiskers at the sides. I soon saw that it belonged with a wide pair of shoulders to a vigorous-looking man in his mid-thirties.

Raskin came to himself with a jerk. He darted one glance at Sam and it was potent with malice. In a frenzy he sprang from his circle of bodyguards. Felling a fireman with a single blow of his thin arm, he seized the fallen man's ax and rushed on the group with the hose. Plunging into their midst, he swung the ax high and severed the hose.

"Well, that about tears it then," said Sam with unnatural calm. His own frenzy was gone. Suddenly cool and purposeful, he reminded me now of the way he was before a jump.

"I'll need your help, old friend. I need to bust through them Rabbits and I'm not fussy how I do it."

I roared with relief. But still he didn't start. He searched the ground. A segment of wrought-iron fence lying nearby caught his eye. He pounced on it and picked it up, hefting it with satisfaction. Without another word we were off.

The surviving firemen and Shirt Tails had been forced back outside the gate again, where they were still locked with the Rabbits in pitched battle. Sam shouted at our side to stand clear, and when I seconded his shout with a full-throated roar of my own, they did—with a jump. The Rabbits were taken by surprise and Sam hit them before they recovered, crashing into them with the segment of fence. Four Rabbits went down under the bars of wrought iron. Dropping the fence, Sam skipped nimbly over it and the four squirming bodies underneath and I followed, less nimbly and unable to resist dawdling a bit on the chests of the fallen Rabbits.

But Sam needed someone to cover his flanks. Already Rabbits inside the gate were converging to stop him. He ducked a blow from a lead pipe that would have made a fine spray of his brains, popped back up and sent a fist into his assailant's throat, then spun about just in time to plant his foot in the groin of a Rabbit coming at him from the other side.

I bellowed and charged. Taking advantage of the distraction, Sam ducked down again and ripped the long coat from the prostrate form with the sore throat. Puddles of water were everywhere from the hose. Sam sloshed the coat in one of these and put it on, narrowly missing being cold-cocked while his arms were tangled in the sleeves—but I wrenched the attacker's arm from its socket in the nick of time and then smashed his face for good measure.

We were through. I reared up to my full height and roared a challenge to any and all Rabbits foolhardy enough to come at me. There were no takers. Appalled, they hung back. I roared again with triumph as help began to pour through the gate.

The fight went out of the Rabbits in that moment. They fell

back, no longer trying to stop help from getting through to the house. Briefly I thought I heard Raskin screaming to his men to stand firm. But they were no longer his to command. They thought now only of their own safety—but too late. They had done too much and stayed too long. The crowd pressed forward like a mighty beast and there was murder in its face. Men streamed through the gate behind the firemen, pulling down the frantic Rabbits with no more regard for their flailing clubs and pipes than if these were willow wands. I saw Raskin drop like a rag, felled by a furious blow from the heavy brass nozzle of a severed hose.

I turned away and looked for Sam—but I was only in time to see the back of the long coat he now wore disappear into the cloud of black smoke that poured from the door of the house. I roared in consternation and ran after him. But I was unable to follow. Heat blasted through the doorway. Blinded and choking, I felt my fur crinkle in that furnace breath and I fell back, sending a terrified wail into the inferno after Sam. The only reply was a crash of falling masonry.

Firemen now had ladders against the walls and were pulling people from the windows and bringing them down while the hoses played constant streams in at the flames below. But the work went so slowly! Few of those at the windows could manage the ladders by themselves; too many needed carrying. And all the while the fire seemed only to wax stronger despite the hoses, the flames lunging fierce as ever into the night air, licking at the ladders, and only acknowledging the puny streams of water by spitting back at them billowing clouds of steam.

I ran distracted back and forth in front of the dying building, howling and roaring, throwing myself again and again at the fatal doorway only to have to recoil each time in despair. The heat was like a great hand, pushing me back. Where was my Sam? I searched the windows with desperate eyes. Once full of people, the windows were emptier now. Some few had been rescued, but more had succumbed to the smoke and heat and lay insensible or dead inside. Even as I looked, the dress of a woman being carried down began to smolder. Elsewhere, too, the firemen were driven back, the flames too intense now to attempt the ladders.

Then my heart gave a leap, and a roar of gladness and terror burst from my lips. There was Sam! His coat steaming about his shoulders, he stood at a window sill bearing in his arms a limp figure.

He shouted, and that beloved voice I'd heard carry so many times over the roar of waterfalls carried now over the roar of the flames. The firemen milled uncertainly. I gnashed my teeth and sped to the spot.

Sam shouted again and motioned with the figure. A tarp! He wanted a tarp! Below, men ran about and soon one was brought. Hoses were concentrated on the seething windows directly beneath Sam, while men formed up around the edges of the tarp and drew it taut. Sam flung his burden clear of the flames. The figure, a woman—not Jenny, I saw—sailed out into the night air, her dress streaming, and bounced on her back in the tarp. The crowd gave a cry like none I'd ever heard.

But Sam had already vanished again. He reappeared, in his arms another limp figure, another woman, this one with dark hair. He readied himself, the vapors rising from his coat looking more like smoke now than steam, and pitched the woman to safety. This time when he'd done he motioned the firemen to train their hoses on him, and he stood there a moment while they soaked him and his coat again from head to foot. I whined to see, for I knew then that he meant to stay in the burning house whether he found Jenny or not, till he'd rescued everyone he could find.

Burying his lower face in the crook of his arm, he plunged back inside. Everyone watching groaned. Long minutes passed in breathless suspense, every eye trained on the empty windows. Coughing and wiping their faces, the firemen on the tarp stumbled back from the heat.

When Sam reappeared this time, he was at the window where we'd seen Jenny. Through the smoke I saw him stagger as he struggled to raise yet another body. I recognized the broad shoulders of the man whose sudden appearance had maddened Raskin. As Sam wrestled with his weight, the man stirred and pushed himself up. An arm around Sam, he managed to stand. The firemen ran over and readied themselves below, but he was refusing to jump. I roared in frustration as I watched precious seconds lost. Sam was plainly all but done in. Leave him! I cried, or tried to.

The man—the crowd recognized him: he was Vanderbilt—pushed free of Sam. He waved his arms heatedly. They argued, then seemed to reach some agreement. Both withdrew once more into the choking depths of the house.

They reappeared together at the topmost window of the blazing building and thrust their heads out, coughing and trying to rid their lungs of smoke as the firemen reassembled underneath. Then Sam lifted up a small bundle and swung it out through the smoke. The child, unconscious, turned in the air and landed, as Sam had intended, on its back in the tarp.

Vanderbilt held another child. He readied himself to throw it to safety but stood at the last unable to do so. Sam took the small figure from him. Soon this child sailed through the air just as the other had done, turning slowly with as practiced-looking a style, and landed flat and safe in the tarp.

With a hideous, shattering crash, the side wall to the left buckled and collapsed, tumbling like flaming surf out across the ground. No one was hurt, for everyone stood in front watching the rescue, but the firemen began herding everyone back. Only the men about the tarp, reinforced now to a double thickness, kept heroically to their posts. The captain whose company had been the first to arrive and who seemed in charge beckoned peremptorily to Sam and Vanderbilt and ordered them through a speaking trumpet to jump.

But first there was another rescue to make—for Sam, the most important of all. Together he and Vanderbilt raised her up. The lurid firelight gleamed red on the rich satin bodice of her dress and on the even richer gold of her hair.

Impatiently, Sam took Jenny to himself and motioned Vanderbilt to jump. Vanderbilt looked down. A freak of the breeze blew the smoke away and I saw his scowl. He hesitated, and indeed who could blame him? There on the ground far below, probably shimmering in the heat and often obscured altogether by intervening clouds of smoke and flame, was a terrifyingly small target which he had to hit just right or he might almost as well miss it. The sight was enough to chill the heart of anyone who wasn't a practiced jumper, and I guessed that Vanderbilt was wondering if it wouldn't be his last.

And then Sam did something that bewildered the crowd but which I understood in an instant, though I marveled that he did it. Still supporting Jenny with one arm, with the other he grabbed Vanderbilt by the collar and hauled him back. He tumbled out of sight. As he rose again, some of his curses reaching us even through the maelstrom of the fire, Sam helped him straighten, then let go and struck him a mighty blow on the jaw. Swiftly lowering Jenny, he scooped up the fallen man, turned, and pitched him out the window, where all unconscious he described precisely the same rotation in midair as had the children, before landing as neatly as they had on his back in the center of the tarp.

Scarcely had the quicker wits among the crowd comprehended when Sam ducked and rose again with Jenny. Sparks blew past his shoulders as he stood a moment in the window, Jenny in his arms. Then, with indescribable tenderness and skill, he lofted her into space. So richly clothed, so beautiful and still was she as she fell in that now-familiar measured turn, that she seemed a princess or some other great lady laid out in state, I thought, until she struck the tarp and bounced, suddenly disheveled, and the spell was broken.

Now Sam alone was left. His name was on every lip, burned in every hoarse throat, as the watchers cried out to him to jump.

Casting off the scorched and reeking remains of the long coat, he sprang to the windowsill and crouched there in his familiar sailor jacket. One moment he gathered himself, half-engulfed in smoke, as upward-rushing showers of sparks streamed past and the flames stretched out to reach him. One moment only did he take, as the crowd, anticipating, pressed forward into the heat as if to catch him in its arms.

Then, in his usual businesslike way, he jumped.

Chapter 25

Jenny came home with us. Wideawake turned up a wagon and a driver only too glad to carry Sam Patch "and his lady," and escorted by noisy admirers we returned to the hide-out in a regular cavalcade. I filed along in my usual place on these occasions—behind—in my mouth the taste, not entirely metaphorical, of dust and ashes. Sam didn't have a thought for me, no more than he had had that other time on the boat when he first met her again. I was better prepared for it this time, of course, but it's not a thing you ever get entirely used to—being superseded, I mean. Even Snooks, though he never left my side, couldn't take his eyes from Jenny and her spoiled finery. "She sure is a looker, ain't she?" he whispered several times in awed tones. I noticed that a relative quiet seemed to have descended on the others as well. They were nowhere near as boisterous as they had a right to be. I even saw Cutaway, who'd refused to be left behind in the race back to Vanderbilt's, tap Old Gooseberry on the arm and borrow his red bandanna, which Old Gooseberry, having moistened it copiously and scrubbed up in the usual way, was about to replace in his pocket.

Sam only had eyes for Jenny. All the way back people thrust bottles on him, but his swallows were as perfunctory as politeness would allow. He was fully occupied with Jenny, attending her as closely as anyone could without actually touching her.

That he never did. No, he left her most scrupulously alone

once she recovered herself enough to sit without his support. I could guess what this restraint cost him, but it wasn't all self-imposed: in part it stemmed from a want of encouragement. As Jenny rode there beside him, though she slumped a little from weariness there was a tension in the way she held herself, and a look almost of bitterness in her face, that I think didn't escape Sam. Now and again she was aware of him studying her and she'd look up and reassure him with a quick smile. But it was a smile with a bitter aftertaste, with a twist of what looked like pain at the corners. I don't know which was worse for Sam: to see her sit there on the hard seat next to him, so close physically and yet so far away in her thoughts, or to see when she did look at him the thinness of that smile.

We reached the hide-out—something of a misnomer now really—and Sam jumped down and helped her alight. The Shirt Tails bustled on ahead to ready things or stood around grinning like wedding guests when the groom prepares to take the bride off to her new home. Still holding her hand, Sam paused before leading her in.

"I reckon you've already figured out it's no accident, my being here, Jenny. Nope, I've been here a while now, looking high and low for you. That's a fact. But something as maybe needs saying . . ."—he broke off and gave her so serious a look that she was startled. "Well," he said, more gently, "this here's where I've been staying, and so this here's where I brought you, figuring you could maybe use a place to stay too and rest up. But there's nothing more in it than that. I ain't keeping you here. If there's some place you'd rather be . . . well—" He released her hand. "Only I will say this. I would take it kindly if you was to bide here a day or two anyways. I reckon it'd mean a lot to me."

This speech clearly took her by surprise. I saw a light of gratitude flicker in her eyes, and the look she followed it with was the kindest he'd had from her yet. But then as he finished, a weight seemed to descend on her again, and she said, sounding tired:

"That's all right, Sam. You were right. I don't have anyplace to go. Thank you for bringing me. Of course I'll stay as long as you like. And thank you for—everything else."

But this last sounded like an afterthought, as if the "everything else" didn't really amount to much.

So she stayed with us at the Shirt Tails', and the original day or two quietly lengthened itself into weeks. I realized with sinking spirits that I had never seen Sam so happy. Hardly drinking or roistering at all, he seemed to soak up contentment just from existing; his happiness, I saw, fed itself just on Jenny's being there. Even his thoughts seemed to go no further than the fullness of the moment. He lived in an eternal present while Jenny was there, an endless springtime with a warm sun benignly fixed overhead.

And Jenny was not insensible to this. During those first few days she showed little change and drifted about listlessly, agreeing to all Sam's suggestions, even anticipating him, accompanying him on walks whenever he invited her, ever obedient to his wishes, express or implied. But she seemed enervated, often scarcely aware of where she was. That quality of remoteness she had, that fascinated even as it chilled, had never been more pronounced. The Shirt Tails spoke in whispers around her, and if called on to address her directly were often so overawed as to find themselves speechless.

Gradually, though, she thawed as the days passed and Sam's attentions never faltered. But what masterfully orchestrated attentions they were. Though no one could know to guard against the mistake better than I, I found that once again I had underestimated Sam. Instead of oppressing her with too much solicitude, he left her much of the time to herself. He never treated her as his guest or his ward or hinted at any claim he thought he had on her. At any time, had she chosen to tell him she was leaving, I believe that Sam, though crushed to an extent perhaps only I could guess, would have been as unruffled and friendly as he ever was on the casual-seeming occasions they were together.

Meanwhile, though, he unfolded himself to her. There, seeing the way he was with the Shirt Tails, and I must say, with precious little else to do, she could begin to take his measure—which of course was Sam's object. Not that he ever talked about himself. If anything, these days he avoided that subject. Instead, with sound instinct and love and perhaps untold invisible labor, he built around the both of them a magical present, and even Jenny's remoteness wasn't proof against it.

And one day she laughed. It was like a beam of sunlight breaking through after a long siege of overcast.

The Shirt Tails were quick to note the change, as quick as animals sensing a shift in the wind. And if they registered the change just as subliminally, they also responded with just the same naturalness. Some few token efforts they had made already to improve their appearance. Now, though, they fairly bloomed, ever exhibiting some new sartorial wonder as the reflected effulgence of Sam's happiness spread and took hold. They began brushing their clothes and sporting bright new neckerchiefs, which they even laundered and changed from time to time, not even excepting Old Gooseberry, who with much fanfare washed his red bandanna. Young Cutaway went so far as to acquire a new coat, which he wore with also new stock at the neck and a dickey, the high starched points of which were forever threatening to blind him and quite prevented him from turning his head.

Even Wideawake one day, glaring dangerously at everyone, showed up in a new hat.

And the weather was indeed changing. The clouds were scattered and breaking up. Jenny laughed often now—with Sam, with the Shirt Tails, sometimes even quietly to herself as she bustled about humming and straightening up. Perhaps for want of much other occupation or perhaps from some deeper reason that chose this way to express itself, she had taken to putting the hide-out in order. Now if an unwary Shirt Tail turned his back on his deck of cards or his bottle, he was apt to find it missing when he wanted it again and to have to go fetch it from the cabinet where everyone soon learned these things were to be kept. Stray boots, hats, and other pieces of clothing had a way of disappearing too, only to turn up, the boots placed neatly together, the other articles carefully folded or otherwise arranged, at the owner's pallet, also mysteriously straightened.

The Shirt Tails seemed dazed. Their own home had become strange to them, albeit in the most delicious way. It had been invaded and taken over by an alien influence, and they were filled with wonder. Small, utterly familiar objects—pipes, tobacco, matches—gained new interest and stature from appearing together now in subtly significant arrangements. Nails and pegs were shifted to new locations on the walls, with surprising results. Then one day all these changes were capped. Returning in a body from some sortie or other and hearing loud cries from the hide-out, a group of Shirt Tails burst in to find Bellows pointing speechless with astonishment at a pair of new curtains, which Jenny had been working on secretly and had hung while they were away.

The hide-out was transformed. Jenny had turned it from a cluttered sty to a cross between a clean barracks and a home, imbuing it in the process with an indefinable femininity. The Shirt

Tails were transformed too. From dirty, foulmouthed roughnecks they had gone to being relatively clean roughnecks who tried to watch their language. I noticed too that they had done an about-face in another respect. The Shirt Tails who had used to be tongue-tied with Jenny now talked with her freely (Cutaway, Old Gooseberry, Snooks), while the Shirt Tails who didn't use to be so overawed (the Brick, Wideawake) seemed to suffer now from a strange new constraint.

For Jenny was transformed too, and had never been so beautiful. Sam and the Shirt Tails had found other clothes for her, and the fine dress she'd come in from Vanderbilt was put away. She went about now dressed simply and plainly, her golden hair her only ornament, and with this change and the thaw in her manner her beauty was even more heartrending. As I overhead Cutaway put it to Mops, it made a man ache just to see her.

That October we spent with the Shirt Tails passed like a fairy tale time for everyone. For the Shirt Tails it was Snow White and the Dwarfs. For Sam, the prince whose happiness underpinned everyone else's, it was Cinderella. And for me, in my ambivalence and self-pity, it was Beauty and the Beast all over, except that I looked for no redemption at the end of the tale.

For in my way I was more tormented by Jenny's beauty than any. The brighter it grew, the more I suffered. Though Sam was as good to me as ever, I could see there was no hope of my competing with Jenny. I had been supplanted in his affections, or if not precisely supplanted, still a new rank had been created above mine and Jenny installed to fill it. To make matters worse, I was finding myself as smitten with her as any of the Shirt Tails. Thus I was robbed even of the consolation of disliking my rival. I could only compare myself to her in point of what I had to offer, and slink away back into my psychic corner despairing, demoralized, and filled with self-loathing.

Then one afternoon late in the month something happened that put a new face on things. I was killing time with Snooks in a desultory game of cribbage while I tried to drown my sorrows in beer—no very easy task for a bear. Jenny, all crisp and neat and smelling of lavender, was passing and paused to watch our game.

"For shame!" she said suddenly, rapping Snooks on the head with her feather duster. "You cheated. That's *two* for a pair and *four* for two fifteens. You pegged ten."

Snooks made a confused show of reviewing his cards. She dusted the shiny red top of his head.

"You mustn't cheat Bruin, you know. He's Sam's friend."

Snooks' eyes widened and he opened his mouth to protest. He'd never looked at it in that light. I sat up straighter.

"You should be especially nice to him, poor bear. He's been through such a lot."

My heart thumped and a lump formed in my throat. She came over to me, slowly reached out a tentative hand and scratched my head. It was an overture. Her touch, so much lighter than Sam's, was not in the least familiar or condescending. Can it be that she knows? I wondered. Suddenly my sorrows, so resistant to drowning, melted under her slim fingers and were gone. Tears welled from my eyes. I was hers to do with as she liked from that moment. I felt no fear, could no longer hold out against her. In abject love and gratitude I thrust my nose up against her wrist and licked her hand.

"Oh Bruin, you seem a very good bear," she said, fondly folding my head in her arms and drawing it to her breast. I was in heaven.

She gave me a last squeeze and a pat.

"There. Now don't you be sad," she said, whisking me on the nose with the feather duster.

Snooks and I followed her with our eyes. When she was gone, we both let our breath out together.

Snooks didn't win again the rest of the day.

Chapter 26

But I wouldn't have you think I spent all my time playing cribbage and mooning about. October was a busy month for the Shirt Tails. The polls would open in early November, and what with their stanch Jacksonian sentiments and their availability at all hours for any sort of work, the Shirt Tails were in much demand to help the local Jackson Committees. There were parades and rallies to drum up attendance for, and dinners and tree plantings—and while Sam declined here to take part in anything so political, just as he had in Paterson, he considered that whether or not I chose to do so was a matter between me and my conscience.

Consequently, wearing a hickory sprig wired to one ear, I went about a good deal with the Shirt Tails to these sorts of events, particularly the barbecues. In fact, my dedication was such that I seldom missed any event where food was served. And I paid my way, too. Not only was I the famous Bruin, Sam Patch's bear, and thus a drawing card, but I soon learned to pitch in and win hearts and minds in the debates. If anyone said Adams went about like a king, spending the people's money on expensive ivory chessmen and similar royal extravagances, I roared my proletarian outrage. And if some troublemaker spoke up and charged Jackson with being an incompetent, illiterate military chieftain, I roared again similarly. Eventually it struck me that so long as I roared at the right times it didn't much matter that I knew what I was roaring about, and I'm afraid that after I realized that, I gave most of my attention over to eating. But I did still manage to comment appropriately most of the time, albeit occasionally with my mouth full, and I consider I gave fair value.

But even with my attention divided, I picked up quite an earful about the two candidates.

Jackson, I learned, was the paramour of an adulteress. Not that anyone accused him of any improprieties before he married Rachel, but alas, in 1791 when he did marry her, Rachel was herself already married to one Lewis Robards, who didn't get around to suing for divorce (on grounds of adultery) until two years later.

The Jacksonians rebutted this telling attack on Jackson's qualifications for office by explaining that it was all a mistake and could have happened to anyone. They then counterattacked in the same vein by unmasking Adams as a procurer who, when a minister to Russia, had delivered up a beautiful American virgin to a life of shame in order to gratify the lust of a Russian aristocrat.

Adams' aristocratic affinities let him in for a number of shrewd blows, in fact. As I munched roast ox I was edified to learn that he had spent a vast sum equipping the East Room of the White House with such trappings of decadence as a billiard table and soda water, and that Henry Clay, his secretary of state, was no better and was an Anglophile besides, even going so far as to use English writing paper in the State Department, along with English penknives and English sealing wax.

To this a minion of the Adams-Clay Coalition responded that Adams was at any rate a statesman of proven brilliance, who had served with distinction as minister to Russia and as secretary of state before becoming president, whereas Thomas Jefferson himself had said of Jackson that he had very little respect for law or Constitution and had a temper that made him a dangerous man. In support of this last we were reminded how in his Florida campaign he had cold-bloodedly executed six militiamen who against his orders had left camp to go home when their term of enlistment was up, though one of the men was a preacher with nine children who had later returned to clear himself.

Unruffled, a speaker for Jackson acknowledged the justice of the charge and said that he was not in a position to dispute it when it was a matter of such public record that Jackson, as commander of the American forces at the battle of New Orleans, had also coolly and deliberately put to death upward of fifteen-hundred British troops on the 8th of January, 1815, for no other offense than that they wished to sup in the city that night.

And so it went, back and forth, while I sat there stuffing myself with roast this and roast that, occasionally roaring an appropriate sentiment, and congratulating myself on being so congenially placed to familiarize myself with the issues.

By the time November rolled around and the polls finally opened, the city was in an unbearable pitch of excitement and I had gained fifty pounds. The rallies and barbecues over, I stayed at the hide-out more now while the Shirt Tails threw themselves into the really strenuous end of the electioneering. There were parades to organize and flags and bunting to put up and wagonloads of floaters to conduct to the polls. These floaters were issued the names of dead men, paid fifty cents a day and expenses plus all they could drink, and trundled about for the three days of voting to as many polls as they could reach. At each they cast their proxies for the dead citizens whose names they had borrowed and clambered with or without help back into the wagons. Snooks boasted to me afterwards that he had voted for Jackson twenty-eight times and each time drunk a pint of beer.

There were also ballots to be handed out. Each party had its own, and nothing persuaded a reluctant citizen to accept the Jackson ticket like the urgings of three or four Shirt Tails armed with stout hickory clubs. Sometimes these arguments were offset to some extent by the blandishments of the Plug Uglies, who were hawking ballots for Adams, and then invariably a lively discussion ensued. The citizen, if he was lucky enough to be able to, generally took this opportunity to crawl away unnoticed.

On the last day of voting, both sides were making their final push, and except for Sam, Jenny, and me the hide-out was deserted. Sam, secretive to the last about his political leanings, had gone out to the polls with Jenny that morning, refusing all offers of transportation and publicity from the Shirt Tails. Now, despite the election parties in every tavern, he was laying low again, but only partly, I think, to safeguard his political neutrality. It was one of the few times he and Jenny had had the place to themselves.

That day, even allowing for its emptiness, the hide-out seemed unusually still. Or maybe "still" isn't just the right word. For while things were certainly quiet enough, there was a strange tension in the air.

Sam sat by the window, reading a newspaper. Jenny was straightening this and that at the other end of the room. She was like a deer, I thought, watching her: her every move had that same daintiness and almost eerie grace. And like a deer she paused often, her hand resting absently on some article she had moved a tiny bit to set right. She seemed to drift away in these pauses and to become somehow more beautiful as she stood there, abstracted and all unconscious of herself. It felt like spying to watch her then. The mundane preoccupations and busyness that normally clothe us slipped away like a robe and left her standing there exposed in herself, vastly more naked than if her dress had fallen from her shoulders into a pile about her feet. And yet I could no more not watch than Sam, whose eyes drank her in over the top of the newspaper and in whose face, as unguarded as hers at such times, was a look of hunger amounting to pain.

Nor were we the only dealers in stolen glances. She stole plenty at him, too, in her more bustling moments, and even quick as they were, each seemed to linger like a caress.

Somehow it came about that her straightening brought her over by Sam. She adjusted a stolen picture in a stolen frame on the wall behind him, then reached up to run a finger over the top border, checking for dust. The other hand she laid carelessly on the back of Sam's chair.

Setting his paper down on his lap, he turned toward her and covered that hand with his.

Neither spoke. At length she tilted her head and, smiling ever so slightly, seemed to draw away. Her arm extended and then I saw that her fingers were closed about his hand. She drew him after her, up out of his chair, the newspaper rustling to the floor. He followed her. She drew him on, as much by her smile as by the gentle pressure of her fingers, and led him thus through the doorway into her room.

Later I heard them talking. The door opened and Sam came out, looking upset. His eyes brushed by me without taking me in. He turned around.

"I don't understand you. I clean don't understand you, Jenny. If you were ready to stay with me before, why won't you stay now? It beats anything, what you say. We get along a hundred times better than back then after the fire. Why should that go *against* me? There's no making sense of it."

Jenny came in, hands behind her back, wrestling with a last button.

"Oh Sam," she laughed with a gaiety that only just failed to be convincing. "Hush. Why don't you sit down. Well, then help me with this button, if you won't do anything else for me.

"It makes perfect sense," she said, as grudgingly he did this, his mind on other things. "Only maybe I can't explain it very well."

"Stay with me, Jenny," said Sam.

She let him hold her. They kissed. Then gently she freed herself.

"I would, Sam. I would if I could. It's because I already . . . care for you so much now that I can't. Please try to understand."

"Damn it, that's what I'm blamed if I understand!" burst out Sam—reasonably enough, it seemed to me.

Jenny's hands slid down from Sam's shoulders to rest on his chest. She seemed to be holding him away, though there was no real force in the gesture, and as if to compensate him for any there might have been, she laid her head on his shoulder. The fingers of one hand toyed with a button on his jacket.

"No," she said softly, "I suppose you couldn't." She sighed and raised her head. "Sam, I can't stay with you now. If I did, it could only be the way I stayed with Corneel." Sam stared at her, white-faced. She looked away. "I don't mean that. I couldn't stay with you that way. Not now." She became engrossed in worrying his button. Sam reached for her. "But," she said quickly, before he could speak, "that's why I have to go. I can't stay with you that way anymore."

She rattled on, speaking, I sensed, partly just to keep Sam from saying anything.

"In the beginning, after the fire, it didn't matter. I didn't care about you so much. I was even a little mad at you because it seemed to me you'd just kidnapped me." She gave a delectable shrug. "But that was all right. It even made it easier, though I was sad because I liked you and staying would mean the end of that, I thought. I was wrong about that," she said, suddenly smiling up at him, but with an uneasiness at the back of her eyes. "It didn't happen that way. And that's why"—she drew away from him—"I have to be by myself for a while."

"Why?" said Sam, refusing to understand—pardonably, I thought.

"Oh Sam." She separated from him with an impatient push and

sat down in a chair. But no amount of dawdling and poking at the frayed armrest answered Sam or made him go away. She looked up, at once exasperated and pleading. "All right: because I'm beginning to like you too much."

"You say it like that's about the worst thing a fellow could try and make you do."

"Well . . ." She bit back something she was about to say and shrugged.

"I guess I still don't get it, Jenny."

And I confess I didn't either.

"Maybe I can't explain. I just don't want to start liking you too much now, Sam. It isn't the right time. I'm just not ready."

"Well, you tell me when, Jenny."

She shook her head.

"You don't want me either, Sam. I'm not right for you. Our lives are too different. What about your jumping?"

That was a good point. All this chasing around was letting the choicest part of the jumping season slip away.

"I guess my jumping would be okay if I could just get back to it."

"There. You see, I'm already in the way."

It took Sam a minute or two to decide which end of this to grab. By then she'd captured the initiative.

"No, Sam, believe me, it's best this way." She stood up. "I'll leave day after tomorrow." Sadly: "I'll tell the others."

"Burn me if you will!" he said, grabbing her arm.

"Oh Sam, please! Don't spoil it."

Now that, I thought, was an odd thing to say. From Sam's end, at least, things appeared pretty spectacularly spoiled already. I wondered what she thought wasn't. Her memories-to-be, I guessed. She had it in view to relegate Sam to memory.

"I'm sorry," he panted, letting go of her. He closed his eyes. "I'm sorry."

She laid her hand against his chest.

"Only it's hard," he told her. "I reckon it'd go easier if you just plain didn't like me. I can't get a handle on this here."

"I'm sorry, Sam. I do like you." She laughed, unsteadily. "I'm afraid I can't help it. But that's just it . . . ." She let the sentence trail off.

Sam studied her, digesting that last look. It had been a veiled look, embarrassed, as though it covered secrets.

"I reckon there's something you're afraid of, all right," he said at last, "but it's nothing you've told me about, is it?" His voice was low. It seemed to come from a different place inside him. Jenny was so still I wondered if she were holding her breath. "Fact is, I reckon it's my jumping, ain't it, Jenny?"

And in the sorrowful look she gave him, he read that he'd guessed right.

Chapter 27

Jenny's leave-taking was a sorrowful affair. Even the weather was lachrymose, a cold November rain misting the air and condensing on surfaces in clammy droplets. It was a day to impart a funereal air to any event, and thus in one sense couldn't have been a better backdrop for Jenny's departure.

Jenny's announcement the day before that she was leaving had rendered the Shirt Tails speechless. Shaved, scrubbed and dressed in their best bibs and tuckers, they had sat there in silent amazement over the remains of the feast Jenny had laid out for them on the row of tables of different heights she had had them place end to end and covered with clean tablecloths. They had stared at her confounded, the jesting and laughter stuck in their throats like a fishbone, the good cheer congealed on their faces. She had told them, haltingly and trying to smile but with eyes that glistened ever more tremulously, that she was leaving on the morrow for Philadelphia to make a new start; that she would never forget them or how good they'd been to her; that the hide-out was another home to her and always would be, and, needlessly, that she hoped they would remember her with kindness and think of her sometimes as they went about their business or found themselves tempted to track across the floor in muddy boots. They had sat there frozen and heard her out, and when she was done they had gazed at her in mute disbelief for long minutes while the lamps hissed and she sat before them so lovely and forlorn at the head of the table, trying to smile though the tears now coursed down her cheeks for all to see.

All heads turned to Sam, sitting beside her. With a ghastly attempt at heartiness, he grinned and opened his mouth to speak. What came out was a croak. Coughing, he reached for and drained his glass. Looking around again, but managing not to meet anyone's eye, Sam said:

"Same here, gents. Bruin and me will be pushing on to Boston now, I reckon. There's a swell there as has been after me to winter with him."

He tried to go on, shook his head and refilled his glass instead, with infinite precision. When he had done, though, he seemed not to trust himself to bring it to his lips. It sat there on the table before him, as plain testimony to heartsickness as if, like Jenny, Sam too had given way to tears.

The Shirt Tails were not so complacent as to suppose that thought of leaving them was the sole ground of Sam's and Jenny's misery. Even with their healthy good opinion of themselves, the Shirt Tails knew the emotion was excessive for that. It was plain that there had been some sort of falling out between their principals, and while they didn't know what had provoked it, they could see what it portended: the unthinkable was to happen. Sam was not to have Jenny. The Shirt Tails were in shock. Bad enough that Jenny should say she was leaving them; incomparably worse that Sam should announce he was leaving them too, and to travel in the opposite direction. How was it possible that the grand events of the fire and Jenny's rescue should come to this? What then had been the point of all Sam's trials and adventures? Not only was every canon of romance violated, but that mainstay of the Shirt Tails' philosophy, the great American creed that grit and determination would see you through, was undermined. As Snooks put it to me later that night, "It kind of shakes your faith in the fitness of things."

So it was a sad, silent company that trooped through the muddy streets under gray skies next morning to see Jenny off. Sam and I were going away too, but it was Jenny's departure that set the tone. Sam and I were leaving the Shirt Tails; that was inevitable and natural, and under different circumstances they would have been happy to speed us along on a tide of St. Croix. Jenny was *bereaving* them, and while not a man of them dreamed of criticizing her for it, they were as saddened, and in much the same way, as if their loss stemmed not from any decision of hers, but from an inclement act of God.

We carried our gloom with us to the station and into the waiting room. There after the clerk went back to sleep the silence was so strained that every sniffle seemed to have a double meaning. At last the Brick could stand it no longer. Jumping up, he glared despairingly at Jenny and Sam and flung off outside with a banging of doors, preferring the chill and wet without to the chill and sadness within. Old Gooseberry was the next to go, dragging himself off so slowly and with so many backward glances that it seemed he would never be entirely gone. One by one the others followed till the three of us were left alone.

Sam and Jenny sat on the same bench, staring at their feet. The space between them loomed so strongly that it seemed almost another person, a flint-hearted duenna neither of them could face. Finally, like the Brick, I could stand it no longer. Scooting over to them on my rump, I sat down, pushed my nose at each in turn and whined my unhappiness. Sam's eyes met mine, then Jenny's did; a minute passed; both stretched out a hand at the same time to pat my head.

Their hands bumped. They pulled them back as if the touch burned. My exasperation at the pair of them overflowed. I gave a loud whine ending in a bark. Shyly, they looked at each other for the first time. Shyly, they smiled, and the invisible duenna vanished almost with an audible pop.

Sam took Jenny's hand and held it consideringly.

"Jumping is my life," he said after a while. "It's what I do."

"I know that, Sam," she answered softly.

He squeezed her hand and rocked on the bench.

"I can't give it up. Not even for you."

"I know, Sam. I didn't . . . I wouldn't ask you to."

He cradled her hand in both of his.

"No."

A gust of rain rattled against the windows. The door banged open and in strode a bulky figure booted above the knees, wearing huge gauntlets and wrapped in several layers of capes and self-importance. Hiding any surprise he may have felt at sight of me, he took a last bite of the chicken leg he had in one hand, flung the wreckage through the open doorway at his back, and said:

"All right, folks. Let's get a move on. Board 'em up," having said which, he gathered up Jenny's baggage, turned on his heel and strode out again.

Bellows stuck his head in cautiously. He saw Sam holding Jenny's hand, brightened, and stepped inside, where he stood gazing at the pair of them and grinning idiotically. Wideawake followed, and then the others. They took in the changed state of affairs and their stiffness fell away. They pressed forward. Finally Cutaway said, blushing:

"We're going to miss you, Jenny."

The rest chimed in with more of the same. The ice was broken. Sam and Jenny arose from their bench, still holding hands. The Shirt Tails all babbled at once.

"Pack it in, gents, and hurry up. I ain't got all day," came the driver's harsh voice. He stood in the doorway, haughtily slapping a coiled whip against his leg. Wideawake scowled. Snooks went up to the man and thrust his face close to the other's.

We went outside. Somehow the rain was just rain now, blank-faced: it had lost its symbolical sting. We slopped through the yard to the coach Jenny was apparently to have to herself. The Shirt Tails clustered around her, incoherently trying to express in these last few minutes their pent-up feelings, which Jenny understood perfectly anyway.

Sam kept his place by her side. Taking advantage of a lull in the Shirt Tails' fervor, he asked:

"When will I see you again, Jenny?"

Nervously she leaned her head into his.

"*All* right. *Let's* go. Burn me if you don't act like this here is your own private rig. Hang it all, shake a leg or stay and be damned, I don't care!" bellowed the driver, affronted, I think, to be taken so little notice of.

Snooks sauntered up to him where he stood by the more patient horses. The driver seemed to swell as Snooks approached, and favored Snooks with a look that would have hurt the feelings of a bug. Snooks came on undaunted, only stopping when another inch would have brought his pugnaciously outthrust chin in contact with the larger man's collarbone.

"I reckon you think you're pretty great," observed Snooks. The driver grinned down at him nastily. Snooks prodded him in the chest with two stiff fingers. "Well, you ain't," he said, turning the prod into a push. Over the man went with a loud "plop" on his back in the muck.

Cutaway jumped to his feet, grinning, from where he'd stationed himself back of the driver's knees. A laugh went up from the other Shirt Tails. The driver scrambled up, began to bluster, looked at us again, thought better of making trouble, and clambered seething onto his box, taking with him his injured dignity and a good deal of mud.

"When, Jenny? When will I see you?" asked Sam, as he and Wideawake handed Jenny into the coach.

"Not long," she told him, reaching her hand out to him through the flap on the window. "Soon."

The driver's whip cracked on the lead horse's back and sent spray flying. The horse bucked and the coach leaped forward.

"When?"

The whip cracked again and again, the driver taking out his ire on the horses. The wheels rumbled, harness creaked and the horses' feet churned up the mud as the coach lurched out of the yard. Jenny waved. The rain and noise of the coach drowned her voice, but we saw her lips form again, like a kiss, the word "Soon."

Chapter 28

Nat Buckerby was a proud man—proud of his wealth, proud of his Back Bay house, proud of his cleverness, and proud of himself generally. Much of this he told us himself, not being one to hide his light under a bushel (as he also told us); the rest was not hard to guess. Other things he was proud of included his not having been to college and his beautiful, though rather proud, wife, whose proud old family, to hear him boast, had found irresistible the proposal of this young go-getter who, starting from scratch as a clerk in a brokerage house, had amassed a fortune of over $100,000 by the time he was twenty. The lady herself, whom he'd summoned to greet us, could attest to the veracity of the tale, and was made to.

"Yessir, sharp as a tack, that's me," chortled Buckerby, who may have been all he said, for all of me, but who certainly looked round as a melon, albeit a melon with very sharp eyes. "Ain't that right, dear?"

The tall, handsome lady at his side gave him a look of disdain only slightly moderated from that which she was bestowing on Sam and me. Under that arctic glare I felt suddenly conscious of the shaggy figure I cut and, what I'd never noticed before, of the poor fit of Sam's sailor jacket. I shuffled uneasily, uncertain what to do with my paws.

Buckerby slapped his leg and guffawed.

"Ain't she great, gents? Oh, she knows me, she knows me!" He pulled out a handkerchief and mopped his brow.

That night we were wined and dined sumptuously in a large company of guests. The faces of most of these had the same glacial cast as Buckerby's wife's, and I noticed that it was only with these persons that Mrs. Buckerby was at all gracious. The others, who for their part were more gracious to Buckerby, were not so well dressed and perhaps for this reason went to greater lengths to show how at ease they were, spitting freely on the carpet and, maybe to keep them clean, putting their boots up on the furniture.

Sam and I were a great hit with this latter group, all of whom shook Sam's hand and greeted him heartily. Mrs. Buckerby's friends hovered on the periphery, staring at us curiously and exchanging remarks sotto voce. Sam grinned as he shook hands. He seemed to be enjoying himself, though he appeared somewhat distracted at times, and bewildered too by the dress jacket Buckerby had found for him to wear. But on the whole he seemed in decent spirits, and I was glad, remembering the dreary ride up, during which he had hardly spoken except to wonder from time to time why Jenny wouldn't say when they'd meet again, or to break out worriedly with some such remark as, "I reckon it's like she says, she just needs time, don't you think, Bruin?"

Then we were introduced to a couple of the Mrs. Buckerby party, and the woman, a Mrs. Kent, looked strikingly like Jenny, though with none of the interest of Jenny's personality. Sam blanched and for a moment could not find his tongue.

Buckerby, mopping away at his forehead, oblivious, babbled on, introducing the pair with a curious mixture of hospitality, deference, and defiance. In the same breath he boasted of the man's family and connections and deprecated these, reminding us that he was even richer and had started with nothing.

"And now these are my friends, same as you!" he concluded, surveying the four of us with inexpressible delight and scarcely forebearing, I think, to hug himself.

Sam had not recovered his speech yet. The woman, flustered by the gaunt way he looked at her, dropped her eyes and simpered.

"Pleased to meet you, I'm sure," said the young Mr. Kent, frowning and extending his hand after a moment's hesitation.

Sam took it mechanically.

"Same here. Right glad to be here," he said, eventually looking at the person whose hand he was shaking. Mr. Kent jerked his hand free and ushered his wife away without ceremony.

"Fine young fellow, there," said Mr. Buckerby, looking after him. "Fine family. I put him onto a good thing not long back and he cleared $5,000. Him and his wife come by regular now. She's a favorite with the missus. Fine young fellow," he said again, sounding wistful. He shook his head. "Wish my boy was more like him."

"You running down Barnaby again, Nat?" said a jovial fellow in a too-tight waistcoat, an old gravy stain decorating his lapel like a medal for valor won in some previous dinner engagement. "You shouldn't ought to do that. Barnaby'll come right."

"Bah!" spat Buckerby with surprising violence. He turned to Sam. "That son of mine! He couldn't learn the business worth a damn, so I figure if he ain't no good at *making* money, I'll send him on to college and he can at least learn how to spend it. Pshaw! You know what he done? Jack Higby, as fine a man who walks, is coming up in the world and he hears that son of mine is going off to Italy to study with some of them foreign painter fellows, so he gives him $10,000 to bring back a load of paintings. Well! You know what Barnaby sends back? Twelve paintings. *Twelve paintings,* for all that." Buckerby clenched and unclenched his hands in honest outrage. "Why, he should have come away with a whole houseful for that much. Old Jack was fit to be tied."

A servant appeared, opened the doors to the dining room, and rang the dinner bell. Buckerby brightened, forgetting the lapses of his son, and clutched Sam's arm as the ladies and gentlemen paired up and we trooped in to take our places. He steered Sam to a seat of honor at his own right hand, a seating which I noticed with vague misgivings placed Sam next to the fascinating Mrs. Kent. A separate table had, at what violence to Mrs. Buckerby's sensibilities I could only guess, been set up for me in the same room not far from Sam. On and about the main table I saw chicken, duck, turkey, beef, veal, mutton, and pork, and it looked like some of each had been served up for me as well. My misgivings about the seating arrangement evaporated, and I ambled over to my place, wondering what my chances were of getting a pitcher of beer.

As soon as we were seated the talk resumed and turned at once to politics. Jackson had won the election in a landslide, a fact which seemed to disgust virtually everyone present, although it was primarily members of Mrs. Buckerby's party who deplored the victory aloud. I saw a smirk on the face of the man with the gravy decoration when a silver-haired gentleman at Mrs. Buckerby's end of the table irately recounted recent headlines in some of the Jackson papers: GLORIOUS TRIUMPH, they were saying; or, not so succinctly, THE COALITION ROUTED, BEATEN AND DEFEATED.

"It's a crime, sir," agreed a heavy-featured man, leaning back with his eyes on his plate while a servant piled up turkey and stuffing. "And it's all the fault of this blamed universal suffrage. Pardon me, ladies. But whenever I think of it, this crazy business of letting every man vote, I get rather warm. Was there ever such nonsense? It'll be the ruin of the country if we don't look out."

"I quite agree," put in Mr. Kent, laying down his fork. "Let me tell you what happened to a friend of mine from Philadelphia just this election."

I saw Sam start at the name of the city and turn his attention momentarily from Mrs. Kent to her husband.

"Now understand first that my friend is a leader of the very first society and worth at least half a million in bank stock, to say nothing of very respectable holdings in real estate," went on Mr. Kent, looking around. "Well, sir, no sooner had my friend deposited his vote in the ballot box than one of your regular whole-hog, hurrah-for-Jackson men, who to every appearance was not worth five dollars in the world, stepped up and announced for all to hear that he intended to *destroy my friend's vote*. There, sir, are the consequences of universal suffrage," he finished sternly, with a genteel thump on the table.

The heavy-featured gentleman, to whom this last was directed, was taken with his mouth full. Hastily swallowing and wiping his mouth on the tablecloth, he said:

"There ought to be separate boxes for the quality."

"Quite so," said someone else. "And they wonder why we're not seen more often at the polls. Why, who the devil's going to put himself out to exercise a privilege shared by every pauper? I'd as soon do common militia duty!"

"I'd be interested to hear Mr. Patch's opinion on the matter," put in Mr. Kent, who had picked up his fork again and, observing Sam's start at being distracted from Mrs. Kent, looked as if he wouldn't have minded sticking him with it.

"Well, I reckon it's for every man to do his duty at the polls as he sees fit," said Sam pacifically, "though," he added as an afterthought, "I don't know as I hold with his doing it more than once."

This piece of fair-mindedness closed out the discussion and was much to Sam's credit, I thought. The topic shifted to the theater, where one of the ladies had lately seen the leading hostess of a rival social set wearing a "shocking" gown, which she proceeded to describe in minutest detail, sending delicious shivers of what can only have been reprobation through all the other ladies present, who hung on her every word.

I looked to see how Sam was getting along next to Mrs. Kent.

Not too well, to judge from his empty plate. Part of the problem seemed to be that the servants had clearly aligned themselves with Mrs. Buckerby's camp and would only serve Buckerby's friends when caught by the arm and compelled under duress or if slipped a half dollar at the door, as we learned later. Sam's unfamiliarity with this convention put him at a disadvantage, as did his preoccupation with Mrs. Kent, who seemed not to mind whether she ate or not.

Finally Sam did capture a servant. Holding on to him, he asked Mrs. Kent what she'd like.

"Why, I really don't know," she said with her charming simper. "I haven't had time to think of it. Goodness, they all eat so fast."

The servant broke away in answer to a summons from Mrs. Buckerby's end. I saw Sam look with envy at the white, tender breast of a turkey promiscuously lying with a fat slice of Virginia ham on a soft bed of mashed potatoes, all nestling cozily with cranberry and applesauce on Buckerby's plate. Buckerby noticed his glance.

"Why, Sam, ain't you eating?"

"Maybe I'll just have some of this wine," said Sam, taking up the decanter. Mrs. Kent let him pour her some, too, and thanked him prettily, but only toyed with her glass.

"You really should try some of this ham," said Buckerby. "It's top-notch." He took a large mouthful. "You know, it's something I've noticed. Folks as are the biggest meat eaters are way ahead when it comes to self-government. You look at the world. It's the beef and mutton countries that are always kicking up a ruckus and conquering their neighbors, and there's never any conquering them back. No sir, can't do it. That's why the nations of the North can never be reduced to slavery, while them in the South, more moderate in their eating, don't you see, are always getting themselves laid by the heels. Yes sir, you've got to eat meat. It's a fact: a country can only stay free and become fit for self-government on a sound democratic basis if its people eat meat."

Sam, his eye on a servant who was careful to pass with his

platter of beef out of Sam's reach, allowed as how there might be something in this.

" 'Course there is," said Buckerby.

"Oh, but Mr. Buckerby, the nations of the South excel in . . . other things," said Mrs. Kent, lowering her eyes and presenting to Sam a creamy expanse of neck.

"They do?" said Buckerby, startled. "What?"

"Why, in love, Mr. Buckerby," said Mrs. Kent, scarcely able to get the word out for blushes. "At least, that's what one hears."

"Caroline!" exclaimed another young woman across the table, with a scandalized laugh. "Really!"

Mr. Kent, I noticed, had stopped eating again. He sat like a pillar of stone, regarding his wife, only his jaws working, though whether he was actually chewing or just gnashing his teeth, I couldn't be sure.

"No, but really," said Mrs. Kent, setting them all at defiance with a very fetching pout. "That is what one hears. And if the men don't go about bashing one another's heads quite so much as they do in Northern climes, perhaps," she said with a swift, languishing look sideways at Sam, "it's because they've learned the joys of . . . surrender." She writhed adorably.

"Just what I said," pounced Buckerby. "It's because they don't eat enough meat."

"Oh, Caroline!" tittered the ladies, delighted.

"I think she's right," said a young woman with a rather calculating cast of feature, seated next to the stupefied Mr. Kent. She looked him up and down and said to the company, "There are ways and ways . . . of conquering."

"No there ain't, there's just one," said Buckerby, agitated to find his principle contested and victory slipping away from him. "Or maybe two. Money's another."

"Buckerby's right," said the men of both parties, united in horror of the young women's thesis.

" 'Course I am," said Buckerby, relieved to have their support. "It's always the strongest as wins. That goes without saying. And it's meat as makes you strongest. So it's always going to be the fellow as eats the most meat who wins," he said with relentless logic. He leaned forward. "What's more, a man can always eat twice as much meat as a woman, so the man will always be the strongest. Unless he goes and lets her start messing with his diet, which he's a double-dyed fool and no real man at all if he does!"

he finished hotly. He sat back, pulled out his handkerchief and set to mopping his brow with a justly satisfied air.

At this point Sam disrupted the conversation by springing up and waylaying an incautious servant who had approached too near with the remnants of an oyster pie. Sam relieved him of this and sat down again. He asked Mrs. Kent if she'd like some.

"Oh dear, no thank you," she dimpled. "I can't bear taking so many things on one plate." She indicated the untouched pâté that lay there already in sole possession.

"But Mr. Buckerby," resumed Mr. Kent's attractive neighbor, with an insinuating smile, "would you carry this method of conquest you defend—I cannot say gallantly—even to your dealings with ladies? Even for men, are there not sometimes methods and . . . methods?"

" 'Course I would," said Buckerby blankly. "It's what I did."

Widespread titters, which the ladies were unable to check. Mrs. Buckerby became very red.

"I beg your pardon, sir," said the young lady, her shoulders shaking and rather red-faced herself. She covered her mouth with her hand. "I see you are consistent to a fault."

"No, but really, Mr. Buckerby," said the irrepressible Caroline, "I must cry shame. It's naughty of you to fib so, just to win your point. You must play fair with us. I refuse to believe that you do not know that we women love gentleness in a man. Let him be hard as he likes with his own kind, if a man would rule in a woman's heart, it must be by softness. Whatever you men may like, we women," she said with another sidelong glance at Sam, whom even the bit of oyster pie, now gone, had not long prevented from staring at her with troubled eyes, "love to be admired, nay, worshipped; deferred to, approached with tenderness, longing—"

She was interrupted by a violent explosion of coughing from across the table. Mr. Kent seemed to have got something stuck in his throat. He choked and fought for breath, his comely neighbor assisting as best she might with one slender hand on his shoulder while, wearing the faintest of smiles, she offered him a glass of water with the other.

Mr. Kent recovered sufficiently to speak and rasped:

"Once more I would be most interested to hear the opinion of Mr. Patch."

Sam looked up, surprised.

"Well," he said, "I don't know as it's a topic I'd ever care to set up as an expert on. But I will allow it's one as I've lately got a particular interest in." He paused, his eyes straying to the suddenly breathless Mrs. Kent. "I guess instead of saying what I think, I'd just like to ask the lady here a question, if that's okay."

Eyes wide, Mrs. Kent nodded. Sam frowned in concentration. Choosing his words with care, he said:

"Suppose a fellow was really gone on a lady as seems so far above him that . . . Well, never mind that. But suppose he has reason to figure she kind of likes him too, anyway, but there's reasons why she can't have him just now. And so he admires her plenty, all right, and he lets her know it, too, his own way. And he longs for her so much that he, well, he just can't stop thinking about her for a minute even. But like I say, there's these reasons why she can't have him right off. And so he goes away, still longing for her and wanting her so bad it hurts, but he knows he has to give her time to work things out. Well, I guess my question is, if this fellow keeps feeling the same way about her and if he lets her be to work things out her own way in her own time, and he doesn't push at her or nothing—is there any hope for this fellow that maybe she'll come around?"

Mrs. Kent returned Sam's earnest gaze with tears in her eyes. Choking back a sob, she tilted her face up at Sam and said:

"Yes! Oh, yes, Mr. Patch!"

Mr. Kent's chair clattered to the floor. Before he could control himself enough to speak, Mrs. Buckerby hastily rose and said:

"Ladies, I think it's time for us to retire."

All rose, the ladies making a beeline for the doors with as much rustling of draperies as if they were all whispering at once, as indeed they seemed hardly able to wait to do.

Sam beamed his gratitude at Mrs. Kent, but with a hint of melancholy that seemed to sap her strength to leave.

"Poor dear Mr. Patch," she faltered. Then with a quick backward glance before fleeing the room: "Yes, you may hope!"

A long, low whistle came from Mr. Buckerby's friend partial to decking himself with gravy—I noticed he had added a second decoration to the first and overlayed the first with a fresh coat.

"Some things can be done as well as others, eh, Sam?" he said admiringly.

But Sam was lost in his own reflections.

Chapter 29

Our stay in Boston was not a success. Even with the encouragement given him by Mrs. Kent (whose abstemious appetite, we learned afterwards, had its ground in her having already eaten at a confectioner's shop), Sam continued to brood about Jenny. I didn't know whether to be fretful or glad that the jumping season was past, even by Sam's generous reckoning. Jumping might have helped take his mind off her; on the other hand, pining for her might equally have turned his mind from his jumping—with disastrous results. I felt a renewed wave of resentment towards Jenny. His low spirits were her fault: why wouldn't she have him? She didn't want to lose him. Well, neither did I. So why couldn't she simply accept him as I did? If she truly loved him, why wouldn't she see that jumping was as necessary to Sam as breath? Why did she have to diminish him in exchange for her love? She was forcing on him a choice that would tear him in two. Better if she simply refused to have him. At least then he would still have his jumping. As things stood, he was robbed even of that: her disapproval turned his pleasure to ashes.

Most of all I resented the grain of sense at the bottom of her objections, that echo of agreement she awoke inside me and the guilt I felt at doing nothing myself to wean him from his dangerous profession. Gingerly, I tried to imagine Sam retiring to rest on his laurels. But then I heard Benjamin Kitchen's voice speaking of endorsements or of starting a store, and my heart sank. It was impossible. What would Sam do? Without his jumping, he wouldn't be Sam.

Not that he was altogether himself just now anyway. Females! How I loathed what they did to a man, turning him from his true outward path, capturing him as a planet captures a satellite. How could a person hope to better himself, to truly become himself; to rise above this endless meaningless round of feeding (however enjoyably) only to feed again later, of reproduction for the sake of more reproduction, to rise up and be free instead of being harnessed with the mere illusion of freedom to a course as unvarying and predictable as the orbit of the moon about the earth? Nature was the enemy, always dragging you back just when you thought you had a leg up. How I resented nature! Nature it was that led to my encounter with Crockett; nature it was that prevented me from assuming the place my abilities merited in the world of men; and now again, nature it was, cunning nature, circling in to take Sam on the flank, robbing his work of its satisfaction, just when he might reasonably have expected to have got the upper hand of her.

How it broke my heart to hear Sam say, as he did to me one day that January, in deepest winter, when we sat in the common room of a tavern, both brooding over our losses before a chill fire:

"You know, Bruin, it's a funny thing. Seems like I've got everything I ever wanted, right down to some things I didn't know I wanted. I've got my work; I've got some money, enough to go on with anyhow; friends; I've even got myself sort of famous, which I wasn't even rightly looking for, though I must be near as famous as Davy Crockett now, I reckon, to hear folks carry on." He paused to consider this, his unexpected fame. It seemed to baffle him. At last with an impatient flick of his hand he took a swallow of St. Croix. He shook his head. "The funny thing is, it just don't add up the way a fellow'd think it would. No sir, not by half."

Sam was right about his fame, by the way—the extent of it. We had only to go outside together into the streets to have every urchin hail us with "Sam Patch! Sam Patch!" and take to jumping over or from everything that didn't lie flat. They jumped from carts and wagons, from horses, from lampposts into snowdrifts, from steps and porches, even from fireplugs. Farmers, we heard, jumped from fences; boatmen from boats; actors from stages; even clerks in the stores had taken to springing over the counters, to the astonishment of their less up-to-the-minute customers. A jumping mania was sweeping the nation. Everyone everywhere, it seemed, was "doing Sam Patch."

When I saw how little all of this excitement affected Sam, I was finally glad it wasn't the season for real jumping. Sam was flattered, of course, but his true satisfaction lay in his jumping, not in the proceeds. None of this excitement of others helped take his mind off Jenny, and I thought it unlikely that his own jumping would succeed any better. And real jumping wasn't a thing you wanted to do unless you could give it your fullest attention.

So I was surprised when one morning late in February Sam came up to me looking more nearly his old self than I'd seen him in a long time and breezily announced that he'd hit on "just the ticket" to pick him up out of his slump.

"I've been feeling poorly and no mistake, Bruin. But I reckon all I need is a little change of scene. So I was thinking maybe we should go on down and take in the inauguration. Give you a chance to introduce me to your old friend Crockett, who I've been itching to meet for a while now anyway. And we can stop off and see Wideawake and the gang while we're about it. It's right on the way," he said carelessly, though eyeing me in a way that should have put me onto his being up to something if the name Crockett hadn't knocked everything else out of my head. I gave a woof of dismay.

"Well, good," said Sam, looking unaccountably relieved, "that's settled then. We'll start tomorrow." As usual, he needed the better part of a day for saying good-byes.

And start tomorrow we did, despite my best efforts to sidestep my fate. First I got drunk, drunk as I'd been only once before in my life, back with Karl, and let me tell you it took some doing. I had hoped that if I could get Sam to follow suit, we might miss our coach. But Sam matched me practically drink for drink, and insofar as I accomplished anything at all, it was only to win his praise for my capacity. So then I tried to straighten him out as to the true state of affairs between Crockett and me by crooning a ballad going the rounds at the time, the refrain of which ran, "Davy, Davy Crockett, king of the wild frontier," and coming down especially heavily on the line, "kilt him a bar when he was only three"—but Sam misunderstood completely, as I might have known he must. So in despair I crawled off and hid, but somehow they found me, and under Sam's direction a party of ten or twelve ignorant well-wishers (allowing for my splitting headache and impaired vision) rousted me out and threw me, covered with feathers and chicken droppings, in the boot of the coach. My fate was sealed.

Snooks was overjoyed to see me, and Sam too, of course, and he threw his arms about my neck with quite affecting disregard for the chicken droppings, though now that I recall the look he gave me afterwards, maybe he hadn't seen them at first. Anyway, he made us welcome. The others were away just at the moment, clearing up some lingering differences with the Plug Uglies.

"But they'll be back any time," Snooks assured us, glowing, "just as soon as they can thrash things out."

So we made ourselves comfortable and Snooks ran off to fetch the cribbage board.

After supper we heard the other Shirt Tails returning. Snooks jumped up to meet them.

"Boys, you'll never guess who's back!"

"Not Sam?"

"Bruin and him both!"

In they trooped, looking weary but pleased with themselves, like men who have successfully concluded a difficult job that had long needed doing. It was gratifying to see how the sight of us brightened their tired faces. After wiping their boots and neatly putting away their lead pipes and cudgels, they flocked around us to shake hands and ask questions.

"Any news from Jenny, Sam?" was one of the first, from Wideawake.

"No, I ain't heard much from her," said Sam. "How've you boys been?"

Busy, it seemed. The Daybreak Boys' territory had at last been absorbed altogether, the Daybreak Boys taking on the status of a cadet branch of the Shirt Tails. This in the end they were glad enough to do, as the Roach Guards were pressing them hard on the other side. The Plug Uglies had given trouble after the election and even tried to muscle in on the Shirt Tails' burgeoning traffic in fancy preserves and smuggled delicacies, but Wideawake was confident that that problem had been finally solved tonight.

"Yep," he said, cautiously leaning back and wincing as he removed his partially crushed-in hat, "things is looking pretty good for us. 'Course it ain't hurt a bit that we busted up them Dead Rabbits like we did. Now we're in solid with Vanderbilt and them too."

For a moment Sam looked grave. Noticing, Wideawake pushed him the bottle and said:

"So where are you two bound for now, Sam?"

Sam refilled his glass.

"I thought we'd go down for the inauguration," he said, again with that false carelessness I'd noticed the first time he brought the idea up.

"Oh ho, so I reckon you'll be stopping off to see Jenny then, seeing as she's right on the way?"

"I thought we might," he said, looking at me.

The Shirt Tails all began talking at once, giving Sam messages to relay to Jenny. I couldn't understand why he'd been so devious about his plans to see her again, unless he'd been partly concerned to fool himself as well as me. In fact, I was cheered. Maybe things would fall out so we wouldn't see Crockett after all.

I woofed my approval and Sam smiled.

"Say, why don't some of you boys come down with us. I reckon Jenny'd be glad to see you, and me and Bruin could sure use the company," he said.

A silence fell on the Shirt Tails. Sam looked from face to face in surprise.

"Well, see, it's like this, Sam," said Wideawake finally, taking up and examining his hat. "We're pretty busy here, what with all the expanding we done, and I don't know as we could rightly afford the time."

The others nodded and muttered agreement, no one meeting Sam's eye.

"Well don't that beat all?" he said at last. The Shirt Tails squirmed.

"It ain't that we don't want to, Sam," put in Cutaway nervously, fingering a large bruise on his cheekbone. "We'd give anything to see Jenny again."

"We sure would!"

"It's just, it's just, well," he said, drawing a breath and looking up with scared eyes, "it's just it's a wilderness out there!"

The Shirt Tails, with the insularity I'd noticed in all true New Yorkers, were terrified of leaving the city.

"But you tell her," said Old Gooseberry tearfully, searching in his pocket for the red bandanna he'd forgotten he was already using as a temporary sling for his arm, "you tell her we miss her, Sam. And we've kept this place up just like she left it."

And so they had, even going so far as to drum Dogs Meat out of the gang for being incurably messy.

Chapter 30

It took two days to reach Philadelphia. This time we rode outside, Sam with the driver and me on the roof just behind, where I could join in the conversation. In the event, though, there really wasn't any. Sam replied to our admiring driver's best efforts with monosyllables till at last, with an expression that as much as said, "The great ain't like you and me," the fellow tolerantly gave up and left Sam alone with his thoughts. These, of course, concerned Jenny, though I couldn't tell if he was more worried about how to locate her or what to say when he did. I suspected the latter, and in any case, the former problem unexpectedly took care of itself. We got out of the coach at the chief hotel of the city, and no sooner had I disentangled myself from the baggage than we heard a glad cry:

"Sam!"

I saw a richly dressed woman leave the side of the man she was with and advance a few steps toward us. Sam looked up.

"Jenny!" he said.

He started toward her, a smile spreading over his face. Then both he and the smile faltered. I saw him take in her fine clothes. The man whose side she had left came up to join her again, his chin in the air, and looked at us inquiringly. Jenny bit her lip. When Sam reached them, she said, as if repenting her outburst:

"Eb, I'd like you to meet a friend of mine. Sam Patch."

Eb's hand was tucked Napoleonically in the front of his coat. He made a show of scratching his chest and left it there.

"Well, well. Not *the* Sam Patch? Well, of course. And there's the bear. Brute, or whatever he's called."

Jenny's eyes never left Sam.

"Sam," she said mechanically, "this is Eb Carmody."

Sam sized up Carmody and dismissed him. *Who* Carmody was mattered less than *that* he was. Sam turned to Jenny with a look of wonderment that I think she found harder to meet than any reproach. This was to follow, though, and it took Jenny with her guard down. The color drained from her face and, reproachful as I felt myself, I found my heart going out to her. But Sam only stood there confronting her, cold and strange.

Jenny's color came back with a rush. Her eyes flashed and she placed her hand defiantly on Carmody's arm.

"We're just leaving for Washington," she said.

Carmody had been watching her. With this he barked a laugh and stuck out his hand.

"And what brings you here, Mr. Patch?" he asked, as belatedly he and Sam shook. "A mite cold yet for a dip in the Delaware, I'd think. Or," he said, slyly turning his head, "ain't it business as draws you?"

"It is and it ain't," said Sam evenly. "I'm heading for the inauguration, same as you, I reckon. Though I allow," he added, turning, against his will it seemed, to Jenny, "I thought I might look up Miss Hansom here too if I got the chance."

Jenny gave her head a slight toss and I saw her fingers bite harder into Carmody's arm. He felt the pressure and said, smiling:

"Well! I don't blame you a bit. Running into us like this then is a real break for you. In fact," he said, his smile suddenly turning crafty, as though he were struck by an idea, "it just could be a bigger break than you know. Let me see," he said, hastily pulling out a large watch. "I tell you what, Mr. Patch. Let's all go back in and have us a drink and get acquainted proper. Miss Hansom here can get you a ticket, and meantime there's a matter I'd like to discuss with you, Mr. Patch, as ought to be of particular interest to a gent in your risky line of work. Yes sir, Mr. Patch, I sure am glad to have met up with you. And Brute here too, of course. Yes, it always makes me proud when I think I see a way of helping folks. And I think this could just be your lucky day, Mr. Patch."

And so, chattering enthusiastically and giving every sign of enjoying himself, Carmody faced about and led us into the hotel, Jenny, her hand resting lightly in the crook of his arm, sweeping along in chill silence on his right, Sam somewhat stiffly attending on the other side.

What Carmody had it in mind to speak to Sam about turned out to be life insurance.

"Sir, has it ever occurred to you that every time you perform one of those justly famous leaps of yours, you set at hazard not only your own life and integrity of limb, but the well-being of those who are dearest to you?" asked Carmody when we were seated at a table. His eyes, bright with honest concern, happened to light on me. "Persons," he added, seeming momentarily confused and accenting the word, "who would be destitute of continued support were some, ah, mishap to befall you, or would in any case welcome a donative in their naturally inconsolable grief as at least expressing your kind remembrance of them in your perils?"

Sam, watching the doorway for Jenny, threw him a glance. Carmody, seeing he had Sam's attention, rubbed his hands briskly.

"Of course," he continued, "it goes without saying that there can be no true indemnification for the loss of a loved one. At least, none which it falls within the merely human resources of us, His willing servants here below, to provide," he qualified piously. "Nevertheless, there are some of us who have made it their mission in life to do what we can in this regard, and if that is not a great deal when measured against divine providence, which alone can apply a balm to the grieving heart, still, to be able to assuage in part the pangs of the injured pocketbook is, I submit, no despicable achievement."

He leaned back, favoring Sam with a smile of heartfelt benevolence.

"Now, Mr. Patch, it just so happens that I represent the City of Brotherly Love Fire, Accident and Life Assurance Company, with offices in Philadelphia, Baltimore and Washington—have, indeed, the honor to be president of that philanthropic concern—and it would warm my heart immensely to be able to place myself and the resources of my firm as a bulwark between misfortune and those you love. Now if I may outline the provisions, the benefits, Mr. Patch, of a policy our firm offers that I think will exactly meet your case, I know you will thank me. True, the premiums may seem a trifle steep, but under the circumstances—"

But just then Jenny appeared in the doorway. Sam, who had long since stopped listening to Carmody, started to stand up. Changing his mind, he gripped the arms of his chair and gravely watched her approach. She moved quickly across to us, eyes lowered, and took a seat by Carmody, opposite Sam. Still without looking up, she removed a ticket from her reticule and placed it on neutral territory in the center of the table.

"Ah, thank you, my dear," said Carmody, irked at the distraction. He shoved the ticket over to Sam, who took it and put some money on the table. "Well, sir," said Carmody, masking his impatience with a smile and struggling to recover his lost momentum, "what do you say? Have I interested you in this matter? Will you let my firm and me be of service?"

Jenny darted him a glance, and another at Sam. She blushed. Some of the tension went out of his face and he relaxed his grip on the chair. I even thought I saw the ghost of a sparkle brighten his eye.

"I'm thinking you've been that already, Mr. Carmody," said Sam, "more than you likely thought to."

Carmody blinked, not understanding. But Jenny looked up, saw the corners of Sam's mouth twitch, and could not suppress a meager smile of her own.

Carmody began to speak again but Sam cut him off:

"But ain't this our coach?"

I drew the boot again this trip, and was lucky to get that. The coach was full on account of the inauguration, and there was a considerable scramble to get aboard, hopeful aspirants for federal office under Jackson sharpening their skills for the competition ahead by fighting each other here for the best seats. Carmody, ordinarily no mean contender, I could see, nonetheless let himself be outmaneuvered. Thrusting aside rivals with truly republican disdain for age, sex, or probable station in society, Carmody managed to occupy the middle of the best bench and plunked his hat down beside him to hold the window seat as well. Turning to beckon Jenny to join him, however, he discovered that Sam had assumed charge of her himself in the interim, having taken her firmly by the arm and pulled her with only the slightest resistance with him into the back. There they sat side by side gazing back at him, Sam placidly, Jenny a bit breathless and beginning to smile. All this I saw through the small window in the back partition, more or less dead behind Sam's head. Then before Carmody had recovered from this surprise, a very bony and determined lady wielding a hatpin scattered the remaining opposition and seated herself uncompromisingly on his hat.

A little demoralized by this setback, Mr. Carmody contented himself with retrieving his hat from underneath his fierce neighbor (who only gave ground grudgingly, seeming to suspect him of still harboring designs on her seat even at this late stage) and turned around to meet the stares of the three bearded and reeking Jacksonians who occupied the bench at the front of the coach facing his. The coach started.

Just then one of the three men gave a yell and slopped a healthy dose of rum down Carmody's front.

"There's a bar! There's a bar in the back! He's lookin' at us!" the man cried, nearly taking out Carmody's eye with the end of his bottle.

Elbowing each other frantically, the Jacksonians all produced huge knives. The bony lady emitted a piercing shriek and went for her hatpin.

I did my best to woof placatingly, but the border of the small window so impeded my muzzle that I'm not sure I got my meaning across. Sam held up his hands.

"Steady on, gents. That's no bear. That there's Bruin."

"Bruin!" exclaimed the Jacksonians. They conferred amongst themselves. "Why, that means—then you must be Sam Patch!"

Sam grinned, as much as to say, "I have that honor." But I thought I detected a faint wryness in the corners, as if he might have added, "though it ain't all it's cracked up to be."

"Well, don't that beat all! How are you, Sam?"

They clambered without ceremony or much care in the placing of knees and feet onto Carmody's bench to shake hands. Sam accepted a drink from each of the three bottles. Then one of them gave a yell again and turned to rub his rump and glare in amazement at the bony lady, in whose lap he was more or less kneeling. She showed him the hatpin.

Retiring rather more gingerly than they had advanced, the Jacksonians took their proper seats again and resumed their drinking, waving at me and seeming much stimulated by our encounter. "Imagine that!" and "Blast my shoes!" I heard many times.

Unconsciously, Sam glanced at Jenny, still wearing the smile with which he'd parted from the Jacksonians. He found her regarding him, her head tilted and such a gentle smile of her own on her lips that he was thrown into confusion.

"Uh, just some of the boys," he said.

She nodded. But it was a nod that encompassed far more than the events of the past few minutes. She turned her head away and gazed into her lap, toying with the strings of her bag.

Then they both tried to speak at once.

She outwaited him, smiling, and Sam began again.

"I'm sorry, Jenny. I reckon I had no right to take on so back there," he told her, though I couldn't see that he had much to apologize for or that he'd even done much taking on that the circumstances didn't strictly warrant. "It's just I was wanting to see you again pretty bad, and I guess I wasn't ready for it when—" He paused, gazing somberly down at her gloved hands. His expression seemed to set; his shoulders twitched. "But I guess it ain't for me to say what you can do."

"No, Sam, I don't blame you for that. I understand." She looked up at him, her eyes roving fondly over his sorrowful face. "But nothing has changed, Sam. I can't help it. I can't put myself at the mercy of . . . what might happen to you. I can't open myself up like that. Not yet, anyhow. You'll have to—"

"I know," he broke in, frowning, unable to hear anymore. "You explained it good enough before, I reckon. You don't like my jumping. And that's what's so hard. Because that's what I do."

Jenny had nothing to say to that, and as the minutes lengthened I saw that she evidently found it beyond her as well to change the subject. I was glad of that, much as I ached for the both of them. As long as she could not content herself with meeting Sam on superficial ground, he still had a claim on her heart.

Sam's face worked and I knew he kicked himself for his bluntness. But he needn't have; this moment was sure to have come sooner or later whatever Sam's conversational agility. It was the one thing that needed to be settled between them, on which all else depended. And plainly neither of them knew how to go about settling it, with the result that they sat there awkwardly together, not estranged in their feelings, but as incapable of behaving naturally as if they were.

The miles jolted by. Outside, the sun balanced precariously on the horizon, burnishing the naked landscape with a one-sided luster and creating deep pockets of shadow. Sam's neighbor to his left, a sturdy, taciturn fellow in rough clothes, took bread and cheese from a cloth bag at his feet and began to eat. My stomach rumbled and a streamer of saliva descended from my muzzle and ran down the partition and onto Sam's back.

Inside, nothing changed. Sam and Jenny sat together in silence, communing only with looks that told me their wordless dialogue continued as fruitlessly as before. The monotony was relieved—or worsened—only by the Jacksonians' singing and from time to time pressing a bottle on Carmody to offer to Sam, which he always declined and never thought to offer to me. A few times Carmody turned around to try to strike up a conversation, casting anxious glances at Jenny, but his voice sounded strained and unnatural, and Sam only shook his head and Jenny looked away. A desultory effort to sell the Jacksonians life insurance coming to nothing, he lapsed at last into a bad-tempered silence.

But Carmody's troubles had only begun.

Outside of Baltimore, in the dead of night, I was awakened from a fitful nap by a series of jolts even more vicious than usual, and I had the sense that we were flying along at speed. Indeed, I could hear the driver's cries and the crack of his whip, and I gathered that he was urging the horses on to their utmost. As we were already going downhill, we passed rapidly from traveling at a healthy rate to what I very much feared was an unhealthy one, and the bumps grew so bad that I seemed to be colliding as often and painfully with the roof of my accommodation as with the sides or the floor.

Suddenly the road leveled out, there was a great splashing, and we slowed as abruptly as if mighty hands had reached out of the mud and laid hold of the wheels. Thumps and curses sounded from the other side of the partition. The driver's voice rose, frantically exhorting the horses, but our speed still fell to a crawl. The driver's whip cracked; I could feel the teams rear and plunge. The coach traveled a few feet farther in sluggish jerks, then settled itself with a patent resolve to move no more. We were stuck.

The driver punished the horses for a few moments longer, then gave it up as a bad job. I heard more cursing from inside first class, then a splash as the driver jumped down from his perch and sloshed around to the side.

He flung open the door. With a good deal of swearing he confirmed what was already no secret—we were stuck—and ordered everybody out.

"It's all the fault of that blasted bear, God damn it to hell," he said. "I never saw such a blame fool thing, packing a bear as freight. Why, he must be all of four hundred pounds if he's an ounce. If it weren't for him, we'd have got across, burn my old mother."

I thought this was unfair. Five hundred pounds is five hundred pounds. He could just as well have left behind two or three of the others. And if he had, I could have ridden inside.

But as he seemed in no mood to listen to reason, I kept these reflections to myself, got out with the others, and took a position discreetly out of the way to the side.

Soon everybody was out except the bony lady, who flatly refused to budge and menaced the driver with her hatpin when he tried to coax her. The others stood about ruefully waiting in the more than ankle-deep mud. Finally the driver threw up his hands and climbed back onto his box, swearing that this was his last run.

"I mean it, by God. The last!"

Cracking his whip over the horses, he shouted and the men put their shoulders to the mud-spattered coach. The horses, indistinct shapes in the darkness, snorted and strained. The coach, mired almost to the axles, shifted reluctantly and advanced a few inches. The men renewed their grip and pushed again, this time under the grim scrutiny of the bony lady, who had stuck her head out the window to monitor their efforts and, I suppose, give silent encouragement.

I heard wet, sucking noises approaching. I turned and saw Jenny, holding up the hem of her dress and picking her way over to where I waited on slightly firmer ground.

"Hello, Bruin," she greeted me softly, trying to read my face in the dark. I stiffened. She took a step closer and gazed down at me. "Dear thing. I hope you're not mad at me too."

To tell you the truth, I was. But it wasn't easy to stay that way in the face of the sorrowful look she gave me. I woofed ambiguously.

"I'm so glad," she said, reassured. "I couldn't stand it if you both hated me." She sighed and my resentment floated away on the night air. "Oh Bruin, I feel awful. I didn't mean to hurt Sam. You know that, don't you? Yes, yes, only please don't lick me, dear. I'm messy enough as it is."

She turned away pensively and for a moment we stood together without speaking, watching the men struggle with the stranded coach. The bony lady watched, too, from her window.

Leaning out as far as she could, she was the spitting image of aggravation. I think she believed the men weren't trying their hardest. Twisting her head sharply this way and that, she eyed them balefully and from time to time urged them to greater efforts with shrill, wordless cries.

"I do love him, I think," said Jenny after a bit, in that tone of a person talking to himself that people often took with me, I'd noticed. "There's something about him. I don't know, a sort of largeness. When I'm with him I feel"—she gave an exasperated laugh—"small. But in the nicest, safest way somehow," she added softly.

I waited for her to go on. But she only stood there watching Sam struggle manfully with the others in the mud.

Pulling her coat together with a quick, nervous gesture, Jenny turned to me again.

"But what can I do? Dear Bruin," she said with sudden passion, her eyes watery and bright in the moonlight, "he loves his jumping. I know I can't ask him to give it up. He couldn't—not really; not in his heart. So what does he want from me? What does he want me to do? Follow him, be with him, live with him loving him more and more all the time as if it didn't matter that any minute he might get himself killed? That his jumping could take him away from me? Does he expect that?" She raised her fists and said with a vehemence I'd never seen in her before: "I hate his jumping. I wish he'd never started it. I wish—"

She broke off. Biting her lip, she turned with a frown to search out Sam again among the men with the coach. Almost now they had worked it to the end of the slough: I could hear the horses' hooves beating on firmer ground and see the coach itself beginning to bounce and rattle with some of its old exuberance.

The bony lady still craned her body from the window. Clearly in the last extremity of fretfulness, she seemed to regard the men's having taken so long as a personal affront and to be holding herself back from actively resenting it only by the greatest effort. Carmody's own halfhearted efforts directly under her window strained her self-control to the breaking point. She hissed at him viciously through compressed lips; I heard him reply something about an "old bat."

Just then the coach, which was almost clear, bounced violently, dislodging the bony lady and sending her tumbling onto Carmody's shoulders. With understandable lack of ceremony, considering the way she was clawing at him, he got a hand under her jaw and stuffed her back through the window like a man bagging laundry. She reemerged, spitting and snarling, as if on a spring and drove at his eyes with her hatpin. She missed, but only because Carmody took the thrust in his forearm. He yelled, staggered, and the coach ran over his foot.

To make a long story short, we unloaded Carmody in Baltimore, a thoroughly demoralized man. The left-hand Jacksonian changed places with him to separate him from the bony lady, and Carmody rode with his badly bruised foot propped on the seat opposite. The whole rest of the way he hugged his punctured arm to his breast and maintained a stubborn silence that was proof against his friendly new neighbor's fiery breath, his best jokes, and even his jabbing elbow.

Needless to say, Jenny didn't get off with him.

Chapter 31

In Baltimore we changed horses, slept a few hours and refreshed ourselves. It suddenly struck me as I stood watching them hitch up the new team that there was no longer any earthly reason for us to press on to Washington. Sam had only hit on the idea in the first place as an excuse to see Jenny. We might never have left Philadelphia if it hadn't been for Carmody's taking Jenny away, and now Carmody was out of the picture. I knew Jenny didn't care to see the inauguration. My heart leaped. Maybe there was still a chance I could avoid meeting Crockett.

I soon saw my error. There were no two ways about it: we had to get back on the coach. There was unfinished business between Sam and Jenny—maybe the most important business they would ever have—and it bound them together and carried them along willy-nilly, taking them where it would go. No, we had to go on to Washington, if only because that was where we were headed and to stop would bring on the crisis Sam and Jenny both dreaded when they would settle matters between them. Neither was ready for that, and neither could tear himself away till it happened, either. And so all three of us were trapped, as much prisoners as if we rode the coach under guard. They would have reboarded, I know, even if the coach were taking them to regions vastly more infernal than Washington.

With a sigh, I got up behind them.

The day was bright and sunny and the traveling much easier. Our break in Baltimore had raised everyone's spirits, and the pretty scenes outside the windows helped keep them elevated. The three Jacksonians, who had left off their singing, gazed with meditative smiles at the cheerful countryside and often even forgot for long periods at a stretch to sip from their fresh bottles. Even the bony lady had mellowed—perhaps partly from a consciousness that she hadn't shown herself in the best light with Carmody. Sitting primly erect with her gloved hands clasped in her lap, she alternately gazed out the window with much the same expression as the Jacksonians, or rotated her head with quick, birdlike motions to bestow on the other passengers looks that seemed to say she forgave them everything.

Sam and Jenny, too, felt the influence of the warm sun, the mild air, and the new mood of amity. They were not so tense now as last night. They still did not speak, but they no longer shrank from looking at each other, and when their eyes did meet, which was often enough now, their glances, instead of being deliberately opaque, said plainly that they both yearned to find some way across the gulf that separated them.

At length Sam, perhaps encouraged by these glances, spoke.

"You know, Jenny," he said, staring down at the piece of leather thonging he'd picked up somewhere and was twisting in his fingers, "it's a funny thing. Before I took to jumping serious, I used to ask myself *why* a lot: why work, why do this, why do that? It came over me so bad sometimes I used to just stand there, forgetting where I was, trying to see the answer. The problem was, there was any amount of answers, but not a single one of them worth a hoot. I mean, I might be standing there working my mule and watching them spindles going round and round and them bobbins going back and forth and them throstles and flyers going up and down, over and over again and never really getting anywhere on account of there was always more spinning to do—and I'd get thinking how I was just like that mule there, just doing the same thing over and over again and never getting done with it on account of there was always more of it to do. And then I'd get to wondering why I was doing it at all, and of course the answer was a fellow had to eat. And that would make me laugh, to think I had no more business being there than that. I mean, if I was fixing to make something and needed a mess of yarn, that would have been one thing. I'd have had a reason for spinning it then. But as it was I could have just as well been out digging a hole in the ground, if I could have got paid as good. There wasn't a blamed bit of sense for me in doing what I was doing, or leastways no more than there was in my doing anything else. The only sense in doing any of it was a fellow had to eat.

"Well, so I'd ask myself, kind of smiling-like, why's a fellow have to eat? And of course the answer is a fellow has to live. And then sometimes maybe I'd ask myself why's a fellow have to live? And you know, Jenny," he said, shyly looking up at her where she listened to him and watched his fingers work the piece of thong, "I never could come up with an answer to that."

We were passing a farmer in his cart. The Jacksonians, as quick as puppies to rise to any new opportunity for fun, hailed him through the window and waved their bottles. The man raised his head. Under his battered hat he displayed a face so lined and careworn that the Jacksonians were dismayed.

They flung back in their seats, away from the dull, unseeing look the man had given them. For a few minutes they were silent. Then one of them, Zeke, said:

"Did you see that team he was driving? Looked like the crows had a mortgage on the horses."

This broke up Jasper and Gordy, the other two. All three in their relief at the joke took hearty swallows from their bottles and dug their elbows into each other's sides.

"But then," resumed Sam, regarding the Jacksonians with a wry gravity that would have perplexed them had they noticed it, "I found jumping, and all that changed." He turned to Jenny. The air around the pair of them seemed to thicken while they held each other's eyes.

Sam looked away and slowly let out his breath.

"I don't mean," he said, going back to toying with the piece of leather, "that I rightly hit on what you'd call an answer. No, I wouldn't say that. But I reckon what did happen was something just as good. And that's just that after I went in for jumping, well, seemed like the question *why* didn't come up anymore."

Now it was Jenny's turn to look away. Sam lifted his head and studied her. Laying aside the scrap of leather, he cautiously stretched his legs.

"The thing is," he said, tucking them under him again, "the

thing is, I went and ran into you there on the boat, Jenny. And ever since, well, even with the jumping, I seem to be back to wondering why again."

She raised her eyes. They met his.

"It's like I won the game and found out there's no prize, Jenny; or what prize there is ain't half what I thought it was," he told her softly.

She closed her eyes and leaned against his arm. He waited. When she looked up again he added:

". . . Without you. I need both, Jenny. You and the jumping."

Suddenly the Jacksonians, more than a little soused now, erupted into shouts and pressed forward to stick their heads out the windows on the bony lady's side, laughing and waving.

"It was me she meant, blame you!"

"No, it weren't, she was looking right at me when she done it!"

"It was me. She was winking at me, you durned fools!"

I saw the bony lady's hand creep in the direction of her hatpin. With a sniff she pulled it back again and clenched it tightly in her lap. Staring into space over the heads of the riotous Jacksonians, she primly lifted her chin, as much as to say she refused to be tempted.

But none of this held any interest for Sam. Only glancing at the Jacksonians, he returned his attention immediately to Jenny and gazed at her, waiting.

She nodded.

"I know, Sam," she said with an effort.

He waited some more, but without result. Leaning back, he took a breath and looked around. The Jacksonians were clumsily finding their seats again under the sidelong vigilance of the bony lady, who for all her resolution could not keep from following their every move with the hungry fixity of a cat watching the antics of three very foolish canaries. Heavily, Sam rubbed his jaw.

"Well, I reckon we'll be in Washington soon," he said, apparently changing the subject. Jenny remained still. Sam nodded to himself. "That'll be something, won't it? Yep, I mean to pay a call on Davy Crockett when we get there. I'm looking forward to it. I reckon I'll ask him how it is he never seems to get tired of hunting bears."

Chapter 32

We arrived in Washington late in the day, just another drop in the flood that had poured into the city over the past several weeks in anticipation of the inauguration and had filled it now to overflowing. By steamboat the people came; by coach, on horseback, or just walking. They came drawn irresistibly by the desire to witness the crowning triumph of their leader, that man of the people, that man whose origin was as humble as their own, who had risen with their help to capture the chief office of the land; that ordinary man who had chastised the Indians in Tennessee, licked the British at New Orleans, chastised some more Indians six years later on the Florida border, and been well on his way to single-handedly (and, alas, without his government's sanction) chastising the Spanish in Florida as well until he was summarily recalled by a worried president: that man, his country's greatest living hero, the man they called Old Hickory.

The city was packed with his admirers, many long-standing and others who I guessed from their handsome carriages and clothes were of more recent vintage. Splendid equipages rattled by on every side, parting the joyous throngs of buckskin-clad supporters who with their long rifles, their jugs and frontier hollers, reeled about deliriously in the streets. These last gave me considerable concern. They all of them had that Crockett look of men who would not count the day well begun unless they could kill a bear or two before breakfast. I whimpered and pulled my muzzle back inside the tarp that screened me from view. Even just a sprig of hickory would have made me feel better. There was no hiding that I was a bear, but it would at least have reassured them that my politics were correct.

But Sam had not forgotten me. Leaving Jenny to wait for him, he came straight back to where the three Jacksonians who had ridden with us had already thrown back the tarp and were trying with some impatience to coax me off their rather flattened luggage. I was having none of it. Then Sam appeared. His sad face crinkled into something like the old smile.

"All right, worrywart, you come on out of there. Is this any way to behave for the bear as fought Crockett to a standstill? It's a fact, gents. You may have heard of it. Only I reckon now he's just feeling a mite tuckered from the trip."

He laughed and grabbed my paw. I clambered out, blinking.

Whoops and shouts! Guns crashed and I dropped down on all fours. We were instantly the center of a grinning crowd.

"No, you blame fool," yelled Gordy, shoving aside the leveled gun barrel that had suddenly extended itself over his shoulder from behind. "Don't you know nothing? This here's Sam Patch and Bruin!"

"Sam Patch! Sam Patch!"

They went wild, discharging their pieces in the air and brandishing their hats and jugs. Two climbed atop the coach. Waving their arms and yelling Sam's name, one of them jumped and one, I think, fell. More cheers.

Sam grinned down at me. Just as he always held his liquor well, so too did he handle this being the center of attention. It bore him up but did not intoxicate. Perhaps once it would have, or more nearly. But a somber strain had entered into him since meeting Jenny, and now it always seemed there was a place inside where this sort of adulation never reached. I remembered how he was after that first leap at Paterson, the one that brought him fame. Then with his rum and his success he had been perfectly happy. Now a much wider fame only had power to make him smile.

"You going to jump, Sam?" shouted someone. Others took it up.

Sam turned. They cheered.

"I reckon not, boys. This time I just mean to watch."

Boos and groans. Sam grinned.

"Well, I'm mighty flattered and that's a fact. But I don't just calculate Old Hickory'd like it much if I up and stole his show."

Laughter.

"Hooray for Sam!" And they did. "There's no mistake in Sam Patch!"

We left the circle of men and rejoined Jenny. There was a strange light in her eyes, and Sam seemed at a loss for a moment how to read it. But then she gave him a smile there was no mistaking the meaning of, and Sam took her arm. We set off in search of a hotel.

We had not gone many steps when there was an earsplitting shriek and a large body cleaved the crowd on my right and struck me at what felt like muzzle velocity. I went down in a heap, certain Davy Crockett had spied me and resolved to finish me with his bare hands. Sure enough, next thing I knew I was hauled up by an ear and clasped in a hug that might have been lethal to a lesser bear.

But it was affectionately meant. Molly Money had found me again.

"Oh my goodness! Goodness, goodness me! Goodness gracious, it's my darling Bruin! It *is* Bruin, isn't it?" she said, holding me away from her suddenly, as if to make certain she hadn't by some chance hugged the wrong bear. Delighted to see her and to discover she wasn't Davy Crockett, I licked her face from her chin to her eyebrows.

"Oh!" she gasped, sputtering, fending me off and wiping her face. "It *is* you. I knew it was. Oh, you dear thing, you remember your Molly?" And here two generous tears welled out of her eyes and ran down her already damp cheeks.

Sam and Jenny had stopped during all this. Now they came back and Sam took Molly's arm to steady her.

"Oh, thank you, thank you," she told him distractedly, not taking her eyes off me. She wiped her cheeks with her fingers. "Oh, thank you, Mr. Patch. You do remember me, don't you? I saw you in Paterson in July. I'm . . . I used to be . . . oh!" And she fished out a handkerchief and pressed it to her nose and mouth, looking at me the while.

"I sure do, Miss Money, and I'm proud to see you again. I reckon any friend of Bruin's is a friend of mine." He introduced Jenny.

"So pleased to meet you," said Molly, her eyes opening wider at Jenny's beauty, her attention for the first time diverted from me. A little flustered, she looked around. "Oh dear, I wonder where Jason is. I mean Mr. Meleager. He's my associate," she explained anxiously to Jenny. "Or that is, I'm his. I did leave him so suddenly. I hope I haven't lost him."

"No fear of that, my dear," came the hated voice, its owner popping up behind her like the proverbial bad penny. I thought of Carmody. I might have known it was a bad omen when he reminded me of Meleager.

"Mr. Patch, this is an unexpected pleasure," Jason Meleager went on, advancing to offer his hand. But he bestowed only the briefest glance on Sam. Drawing himself to his full height in a way that somehow called attention to his elegant new clothes, he removed his hat to Jenny and said, "Miss Hansom, permit me to say you look ravishing. I'm delighted to see you again."

This speech pleased no one, not even Jenny, who returned a slight nod of thanks but looked away. I think she was unwilling to be reminded of Carmody, to whom she owed her fine clothes.

Seeing his error, if perhaps not understanding it, Meleager adroitly shifted the focus to me.

"Yes, and here's Bruin. My word, if he doesn't seem positively to thrive on the rigors of jumping. Will you look at the fat on him?" He laughed good-humoredly. Molly frowned and gave me a consoling pat. I worked as much contempt into my features as I could, in the hope of disguising my terror. I think Meleager scared me even more than Crockett did, in the same way someone might shrink more violently from a snake or a spider than from a lynx or a wolf. "Well," said Meleager, his ironical eyes boring into me, "I suppose it helps him to float."

Meleager soon learned we had no place to stay.

"What, no hotel?" he said. "But my dear friends, you'll never find one now. It's much too late. The inauguration is tomorrow and there isn't a bed to be had at any price. Good grief, what shall we do?" He pondered. "I see only one solution. You must stay with us. Miss Money, you share your quarters with but one other lady. Do you suppose that by any chance there would be room . . . ?"

Molly, forgetting again and calling Meleager Jason, agreed immediately to share her bed with Jenny, like the good soul she was.

"Well, that's fine," said Meleager. "Mr. Patch, I'm afraid that my bed has three occupants already or I'd make you a comparable offer. But you're welcome to sleep in our wagon." He smiled. With Meleager you never knew if you were being insulted, though there was generally a strong presumption that you were.

That evening we could not get away from our benefactors, though it must have been plain to the meanest intelligence that that was what Sam and Jenny wanted to do. There was nothing mean about Meleager's intelligence, but as the same couldn't be said for the rest of him, he attached himself and stuck like a leech, oblivious to all hints that we could have managed without him. Patting and stroking me, Molly sat quietly by his side, used to accommodating herself to his lead.

Only once did she become animated—early on, in response to a polite question from Jenny as to what had brought them to Washington. Had they come just as spectators?

"Oh, goodness no. Jason, I mean Mr. Meleager, is going to see the president about a position with the government. Isn't that so, Jason? I mean Mr. Meleager? Yes, he has a proposal. He wants to set up a United States Phrenological Institute. I think it's a wonderful idea. Why, wasn't one of the big issues of the election *internal improvement?* And his institute would improve everybody everywhere, not just people in the Northeast with their factories and things. Though he's promised me he'll try to have it located in Boston."

Her Jason was regarding her sourly.

"Ah, yes, it did cross my mind to seek funding for a project somewhat along those lines. I can't say that I'm as sanguine about my chances of success as Miss Money here, but we'll see, we'll see. In the meantime I've been pursuing certain other possibilities . . . But tell me, Mr. Patch, what are your plans for after the inauguration?"

Sam's eyes strayed to Jenny.

"I don't know as my plans are that set."

"But I suppose you do mean to press on with your jumping?"

"I reckon," said Sam, this time not looking at her.

"Well, that's wonderful. I'm glad to hear it," said Meleager, glancing at Jenny in his turn. "You know," he said, still watching her, "I take more than an ordinary interest in your career, Mr. Patch. After all, I credit myself in some measure with having started you in it. Why, even your famous companion here," he said, indicating me where I sat on the other side of Molly, getting my muzzle scratched, "is a discovery and alumnus of mine, as you undoubt-edly recall. Yes indeed. I should be most disappointed to hear of your giving up your jumping."

Cocking an eyebrow at Jenny, he smiled and shook his head to show how disappointed he'd be. There was no answering smile, but far from having his spirits dampened by this, he seemed ac-tually encouraged. He leaned back. Jenny's eyes were averted, but his flashed with a bold, triumphant light. He had opened his mouth to pursue a topic so strangely gratifying when I woofed, gaining his attention, and bared my teeth.

"Hm. Yes," he said after a moment, thoughtfully and looking a little shaken. He glanced at me again, askance, and I gave him another view of them and of a good deal of gum. "Well, we'll have to speak more of this another time, when we're not so tired. I have a message for you in fact, Mr. Patch, from some gentlemen who are admirers of yours, and a business proposition of my own as well. But all that can wait. It's late now; there will be time enough tomorrow, after the ceremonies. I'm looking forward to them. Aren't you? This Jackson is said to be quite a wild man. It will be inter-esting to get a look at his head."

He stood and Molly rose with him. She bent to give me a last pat, and Meleager turned again to Jenny. He bowed, all sinister charm.

"Miss Hansom," he said, with a smile that was rather too knowing to suit me; "Mr. Patch. Till tomorrow." They left.

The racket in the crowded dining room bore in on us, and I looked around at the people talking and laughing at the other tables. Jackson's name was on everyone's lips; no one had a care for anything beyond the events of tomorrow. Only at our table was there no boisterous conversation, or any conversation at all. And if Sam and Jenny were, as I suppose, as preoccupied by what would happen tomorrow as anyone, it was not the inauguration specifically that concerned them. No, it was the approach of that moment they had postponed once already by reboarding the coach in Baltimore. Now it was upon them. Both sensed that the unnat-ural hiatus in which they had floated so poignantly for the past two days was a period of grace that could not be further prolonged; that a decision had to be taken, and would be—tomorrow. And both sensed too that this decision would be made almost despite them, even though they alone would make it.

Chapter 33

The momentous day, March 4, 1829, the day of the inauguration, dawned clear and chill. From my old spot under Meleager's wagon I watched it progress from the first uncertain brightening, not yet enough to hide the stars, to a definite glow above the buildings to the east, and then to an early stage of maturity, a direct shaft of radiance striking and setting alight the topmost roofs and chimneys. Rising restlessly, I watched it come on in defiance of my best efforts to wish it away. I had lain awake most of the night wondering what this day would bring; now here it was in person, so to speak, chipper as a Jacksonian and cold as Meleager, and my one desire was that without more ado it would just take itself away again.

I had too many reasons to mistrust this day to feel any different. Everything about it was ominous, right down to its cheerful appearance. In view of everything I expected to go wrong today, I would have found a decent overcast more sympathetic and considerate.

First there was Crockett. I was due to meet Crockett today; *would* meet him if Sam had any say, and what Sam wanted had a way of coming about. What would happen when we did meet had given me much food for reflection while waiting for the sun to rise.

That Crockett wouldn't remember me I regarded as too faint a possibility to pin any hopes on. Anyway, should he have forgotten, Sam could be counted on to remind him. That moving little story Meleager had invented for Sam about my encounter with Crockett had stuck; I worried it might yet prove more hurtful to me than any of Meleager's acts of conscious malice.

Then there was the inauguration itself. Even if I survived Crockett, there were countless thousands of others just like him about, all only too willing to correct any little oversights of his in the bear-killing line. It was some consolation to know that they would never harm a hair on my hide if they knew who I was; but there was also a distinct possibility that I would be well on the way to being a rug before anyone could do introductions.

Finally, there was the matter of Sam and Jenny. I trembled for the result of that. I had a feeling, a horrible feeling, that this time what Sam wanted was not going to come to pass.

No sooner did the sun touch the canvas top than I saw the wagon shake and Sam appeared at the back. I gathered from his hollow eyes that he hadn't slept any better than I had. He threw me a preoccupied glance and passed a hand over his stubbly jaw. Uncurling myself from the spot in the yard where I had left off my pacing after the light goaded me from under the wagon, I went up to Sam, rumbling plaintively. He dropped his hand, seemed to relax a little, and smiled.

"Morning, old friend. Already up, are you?" He jumped down and tugged at the front of his sailor jacket. I thrust my head under his hand. He gazed at me intently for a moment, then scratched me between the ears. "True blue, ain't you, Bruin?" he murmured, his eyes probing mine. "All right, I know you are," he laughed, throwing his arm around my neck and evading my attempts to lick him. He squeezed my head and held me still. "It's sure the damnedest thing, the shape a man's friends come in. And all you've ever had from me is a sight more baths than a fellow of your sort is generally accustomed to. Well," he said, smiling away my protest, "let's go get something in our bellies. I've a feeling we'll be needing all our strength before this day is through."

After a quick wash-up at the pump we went inside and found many of the hotel's other guests stirring too. Everywhere we heard Jackson's name. He was the subject of every conversation and of any number of boisterous toasts.

A little later Meleager, Molly, and Jenny came down. Meleager was in the middle, with one of the women on either arm. But there his impartiality ended. Molly, looking around apprehensively at the teeming lobby, had Meleager's arm and nothing more. Meleager's attention was given entirely to Jenny. Very debonair today, he hovered over her, keeping up a stream of what, from his face, was bright and amusing chatter.

I glanced at Sam. I think he didn't notice Meleager at all. He only had eyes for Jenny.

And Jenny seemed to forget everything else on spotting Sam. Greeting him with a smile I know Meleager would have given his eyeteeth for, she quickened her step and came down to where Sam and I were waiting.

Sam's face was radiant. I began to wonder if perhaps the day wouldn't turn out so badly after all.

Something had changed in Jenny overnight. Some decision had been taken—while she slept, I thought. She didn't look as if she'd passed a night like Sam's and mine. I think the matter of Sam and his jumping had been in some sense taken out of her hands and considered by a higher court while she was unconscious. For a lot goes on while we're unconscious. It's often then that the great inarticulate beast within us, which we flatter ourselves either doesn't exist or is tamely broken to our will, exerts itself to tell us what things really mean. I could only guess that in the womanly depths of her the ledger on Sam had been sized up and a judgment rendered; that the various entries for and against him had been weighed and counted and that some things that perplexed in the proverbially more reasonable light of day were set aside now as being not so important after all. So when she opened her eyes, she saw Sam transfigured, as if he were the one who'd changed. And Sam, looking back at her all through breakfast, found a new light in her eyes that seemed amazingly to promise the consummation of all his hopes and left him thoroughly flustered and capable of scarcely anything but a wordless display of happiness.

After the meal Meleager and Molly hove up beside us in the lobby. Plying his gold toothpick, Meleager waited a while to be noticed, then cleared his throat. No result. He put the toothpick away and took out a cigar case.

"Cigar, Mr. Patch? No?"

He put the case back, saving out a cigar for himself. This he lit with a match he struck ostentatiously on a handy table. He might have fired the table and the cigar together and still not got their attention.

"Shall we go for a stroll, then?" he asked next, sending gouts of smoke in their direction. No response. Sam and Jenny only continued to gaze at each other.

Now, though, Molly woke to the situation; her sympathies ranged themselves at once with Sam and Jenny. Her expression melted.

"Jason, hush!" she said softly, tugging at his arm. A shiver of delight and embarrassment shook her ample frame, and perforce Meleager's too. "Can't you see. . . ?" she said, giggling and blushing, stealing another glance at the two lovers and blushing some more.

For once Molly prevailed, the poetry in her kind soul proving stronger than Meleager's baffled malice. With a gargantuan sigh she freshened her grip on Meleager's arm and led him away. And oddly enough, as they retired with many a backward glance, I thought it was Meleager's face that betrayed the most envy.

By noon the whole city had gravitated to the Capitol building and was waiting with surprising complacency for the appearance of their hero. Buckskin-clad figures were everywhere, and some did give me odd looks, but I seemed to have overestimated my danger. Apparently the attraction of slaughtering bears was eclipsed by the desire not to miss anything and a tacit amnesty was declared. Anyway, good feeling clearly ran high. It must have been one of the few times when Old Hickory actually had a tranquilizing effect on anyone.

Also, I take some credit for my own precautions. First, I made sure to keep myself wedged in so tightly between Sam and Jenny that Sam, till he understood, was a little irked. And then too there was the coonskin cap I'd appropriated from a late-sleeping guest at the hotel. More than any hickory sprig, which after all might have stuck to my fur only by accident, I think the cap went a long way toward helping me blend right in.

So there we waited, in front of the steps of the east portico of the Capitol, surrounded by the homely flower of the frontier, all of them simmering with happiness and excitement. Flags and bunting fluttered in the crisp air, and buckskin fringe on many a sleeve; laughter and voices bubbled around us. Sam, and Jenny, too, wore the same look of happiness and expectation as everyone else, although its basis in their case was anything but political. I found myself yielding to these benign influences. Maybe, I thought, Davy Crockett would turn out to be in a good mood, too.

Suddenly the band struck up and the door leading onto the portico opened. A party of dignified-looking figures emerged, and the crowd broke into a cheer. A man taller than the rest appeared, with an imposing mane of graying hair. The crowd went wild. I saw hats, bottles, and even an infant thrown into the air.

I studied Jackson closely, a little confounded by his appearance. I don't know what I'd expected, but this tall, rather courtly-looking gentleman gravely surveying the crowd from the steps didn't match up at all. I suppose I'd thought that Jackson would be a kind of quintessential Jacksonian—fierce of eye, clad in buckskin or homespun, a gun in one hand and a jug in the other. Except for the fierce-of-eye part, nothing could have been further from the truth. He looked at least as much a gentleman as any of those bona fide samples I'd seen drink themselves into relative stupor in Boston. But his eye did have a nasty glint, I thought, even now with nothing to meet it save a throng of adoring supporters. Its affinity to Crockett's was obvious. I didn't have to try hard to imagine how it would kindle in that thin, severe face of his at sight of an Indian or anyone else who might make so bold as to oppose him or to whom he might take a dislike. Thoughtfully, I pulled my coonskin cap lower over my face.

The dignitaries formed themselves up around Jackson. Briefly a speaker addressed the crowd, then someone else stepped forward with a large Bible, which Jackson bent over and kissed, setting off the cheering again. Then Jackson faced us to read his address. The crowd hushed and the new president began to read. For perhaps ten minutes he read, and you could have heard a pin drop throughout, so intent was the crowd on catching every word— or any word. For the truth was that Jackson's speaking voice was as little Jacksonian as the rest of him, and I don't think anyone but those standing to either side of him on the portico heard a bit of it. I also don't think anyone minded.

Then he was done and cannon crashed close by, followed by an answering thunder of guns on the river, all barely audible over the roaring of the crowd. People surged forward, everyone wanting to shake the president's hand; and I think everyone would have done it, too, if the group around him had been any less deter-

mined. They managed finally to wrestle him away and into a waiting carriage. This, surrounded by an honor guard of somewhat
decrepit Revolutionary officers, set off immediately down Penn-
sylvania Avenue to the White House. The crowd gave way, cheering and waving, straining for a glimpse of their new leader, and he,
with his wintry smile, nodded and comparatively graciously waved
back.

So that was Jackson. My first reaction, that he was nothing
much, changed even as I watched the crowd chase his departing
carriage. The image of his face lingered, grew more impressive as
I thought about it. There was iron in him. He was a man whose
outlook had a primeval simplicity: the world was full of enemies. It
was a man's task to cut his way through them and remove them
from his path. Friends weren't so much a radically different sort of
being as just a more congenial variety of nonenemy, hence not
requiring such concentrated attention. There was no second, independent category of entity. Indians, live ones anyway, were enemies by nature, incapable of being friends; and bears, I feared,
were more like Indians than like anything else. I could see it was
a system with much to recommend it to the grasp of his equally
simple friends.

"It's Sam! Old Sam! Did you see him, Sam? Weren't he just
great?"

I jumped, startled, and almost lost my cap. Gordy, our fellow
passenger on the coach, had somehow spotted us in the crowd. He
swarmed up to us, closely followed by Zeke and Jasper. The three
of them grinned at us, weaved happily on their feet, trying to keep
us in focus, and pressed their bottles on Sam.

"What did you think, Sam? Ain't he something? Old Hickory
himself! Was like I died and went to heaven!"

"I reckon he's a pretty impressive gent, all right," allowed Sam,
grinning back and taking another friendly swig from Gordy's bottle.

"You bet! Won't be no more nonsense with him around."

Jasper, whose fullness of heart seemed to have impaired his
speech, was tugging at Gordy's sleeve and pointing down the avenue, where the crowd was streaming on its way to the refresh-
ments waiting at the White House. He managed to get out two
words that sounded like "ice cream."

"He's right, Sam. Let's go. We don't want to miss nothing!"

There was a good deal at the White House I personally wouldn't have minded missing. But Sam was as drunk as Gordy, though, as I say, from a different cause. He gave Jenny a look of good-humored inquiry. She laughed and squeezed his arm.

We set off at a lope, urged to go faster by Gordy and company, but prevented by the crush around us. Gordy, I think under the impression that he was going a lot faster than he was, spent as much energy blundering into people on either side as on trying to pass them in front. At length he subsided, panting, and gasped to me as I came up: "How in tarnation far is it?"

Jenny skipped along at Sam's side, holding his hand and laughing breathlessly. I had to woof at the sight. They were so happy, the pair of them. Sam was grinning and laughing . . . His face when he looked at Jenny practically shone.

We reached the lawn of the White House and kept right on going. The crowd was so dense by now that we hadn't much choice; regardless of anything some of us might have preferred to do instead, we found ourselves flowing toward the White House like water running toward a drain.

We gained the steps. There the crush was so great that people who fainted had no place to fall and were carried along off their feet. The very door timbers creaked under the pressure of so many shoulders.

Jenny gave a cry. She was having the breath squeezed out of her. I myself was seeing spots. Deciding it was time I took a hand, I reared up glowering and threw some bodies about. The effect was magical. People fell all over themselves to give us room. Encouraged, I pushed again, starting a chain reaction that spread outward behind us until it had knocked down half of the farthest edge of the crowd. Ahead, the logjam in the doorway suddenly eased and people who had been stuck before slipped through like greased pigs.

Then we were inside. It was pandemonium, people romping, fighting, and caterwauling like madmen. And ever above the shrieking and whooping came the crash of breaking crockery and glass, destroyed as the crowd scrambled to reach the buckets of hard liquor. Two men in white jackets appeared bearing a cut-glass bowl of punch. In seconds they were knocked sprawling, the bowl dashed to the floor. A spicy odor of oranges filled the air.

Against the far wall was Jackson himself, an object of attraction second only to the liquor and looking in imminent danger of meeting the fate of the punch bowl. He was protected by a desperate band who struggled with all their might, their clothes torn and disheveled, to keep off the heedless stream of well-wishers. In the vanguard of this band was an overheated face I recognized. My heart stopped: Crockett.

He looked in a positively foul mood, too. I don't know why his eyes alone didn't keep off the crowd. But no, impelled partly by enthusiasm, partly by the pressure behind, one grinning bumpkin after another pushed forward, intent on congratulating Jackson personally, only to go down under the fists of Crockett or one of the others.

And, to my horror, Sam, Jenny and I were in the greeting line, moving steadily toward our own confrontation with those redoubtable eyes, not to say fists. And Sam, with Jenny safely in tow, was as oblivious of any danger as the most heedless Jacksonian.

In the middle of everything was a very stout woman seated on the floor, eating an aspic with a gold spoon. People stepped considerately over and around her and the line moved on, sometimes slower if those at the front had time to exchange blows with Crockett and the others, sometimes faster if they didn't. I cut my foot on a shard of crystal. The pain hardly registered. I was too distracted by Crockett and by my mounting desire to flee before it was too late, before he spied me and left Jackson to fend for himself while he, Crockett, found his gun, which I knew he'd have handy someplace, and came after me to settle scores . . .

I tried to take heart from how hard-pressed Crockett and the others were—they were beginning to droop from exhaustion, and now and again someone actually got past them and had to be knocked down by the president himself, which only sharpened the competition to be punched by Jackson personally.

But Crockett never flagged. His blows continued to rain down as tirelessly and with as good effect as if he found cracking heads a tonic.

Then we stood before him—or Sam did, anyway. My protective coonskin cap long since gone, I was crouched down trying to hide behind Jenny's skirts. Above the din I heard Sam say:

"Howdy, Colonel Crockett. I reckon this ain't the best time for talking, but I just want to say I'm mighty pleased to meet you. My name's Sam Patch."

And I heard Crockett say:

"I know that bar."

How this conversation might have continued we'll never find out. I'd heard enough already. It may be, as Sam accused later, that I have a deficient sense of history, but there was certainly nothing wrong with the way my instinct of self-preservation worked. With a howl of sheer terror, I forgot reputation, Sam, everything and just bolted for the nearest window, scattering Jacksonians broadcast. The men in my path obligingly smashed the glass and leaped through before me to clear the way, and out I jumped into the yard. There I noticed in passing that—apparently in the hopes of drawing people off from inside—they were indeed setting up tubs of ice cream, as Jasper had presciently hoped they would.

Chapter 34

The events of that evening are burned indelibly in my memory.
They're so painful to recall that it's all I can do to relate them. Even
so, I've gone over and over them, reviewed every word, every
nuance, a hundred times—all useless labor, of course. What difference can any of it make now? Sam is gone, there's nothing to be
done. Still, I find I can't help myself. That night holds a terrible
fascination for me. I return to it like a ghost who can't keep from
haunting the scene of his last moments on earth. For that night I
think we came within sight—sight? no, within smell; within a kiss
or a single word—of escaping the events that followed.

We had come back to the hotel. I was in my usual place beside
Sam, feeling a lot more cheerful than I looked but sedulously cul-
tivating an appearance of intense remorse for reasons I'll explain.
So I was keeping very still, not even agitating for a refill on my
beer, which nobody seemed to notice I'd finished some time back.
Sam was mad at me, you see. It seems that—quite inadvertently—
I had managed to forever bollix up his chances of hitting it off with
Crockett . . .

It happened this way. When I took off for the window, Crockett
evidently made a move to come after me—maybe just for a closer
look, but maybe to grapple with me and settle things right there, if
you ask me. So anyway, Sam happened to be in the way and

Crockett shoved him. That didn't do much on account of all the people backed up behind, so Crockett slugged him. Sam, not unreasonably finding a certain lapse from courtesy in this, slugged Crockett back (oh joy!). What's more, Sam *knocked Crockett down!*

Well! I leave it to you to imagine the sequel—how Crockett's eyes blazed as he glared at Sam; how Sam stood there at the ready, prepared to give whatever satisfaction was required; how the crowd surged forward when Crockett fell, forcing Crockett to postpone settling personal scores to protect the president; and how Sam's heart must have sunk as he watched Crockett scornfully turn his back on him and realized just how unlike the picture in his mind the long-awaited encounter had turned out to be.

It's true, I wasn't so terribly unhappy for myself, but I did feel bad for Sam. There was no way he could make up for what he'd done. Apologies would only make things worse. I had forever ruined Sam's chances of getting close to his idol.

Worst of all, I'd in some sense dismantled the idol himself. As Sam put it, shoving aside his St. Croix and leaning forward, fuming:

"It's plumb bad enough you made me knock him down, blast it. But that's only a patch on what you done. Burn me, I'd have swore up to now there weren't a man as *could* knock him down. It's like . . . why, it's like the whole world is just a meaner place somehow."

Jenny, amused, tried to smooth things over.

"But Sam, it wasn't just anybody who knocked him down. It was you."

"Right. And that there's the worst thing about it."

He was inconsolable. We sat there in silence over our drinks, Sam bitterly, Jenny still amused, me with mixed emotions.

Sam brooded a while, then said:

"You don't understand, Jenny. It's more than just I didn't get to meet Crockett proper. A whole lot more. It's like I'm feeling there ain't nothing is what it's cracked up to be. There's this here with Crockett, who I've looked up to for so long. And there's the jumping, too. Don't get me wrong, I'm as stuck on it as ever. But it's a curious thing: when I was getting started, I figured it would just keep getting better as I made my mark. Now I reckon I've made that pretty fair and somehow I ain't half so pleased as I thought I'd be. Instead of being on top of things, the fact is half the time lately I don't even know which end is up.

" 'Course," he said, looking up, "I reckon a lot of that is I ran into you."

Jenny still wore her smile. But was it a little softer now? I held my breath.

"Jenny. . . ," said Sam at last.

Just then of all times a jarring new voice broke in on us:

"Ah, there you are. I was hoping I'd find you. Good evening, Mr. Patch. Miss Hansom. May I join you?"

Looking fresh as a daisy, Meleager nodded to Sam and gazed hungrily at Jenny's now-fading smile.

"Actually," Sam told him rather coolly, "this ain't just the best time, Mr. Meleager. We're sort of talking over something important."

"Ah. I beg your pardon. Of course I don't wish to intrude." He hesitated. "Still, I wonder if you could give me just a minute anyway. As I mentioned last night, I have a message for you from some gentlemen in Buffalo and also a matter of my own I'd like to discuss, and Miss Money and I plan to leave early tomorrow morning if Miss Money is well enough to travel. We were paying our respects to the new president this afternoon when one of his associates accidentally struck her," he explained to Jenny. "That is, the man meant to strike someone else"—here I thought I saw just the shadow of a smirk—"but that person ducked."

"Perhaps another time would be better, Mr. Meleager," said Jenny.

"Alas, I doubt that very much. Another time may not offer."

It was here, this deceptively ordinary moment, its true significance unremarked by anyone, that I sometimes think the issue hung by a hair. If they had known what a crisis it was for Sam Patch, every soul in that noisy dining room would have stopped cold whatever he was doing, a hush would have fallen, and all eyes would have turned to us. Dear Sam, why didn't you send him away—push him, knock him down if you had to (not a bad idea in its own right)? Then you could have finished what you were saying to Jenny and she at least might have said yes. And then, who knows, with Jenny by him Sam might have turned aside, stopped short at last, not pushed things to conclusions.

I don't know. Maybe the hair was really more like a strong rope after all and the end would have been the same. It would have been most unlike Meleager to allow himself to be turned away, and even if somehow that were managed, Sam's own ambition, if I can call it that, might have led him over the same course in time. Could even Jenny have taken the place of his work, the jumping that made sense of his life?

I don't know. These are waters too deep for me. I only know that in the event Sam motioned impatiently for Meleager to speak, and Meleager did.

"Mr. Patch, I bear an invitation to you from a group of sporting gentlemen in Buffalo. On learning of our past connection, they asked me to convey to you as strongly as possible their desire that you visit their city and take part in a certain entertainment they have planned. In short, they would like you to come and jump Niagara Falls."

"Niagara Falls?"

"Indeed, sir, the mighty Niagara. The prince of waterfalls. The"—he smiled—"*ne plus ultra* of jumps."

Sam sat thunderstruck. I stared in dismay. Why hadn't he ever mentioned these falls? What must they be like if their name alone could strike him speechless?

But then—and this made me tremble too—his color returned and I saw how excited he was.

"It sure would be a fine jump."

Meleager laughed.

"A fine jump! My dear fellow! It would be a crowning achievement, a jump the fame of which would echo down the ages. It would make your other jumps look like child's play. You mean you'll consider it?"

He hardly needed to ask. Sam *was* considering it; was so rapt in considering it that, just watching him, I could practically feel the earth quake from the pounding cataract and see rainbows shimmering hundreds of feet in the air over jagged rocks.

Indeed, to say Sam was considering it is a misnomer. There's no considering where there isn't any doubt, and I could see at once that there wasn't any doubt about what Sam would do. Before Meleager mentioned them, these falls weren't on the roster of possible jumps, but only because Sam hadn't thought of them. Now everything was changed. The falls were there, hence must be jumped. To turn away would be a defeat, an admission that Sam had reached his limits. More, it would reduce other lesser jumps to feats that others might imitate or surpass. If Sam shrank from this, then in the future a jump of thirty feet would be just a jump of thirty feet, not the glorious sample of jumping qualities whose full measure still had yet to be taken.

No, I can't hold Meleager to blame for this. The idea must have come up sooner or later, and I can't imagine that it would ever have failed to fascinate.

Somehow we all wound up looking at Jenny. White-faced, she regarded Sam, her hand clenched and pressing on the table. She spoke not a word. As he gazed back at her, I saw that the two of them were locked again in silent communion as they'd been in the coach; that while all else fell away they burned and became transparent to each other, saw through each other past all pretense or politeness and assessed directly their love and each other's requirements. The moment of decision, so long deferred, had come. And now that it had come, both realized that the decision was after all not theirs to make—not freely; no, that their will in the matter, however much they yearned for the same result, must in the end count for very little.

Meleager watched them, astonished. Always before he had frightened me, even when I knew I had no harm to expect. Just his presence was threatening, seemed to crush my spirit with evil portents and intimations of malice. Momentarily now his fangs were drawn. Against the bright background of Sam and Jenny's emotion he appeared impotent, a weak, blinking thing, helpless in the light.

"Uh, they also plan other attractions," he said at hazard, just to be saying something, I think. "Table Rock is to be blown up with gunpowder and a schooner sent over the falls . . ." His voice trailed away.

At last Jenny lowered her eyes. Hours seemed to have passed. Her face was very beautiful—not even sad, really; rather, her features had arranged themselves in a kind of repose. Meleager was staring at her entranced.

Then, gracefully, she arose, her eye still meeting no one's. Standing, she paused a moment, then murmured:

"Excuse me, it's late."

"Jenny," said Sam in a voice that was strange to me.

I wrenched my eyes from Jenny. Sam stared at her. Somehow great circles had formed under his eyes. In just these few minutes he had aged.

"Jenny," he said again as she looked at him. She waited. He couldn't speak.

At length she nodded once, ever so slightly. There was nothing more to say. Composedly, she turned to go, the motion wafting a wave of her scent to me. The tears rose to my eyes.

Hastily, Meleager stumbled to his feet. He said something about allowing him to accompany her and started round the table. Before he reached her, though, she changed. Her face, her whole bearing, now expressed that chilling remoteness of earlier days. It was the look she'd worn when first I saw her on the boat from Albany. It was the look she'd worn with Sam way back in the beginning, and subsequently with Vanderbilt and Carmody. Now, not inhospitably, she turned that look on Meleager.

I saw him falter as his eyes met hers and registered the temperature there—cold beyond reckoning. But he approached again, recovering his confidence. For he saw that her indifference had as little concern or care for its subject as for its object, in this case himself. Thus I suppose it was an indifference holding, in its utter passivity and compliancy, no slight allure for a certain kind of man.

Chapter 35

I'm brought to my miserable present again by a startling visitation from the past. It seems to my bewildered brain that my mother has just reconstituted herself from the nameless humus and licked my cheek, soothing my anguish with her love. I turn and stare astonished into a pair of golden eyes. The eyes widen and my pretty penmate, alarmed at her own boldness, draws back in confusion, watching me. My own confusion is not small. Where are Sam, Jenny, the hotel where we parted that fateful night? My eyes, I realize, are filled with tears; my unlicked cheek is stiff with them.

My pretty penmate regards me, cocking her head. I am empty—empty of strength, empty of will, now even empty of feeling. She cocks her head the other way. I am a puzzle to her, one she never doubts it is her right to solve. I gaze back meekly, momentarily grateful to her just for existing. Her interest is the one thing, however foolish, that relieves the world of emptiness. I marvel. Dimly it comes home to me that my present has darkened to this one serendipitous spark. And without the least inkling of the absurdity of the idea, or even any invitation, she offers, this little spark, to roll back the shadows that beset me. Give her her head and she would brush them away like so many cobwebs. Her absurdity is sublime, but there is certainly no nonsense about her.

The thought makes me smile. Seeing, she is encouraged. Before I know what is happening, she woofs happily and lands with a bounce at my side, there to snuggle with proprietary complacency. I stare again in astonishment, but she only turns those great eyes on me trustingly and, as I still stare, licks my nose. There, she's thinking, it's about time we settled that. Her warmth spreads against me, reaches inside. Serenely she sits there, gazing out over the waste, confident everything is all right now.

It was a different Jenny who came down with Meleager next morning, a Jenny no longer hopeful and happy, no longer smiling—no longer Sam's. All the softness that had grown upon her in her time with Sam was gone; in its place was the old detachment, looking firmly established and quite at home.

She nodded to Sam, but, again, so coolly that I think he'd have been better off if she'd snubbed him. On the other hand, I don't know what he'd have done if she'd cried. But then, if she'd cried, she wouldn't have been Jenny.

No, she didn't cry. Instead she behaved as if she had managed to wall herself off from him to a degree that was hardly flattering. I think he'd have preferred to see more sign she was angry or hurt, though it may sound odd to put it that way. The smooth surface she showed left him nothing to cling to, no foothold, nothing to bring away. She'd abstracted herself, absconded. The warm woman of only a day ago was gone as utterly as if she'd changed to a wraith of smoke or a chill cloud of vapor.

But if this change left Sam desolate, it had the opposite effect on Meleager, who skipped along at her side, eyes glittering, babbling away and not the least downcast that he knew Jenny paid no attention. What crushed Sam affected Meleager not at all. He had never aspired so high as Sam in the first place, and he saw progress in the fact that now, in a perverse way, he had come up with him.

But poor Molly! For she was there, too, trailing along behind; and if yesterday she hadn't remarked Meleager's attentions to Jenny, or if she'd tolerated them, today was a different story. Her face puffy and a large bruise under one eye, she seemed to find it painful even to look at the pair in front of her, though look she did from time to time, and then her glance was filled with such heartache that it was a wonder it didn't penetrate straight through to Meleager's organ of Conjugality, or of Friendship at least, and so silence him though he never once met her eye.

"Ah, good morning, Mr. Patch," sparkled Meleager, cheerfully coming up to us and even bestowing a comparatively benign glance on me. "You slept well, I hope? You could hardly have fared worse than I did, I'm sure. I tell you, I very nearly got up and came out to the wagon myself. One of the gentlemen sharing the room with me spent three-quarters of the night giving a highly circumstantial reenactment of the entire inauguration in his sleep. It was all there, I swear, down to the speeches and the firing of cannon. I wouldn't have slept at all, I believe, except that he was evidently one of those frightened by our hirsute friend here" (meaning me) "at the reception. When he came to that part, he suddenly gave the most astonishing leap, fell on the floor, and finished the night under the bed."

As no one had anything to say to this, Meleager laughed and turned to Sam.

"So. You've had the night to think matters over. What have you decided? May I send the Buffalo gentlemen an encouraging reply?"

Sam's eyes had never left Jenny. She looked at him now and the mask slipped. But there was no reproach, only understanding. Nor was there any suspense. She knew what he had to say, and in that gentle, sorrowing gaze she even encouraged him to say it.

"I beg your pardon?" said Meleager, not hearing him. Sam drew a breath.

"I said I reckon."

"Excellent. Ah, there's the bell. Shall we go in?" said Meleager hastily, anxious to prevent further erosion of Jenny's estrangement. Meleager looked at her as if he wanted to give her his arm; but he didn't dare yet. With a strained smile he stood by as Sam approached her. Jenny hesitated a moment, then went in with Sam.

After a breakfast that not even Molly or Meleager seemed to enjoy, or me either for that matter, we came out and Meleager resumed his conversation with Sam.

"Mr. Patch," he said around his gold toothpick, eyeing Jenny the while, "I mentioned last night that I had a proposition of my own to make you." He paused. I sensed that Jenny's presence was causing him to choose his words with special care. "It's just this. There are some months before your Niagara debut in October, and it strikes me that they mark an opportunity for unusual profit for both of us, rightly spent. Here's my idea. What would you say, you and Miss Hansom, I mean, to joining forces with Miss Money and myself for the duration? You have an enviable way of drawing crowds, and they should be positively enormous as the news of your Niagara plans spreads. And while admittedly my experience with your crowds has not been an unalloyed success, I'd be game to try again if you were willing to assist me. Do you see? Both of us stand to benefit enormously. My difficulty is drawing crowds, and yours is profiting from them. Working together with me, you could turn your notoriety—I mean your fame, of course—to advantage, and so could I. You wouldn't have to do anything, really. Just let me announce that you'll be there to greet those attending my lectures from the stage. That should do, I think. Once they're inside, trust me to make them pay for the privilege of meeting you. And I would of course, ha, ha, be willing to share with you most generously in the proceeds.

"And Miss Hansom," he said, quickly turning to Jenny, "you could be most useful to me too, if you were willing. I can always find a place for so attractive an assistant."

Poor Molly gasped. Meleager ignored her, or maybe never even noticed her. Hungrily, anxiously, he made his pitch to Jenny.

"You could help me on stage, displaying the skulls and such, freeing Miss Money to concentrate on her singing. I know many would come just to see you. And again, believe me, I'm prepared to be generous."

He waited, but she didn't say anything and he couldn't read her expression. Reluctantly, he turned back to Sam.

"Well, Mr. Patch, what do you say?"

But Sam was having better luck with Jenny than Meleager was. During the meal she had unbent a bit, and now his eyes probed and held hers and overcame her attempt to look away. I saw him draw strength from this. I thought he even began to look something like his old self again as he read that she did not, could not, hate him and still wished him well, for all that she couldn't stay with him. A peace seemed to descend on him; he didn't look so haggard. That he loved her more than ever and that she saw this and was unable to root him out of her own heart was written in their faces. It seemed to dawn on them that once again matters were out of their hands, but in far kindlier fashion than before; that if they could not yet have each other, neither was all between them ended, despite any conscious decisions of theirs. For good or ill the bond between them still held. Their time was not come, but it might yet. This was only an intermission. Negotiations would proceed.

"I reckon not, Mr. Meleager," said Sam. "I reckon I'd better just go my own way for a spell."

Meleager chewed his lip. I couldn't tell what he thought about losing Sam, but that he felt chagrin on some score or other was plain enough from the way he looked at Jenny.

"But October, you say?" said Sam. "That's when they're having this shindig? I guess a world of folks will be there to see," he mused. "Why, I expect they'll come from all over to take in a show like this here one shapes up to be. Even them Shirt Tails out of New York might stir their stumps for this one, I wouldn't be surprised. Why," he said softly, eyeing Jenny, "I calculate a fellow might figure on seeing just about anybody show up for this one, ain't that so?"

Despite herself, Jenny smiled.

All in all, then, Washington was more anticlimax than crux in Sam and Jenny's relations. It had seemed before that matters must be resolved there; instead the result was another postponement. Against all odds, Sam still progressed in his campaign to win Jenny. Indeed, he had won her heart; only her head held out against him, and perhaps her pride. She still rebelled against submitting herself to the chances of his career and her vulnerability there. But the party of her heart seemed to gain strength daily, and so Sam still hoped. Indeed, he had if anything more cause for hope than when she'd left him in New York.

Meleager, too, wasn't entirely unhappy with the turn of events. Jenny agreed to travel with him—or rather, with "Miss Money and you," as Jenny was careful to word it—and on the principle that half a loaf was better than none, Meleager accepted her terms. We parted, then, everyone feeling he had gotten less than he hoped, perhaps, but rather more than he expected.

The days and weeks flew by for Sam and me, and they were the happiest in a long time. It was like when we were just starting out. Once again hope loomed on the horizon and life had a purpose. Niagara had brought things back into focus for Sam. As he said to me one night over drinks in a small town on the Massachusetts coast, where we'd worked our way, jumping, from Washington:

"You know, Bruin, I was a blamed fool. There I was, feeling lower and lower on account of the jumping was getting to seem more like a job than something I plain wanted to do, and the way out was there in front of me only I didn't have the wit to see it. It goes to show, it's just wrong in a fellow ever to give up hope. You can't ever prove anything about how there's nothing left to live for, can you?"

I mumbled something equivocal, just to keep him happy. Truth was, I thought this insight of his fell a little short of brilliance. It seemed both platitudinous on the one hand and doubtful on the other, and that didn't leave much to admire. But I'd happily have seconded sappier sentiments than this if it would have done Sam any good.

But then, just as I was starting to feel all sad and wise and superior, Sam said something that brought me up short. I'm not sure I've entirely figured it out to this day.

"I ain't so much saying you can always plan on something like Niagara to come along and pull you out of a hole, though it's true, you never know but it might," he told me, regarding me reproachfully over his glass as if he sensed I'd been underestimating him. "Take jumping, for instance: there just *ain't* nothing to beat old Niagara, so there's no way that trick can work twice. If I've always got to have something bigger and better, well then, after Niagara I may as well go hang it up." He took a large swallow, eyed me, and set down his glass.

"But listen here: I'm thinking if the mountain won't come to Mohammed, maybe Mohammed can still go to the mountain. I mean, here's the thing. Maybe it's true there's only so many jumps; but maybe there's lots more ways than one to look at jumping."

He rolled his eyes at his cleverness in making this out and leaned closer.

"What if there's as many kinds of jumps as there's ways of thinking about jumping? What about that? Why, then a fellow would never run out, would he? It sets me thinking, and that's a fact. Here I am and jumping is my life. But it's like I'm only just finding out what jumping *really is*."

Here he bent on me a look of the greatest significance. I tried to bear up under it respectfully, but if you want the truth, I didn't have the faintest idea what he was talking about. Jumping, I'd have said, was jumping, and that was about all there was to it. But I'd learned already not to sell Sam short, and if he said jumping might be something it wasn't, I'd try to entertain the possibility. What counted was that Sam's mystical insight seemed to give him a new hold. If those were the terms, he could have any five crazy notions without complaint from me.

We spent most of that summer touring up and down the coast, jumping from mastheads, yardarms, and rooftops. I never saw Sam in better jumping trim, and I was getting pretty good, too. I'd learned that a little technique saved a lot of aches and pains, and now I generally managed to hit the water hind feet first instead of on my rump or my back or, worst of all, on my belly. The crowd loved it. They'd liked it well enough back when the splash I made doused everybody, but they seemed to like my new style even better. I wonder if they noticed how much it was like Sam's.

They'd have liked anything, though. Word of Sam's Niagara plans had spread, and we were heroes everywhere we went. Sam took to refusing to perform from anything under thirty feet (he said less than that was more of a hop or a skip and he was strictly a jumper by trade), but people loved even the short jumps and just generally couldn't get enough of us. And Sam took every jump seriously. The shadow of Niagara fell on everything we did that summer. Even the least jump became a sort of Niagara in minia- ture, hence something to be approached with proper gravity; and after the joking and cavorting, Sam always delivered the same little prologue. The point of what they were about to witness, he'd tell his audience, was to show how some things can be done as well as others. And if nobody really knew what he was talking about, they all heard him respectfully and did their best to take what he said to heart.

In September we finally turned inland. Sam had had a message from the Buffalo organizers giving the Niagara date as October 6, and while they had urged him to come on early to allow time for publicity and carousing, Sam seemed reluctant to oblige. In fact, as the date approached, I saw signs of nervousness. It wasn't the jump; Sam had been ready for that from the minute Meleager proposed it. But when he got to Niagara, Sam would see Jenny again. How this meeting would go preyed on his mind consider- ably.

One day we got a letter from Molly. She sounded much happier and apparently the reason was Jenny. Jenny was wonderful, wrote Molly. Not only did crowds flock to see her, but she exerted an influence over them that Molly described as nothing short of magical. As soon as Jenny appeared on stage, even the rowdiest were converted into gawking gentlemen, disguising their belches, tippling with little finger raised, and careful not to spit on anyone's feet. Jenny always stayed on stage, and if anybody did misbehave, as sometimes still happened during Molly's sets, Jenny only had to give him a glance and either the troublemaker subsided directly of his own accord or he was straightaway helped to by his more considerate neighbors.

In fact, it sounded as though Jenny and Molly were thick as thieves. I inferred that Meleager's own designs in this line had fallen through. I'd thought they would from the way Jenny and Sam had parted, but the confirmation was welcome all the same. Carmody had been a negligible rival, but the recollection of what he'd put Sam through was still fresh enough to smart. Actually, it sounded from Molly's ingenuous account as if Jenny was even obliging Meleager to be more loyal to Molly. Insofar as he hoped to win to Jenny's good graces, he had to please her, and evidently she had let him know that it didn't please her to see him treat Molly the way he did. I thought that was a delightful paradox and wondered if Meleager appreciated it; certainly Molly did, or the better treatment, anyway. That much was clear from the letter, which bubbled along for ten closely written pages and more than once brought moisture to my eye. Nor could Meleager rebel: he was doing too well; Jenny had become necessary. Not only was attendance up, but the phrenological aids were moving so briskly now, Molly wrote, that Meleager had had to stoop to selling knucklebones and refuse from butcher shops, which he advertised as having been formerly attached to notably interesting skulls. It was the only way he could keep anything in stock. The crowds would buy anything, so long as they could take it from Jenny's hands.

Sam warmed himself on the feelings he knew Jenny had for him, but he knew he enjoyed them on borrowed time. I never saw him flinch from anything, but I think he came close to flinching from meeting up with Jenny at Niagara. I think he sometimes wished that summer would never end, that he could spend his days perpetually loving Jenny, even at a remove, and jumping in the shadow of Niagara.

But the summer trickled away till there was only a little left, and so Sam had finally to turn his steps in the direction of the rendezvous. Late September found us in Utica, where we took a canal boat for

Rochester. The stage would have been faster, but I think Sam chose the canal boat as much for that very reason as because, as he said, it would be nicer for me.

Our steersman on the trip was one Erastus Bearcup, as hairy a man as I ever saw. Except for his eyes, which glittered like zircons, and a light patch I took to be the end of his nose, only the positioning of his body announced that a person wasn't looking at the back of his head. His forearms and even the backs of his hands were covered with a thick mat of fur, and when later in the day he stripped to the waist, he exposed such a rich pelt front and back that I wondered he didn't find a shirt altogether superfluous.

Ordinarily Bearcup and his two crewmen only carried freight, but Bearcup's slow-moving *Belvedere,* as his dingy barge was somewhat grandly named, was fast enough for Sam, and traveling with Bearcup meant we had the boat to ourselves. Bearcup was only too glad to make accommodations, and in no time I was happily ensconced with Sam in the stern on some soft bolts of cotton. Bearcup managed the tiller and we passed a pleasant if not altogether uneventful trip trading round bottles of St. Croix and, in the case of Bearcup and me, admiring each other's coat. By the time we got in to Rochester, about seven o'clock, we were all fast friends, so instead of striking off on our own Sam and I stayed to help Bearcup unload and then went with him to a haunt of his, the Recess Tavern, on Exchange Street, to meet "some more of the boys."

At the Recess, Bearcup, in an excellent humor, banged open the door and cried:

"Lookie here, boys! Look who I got. It's Sam Patch!"

Chapter 36

I awoke next morning to a splitting headache and the consciousness that we had just two weeks to the day till our October 6 jump
at Niagara. As the biggest event of Sam's career, it should have
been something to look forward to, but somehow the closer we got
to it, the more it cast a pall over things. It almost seemed to be
stalking us. Just an idea at the beginning of summer, it had been
quietly putting on flesh and creeping up on us till now it was hard
to think of anything else. And every day it loomed larger. We
dragged our feet, we laid over whole days; nothing helped. It just
kept gaining on us no matter what.

There was too much going on at Niagara for me not to feel
apprehensive. Sam was to meet Jenny there, and Meleager, and not
least of all there was the jump. Even if it didn't kill him, it was
bound to mark a turning point. For after Niagara his jumping could
never be the same. Waterfalls wouldn't be the same. It was as
though in jumping Niagara he were to jump all waterfalls together,
at once. Afterward he could only repeat himself in that line. Jumping itself, the way it had been, would be lost to him. And however
much he consoled himself with mystical delvings into the true
nature of jumping, I worried about him.

I think Sam himself had some sense that Niagara represented
a swan song of sorts; that no matter how he tried to fortify himself

with metaphysics, jumping Niagara would likely forevermore rob him of jumping.

In fact, I think this may have been on his mind that morning when he came down late (they'd put us up at the Recess—wouldn't have it any other way) and grumpily seated himself without even giving me the usual scratch.

Bill Cochrane, owner of the place, and some of the boys who'd helped welcome us last night came up and renewed their urgings that Sam have a look at their own falls there on the Genesee. A hundred feet high it was, and right close in to town. They'd wanted to drag him out there last night for a jump, and it hadn't been easy for Sam to persuade them that after our ride with Bearcup he was in no condition to do it justice even if there'd been any light, which there wasn't. Now they were starting in again.

Sam heard them out over a plate of sausage and eggs.

"All right," he said, without looking up.

So we went, traipsing on over when Sam was done with breakfast.

It was a hard falls to get to, sandwiched between the high walls of mills and factories. But I gasped when I saw it. Nearly a hundred feet across and tumbling mightily into mist-veiled depths hidden by the angle of the bank, it was the most massive falls I'd ever seen.

And still everybody said it wasn't a patch on Niagara.

I heard Sam suck in his breath too. As soon as we came out on the grassy strip at the water's edge, he hopped out on a treacherous-looking ledge of rock washed an inch deep in water.

"Careful, Sam!" Bill yelled before he could stop himself. He bit his lip and looked at the other two who'd come along. They hooted and Bill laughed too. Then the one name Orson stepped out after Sam. He turned around.

"Hey, look at me!" he said, splashing his feet.

"Aw, that ain't nothing," the third man said, though without going so far as to try to improve on it.

Meanwhile Sam was examining the falls. Unconscious of the water pushing at his ankles, he walked to the edge and looked over. Mist billowed up in his face as he searched below for rocks, snagged trees, or peculiar eddies that might mean unseen hazards beneath the surface. A full hundred feet the water plunged in wavy tresses of foam before exploding at the bottom with an ominous roar. But Sam was in his element. He was as cool leaning over that slippery bit of rock as Bearcup was sitting by the tiller of the *Belvedere*.

Straightening finally, he put his hands on his hips and squinted across to the opposite bank. I saw his eye take in the slight curve in the lip and the interruption midway where a split of rock broke the water's surface. He shaded his eyes. But professional scrutiny was yielding now to aesthetic pleasure. He gazed at the water rushing over the edges of the spit and I could see that he liked what he saw.

"What do you think, Sam?" asked the bold Orson, knees bent and feet carefully planted. "Can you jump it?"

Sam treated this question with the contempt it deserved. Intently, he surveyed the feathery-looking foam, the rainbows and clouds of spray. He seemed to be trying to fix the look of the falls in his mind, as if he wanted to treasure it up against future need.

"I reckon we'll save this one out," he said to no one in particular, his voice barely reaching me over the water's thunder.

Absently, he took out his watch.

"Here, will you hold this a minute?" he said, giving it to Orson.

Then he stepped off the rock and vanished.

Impossible to describe the scene back at the Recess when we returned. Word of Sam's jump had gone out like lightning and the whole town was wild. If Bill had owned a Recess as big as a circus tent, he could still have packed it to the rafters. Even the upper crust came to gawk and shake Sam's hand. I hadn't seen so many beaver hats since the inauguration. But Sam, good-humored again, bore it all modestly.

"Jump?" he said, deprecating the whole thing with a wave of his hand. "That was no jump, that was just practice!"

We spent the rest of our two weeks in Rochester carousing and otherwise enjoying ourselves by way of getting in shape for Niagara. At least once a day Sam went off to visit the Genesee Falls, for which he'd developed such an attachment. Everyone hoped he would jump it again, too, but he only said no, he was saving it out. He refused to explain what he meant by this, but finally he pacified his admirers by telling them he would come back to Rochester after Niagara and jump it properly then. This promise he solemnized to everyone's satisfaction with a drink, and then we moved on to drinks in honor of his upcoming feat at Niagara.

In fact, we stayed up so late and had so many drinks that we missed our coach the next day and arrived at Niagara on Tuesday too late to jump.

Chapter 37

The exhibition at the Falls on the 6th was a disappointment for the attending crowd, which pronounced it a hoax. The British authorities refused to permit Table Rock to be blown up; and in lieu thereof an effort was made to cause an explosion on Goat Island. It was an abortion—"a mere flash, scarcely audible ten rods," according to one onlooker. The vessel which was to have crossed the Falls, struck on some rocks and remains stationary some distance above the cataract. Sam Patch did not show until the next day, when he jumped into the Niagara River from a rock about 70 feet high. The "exhibition" was altogether a failure—although the natural beauties of the scene doubtless repaid the curiosity of the throng.

Lockport Gazette
October 13, 1829

Meleager, Molly, and Jenny sought us out right after the jump.

"Oh!" shrieked Molly, blubbering on my shoulder, "dear Bruin, thank goodness you're safe! I was so worried. I thought surely you were going to throw yourself in after Mr. Patch. You dear thing. I'm so glad you didn't. You're such a nice, sensible bear."

Meleager stuck out his hand.

"Yes indeed, a fine performance, Mr. Patch, very fine, under the circumstances. I suppose you really couldn't do any better on such short notice, could you? A shame you didn't arrive sooner before people went home, though. I'm afraid many of your devotees must have left disappointed. Well, you've recouped somewhat today—at least with those who stayed to see you. I shouldn't worry if I were you. I'm sure you haven't done your reputation any lasting harm."

"It ain't my reputation I'm concerned about exactly, Mr. Meleager," said Sam. "It's the folks who left thinking the whole thing's a hoax. I'll have to find some way of turning them around on that, I reckon."

Indeed, we had already spent the better part of last night trying to do just that. Mortified at having come in late and let people down, Sam had dragged me around to every saloon in town, spreading word that he meant to perform at least a token jump on the morrow. And I suppose it was well he did. In some of these places we met with heckling. This was a new experience for me, at least since joining Sam, who hadn't had to contend with anything like it since that first jump in Paterson when he saved Tim Crane's bridge. But Sam seemed to feel he had brought it on himself, and instead of going up and knocking the heckler's head off, as I must say I was inclined to do, he just bore up and reiterated that he meant to do a jump tomorrow that "wouldn't be nothing much, but wouldn't be nothing, either," and skeptics could come and satisfy themselves as to whether or not he was "the real Sam Patch as advertised."

Wiping some stray droplets from his forehead, Sam turned back to Jenny.

"Hello, Jenny. You look good."

Jenny had been studying him too, especially when he wasn't looking at her. Her eyes probed every nook and cranny of his face, as if she hoped to find in the shape of an ear or the stubbly outline of his jaw some key that would enable her to give his love and his jumping a proper construction. He baffled her, and if anything he baffled her more as she knew him better. The things he did didn't add up. The man shimmered in and out of focus; she mistrusted the images that formed. Meleager, vastly more complex, must have seemed in many ways far easier to read.

But for all that he was a puzzle, I could see that something in her still responded to him. And she couldn't hold back the smile Sam had been waiting for.

Sam went up and took her hands.

"Well, you'll be wanting to change into dry clothes, I expect. And then doubtless these gentlemen here have the usual reception for you in mind," broke in Meleager, indicating the small crowd around us, who were indeed equipped with the usual jugs and bottles, but who were also presently so rapt in gaping at Jenny that they seemed to have forgotten their thirst. "Miss Hansom, will you come with us back to the hotel then? I'm afraid if we don't leave now we'll miss the packet."

"Tell you what, Mr. Meleager," said Sam, not bothering to look at him. "You and Miss Money go on and catch your boat. I reckon there'll be another along—right, boys? That's what I thought. Well, me and Miss Hansom will follow on that. I guess I can put off the usual celebrating till there's something proper to celebrate. This here little business was just nothing. In the meantime me and Miss Hansom have some catching up to do."

So after Sam changed we passed the afternoon strolling about in the vicinity of the falls. Looking rather glum about it, Meleager left with Molly to ride the boat back to Buffalo, and those other men about us too obtuse to see by themselves that their company was in no great demand Sam good-humoredly shooed on their way, promising to give them something to really drink about before he left town, and promising to help them drink about it, too.

When the last of them had been sent packing, Sam turned to Jenny. Absently scratching the top of my head, she stood gazing out over the river. Sam joined her, and for some moments the three of us just looked at the falls.

They could stand a lot of looking at. I'd never seen anything so big before that moved. I don't know how to describe them. Maybe I can't do better than to say they're indescribable. And plunging through space nearly two hundred feet, the weight of them fell equally heavily on the rocks at the bottom and on my self-esteem. I was abject in the face of them. I thought of my sometime flattering speculations about my importance in the general scheme of things and I was filled with shame. As well inquire into the uniqueness and irreplaceability of a flea or a maggot. Of what conceivable importance could I be beside this sublime monster, however mindless it was? It was a god, a divinity of the old school, classmate of Thor and Ra. I wasn't even a man. To jump such a falls was either an act of worship—and a properly dangerous one, for any god worthy of the title ought to be approached with fear and trembling—or an act of hubris as sublime as the waterfall itself.

I stole a glance at Sam. My last thought had me teetering on the brink of what felt like an insight . . .

Yes, there was truth in my worm's-eye view of these falls. They were indeed resistless, implacable. They were a terrific antidote to that primitive complacency that locates oneself and one's own at the center of things. Nothing like them for gaining a proper sense of scale. But to the worm, even a worm is and must be important, and the falls' brand of truth isn't a comfortable one to live with. It requires palliating, something at least to wash it down with. Impossible to accept that all life ends in mineral insignificance and that to know that is the sum of wisdom.

I gazed at Sam and found myself taking new heart. His maxim "Some things can be done as well as others" occurred to me in a new light. My scalp tingled; I wondered if once again I hadn't underestimated Sam . . .

Was it possible that some such revelation as the one the falls had inflicted on me was a precondition of really understanding Sam? That his maxim and his work reflected a hitherto unsuspected philosophical penetration? What if the only way to read him properly was against the background of the falls' brand of truth and, specifically, as a response to it? Was he saying maybe that there are other measures of importance beyond mere size, being at the center of things, and lasting forever? That the old quantitative, spatial way of looking at things was as primitive and false as the related error of thinking that we in fact do endure, are the eternal centerpiece of the universe—the notion, in short, which viewing Niagara Falls tended so effectually to disabuse me of? Was he perhaps plumping for a subtler view, not so much quantitative as qualitative—an *adverbial* style of valuation, and a route back to self-esteem?

"Some things can be done as well as others," he said. What if this didn't mean that some things can be done *in addition* to others, but *as properly*—so as to have as much merit? Had I been overlooking the real significance of Sam's having picked a line of work that produced artifacts even more evanescent than snow sculpture? Was he trying to show that it's not *what* that counts, but *how?* Yes, he made a splash, so to speak—but does anything leave less trace than a splash? The point is—who cares? It doesn't matter! How is Sam any the less for the fact that he, like the rest of us, can't leave a footprint in a river?

But Jenny was speaking. She seemed to be having trouble getting the words out.

"I'm glad I saw you jump, Sam. I think I understand better now. And I think I see now that it would be wrong of me to try to stop you.

"But Sam," she said, shushing him as he started to speak, "when you're not jumping, you must be very good to me. I want you to make me feel important too. Will you try to do that? If I have to share you with your jumping, and maybe someday lose you to it, you have to make that up to me. You have to show me that you need me, too, so I'll have something if . . . if . . ."

Sam folded her in his arms. He kissed her neck, her cheeks and her eyes. A little later, when she'd stopped her sobbing, we took the boat back to Buffalo.

Chapter 38

That weekend Meleager had an idea.

Actually, it was quite a striking idea, and as natural in its way as Flexible Grummett's suggestion way back when that I should follow Sam and jump, too. I also suspect that it was inspired by similar motives.

The idea was simply that to recover as dramatically as possible from the ignominy of having missed his initial appointment to jump, Sam should leap next time from a platform built out over the falls to give him greater height.

"Actually," said Meleager, turning to Jenny, who had stiffened angrily at the proposal, "it would be much safer. The platform could be angled out over the river, past the rocks. That's where the real danger lies. Mr. Patch has already demonstrated numerous times that mere height by itself is no difficulty." He smiled reassuringly.

Sam liked the idea. Snapping his fingers, he declared he'd take it right up with the boys. He called for pen and paper and then and there, with Meleager's assistance, he drafted the following handbill:

> ## TO THE LADIES AND GENTLEMEN OF
> ## WESTERN NEW YORK AND OF UPPER CANADA
>
> *All I have to say is, that I arrived at the Falls too late, to give you a specimen of my Jumping Qualities on the 6th inst.; but on Wednesday, I thought I would venture a small Leap, which I accordingly made, of Eighty Feet, merely to convince those that remained to see me, with what safety and ease I could descend and that I was the TRUE SAM PATCH, and to show that some Things could be Done as well as Others; which was denied before I made the jump.*
>
> *I shall, Ladies and Gentlemen, on Saturday next, Oct. 17th, precisely at 3 o'clock, P.M., LEAP at the FALLS OF NIAGARA, from a height of 120 to 130 feet (being 40 to 50 feet higher than I leapt before), into the eddy below. On my way down from Buffalo, on the morning of that day, in the Steam-Boat Niagara, I shall, for the amusement of the Ladies, doff my coat and Spring from the Mast head into the Niagara River.*
>
> *Sam Patch*
> *of Passaic Falls, New Jersey*
> *Buffalo, October 12, 1829*

In the interim we spent much time at the falls. In fact, they drew us like a magnet, though each of us, I think, saw in them something different.

Sam, I would say, at once liked them best and was least impressed by them. He took in the falls' sweep and furor more with the eye of a craftsman who admires a fine piece of handiwork. He seemed to feel Niagara had been made expressly for him and matched his specifications in every particular. The falls were merely perfect. Had it been any but Sam who viewed them this way, I'd have said his perceptions were a bit pedestrian.

But Jenny was awed. The falls filled her with dread. But even she didn't mind coming back again to see them, and a couple of times suggested the visit herself. They held a fascination for her. It seemed to me she gazed at them as if trying to unlock some mystery. Then from time to time she'd steal a glance at Sam and study him with much the same look she gave to the falls.

For myself, I liked them less and less. They gave new meaning to Sam's distinction between a full-time jumper and one, like me, who only jumped part-time. The difference was no mere matter of degree. There was only the most superficial likeness between Sam's jumps and mine, and the difference was not to be explicated just in terms of expertise. Not all verse is poetry, and next to Sam I was the veriest poetaster, most noticeably when we tackled the same subject.

Molly Money enshrined this insight in an innocent remark. The pair of us came sometimes on our own to wander about the falls when Meleager was out of sorts, which was often enough, and when Sam and Jenny were minded to spend the day by themselves in their hotel room, which also happened not infrequently.

"I'm so glad you won't be jumping Saturday with Mr. Patch, my dear. I do worry about you so. It isn't that I don't worry about Mr. Patch, of course—I do. But he seems so in his element somehow, as if it's hard to believe anything really bad could happen. And even if it did, it would be very sad, of course, and poor Jenny would be desolated; but it would seem almost natural, somehow. Is that a terrible thing to say? I don't mean it that way. I'd be as sorry as anyone. You know that. But if something bad did happen to Mr. Patch, it would be very grand and awful. If it happened to you, dear, I'm afraid you'd only look foolish."

Saturday came, and with it the preparations for Sam's jump. Four long trees were stripped and brought to the base of Goat Island, where they were lashed together and guyed with ropes. The first attempt to raise the platform failed when one of the ropes broke and the whole structure came crashing down. Under Sam's fretful direction the damage was repaired and the platform haltingly rose again, bobbing and swinging, looking each moment in imminent peril of snapping in two. The men moored it in place extending out over the current at a slight angle from the perpendicular, 120 feet above the water. There it swayed, creaking and groaning, as though it still must topple any second, and made a strangely breathtaking sight just in itself. For though it reached only two-thirds of the way to the top of those gargantuan falls, still it was at least of a scale with them. From the other shore the men on the ropes and at the base of the platform looked like ants swarming about a stick in the ground. And just to look up along its length from the base of the platform, as I did, was to make oneself liable to an attack of vertigo that left the palms of one's hands tingling so they almost hurt and raised the fur on end all down one's back.

Unfortunately the day was lowering and rainy, but I think at that point Sam would have jumped in a blizzard. Not holding his earlier default against him, thousands had come to see, and Sam would have done anything rather than disappoint them a second time. And for their part, his audience seemed just as bound and determined to watch. When three o'clock came and it was still pouring, Sam sent word to those on both sides of the river that he earnestly begged their indulgence, but that he feared it was still raining too hard to jump just at present, inasmuch as he might get wet; but if they'd wait right there a bit till the weather cleared, he'd wait right there with them, and then they'd see something they wouldn't forget in a hurry and they'd know whether he meant business or not. To a man, I think, they all faithfully waited.

An hour later the rain slacked off and Sam emerged from a cleft in the rock where he'd sheltered himself. After taking brief stock of the sky, he kicked off his shoes, gave his jacket to someone to hold, and began a swift ascent of the platform by means of crosspieces nailed to its length. A collective sigh went up from the watchers. Molly, next to me on the edge of the bank across the river, squeezed my shoulder till it hurt, while Jenny, on the other side of her, bit at a handkerchief.

Finally, Sam gained the top of the platform, which reeled under his weight. He stood and spread his arms. Then, turning our way and looking directly at us, he took out a black scarf and tied it around his neck. The crowd sent up a cheer barely audible against the background roar of the falls, and I looked sharply at Jenny. The tears were in her eyes now. But she seemed to collect herself; her handkerchief fluttered bravely as she waved. I was certain I recognized the scarf as hers.

Then, after some cautious stamping and jumping to test the platform, Sam stood still. Bestowing only two glances on the seething water to either side of his perch, he studied the eddy directly beneath him for a while, then lifted his face again to us. To Jenny,

I should say. For though the distance and the spray and mist that intermittently filled the immense gorge made vision uncertain, there could be no doubt of the object of his attention. She lifted her chin and gazed back at him. Motionless, the two of them communed this way across the gulf as if only they two were there; as if Sam were dedicating the jump to her from the tiny, precarious top of his platform of skinned trees and soothing her with his glance; and as if she accepted the offering finally and was soothed.

A full ten minutes passed. Then Sam disengaged and glanced at me, I thought. He took the scarf from his neck. Tying it around his waist, he waved, kissed an American flag that hung above him, and stepped off to plummet into the flood.

I've described before how he jumped. Always it was a marvel of precision and control. But never before had I seen such perfection, such technical mastery. Like an arrow, the newspapers were fond of saying. Yes, like an arrow he sped down to the gray-green, foaming water, to strike, with never a quaver, feet first, his hands coming down from over his head to below his hips, his feet drawing up, his knees straightening just before the impact. Then he was gone with scarcely a splash.

I'd swear that not a soul breathed while he fell and that not a soul but gasped when he struck and vanished. Molly staggered and looked faint. Jenny, her fingers clenched on the rail in front of us, stared at the river in disbelief.

For long moments the boat plied the eddy where Sam had disappeared. Whether from his sense of showmanship or because the current had him, he didn't reappear right away and people began to murmur. I could see them stirring, putting their heads together. But I wasn't worried—too worried, anyway. The jump had been perfect, and I was able to endure the suspense with something approaching professional detachment. Molly's fingers were digging into my shoulder. I slipped free and licked her hand.

And sure enough, next moment a cheer announced that Sam was discovered. We saw him wave the boat off and begin swimming strongly for the nearest shore. Then he was clambering onto a rock as men raced toward him along the water's edge. Hats soared, handkerchiefs were brandished aloft. Sam greeted the men as they came up with him. He waved at the crowd on the banks high above. Then he faced our way particularly and looked up at us. Jenny raised her handkerchief and waved, slowly and awkwardly at first, then excitedly. I woofed and Molly enveloped her in a tremendous hug and she hugged Molly back, her lips trembling, the tears running freely down her cheeks.

As a newspaper editor put it later, not understating the case too badly:

"This jump of Patch's is the greatest feat of the kind ever effected by man. He may now challenge the universe for a competitor!"

Chapter 39

Over and over I rehearse that scene of triumph, cling to it, try to fix it forever in place. But I'm as frustrated in the recollection as we were in the living of it: to have the scene at all, it must be played, and the very playing spins it out and puts it behind. Just now, in fact, it seems to be fading even more resolutely than usual, and I wake to the fact that the daylong hiss of the rain, background accompaniment to my reveries, is slackening off with the light.

I look about me. The droplets are few enough now that I can see the individual rings they form in the puddles. They gather in shining globules on the underside of the fence slats and rest there instead of hurrying off in streams. The sky is as gray as ever—grayer—but the drops falling now seem almost inadvertent, their initial impulse spent.

My side is warm where my pretty penmate has been faithfully keeping her station. I'm surprised and ashamed at how good the warmth feels. For me to enjoy anything seems a mark of disrespect to Sam and a reproach to my grief. How can my mourning be genuine and deep and I still be sensible to pleasure? But the truth is that it's only my body that registers the pleasure, and the body has no finer feelings, no empathy or respect. It's an entirely selfish thing. Yes, Sam is dead, it says; when do we eat? The king is dead, long live the king.

There, I think, in a nutshell you have the true burden of the consolatory phrase "Life goes on": we still get hungry.

Yes, we still get hungry. And even more than most this draggled creature at my side is little else than an agglomeration of appetites. I gaze down at her in wonder, almost in fear, where she sits hunched over, attending to her injured ankle. She licks it repeatedly with a soft slurping sound. Her eyes are half-closed; she has licked and lulled herself into a trance. In the purity of her concentration, consciousness itself sunk in instinct, she seems to me an avatar of deity.

She looks up. Finding my eyes on her, she pants, sits up and preens herself complacently, never doubting the security of her tenure, the brightness of her prospects. She turns her head to look at me again and I know what she's thinking. Without the least impatience in the world, she's wondering how long I mean to keep us sitting here in the wet like this.

My superior knowledge and, yes, finer feelings are no match for her simplicity. How explain to her the impossibility of the odds, the hopelessness of the case? Her trusting optimism would be proof against my demonstration. She doesn't even know enough to realize we have to escape; she just wants to leave. Oh, invincible ignorance! I feel my spirit descending from lonely reaches of freedom and enlightenment, drawn by those golden eyes. Banality besets me again, wraps me in its comfortable embrace. Grumpily, but with a grateful stirring of something else to which I won't just now presume to give a name, I bend to look more closely at her ankle.

Yes, I suppose she could travel if she had to.

Once again we were the toast of the town. Despite the rain, thousands had turned out to see the Great Leaper redeem his pledge, and through them thousands more soon heard the tale of it. The entire city was convulsed: Sam's feat had sandbagged them, left them gasping. Always the mighty Niagara Falls had been a fearsome presence just outside of town, a distillation of the surrounding wilderness, glowering on their doorstep. Like the citizens of ancient Athens with their Minotaur, the pioneer residents of Buffalo had learned to live with and even take a certain proprietary pride in the monster; but it was an uneasy neighbor at best. Now Sam had bearded it. If he'd diverted the river, he could hardly have impressed them more.

People's enthusiasm stunned Meleager and provoked him. He'd stayed away from the jump, pleading indisposition; now the fuss over Sam seemed to make him sick in earnest. The excitement went beyond anything he'd ever seen. This time the whole town was carried away, not just the more excitable orders. People Meleager would have given his eyeteeth to impress were fawning on Sam, and it cut Meleager to the quick. Not least of all, Jenny, too, was frankly fascinated. He writhed to see her happiness, how she couldn't take her eyes from Sam. Her complete capitulation, her undissembled dropping of Meleager from any consideration— if indeed she ever held him in any—was salt in wounds that smarted no small amount already.

I knew what he was thinking. Like other people given to jealous envy, Meleager chafed at the apparent lack of justice in this life. Here he was, so plainly superior to this upstart bumpkin by any objective measure, yet Sam bested him at every turn. Sam won fame and honors while Meleager's efforts went unrewarded; Sam took me away from him, somehow got my cooperation, and used me to advantage when Meleager never could; and lastly and most palpably an outrage, Sam had even captivated Jenny, stealing her from under Meleager's very nose and so bewitching her that she was blind to all Meleager's patently more lustrous qualities. It seemed that everything Sam did had a corrosive effect on Meleager's self-esteem.

I might have laughed to see his discomfiture, but the light in his eye when he looked at Sam or Jenny was too hot and desperate for gloating over. In fact, with his drawn face and his quick, snarling smiles he began to remind me increasingly of Flavius Raskin.

All that first night of celebrating he sat at our table with us, not saying anything, holding his end up just with those snarling smiles. The stream of people that came by to see Sam he surveyed with contempt when he looked at them at all; for the most part he had eyes only for Jenny and Sam.

I think Jenny's defection, if you can call it that, obsessed him. He coveted her more for having passed him over than he ever would have had she accepted him. Besides finding her desirable in herself, I think he projected onto her his other frustrations. She became a living symbol of all the humiliations he imagined he had suffered at Sam's hands, all the good things rightfully his that Sam had somehow bilked him of. The hunger in his face when he looked at her alarmed me, and the veiled, considering looks with which he appraised Sam alarmed me more.

Next morning after breakfast he strolled up to us with Molly. We were on the hotel porch, Sam, Jenny, and I, taking the air and returning the greetings of passersby. None of us was exactly delighted to see him, but Sam and Jenny anyway returned his salutation cordially enough. I regarded him narrowly but couldn't see any sign of last night's turmoil. His tone was free of rancor as he addressed Sam, and even the "good morning" he gave Jenny seemed relaxed and natural. He appeared to have come to terms with himself in the night and to have purged himself of bitterness.

In my book that made it certain he was up to something, and I settled down to watch him like a hawk.

He made some comment on the day and offered Sam a cigar, which Sam accepted. Molly came straight up to me and began to scratch my ears. After making an unusually bland pleasantry on this, Meleager said:

"Well, Mr. Patch, you have slain the dragon. The world lies at your feet. You seem to have a firm grasp of what few men even come within sight of—renown, the realization of your dreams, riches for the asking. You've done it all unaided, starting from nothing, and done it in a remarkably short time, too. Really, I'm quite speechless with admiration. I still remember our first meeting, when you'd taken just the first step on the path that was to bring you your success. How little I thought then that I saw before me such a hero, such a man of destiny, Mr. Patch. Yes, I've often reflected on that, how I could have misread you the way I did. All I can think is that your very singularity deceived me, Mr. Patch. The unique must always be unpredictable, I suppose. It follows its own laws, and the rest of us, having nothing to compare it to, have nothing on which to base a forecast. Indeed, I confess, you're an enigma to me still, Mr. Patch."

"Is that right, Mr. Meleager? It's a curiosity to hear you say so. I never made a secret what I was about," said Sam.

"No," agreed Meleager, puffing thoughtfully, "no, I suppose you didn't. Still, appearances have been known to be misleading. I confess I'm far less inclined to skepticism about them in your case than I once was, but even so, it's not always easy to know just what they're appearances *of,* if you take my point. But that aside, may I ask what you intend doing next? The dragon you've just slain was, if not the last, certainly the largest of its kind. I'm curious," he said, echoing Sam's own concern of not so long ago, "how you mean to avoid the horrors of anticlimax. I believe I do know you well enough to know you have no intention of retiring."

Sam took his cigar out and considered the glowing end of it. Jenny stood tranquilly by, watching him. I wondered if she had even heard Meleager's question.

"Well, Mr. Meleager," said Sam finally, frowning slightly as he rotated the cigar to discover any hidden features of interest, "I don't mind admitting that's a question I don't rightly just know the answer to. But I ain't worried much. It strikes me as there's jumping and there's jumping, and the subject is maybe a bigger one than I took it for at first. I reckon I'll see deeper into it by and by though, and something new will come along same as old Niagara did." And so saying, he smiled at Jenny, replaced the cigar in his mouth, and took a deep puff with every sign of satisfaction.

Meleager paled at Jenny's answering smile.

"No doubt, no doubt," he said, turning away. When he turned back, except for a tremor of the lip he was his new bland self again. "But I gather then that just at the moment you don't have any concrete projects in view? I ask," he continued, as Sam opened his mouth to speak, "because I have another proposition for you. You must admit," he said with a somewhat bitter smile, "that my ideas haven't turned out so badly for you."

I growled and shook off Molly's hand. Now we were coming to the meat of it. I thought of Meleager's other ideas: to jump Niagara; the platform. It was hardly owing to Meleager that they had worked out as well as they had; indeed, I suspected their success had caused him no little chagrin.

But Sam, finding no harm in hearing him out, signaled Meleager to go on.

"Once," said Meleager, gazing absently at two teamsters who had come to grief in the street through waving and shouting at Sam when they should have been guiding their horses, "I asked you to join me that we might tour together for our mutual profit. Much has changed in the short time since then. It would be presumptuous of me now to repeat that invitation. Instead, if this isn't equally presumptuous, I'd like to request to join you." He smiled. "Hear me out, please. I think you'll want to consider this.

"It has struck me, Mr. Patch, that our ways seem curiously bound up together. Indeed, it almost seems to be my destiny to advance your fortunes. So be it. I—we—have missed important opportunities through my having underestimated you and overlooked ways I could be of service that would have benefited us both. Now, as I say, I have an idea, and from what you tell me, it's an idea that may be just the 'something new' you've been waiting for.

"Mr. Patch, you've reached the top of your career in your present line. In the whole country there's no jump for you to try that can add so much as a whisper to your fame—and without refurbishing, this will fade. *So why not leave the country?* Go abroad! At a stroke you would open a whole new world of prospects. It may be that there are no waterfalls in Europe to compare with Niagara. What matter? There are none here either, and there at least there are other things to do and whole populations to do them for who have never had the advantage of witnessing one of your astonishing performances. I can think of no more promising sphere in which to carry on with the business of demonstrating how some things can be done as well as others.

"Think of it, Mr. Patch!" said Meleager, with a wave of his cigar. "You could continue in the work you love and have shown such amazing proficiency in. Whole new audiences would flock to see you perform whole new jumps. London Bridge! Why not? Gibraltar and the Pillars of Hercules! How does that sound for a jump? In company we could seek out the crowned heads of Europe. You could jump for them and I could feel them. Instead of a provincial hero you could become a living wonder of the world. And we'd both grow rich in the process."

He stood back, clamped the cigar in his teeth again and chewed the end of it with an agitation that told how he'd worked himself up. Sam's eyebrows climbed. He scratched his stubble. I thought furiously, but for the life of me I couldn't find a catch. Only Molly had an objection. Evidently Meleager hadn't cleared his proposal with her first.

"But Jason, what about our institute?"

Biting back what would doubtless have been a more peremptory response, the new, considerate Meleager answered patiently:

"Plenty of time for that, my dear, when we return from our tour. Indeed, it will hardly hurt our prospects to have been associated with Mr. Patch and received by royalty. Who knows," he said to Sam with a nervous little laugh, "with your permission we might even consider working your name into the title."

The Sam Patch, Jason Meleager Institute for Jumping and Phrenological Studies? I thought, aghast, until I realized he was only joking. Molly, though, who I remembered entertained her own ideas for a suitable title and who didn't have much sense of humor, looked considerably put out.

But Sam, I could see, was plainly taken with the idea—of Europe, if not of lending his name to Meleager's institute—and Meleager worked to consolidate his advantage. He spoke both French and German, he told us; had studied in Europe and knew his way around. Sam could leave all arrangements to Meleager and devote himself just to jumping. He wouldn't have to have anything to do with Meleager's phrenological sideshow unless he wanted to—in which case, of course, he would be more than welcome. But he was the star; it was for him to decide. Meleager even thought to highlight one feature of the proposal that would appeal to Jenny: the European jumps would all be comparatively safe. Sam would encounter nothing to test him like Niagara.

Sam was watching Jenny. He flashed Meleager a glance of gratitude.

"Well, Jenny," he murmured in the pause after Meleager finished speaking, "what do you think?"

I think Jenny thought quite a few things in the moment or two she took before answering, but she only asked:

"Is it what you want?"

"Well, it sounds pretty good, Jenny. I think maybe it is."

"Well, then, I think we should go."

Beaming, Sam turned to Meleager, not half so happy with the Europe idea as he was with Jenny. Even Meleager seemed momentarily distracted. Taking no notice of the approval of his plan, he feasted his eyes on Jenny with the same wild intensity I remembered to have seen Raskin give to the job.

But his idea seemed sound enough; at least, I still couldn't find a flaw in it beyond the necessity of taking along its author. I wondered if just this once Meleager had decided the rewards were greater from playing it straight.

So, after a little dickering over a further proposal to try to charge admission to the jumps—Sam wasn't having any until Meleager hastily explained he only meant for special seating—the thing was settled. We would leave immediately for London.

"Except," said Sam, "we have to stop off in Rochester along the way. I made the boys there a special promise I'd come back and do a proper jump. And the fact is, they sure do have a pretty falls there on the Genesee. I reckon that's as good a place to make one last jump before I go as any."

Chapter 40

Rochester loved Sam. Celebrated as we'd been at Niagara, that was nothing to the reception they gave us in Rochester, where because of Sam's earlier jump and his remembering his promise to return they showered us with attentions and embraced us as their own. Niagara had swelled Sam's fame past belief, and those who hadn't witnessed the jump seemed even more awed, I noticed, than those who had—maybe because they supplied the details from their own imagination. I guessed even Davy Crockett must have heard of Sam now.

We arrived in Rochester by coach one cool day at the end of October. Our driver, setting aside the haughtiness peculiar to his fraternity and generously owning Sam an even bigger celebrity than himself, lashed his horses up Main Street at a breakneck pace, slowing for nothing and hollering to everyone that Sam Patch was here—"Sam Patch! Look out, blast you! Make way for Sam Patch!"

But fast as we drove, word preceded us. Our driver finally had no choice but to stop in the street in the center of town, where so huge a crowd had collected that his most profane efforts couldn't get us through. Sam grinned out the window at everybody. Still rolling, the coach was boarded at every point a man could hang onto, several enterprising fellows even invading the boot where I was, which, however, they considerately evacuated posthaste on finding it occupied. Meanwhile, as Molly quailed and even Jenny shrank back, others wrenched the door half off its hinge, fairly tore Sam out of his seat and bore him away.

We were hemmed in by wild faces. Beckoning fiercely, one of them said:

"Hurry up there, ladies and gents. We're going on down to the Recess. You don't want to miss none of the drinking!"

Eagerly assisted, we got out of the coach and were half carried, half dragged down the street after Sam. Outside the Recess another crowd blocked our progress. Our escort surrendered us, and like so many sacks we were bundled forward from hand to hand and stuffed through the door. I landed on something yielding which on further inspection proved to be Molly. She in turn rested, none too comfortably from the look of things, on Meleager, who appeared to be unconscious. By us, rumpled but intact and laughing despite herself, stood Jenny, a flush of excitement in her cheeks and around her a cluster of men who seemed momentarily to have forgotten all about Sam.

Sam himself sat on the bar in a pose that reminded me of the first time I'd seen him up close, in Fyfield's tavern in Paterson after his first jump, except that this time he wasn't dripping river water onto the floor. But he wore the same grin and clutched what might have been the same bottle of St. Croix, though of course I knew it wasn't. And here I was again making my entrance with Molly and Meleager, too. But these parallels only emphasized how much things had really changed. That earlier time I'd had a certain notoriety, but now in a way I was nearly as famous as Sam. And while Sam was the man of the hour even back then, for all anyone knew, that one hour might have measured the extent of his glory. Back then, too, it was still possible for Meleager to upstage and condescend to him; Meleager was the person of real consequence. Now, though, the tables were turned, and if Meleager was noticed at all—which so far he hadn't been: only Molly, trying with a stricken look to revive him, was paying him any attention at all—he was noticed only as a lesser appendage of Sam.

As Meleager began to stir and opened his eyes, I saw what could only be a bitter consciousness of these altered circumstances flash through his mind.

But Sam was oblivious to Meleager's baleful stare. Bearcup had buttonholed him and was recounting a run-in he'd had with a man who bragged of once having met the notorious brawler and riverboatman Mike Fink.

"But I straightened him out all right, I guess. Before I was through he'd have swore to Mike Fink himself that next to you old Mike was nothing, just nothing at all," he concluded reverently. Overcome with emotion, he wiped his eyes on his sleeve.

"But tell us about Niagara. How was it, Sam?" Bill Cochrane called out. Sam grinned, happy to oblige.

"Well, it went off pretty good, I guess. I can't complain."

Cheers and laughter. "Tell us!" Sam took a swig from his bottle.

"Well, all right then, I'll say it: it was a humdinger."

"A humdinger!"

"It was. First off it was a first-rate place for a jump, the equal to which I never saw in all my days. And if I do say so, I've seen some first-rate jumps."

"Hooray!"

"You bet. There she was, that old Niagara, just as mean and nasty as three cats with their tails spliced, and it was like she was waiting for me since the beginning of time, practicing up ways to make things turn out bad for me. Boys, there was rocks as would grind a fellow up quicker than you could chomp an oyster and currents as would sweep away the leavings. The spray was so thick I didn't hardly know which way was down, and the thunder she made, boys, well, it just shook your bones. A mighty ticklish business, you can take it from me." He shook his head. Nobody seemed inclined to dispute his assessment.

"And if that wasn't enough, it was raining. That's right, just coming down in heaps. I thought for a time there I was going to have to send out for an umbrella just so I'd know when I hit the water. It was like that old falls saw me coming and got worried maybe she wasn't big enough, so she laid on something extra to try and double her size.

"But I'll tell you, boys, that was where she went wrong. It set me thinking, it did. See, I reckoned there was only one way she'd get so all-fired excited, and that was if she knew she'd finally met a fellow who was her match. So I said to myself, 'Sam, this old Niagara sure puts on a fine show, and she's trying her damnedest to get you buffaloed, which is a thing you're not often in the habit of, for a fact. But it's likely all smoke or she wouldn't have to work it so hard, and I'm guessing she knows you for a fellow without a mistake in him and she's plumb running scared. So just step out bold and show her what you're made of, and I calculate that'll settle her hash.'

"Well, gents, I don't mind saying that little speech put the heart in me again so I must have rose up forty feet in my esteem. So I just set out cool as could be to give her a taste of my jumping qualities, and I reckon you all know the rest of it."

They did. Oh yes they did. They signified as much with a roar that must have carried all the way to Niagara.

They wanted to know when he would jump for them there in town.

"Well, how about in a week?" said Sam, looking around agreeably. "That'll give folks as want to see a chance to get here."

All of them present wanted to see. They pointed out that they were already there; Sam didn't have to wait on their account. But Sam stuck to waiting a week, even rejecting a compromise proposal that he do just a practice jump for them as soon as it was light.

"Boys, I don't need any practice and I don't rightly want any. It would take the blush off it. Now what I do want is for you to just let me rest up a mite and catch up on my drinking, which I've been somewhat neglecting of late."

To take their minds off their disappointment, he told them of our plans to travel abroad. When they got over their astonishment, they were if anything prouder of him than before.

"I guess you'll show them popes and kings a thing or two," they said. "I reckon they'll see how we do things in the Yew-nited States!"

Almost ten thousand people gathered to witness Sam's jump. It took place Friday, November 6, 1829, a cool, blustery day but a clear one Sam pronounced ideal for the business at hand. And the crowd seemed to think so, too. Hours before the event was scheduled to take place they had lined the high banks and buildings on either side of the falls, as well as the flats below for some ways. According to the papers the next day, it was the largest assemblage the town had ever seen.

We got to the falls late, but it wasn't entirely our fault. Eager though the boys were to see the performance, they couldn't bring themselves to curtail the pleasurable business of toasting Sam's luck even to let us get on with it. Then Sam had no sooner declared that this was the last round when Bill Cochrane had the inspiration that Sam should appear in a style more befitting his dignity. He rushed off, to return, eyes alight, with a fancy white suit which he urged Sam to try on. Sam did, and the result exceeded everyone's expectations. The suit was Bill's band uniform, and draped and decorated in its braid, frogs, and epaulets, Sam really looked splendid. Meleager, watching somewhat sulkily from a table in a corner, remarked Sam looked just like Napolean, the Little Corporal; only Meleager actually said "a little corpulent," which I thought was unkind even if the uniform jacket was maybe a bit too tight. Jenny, saying it looked very handsome, got up and kissed Sam in front of everybody; but Sam was ill at ease and would only keep the pants, preferring his old sailor jacket to the other, which he said made him look "like an admiral, at least." But this change in his outfit called for more drinks, so what with one thing and another we didn't get to the falls till around 2:45, forty-five minutes late.

The crowd, though, had been content to wait and had even received some unscheduled entertainment. In fact, the jump almost went forward without us. About fifteen minutes after we were due somebody stepped out, reeled to the edge of the falls and, waving his arms and bouncing unsteadily on his feet, announced he was Sam Patch and was going to jump.

"Look at me! Whoopee! Here I go! Watch me jump!"

The crowd, taking him at his word, was all for letting him do it, too, but after a swaggering look over the edge he changed his mind and fled in a last-minute access of sobriety.

Not so the real Simon Pure. Though probably he'd had more to drink than the imposter, Sam was as steady as if hung in gimbals. If what he could hold without getting the staggers was the measure of a man's capacity, I'd never seen Sam drink too much. Even Jenny wasn't worried, or too worried anyway. Or maybe she was, actually, but having made her choice was too proud to show it. That's possible, now I think of it. But anyway, she *didn't* show it. She only returned the pressure as he squeezed her hands, and gave him a smile that would have brought him back, I think, even if he'd killed himself.

Then Sam turned and grinned at the crowd ranged all down the river. He waved and they roared back loud enough to drown out the falls. He stripped off his jacket and tossed it to us. Bill caught it and took charge of it with such devotion that I think he would have missed seeing the jump if Bearcup next to him hadn't begun pestering him to let him hold it, too, "just for a minute." I caught a glimpse of Meleager standing behind them, sneering.

A hundred feet was the drop, but to Sam that was nothing. Ignoring the treacherous current that tugged at his ankles, he waded out with the aplomb of a man crossing a muddy street. Stopping when he'd gone as far as he could, he glanced over the edge and took some deep breaths; then he stretched, waved at everybody, and jumped.

The jump was, as usual, another marvel of precision and grace. He struck with hardly a splash and this time reappeared in seconds. Disdaining, again as usual, the waiting boat, he swam swiftly to shore, climbed out, showed himself whole to the crowd, and headed back up our way. Arriving, he embraced Jenny, then Molly, shook hands with Meleager (who dried his hands elaborately with a handkerchief after), accepted his jacket back from a proud Bill, heard with a grin Bearcup's complaint that he "would have held it only I couldn't make him give it to me," and at last turned panting to me.

"Well, fussbudget, will you take a turn?"

I screwed up my face to intimate I hardly thought it necessary. Sam laughed.

"Come on, old fellow. She's a sweet one. I won't stand by and see her snubbed. Out." He pointed.

I whimpered and appealed to Molly, who took a half step forward but stopped, overawed by Sam. Meleager grinned maliciously. Jenny looked sympathetic, but the smile that hovered about her lips signified I could hope for little real help from that quarter.

"There's things we all have to do, old fellow," said Sam, "and some of them are risky and nobody can do them for us. But you'll be a better fellow for it."

I questioned that, in the present instance. Nor did I see why I had to jump just because he did. Were the things we all had to do always the same things? Even granting he was onto something about a form of jumping being obligatory for everyone who grounded his search for meaning in *this* life instead of in some problematical future one, I thought it was a kind of category mistake to take the maxim so literally.

But Sam seemed in no mood to take the question up on a suitable level of philosophical generality.

"Out you go, old friend," he said, and poked me in the ribs.

So out I went, to get it over with. I waded out to where Sam had stood, looked over, shuddered, and launched myself resignedly into the abyss.

Despite my resolution, I opened my eyes on the way down. Twice the piercing blue sky with its scudding clouds alternated with the more ambiguous blue of the water. I landed in a workmanlike way on my rump with a splash that must nearly have emptied the river, though I can't swear to it as my eyes were closed again by this time. Finding myself still alive, I let nature take over once more—highly incensed at the cavalier way I'd ignored her promptings in the first place—and mentally sat back while my body swam for shore.

There I received the usual hero's welcome. Then Sam came up, and Molly close behind, and he put his strong arms around me and I began to glow, and I saw he was right again, the whole thing had been worthwhile.

Chapter 41

You might think we'd leave immediately for London after that. What was to stop us? We'd fulfilled our promises, said our good-byes, and generally wound things up with a bang. Jenny, for one, chafed to go; for all her growing faith in Sam's jumping prowess, she ached to see the last of real waterfalls and to have Sam fill his sights instead with the more genteel challenges of Europe. Molly, too, was ready. Life at the Recess exhausted her. Besides having to contend day and night with the roistering of the boys, who weren't above playing affectionately intended practical jokes on her, she lived in constant terror of Bearcup, whose idea of the perfect woman she apparently matched, poor thing. Conducting a singularly dogged courtship, he had taken to following her every-where, snuffling amorously and looking for opportunities to pinch her.

Only Meleager seemed in no hurry to go. For the whole week before the jump he was ever to be found somewhere close by Sam and Jenny and me. Neither joining us nor ever leaving us alone, he was a relentless presence we soon came to find about as welcome as a ringing in the ears. When he knew we were aware of him, he kept up a genial front; but many times when he forgot himself or thought we had forgotten him I surprised him, lips curled, staring at Sam with unpleasant intensity. Sam seemed to hold a morbid fascination for him that eclipsed even his eagerness to harvest the riches of Europe.

The jump itself seemed to mark a crisis for Meleager. Forgotten by everyone else but me, he sat all that night at a table in a corner, hunched over a glass I never saw him touch, eyes blazing with rage and contempt whenever one of the crowd thumped or jostled him, and otherwise more or less glowering at Sam. He spoke only once. This was in answer to an appeal from Sam that he confirm what Sam had unsuccessfully tried several times already to get across to his potted and besotted admirers—namely, that we were through jumping in the States for a while; that we were off to show the degenerate sons of old Europe now how some things could be done as well as others.

"Boys," said Sam, "it makes me feel low as a skunk to think I'm letting you down, but the fact of it is we've got plans. We're heading for London just as soon as we can get on a packet. You boys know that. Now, I'd take it kindly if you was to quit hollering for me and Bruin to lay over and do her again. It's real flattering and all that, but there's others involved, and I reckon there's no help but for us to push on. Ain't that right, professor?" he said, looking for Meleager through the smoke and racket.

Meleager blinked. I thought then he was only surprised at being addressed; now I know to my everlasting sorrow that Sam had given him an idea.

He sat back, smiled lazily and pinched at his shirt cuffs.

"Oh, I don't know . . . ," he said. "Actually, it does seem a shame to disappoint so many good people."

Sam stared at him a moment, then waved down the noise and called for a song. We launched into "The Wee Cooper o' Fife," sung at ear-shattering volume. Even Meleager joined in on the "nackety-nackety, noo-noo-noo's," no longer seeming to mind being thumped on the back, and grinning about with the look of the cat that ate the canary.

In fact, though, the next day made plain the impossibility of leaving. Huddled together in the midst of the new arrivals still belatedly streaming into town were the Shirt Tails, at long last venturing forth from the safer, more civilized precincts of New York City to witness a jump.

"Well, I'll be a son of a gun," said Sam as Bellows and Cutaway pushed cautiously through the doorway into the Recess that morning. "Will you look at who's here!"

Jenny and I looked up. The two Shirt Tails saw us at the same time. They beamed and motioned behind them. The Brick, Wideawake, and Old Gooseberry spilled into the room, and after them Snooks and Mops, guarding the flanks. Scowling belligerently and with their hands hidden in their strangely lumpy jackets, they advanced on us in a wary body.

"It's all right, boys," laughed Sam, "you're with friends."

Bill Cochrane's astute offering of drinks on the house at length convinced them of this, and disencumbering themselves of a considerable arsenal on our table, they relaxed and gathered around to greet us. While Sam and Wideawake shook hands, Cutaway gazed blushing at Jenny, and Snooks placed himself in front of me, appropriated Old Gooseberry's already damp red bandanna, and dabbed at his eyes.

"We figured we had to see you again, Sam," explained the Brick, darting glances at Jenny. "It ain't been the same since you went, and after you jumped that Niagara, well, we was all so full of thinking about you that it was hurting business. So we thought we'd come on up and pay our respects."

"Well, I'm sure glad you did," said Sam, delighted. "Many's the time I've wondered how you boys were making out." Then he told them about how we were leaving for London. They turned to Jenny, looking a question.

"Yes, I'm going too," she said, though I think they might have guessed it just from the look in her eyes. She laid her hand on Sam's arm with such pride and contentment that Old Gooseberry was overcome and had to reclaim his bandanna. After some initial confusion Cutaway flung his hat in the air with a yell. The others chimed in.

"Yep," said Sam, "we're leaving directly."

Snooks was the first to see the implication of this.

"You don't mean right away?"

"Well, that's just about it."

There was a silence for a moment while this information sank in.

"You mean we've got to keep on all the way to London before we get to see you jump?" said Cutaway.

"About how far is that from New York?" asked Old Gooseberry doubtfully, casting an eye at the heavy lead pipe he'd armed himself with just for the trip to Rochester.

Sam scratched his head.

"Now listen, boys. I made sort of a promise. I was just going to stop off here first on account of I said I would, and then it was straight off to London. Burn me, why couldn't you have made it here Friday?"

The reason, it seemed, was that they'd lost a day hiding out from the constables, who wanted them for questioning in the matter of who had broken into Flanagan Brothers and stolen a number of articles of expensive men's clothing. For the first time I noticed that they were all remarkably well turned out.

"We wanted to look spruce for the trip," mumbled the Brick, dropping his eyes from Jenny's.

"It was that Dogs Meat as peached on us," said Snooks. "You should have finished him, Bruin. He don't have an ounce of good in him."

Gradually the talking died. One by one, everyone but Sam turned to look at Jenny, who resolutely looked at no one.

"Why don't you, Sam?" said Bill Cochrane. "It ain't just these here Pantywaists as want to see. The whole town's full of folks coming in. Even the professor said it'd be a shame to disappoint them."

After ascertaining that Bill's calling them Pantywaists was only an honest mistake, the Shirt Tails asked who the professor was. Badly shaken, Bill meanwhile retired to lie down.

Sam shrugged off the question. But just then, in walked Meleager himself with Molly, closely followed by Bearcup, who'd gotten up early to lie in wait for her outside their hotel.

"That there's the professor," volunteered a Recess regular.

Divining instinctively that he didn't mean Bearcup, the Shirt Tails bent on Meleager the full force of their critical scrutiny.

It was an inspection that might have rattled a better man than he. Meleager's step faltered; his eyebrows shot up. I saw Bearcup move in, positioning himself to protect Molly.

"He's a fellow I'm fixing to travel with," explained Sam, giving Meleager no very warm look. "The boys here are friends of mine," he told him. "They were just asking about you."

Meleager still seemed to think this had an ominous sound. Then someone explained that the real topic was Meleager's remark that it would be a shame for Sam not to jump. Meleager relaxed.

"Yes, well, I did say that. It's true, my heart misgives me to think of frustrating so many of your admirers, Mr. Patch, especially when they've traveled such a ways to get here. It seems too bad, that's all. Of course, perhaps it's none of my affair, and I never would have spoken if you hadn't asked my opinion. But as you did ask, I thought I'd say that I for one see no special urgency connected with our leaving for the Continent. The pyramids, which admittedly aren't in Europe, have waited some three thousand years without undue hardship, and they still don't even have any water under them. I don't see any harm in letting them wait a little longer."

I didn't see the significance of his bringing the pyramids into this at all, but the Shirt Tails eagerly fastened on the point.

"Yeah, it won't hurt them none to wait!"

"Similarly," continued Meleager, thus encouraged, "with the castles along the Rhine. They might furnish some interesting jumps. But they've waited five hundred years and more, some of them, without a taker, and I hardly think another week or so will rob them of their attractions.

"Yeah, nobody's going to rob them of nothing," said the Shirt Tails, albeit with an air of thinking that the matter might bear looking into.

"Oh, hell," said Sam. He turned to Jenny.

She'd been listening, her face lowered. Now she looked up with a hint of desperation.

"Wideawake, Gooseberry, . . . I'm the one who didn't want Sam to jump again. It's because of me that he won't. I know you don't believe anything bad could happen to him—but I worry. Can you understand? I . . . I don't want to lose him. I just feel that if we go to Europe, things will be easier, not so dangerous. Do you really want to see him jump so very badly?"

"Yeah!" said Bellows. Cutaway and the Brick jabbed him with their elbows. "Oof!" he said, and looked at them, baffled.

The Shirt Tails shuffled their feet.

"Naw," said Old Gooseberry, staring at his toes, "we don't want to see it much."

"No."

"Not us."

"We can see it any old time. When you come back."

"Sure, when you come back. We'll see it then."

"I reckon we can wait. That'll be soon enough. Damn, won't it be something, too?" said Cutaway, slapping his thigh.

"Yeah. First-rate!"

"It will, or I'm a Mussulman!" averred Snooks.

"Hey, why don't we go too? We could make sure nobody pulls nothing."

"Look into them castles, too!"

Their glances converged on Wideawake. He took a breath and looked at Sam, who for once in his life didn't seem to know what to say.

"It's all right," said Jenny, unable to keep from smiling even though her eyes glistened with tears. "You . . . you're busy here. Sam, why don't you jump again? And then we'll go."

Sam heaved a sigh. He put his hand on her shoulder.

"All right, boys, we'll do her. But this here one's the last for sure, and if you go and sleep through it, you're going to have to track me to the pyramids!"

Meleager, may he rot in hell, had another idea.

"Why not jump this time from a platform, Mr. Patch? It wouldn't have to be the sort of ramshackle affair they put up at Niagara." He smiled at Jenny. "Simply climbing that thing was not the least dangerous part of the jump, I believe. But here they could build you a proper one. I've been thinking: if you increased the height by only twenty-five feet, Mr. Patch, you'd outstrip your Niagara distance by five feet. That would be a new record. It would save you from repeating yourself and be a truly fitting encore, don't you think?

Sam, needless to say, was taken with the idea, and Jenny offered no objection. But when Sam turned back to Meleager, she continued to study him, and again I saw that her eyes were filled with tears.

Once, too, Meleager found her gazing at him. So bleak was her stare, so implacable, that it shriveled his phony gaiety on the spot. He took care not to look her way again.

Sam and Meleager drafted a handbill.

"And I sure hope this one holds them," said Sam, meaning the jump, "because after this it's London and no mistake."

Smiling, Meleager asked why not simply bill the event as his last jump?

The headings framing a picture of a starved-looking American eagle, this is what they came up with:

HIGHER YET!
Sam's Last Jump

"Some things can be done
as well as others"

There's no Mistake
in SAM PATCH

Of the truth of this we will endeavour to convince the good people of Rochester and its vicinity, next Friday, Nov. 13, at 2 o'clock P.M. Having determined to astonish the natives of the world before he returns to the Jerseys, he will have a scaffold twenty-five feet in height erected on the banks of the Genesee Falls, in this village, from which he will fearlessly leap into the abyss below, a distance of 125 feet. At 3 o'clock precisely, Sam's bear will make the same jump and follow his master, thus showing conclusively that "some things can be done as well as others." Moreover, Sam hopes that all the good people who attend this astonishing exhibition will contribute something toward remunerating him for the seemingly hazardous experiment.

The last sentence was Meleager's idea. No time like the present, he said, for putting things on a more businesslike footing.

That next week was a busy one. Besides the jump to think about, there were also the preparations for London. Molly, now that she'd had time to digest the idea, talked of it constantly.

"Oh, Bruin, won't it be fun? We'll travel everywhere and see everything, and Jason will introduce us to kings and queens and all the best sort of people, and Mr. Patch will jump for them and take their breath away just like he does mine, and we'll be together again, you and me, and we can introduce you to Dr. Gall and Dr. Spurzheim, and I know when they feel your head they'll say, 'Well, I never!'—and we'll be in Paris, and I can hardly wait to see all the fashions!"

Jenny tried hard to match Molly's enthusiasm, but only someone as distracted as Molly could fail to see through the attempt. The jump overshadowed everything for Jenny; till it was done, she could think of nothing else. Her anxiety was such that Sam, who felt bad enough already for having gone back on his promise, was infected with a like anxiety for her and went to some lengths to try to cheer her up. His attentions were pretty constant already; on Wednesday, though, he brought her a special cake he'd had baked in the shape of the London Bridge—or so he'd been confidently assured by the baker, who had enlisted the aid of "a gent as once went there and saw it."

"He wanted to do me one of Niagara, but I said nothing doing. It was this here or nothing, and I reckon it didn't turn out half bad, though I allow it must be a pretty funny-looking bridge, to judge from the model. He said these here things were houses. Aw, Jenny, don't cry."

For a great sob had shaken her body. She closed her eyes and turned her head away, but not before a tear fell and landed on one of the bridge's peculiar stanchions. It glistened there on the icing, a tiny, ill-omened drop of brine.

To my surprise, Meleager seemed strangely affected. In better spirits since Sam agreed to jump, he was always hovering about now, as giddily talkative on the subject of what he liked to call Sam's last jump as Molly was about Europe. A kind of wildness came into his face.

"It'll soon be over," he told Jenny. He sought her eyes. "Then we'll leave for the Continent. You'll like it there. We'll put all this behind us." But Jenny never looked up.

Jenny wasn't the only one with misgivings. The Shirt Tails weren't entirely happy either, for all that they were the ones Sam was principally jumping for.

"Sam," said Wideawake over drinks that night, "maybe the whole thing ain't such a hot idea after all. Me and some of the boys are feeling kind of funny about it."

Sam had been brooding all day over Jenny's reception of the cake. He shot Wideawake a glance that was anything but friendly, and Wideawake retreated behind his drink.

A moment later, though—a moment filled with much unconcerned drumming of fingers, humming under the breath, and several covert glances at Sam—Wideawake cleared his throat and said, staring at the table:

"It's just, well, like I say, there's kind of a funny feel to it. I mean," he hurried on as Sam began to smolder, "it ain't we changed our minds or nothing. No, it ain't that. We want to see you do it as bad as ever. But maybe couldn't you move it back a day or something? I mean, why's it got to be on Friday the 13th, for chrissake, and you calling it the Last Jump and all? Burn me if it don't give a fellow the willies!"

"Now you listen to me, Wideawake," said Sam in such a way that not only Wideawake but everyone else turned to listen. "That there jump is going off Friday as planned and not a jot later. I ain't moving it forward because I said it would be the 13th and I don't want folks coming in then and finding it over and done with. And I ain't moving it back because I ain't drawing the business out a minute longer than I said, and I reckon you can figure why for yourself. And as for it being Friday the 13th, why, I don't give two pins for that. I'd jump if it was Halloween and I had to walk on black cats all the way there. It don't make no never mind. Jumping is what I do, and there ain't a mistake in me today and there won't be one Friday. Now that's the last I care to hear about it!"

In the corner where he was watching, Meleager wrinkled up his face in an unreadable grimace, which however he took pains to hide behind his glass when he saw my eyes were on him.

Thursday they built the platform. Put together of heavy timbers on the bare rock that jutted into the falls, it looked like the speakers' stands I remembered from the Fourth of July, only taller. It even had its own flagpole. What it didn't have was a handrail, and that, taken with the flagpole, gave it a rather unsettling resemblance to an unfinished gallows. I think Jenny had the same thought. We'd gone down together to watch them build it. Sam stood a few feet away, joking with his ever-present admirers. Jenny's eye happened to meet mine. With a tight shake of her head, she said:

"I can't stand to look at it!"

Molly was standing with us and heard. As I growled my frustration and for some reason thought of Meleager, Molly folded Jenny in her matronly arms.

"It'll be fine, dear, you'll see. That man of yours, I think he could jump from the heavens themselves and not take a hurt. It's just as he says, dear: there isn't a mistake in him, not from beginning to end. Or from head to toe, I should say. He knows what he's about. I never saw anyone who knew better, not even Jason, who's very clever and knows such a lot about people and about what he wants to do, although he does keep having disappointments. But even Jason says Mr. Patch is extraordinary. Just last time he jumped I heard him say, 'There's no stopping him.'"

Chapter 42

Friday the 13th dawned bitterly cold. Even inside the Recess, so warm last night from the fire and the press of bodies, the air had an arctic bite that caused the sleepers on the floor to toss restlessly and hug themselves as if trying to draw up nonexistent blankets. Bill, shivering in his coat, was building up the fire, but the flames only flickered feebly and seemed to have lost the power to warm. Even I was cold, though not entirely from the air. I'd waked with a terrifying image before my mind's eye. It seemed to me I saw the platform for Sam's jump rearing up against the night sky, and there was something so indescribably eerie about the patient stillness of those skeletal timbers waiting by the falls, something so uncanny, that a chill that had nothing to do with the weather clutched my heart and gave me the shivers as bad as Bill.

But the Recess was stirring; the Shirt Tails were rousing themselves.

"Colder than a witch's tit," muttered a voice in my ear. Startled, I looked up and poked Snooks in the eye with my nose. He sat up from where he'd curled himself around me for warmth. Out of sorts, he scowled at me, rubbed his eye, and took stock of the light from the window. It was his turn to shiver. "Hanged if I don't wish I was home," he said. "Even mixing it up with the Plug Uglies is better than freezing on a floor like this."

But spirits revived a bit when Bill set out a pot of coffee. By

then the fire was gaining on the cold and the windows had acquired a cozy fogging of condensation. I began to hear talk of Sam
and the jump.

"It'll be first-rate, all right," said Cutaway.

"I reckon," said Mops.

Still, neither could forebear a glance at the gray sky through
the windows, and the voices of both lacked some conviction.

Bill fed us, and then Sam came down with Jenny. We all saw at
once the strain in her face, though she tried to hide it. But Sam
looked himself, if a little bit tired, and threw us all a wave.

"Morning, boys. Bit nippy, ain't it? Now, who's got that coffee?
That's just the ticket for thawing a fellow out on a day like this."

Bellows waved a bottle of rum from last night. He smacked his
lips a few times to help organize his thoughts, then managed to get
out:

"This here's warming enough for me, Sam!" And he tilted the
bottle to his lips and drained off enough at a go to set a polar bear's
innards afire.

"Well, I guess there's something to be said for that method
too," allowed Sam, accepting a bottle from Old Gooseberry. But I
noticed he drank only a little.

Indeed, the drinking didn't really seem to catch on, or not like
last night anyway. Toasts were called, but they were drunk half-
heartedly, and Sam, pacing himself, refused almost half of them.
There seemed a staleness to the whole business. In any case, it
was hard to be festive in that bleak early light.

Then Meleager entered with Molly and Bearcup, whom even
Meleager's exasperation had been unable to drive from Molly's
side since their introduction to the Shirt Tails, and whom Molly
herself tolerated now, partly because of that piece of gallantry and
partly because she had gotten Bearcup to swear off pinching her as
inconsistent with the duties of a protector.

"What, is this how we send off Mr. Patch, gentlemen? Our own
Great Leaper, who's going to make his greatest jump ever for us
today? Fie, I've seen better cheer at a wake! Bill, break out new
bottles. We must do something to build a fire under this crowd, it
appears."

He sauntered in, his eye glittering strangely, I thought, and
took a seat beside Sam and across from Jenny. Molly and Bearcup
followed.

As Bill went around handing out fresh bottles, Meleager produced a bottle of his own from under his coat.

"I have a present for you, Mr. Patch; a little something special to suit the occasion. As we're leaving for Europe inside of a week, I thought it wouldn't be amiss to anticipate our getting there by a bit, and I've brought you this." The gift was a moldy-looking bottle of Courvoisier from which Meleager hadn't even troubled to wipe the cobwebs. This he began to do now, with loving care. "Wait till you taste, Mr. Patch. You'll never want to drink anything else. And," he said with an ambiguous gleam, "with any luck you never will."

He drew the cork and called for glasses. Sam took one and let Meleager pour.

"Thank you very much, Mr. Meleager. I reckon that'll do. No call to try to fit the whole bottle into the glass all at once. If it's as good as you say, it'll be useful to keep a store to celebrate with when I get back, same as now."

"Miss Hansom?"

Mechanically, Jenny took a glass. I noticed as Meleager filled it that his hand seemed to shake.

Bill had set out glasses enough for all. Now Bearcup pushed one forward. Meleager glared, but as Bearcup was easily proof against this sort of intimidation, Meleager had no choice but to serve him with a splash of the cognac, too.

Molly refused; Meleager helped himself. He raised his glass.

"A toast! To Sam Patch, the Jersey Leaper and the world's greatest jumper, who's going to make for us today the world's greatest jump; who's going to leap into such a gulf as no man has ever plumbed to date and returned to tell the tale of it. To Sam Patch, ladies and gentlemen, who makes his last jump today"— Meleager paused; he grinned—"before departing the country for an extended tour abroad."

There was a moment's silence. Bearcup swallowed his cognac at a gulp and sat ramrod straight, as if holding himself alert for novel effects. Jenny, on the other hand, set hers down untasted and pushed the glass away from her. She looked sharply at Meleager, who smirked and dropped his eyes. Avoiding her gaze, he sipped appreciatively and swirled the liquor under his nose, smiling and savoring the bouquet. He glanced up at Sam with a sort of secret glee.

"Am I not right, Mr. Patch? Is this not a fit stirrup cup for a hero? True nectar?"

"It's mighty fine, Mr. Meleager," said Sam, who had not joined in the toast with much enthusiasm, "and I thank you for the thought.

It does warm a man, and no mistake. But I reckon I could do with a little less talk of this being the last jump and all. I guess it feels that way enough already without your making such a to-do of reminding me. Even allowing for the time we mean to have in London and all, it's a sad thing for a fellow to be saying good-bye to all he knows and cares about."

"But Mr. Patch, that's precisely why we owe it to ourselves to be merry," replied Meleager, with something of that fey giddiness he'd exhibited all week. "Look beyond the present, Mr. Patch. It's a measure of your success that you've left yourself nothing more to do. It would be merely tasteless to stay on now. Leave the work when it's done, Mr. Patch, or you'll ruin the effect. That's the counsel of a true friend.

"Of course you're sad. That's only natural. You're closing a chapter, rounding off an important episode in your career. But you've finished what you set out to do: you've shown the world that indeed some things can be done as well as others. Now you must let go; retire gracefully and remove yourself from the scene. As an artist, you must keep perspective on the larger work and not let the merely human in you spoil it."

"Well," said Sam, "I reckon there's something in what you say, all right, and I never thought of it that way before. But for all that, I can't help feeling a little low. Gents," he said, looking around, "and Miss Money, I'm thinking I'd like a word or two with Jenny now, if you folks don't mind."

When the three of us were alone—for Sam never minded me—he said:

"Well, Jenny, I reckon this is it, like Mr. Meleager says: the finish, in a way." He shook his head. "When I got started, I never thought there'd come a day like this. But I reckon he's right. It feels done, somehow; like it's already over with. Like I said my piece and made my mark and got nothing more to add. I don't know, though, it feels pretty strange—like I've been lied to, sort of. Like an old friend wasn't the friend I thought he was. Why, jumping was the answer to everything, Jenny; I thought it was all laid out. But here I am at my peak and I've clean run out of jumps. I mean, it's only jumping that made everything make sense, and now I've gone and run through it and come out the other side, and it turns out the jumping just ain't big enough to last. Jenny," he said, reaching out for her hand, "it's a curious thing, but I don't mind telling you: I'm even wishing I didn't have to do this jump."

"Sam. Oh, Sam." She pressed his hand in hers, then held it to her breast. "Then don't, Sam. There's no need. You don't have to anymore. My darling, don't you see? It's just as you say. Jumping's given you all it has to give. It's made you what you are, and that's so precious, so wonderful; and now at last you're free, Sam. You've come out the other side. And I'm here, Sam. The two of us are ready for each other now. Oh please; please, my darling. For once Meleager's right. You mustn't look back. You're done with that and you don't need it anymore. Let's make a new start. We can be together now."

A long moment passed, during which Sam gazed with utmost seriousness at Jenny—at her lovely hair, so soft and fragrant; at her pleading eyes; and at her lips, still parted in entreaty.

"You know," he said at last, "it used to be there were just two things in this world I wanted. Jumping was the one, and you, Jenny, well, I reckon you know you were always the other one. Now that's changed around some. It's like you say, about the jumping. I've sort of got it inside me now. It's there to stay and I'll always have it, some way or other. And now it's just you I want, Jenny; you more than anything. You're the only thing. You're what everything's about."

"Then, Sam . . . ," she whispered. He interrupted her.

"No, I've still got to jump. There's things," he said, echoing what he'd told me a week ago, "a fellow just has to do."

She might have been turned to stone, if ever stone could be found one-half so lovely. Then, almost imperceptibly, her shoulders drooped.

After a time, she lifted her head.

"I know, Sam." He waited. "And, the funny thing is, I'm not really even afraid." She drew her finger over the back of his hand, tracing the veins, gently rubbing the skin. "I'm not the same either anymore. Maybe a little of your jumping's worked inside me too. I don't know. Maybe I just see you more clearly now. But Sam," she said, covering his hand and putting her whole heart into the plea: "come back to me."

The others, even Meleager, left them alone together until it came time to get ready for the jump. Sam dressed again in Bill's white band uniform, Jenny's black scarf at his throat—how brave he looked! We were about to leave when suddenly Sam turned to her at the door.

"Jenny, I've been thinking. This jump ain't like the others. I ain't proud of it the same, and I reckon I'd sooner you didn't come along to see."

"But Sam—"

Tenderly, he shushed her.

"You stay here, with Bruin. That'll be best. Bruin," he said, throwing his arms around me in a quick hug, "you keep her company." My dismay was equal to Jenny's. He flashed us his smile of former days.

"Now, let's have none of that. The both of you can watch the next one," he said.

But there was no jumps after that, and that was the last hug Sam would ever give me. For there never was a mistake in Sam, and it happened that he made that day both his highest jump and his last, just as he'd said he would.

Chapter 43

Dear Sam. So now you're gone and the little world you made has fallen apart. Your vision at last proved too small to contain you. Alas, when you sought to transfer your loyalty to another mistress, you found what a jealous mistress jumping was.

Yes, nature struck again, at last. She has ever been my nemesis. From the date of my earliest, most naive reflections on my place in this life, I've had to contend with nature. Once I felt secure with her; I thought I was her favorite child. Crockett disabused me of that, and I learned she loves all her progeny equally, if at all, and that the only way to curry favor with her is to behave as she expects: be conventional, remember your place; if you're a bear, be a bear; if a man, well . . . In any case, don't ask questions. Eat and breed.

And to see that we do, to see that we follow this iron law, she's attached some strings. Thus she leads us always and everywhere by the belly and by another organ less permissible to mention, and if we would forget what's expected of us, she brings us up short with a tug on one or the other leash.

But now and again someone comes along who prefers to set his own agenda even so, someone who cannot rest content with the career mapped out for him and shared by every plant and animal. Now and again someone comes along who wants to do something on his own account instead, wants to arrogate nature's own pre-rogative—to create, not merely procreate—wants to raise up

something other, *something* unnatural, *that will stand above na-*
ture's inexorable cycle of generation and decay.

Perhaps, indeed, I describe us all.

In any case, such a one was Sam. And really he fared quite well
and got off rather easily, considering.

Yes, Sam, in your case nature was uncommonly civil. You had
quite a ride of her. Partly she may have been baffled by your talent,
but partly too I detect signs of a rare considerateness, of a fondness
for you, even. How else explain the astonishing coincidence of her
waiting to claim you until what you yourself had announced to be
your Last Jump, and on Friday the 13th at that—notoriously a day
when accidents will happen? Had she acted sooner—in Paterson,
for instance—your memory would be rather different. I think she
intended a compliment, Sam. I think that despite all you were her
darling. It's not the sort of accommodation she makes for everyone.

Yes, and you used her indulgence, if such it was, to good pur-
pose. What a man could do, you did. Having found at last its proper
channel, the amazing energy in you burst out and you accom-
plished wonders. For a time you were invincible. You showed all
and sundry—and not least of all, me—how indeed some things can
be done as well as others. And when at last a mischance did bring
you low, it was before a crowd of twenty thousand, some of whom
had traveled hundreds of miles to see you make your demonstra-
tion. Davy Crockett himself was never idolized more. You were
everybody's hero, Sam; they trusted you—half-worshipped you,
some of them. You spoke to something in each of them. When they
saw you begin to tilt in the air so fatally, saw you lose that famous
arrowy precision and spread your arms, saw you clutch at nothing
and plummet out of control—every heart was squeezed in a vise of
terror, every watcher felt that he himself was lost. Not a soul who
heard it will soon rid his dreams of that awful crack when you
struck, on your side, to rise and jump no more.

Wideawake and the Shirt Tails brought us the news. They didn't
have to say a word. The disbelief and horror stamped on their
faces told us everything while they yet stood in the doorway.
Terrified, they gazed at us, and I felt a weakness seize my limbs. I
searched their faces for the least sign of hope, but none was there.
They had come back without Sam. They scarcely believed it themselves, but Sam was gone.

I threw back my head and howled. What treachery! At least,
what a cosmic, bald mistake! There was no point to this, no justice,

I thought. It was a blow that shattered sanity, holed the fabric of sense we stretch over our days. The game, so superlatively played and on the point of being won, was botched.

By me Jenny sat motionless. At last Wideawake stepped forward, drawing off his hat. But Jenny forestalled him with a tiny shake of her head. He stopped in his tracks and stood there, not knowing what to do. Still Jenny made no move. Only her face had changed since the Shirt Tails' appearance, growing in an instant sharp and haggard.

The Shirt Tails were shuffling nearer and ranging themselves behind Wideawake when Molly Money burst through the door. She saw only Jenny.

"My poor dear!" she cried. The Shirt Tails parted ranks for her. She rushed up to Jenny, enveloped her in an embrace and filled the room with her weeping. Jenny sat a moment, rigid. Then she gave one terrible sob and buried her face in Molly's shoulder.

Behind Molly came Meleager, and he too seemed in the grip of some violent emotion. What it was, though, was slightly problematical, for he was making a strong effort to suppress it and what signs escaped didn't accord very well with grief. If anything, I thought the wild light in his eye sometimes was more expressive of triumph. But at least there was no doubting his distress over Jenny's suffering. Indeed, he staggered on catching sight of her and seemed almost afraid. His face a mask of contending feelings, he flinched away and his glance met mine. Then for an instant one emotion did become uppermost: he shot me a bolt of purest malice.

Recovering himself, he wiped his hands and advanced a few steps nearer Jenny. Somehow she sensed his approach. She looked up, and her face was dreadful—but not just with suffering. No, it was loathing she met him with—such loathing as verged on madness.

"*You!*" she hissed, so that even the Shirt Tails drew back and the color drained from Meleager's face. *"You would comfort me?"*

Rising so suddenly that Molly was astonished, Jenny seemed to tower a moment over everyone, a monstrous cobra about to strike. She advanced on Meleager with a step so slow and deadly that the fur on the back of my neck stood up. He shrank back.

She halted, looked at him and laughed.

"Yes, creep away, little man. Plotter. Snake. If I see you again, I—"

Unable to finish, she spun about and ran upstairs.

Slowly, Molly rose to her feet from where she'd been kneeling.

In her turn she looked at Meleager, but with none of her accustomed deference. Instead I read pain in her expression, and sorrow, and more than a shade of horror.

Somehow the rest of that awful afternoon dragged by. In a daze, I barely registered when Molly came down from Jenny's room and announced in a broken voice that Miss Hansom requested not to be disturbed. I was scarcely conscious of the caresses Molly gave me, and which she broke off finally with a sigh and a kiss on seeing I was insensible of them. She left, followed half a moment later by an agitated Bearcup, and I was alone with Bill, some few of the regulars, and the Shirt Tails, all of whom seemed struck by paralysis.

Bellows cleared his throat. No one taking any notice of this, he looked around and cleared it again, louder. A couple of heads turned.

"I wonder," he said.

A few more faces looked his way, though without much curiosity. Making a supreme effort, so as not to lose his audience, he blurted:

"I wonder, you don't reckon it could have been a rum go?"

Now he had everyone's attention, but that very fact alarmed him so that he couldn't get another word out and was reduced to goggling back at all the sharp looks directed at him.

"What in hell do you mean, a 'rum go'?" demanded Wideawake, never noted for his patience and just then more than usually out of sorts.

"Well, like a hoax," stammered Bellows, clearly regretting ever having brought the matter up.

"*A hoax?*" they all shouted.

Bellows cringed.

"Well, you know, a joke, sort of," he offered, desperately. The Shirt Tails were thunderstruck. Bellows reminded them: "Sam was always joking."

"That's true, he was," remembered someone. A ripple of excitement swept the room.

"Why," said Bellows, gaining confidence, "you remember the time we was out walking and he jumped off the Fitzhugh Street bridge, don't you? We must have looked for him half an hour and never did turn him up. Then just as we was leaving, why, there he was.

"I remember that. He was floating under the bridge," said the Brick.

"He was," said Cutaway. "And he hollered out if we'd lost something."

They all took turns looking at each other.

"Huh!" snorted Wideawake. But even he looked thoughtful. The idea began to take hold.

"Why, it's a capital joke!" cried Snooks, snapping his fingers.

"It is!" grinned Cutaway.

"I'll bet he's out there still, just laughing at us."

But this suggestion seemed oddly to dampen again their reviving spirits. They looked coldly at Bellows, who'd made it. He blinked back at them, not understanding the sudden change. Wideawake undertook to enlighten him.

"And just how in hell does a fellow go about laughing under water, or even sit around scowling there, for a matter of hours, will you tell me that?"

"Well," said Bellows, reflecting, "I reckon he must have found someplace."

"What do you mean, 'found someplace,' you blamed fool?"

"Well, like a cave or something, with air and all, under the water. Why, that's probably what would have gave him the idea."

It was Wideawake's turn to be brought up short.

"Why, sure!" said Cutaway, eager to believe. "Sam was down there a couple of times. He could have set it up easy."

"So why in hell ain't he back then, if it was all a joke?"

"Why . . . well . . . ," floundered Cutaway.

"On account of the hoax went off so good!" said Snooks, coming to his aid. "Why, don't you see? He likely didn't want to spoil it. I reckon his plan is to show up in London, maybe, and just plain have the laugh on us. That Sam," he said, shaking his head in admiration, "he sure is one hell of a card."

"But now we know the joke," said Old Gooseberry, raising his eyebrows as if his own observation surprised him. "It's like we're in on it."

"You bet!"

"We sure are!"

"So I reckon there ain't no call to be feeling low after all," he continued, drawing the obvious inference.

"Why, damn if there is!"

"I reckon not!"

"Well," said Old Gooseberry, giving his eyes a last dab before putting his bandanna away, "then I reckon I'll have another drink."

This proposal struck everyone as being too sound to resist, and the atmosphere lightened by several shades as new bottles were broken out and everyone, even the doubters, drank to the promise of Sam's resurrection.

By evening I'd had all I could stand of the hoax idea. It wasn't that I objected to the Shirt Tails' deceiving themselves, only they deceived themselves so well that they became positively uproarious, thinking it a terrific joke on Sam that they'd found him out. Under the circumstances, their hilarity was grotesque, and it made my own suffering a hundred times worse. I shuddered, too, to think what would be the effect on Jenny of hearing that Sam hadn't met with any mishap at all, but was presumably this very moment chuckling to himself over his joke in a secret cave under the river.

In fact, Jenny's knowing nothing about it was a chief objection to Bellows' theory. Snooks proposed that maybe Sam had acted on the spur of the moment, or maybe he knew that if he told Jenny, she'd give the game away. This plausibly disposed of part of the problem, but what about me? The Shirt Tails were divided over whether or not I was in on the secret. The upshot was that those who thought I wasn't tried to cheer me up with the cave hypothesis, and the others, who thought I was, closed in when the first set got tired, slapping me on the back and calling me a sly dog for the way I tried to fool them. All in all they were making me about as miserable as a bear could be, and I knew if I didn't get away, I was going to do something I'd be sorry for. So, taking advantage of a lull in their attentions when everybody was engrossed by some particularly difficult point of their new eschatology, I stole away outside.

The relief was tremendous. But then the solitude of the night closed around me and brought home how truly alone I was. Stifling a whimper, I set out with no clear end in view for the falls.

Soon, though, I found myself loping down the strangely quiet streets with an unaccountable sense of urgency. Something drew me on, compelled me to make haste. I began to feel as if I had a rendezvous, as if the falls themselves expected me and had some communication to make. Padding along soundlessly, I flitted by the darkened buildings like a shadow. I didn't see a soul, and I don't think anybody saw me—or if anybody did, he kept quiet about it. I sped through the night like a ghost, and as if I'd been a ghost in earnest, I seemed invisible and capable of penetrating anywhere.

Before long I reached the river bank, where the sound of the falls smote me like a fist. There seemed a ghastly pall over the night, a sinister expectancy. I pushed on, the moon lighting my way intermittently through racing clouds, painting the sinuous surface of the river with oily sparkles.

Feeling myself more than ever in the grip of a compulsion, I followed the bank downstream till the noise of the falls filled my head. Tears blurred my vision and made me stumble. The falls' roar reminded me so of Sam. It might have been his voice, it was so familiar. It brought him unbearably close. Impossible to believe the falls could still sound that way and Sam be gone forever.

I kept on, and then the moon broke through again and showed me, stark and hideous, that grisly platform rearing against the sky.

And under its naked timbers stood the last person I'd have thought to meet there: Jason Meleager.

I stood rooted to the spot. But why shouldn't he be here? the reasonable part of me asked. Wasn't I here myself? Yet somehow his presence, innocent enough on the face of it, filled me with dread.

No power on earth could have made me go up to him. Neither, though, did I dream for a moment of slinking away. I was in a quandary, when suddenly a newcomer appeared, startling Meleager as much as me. I recognized Molly.

Impelled by the same instinct that had drawn me to the falls in the first place, I crept closer to listen.

"Well," he said, greeting her with a forced laugh and asking her what I'd wanted to ask him, "what are you doing here? Come to pay your last respects? Or did you follow me?" He stiffened and stared behind her. "Is that fool Bearcup with you?"

"No," said Molly. "I made him promise to stay."

"Ah." Meleager fidgeted. Molly's presence seemed to make him uneasy, but indeed, there was something unnatural in their meeting and speaking there at all by that awful tower. "Well, how long have you been spying on me?"

"I wasn't spying. I came to find you because"—her voice shook; she seemed to have to make an effort to go on—"because I wanted to speak to you."

"Ah! Well! All right then. Here I am. Speak away."

She was silent for a moment. Her eye falling on the leg of the platform, she glanced up to the top. With a shudder, she turned again to Meleager.

"Jason, I don't want to make you angry, but there's something I have to ask you. You were with Mr. Patch right up to the moment of his jump."

"Of course I was. You know that."

"Why, Jason? Why were you?"

"Eh? What are you talking about?"

"I want to know why you were with him, Jason. And not just today; I mean over the whole past week."

"Bah! What kind of question is that? Why do you suppose? Good God, woman, why not ask any of the other fifteen or twenty thousand people who came to see him jump why *they* were here? Why do you persecute me?"

"I'm sorry, Jason. I said I didn't want to make you angry."

"Then don't hound me with your stupid questions," he snapped.

She flinched. A moment went by.

"It's only . . . it's only that—"

"Yes, yes. Speak up."

"Well, it's only that you didn't like Mr. Patch very much."

"What's that?" he said, startled.

"You didn't like Mr. Patch, Jason. In fact, sometimes I've thought you almost hated him. And so I wondered—I wanted to ask—why you kept so close to him these last few days."

I could see him peering at her, trying to make out her face better. He jerked his hand.

"That's nonsense. Of course I liked him. I liked him well enough."

"Oh, Jason!"

"Well, now what?"

She had drawn out a handkerchief. She wiped her eyes. Meleager grew agitated.

"Well?" he repeated.

"Jason, why won't you tell me the truth? You didn't like Mr. Patch. I know you didn't. I could see that you resented him for being so celebrated and successful when you'd worked just as hard; I could see you thought he had things you should have had."

"That's enough!" he stopped her. She gazed up at him meekly. He looked away.

"All right, I didn't like the man much. What of it? As you saw, I tried to hide my aversion, such as it was, for the sake of our working together. I never said there was anything wrong with him. I'd have thought I was more deserving of praise than censure, Miss Money," he said, in that ironical tone he so often took with her, "for mastering my feelings so well."

She only looked at him. He dropped his half-mocking pose of injured pride and shrugged fretfully.

"Then why are you here now, Jason?" she asked him, so softly that I had to strain to hear.

"Now? Why shouldn't I be? Aren't you here yourself?" he said, making me start at how closely his words echoed what I'd imagined he would say.

"Oh, very well," he said after a minute, unable to bear up under her patient scrutiny. "If you must have all my dirty secrets, it's true, I came because I didn't like him. Yes, I came to revisit the scene where he finally met the fate he'd courted for so long, and so richly deserved besides, I might add. Now you know everything. I trust you don't blame me for trying to conceal sentiments so unsavory."

"No, Jason," she told him, her eyes wide. "Not for that."

"Ha! Well, for what then?"

Without taking her eyes from him, she only shook her head.

"So then your show of friendliness over the past week was just hypocrisy?" she asked.

"I believe I've told you what it was. Put what name to it you like."

"And your idea that he jump this time from this terrible platform—that was only apparently friendly, too? And the drink you gave him from the flask, just before he jumped?"

"What drink? Oh, that. I thought it would warm him up."

Molly gazed at him.

"Jason, I've never seen you carry a flask before."

"They're not so hard to come by."

"What was in it, Jason?"

"Brandy, for God's sake. Cognac. From the bottle I bought. What's the meaning of this?"

He seemed to want to break away from her, but could not.

"I saw you speak with him after he drank. You held him back for several minutes, in fact, when he wanted to climb up. You were excited, seemed to be so intimate with him that I wondered. What were you saying, Jason?"

—355—

"Nothing." Then he smiled—despite himself, it seemed. "I was encouraging him, that's all; reminding him of our fine plans, of all he had to live for. As I recall, I told him to be sure to make this a jump people would remember." He cocked an eyebrow at her, the smile still on his face.

Molly shook her head again, as if to clear away cobwebs.

"Yes, I believe you, Jason. I believe that." She closed her eyes. "Was there something in the brandy? What was in the brandy, Jason?"

He hesitated hardly at all.

"Laudanum," he said, with that mirthless smile. "Quite a lot of it."

The earth seemed to open under me. I felt as I'd felt those first times when I jumped: as if the whole familiar world were only painted scenery I'd just been granted a glimpse behind. I saw wheels and engines of impossible description, huge pulleys and blinding lights.

I rose up. I rose up like a ball of smoke. I was unaware of any volition. Lightnings flashed and a roaring drowned the falls. I was at Meleager's side in an instant. Night was day. I saw as clearly as if a burning sun had lowered itself from the heavens to light my vengeance. Every line in Meleager's face was sharply etched. I could have counted the white teeth in his mouth as he opened his lips to scream. Then his head was above me, the ends of his hair on fire against the moon. He swung up, up, in that deathly roaring radiance, his mouth round, his eyes starting from their sockets— and then down: down and away he sped, his figure swiftly dwindling, legs awry like a rag doll's, to vanish in the roiling maw of the falls.

"No, don't come near me, dear," said Molly faintly, not seeming at all surprised by my sudden appearance. I hung my head. My rage was already passing off, leaving me weak and trembling. I seemed to be two people. One of them felt remorse on account of Molly; the other part of me still shivered with satisfaction at what I'd done.

"I forgive you," she said, after a long interval in which we stood staring out over the falls, listening to its rumble, watching the water at the bottom perpetually composing itself to resume its silent course through the night. The moon glinted tranquilly on the freshly smoothed waves.

"I suppose he only met the fate he deserved, poor man. I don't blame you, Bruin. It was the hand of justice. Only, no, you mustn't come any closer. Please."

She wouldn't look at me. I burned with ... what? Shame? Sorrow? Remorse? All of these and none of them, for much as I regretted killing *her* Meleager, I could still only rejoice at having killed mine. Molly and I were irreparably estranged.

"I'm afraid he wasn't strong enough to contend with Mr. Patch," Molly was saying in a voice that momentarily threatened to break. "Mr. Patch always made him feel small. In a way, your Mr. Patch killed my Jason, Bruin, as much as the other way around." She heaved a quivering sigh that caught in her throat. "And now here we are, the pair of us."

When she could speak again, she said:

"You know, there were times when he was good to me. He wasn't always difficult. When he wanted to, he could make me happy. And he used to, sometimes—make me happy—really he did—before he became so jealous of Mr. Patch. Sometimes he was prickly and arrogant, but ... oh, I don't know." She sighed again. "I guess it was always just that it's easier to suffer and hope than to have no hope. Yes, I did let him mistreat me, dear. But it was a small price for all those wonderful dreams of what our life would be someday."

At last she turned to gaze at me. Tears had wet her cheeks, but she took no notice. Her round, ordinary face bore its sorrow as though accustomed to the weight.

"Now whatever will become of us? Actually, I guess I'll be all right. The other day I stumbled on his secret savings. Oh dear, I can hardly think of it even now. Do you know, Bruin, that all those years, he was stealing from me, setting money aside? Well, he was. We could have had our institute long ago. If I'd only known. Well, I guess I'll go back to Boston now. I don't know what I'll do.

"I'd take you with me if I could, my dear. I wish I could. But somehow I think you'll be all right," she said. "You're a very clever bear."

Next day, Jenny came to say good-bye.

"I've decided to go back to New York with Wideawake and the others," she told me, watching my face. "They've invited me, and they're all the friends I have."

I had nothing to say to that. Dully, I noted the dark patches under her eyes. She was not beautiful today. Today she and Molly might have been sisters. I suppose in a way they were.

She stretched out her fingers and gently stroked my cheek. The tears welled up. She bit her lip.

"Bruin, they mean to bring you with us, too, if you'll come. Would you like that?"

It took a moment for her question to penetrate. I looked up and found her regarding me almost fearfully. I had no idea why. Nor did I care to try to figure it out. A heavy fog seemed to have settled over me since last night, muffling my senses, clouding my brain. I felt a pang at the thought of Jenny's leaving me—Jenny, whom Sam had loved and whom even I had grown rather fond of. But that's all it was, a pang. I seemed to have run out of stronger feelings, apart from a certain ache even the fog couldn't altogether dissemble. There was even relief in the prospect of her going away: she was too vivid a reminder of Sam and of our buried rivalry, hers and mine. In several ways, she made that somber ache under the fog throb more painfully.

Then I thought I understood her look. Yes, she was afraid. I gave a low woof and licked her hand. Before she could misunderstand, I shook my head and pulled away.

She blinked uncertainly.

"You don't want to come?"

I repeated my performance with the lick and the shake of the head.

"You're not coming?"

This time I nodded.

Her eyes widened.

"Oh, Bruin," she said, and then words failed her.

Chapter 44

And so I stayed. It took some doing—the Shirt Tails were deter-mined to have me. I actually had to bare my teeth at Snooks. But Jenny interceded, suggesting that perhaps Sam had instructed me to wait for him here, and that gave them pause. On no account did they want to violate Sam's wishes. And then finally, if Sam were dead—a possibility they still steadfastly refused to admit, offi-cially—my loyalty was more moving still. So their leave-taking was a tearful one; Old Gooseberry's bandanna was in great demand. But at last they filed out, Jenny last, to return to the less barbarous City, taking what consolation they could from the thought that Sam's death was all a prank, albeit one not half so humorous as it had seemed the night before.

And, yes, I stayed; I stayed with Bill, devout believer that Sam was coming back. This belief sustained him for a long time, and he used to rehearse it on visits to me when he came to comfort and be comforted. But then the visits fell off and I was left more and more alone. And finally, just a week ago—March 17 it was—a farmer found Sam's body near the mouth of the Genesee. It was frozen in a block of ice, and it was Sam, all right. He still had Bill's white pants on, and Jenny's black scarf about his waist. Bill said there was hardly a mark on him; it was a miracle: as if the river were hard put to find a mistake in Sam even in death.

They buried him nearby. Not even Bill attended.

And now for me. The last embarrassing bit of Sam, I suspect they'll come soon to sweep me away. I wonder how I'll like my new career as Sears Famous Bear Grease, whether I'll find it a restful change. It seems a long way to fall, and rather demeaning—a job that any bear could do. I'm used to better. I'm used to being special. I used to know the heady excitement of life on the edge, of acclaim for my talents. I was a member of the aristocracy, had won through so that I lived for myself. I sense that this new role blocked out for me will require a difficult adjustment.

Yes, the last few months have stripped away my distinction, my humanity, and soon . . . But what's to do? I feel as Sam must have felt when jumping let him down and proved to have an end. I still have life left over, an embarrassment of riches. But how begin again? How depreciate that old life by supposing anything could follow it? And in any case, what *could?*

At this important juncture in my thoughts I'm startled to feel my cheek nudged by a cold nose and to have a tongue thrust in my ear. I come awake. It's dark; my pretty penmate is regarding me with devotion but with some impatience too. It seems the slops they feed us have been set out and she wants to eat. I wonder for a moment that she waited, but then I remember, she considers me her mate.

My stomach growls. She has an ally in my own camp. I must eat. Life, I see, will go on, with me or without me, however rudely and with however little consideration for a person's feelings.

She sees me stir and joyfully skips over to our trough. I can't help noticing that she hardly limps at all.

Then, as I watch her, something gives way inside me. My eyes open in surprise. I look round at the night with suddenly quickening interest, at my penmate invading the trough with her frequent backward glances. I feel a strange excitement. In fact, I feel newly hatched.

Dear Sam, I think I can't let them make bear grease of me. It's too great an affront to put on your memory. I'd sooner die. And since that way lies the bear grease, I have to live. I hope you'll forgive my logic. I confess, I think it's helped along a bit by my penmate, feeding so prettily, and by the bright eye she keeps on me.

Yes, tonight we'll slip away. I know enough, it won't be hard. We'll find our way to real wilderness, far from man, and as we roam the dim corridors and bright glades of the forest, I'll think of you, of how there never was a mistake in you, and of how you demonstrated past all quibbling how some things can be done as well as others.

And if Davy Crockett comes after us, well, he'd just better watch out, that's all.

THE END